INTRODUCTION TO THE
SHORT STORY

HAYDEN SERIES IN LITERATURE

Robert W. Boynton, Consulting Editor

Former Principal, Senior High School
and Chairman, English Department
Germantown Friends School

INTRODUCTION TO THE
SHORT STORY

SECOND EDITION

Robert W. Boynton

and

Maynard Mack

HAYDEN BOOK COMPANY, INC.
Rochelle Park, New Jersey

Library of Congress Cataloging in Publication Data

Boynton, Robert W.
  Introduction to the short story.

  (Hayden series in literature)
  SUMMARY: Text and selected works introduce the art
of the short story.
  1. Short stories, American. 2. Short stories,
English. 3. Short story. [1. Short stories.
2. Short story] I. Mack, Maynard, 1909–   , joint
author. II. Title.
PZ5.B676In 1978   813'.01 [Fic]   77-28388
ISBN 0-8104-5050-X

Printed in the United States of America

16 17 18 19   PRINTING

81 82 83 84 85   YEAR

CONTENTS

INTRODUCTION

This book is an introduction to the art of the short story—the art of the writer as the creator of the experience the story deals with and the art of the reader as the re-creator of that experience. Since few of us will ever be writers of short stories, the main purpose here is to help you become a more skilled reader. We assume that users of this book have already read a good many short stories. Our hope is to widen and deepen that experience and place it on a solid basis of critical understanding.

It is said more often than it should be by both students and teachers that analysis of an art form deadens appreciation. That is nonsense. It is certainly true that naming parts or hunting symbols as teaching and testing devices deadens art and people, but *how* a work of art is put together is an integral part of *what* the work means. We go to some pains here to spell out one way of looking at the form of the short story, and we refer to points of our analysis throughout the book. At the same time we are aware that the stories we have included are not just vehicles for analysis. Above all, they are superb examples of the storyteller's art, and they illustrate the modern writer's intense concern with people, and with probing the complexity of the human personality in seemingly trivial incidents as well as in matters of life and death.

PART ONE

An Analysis of the Form

The first part of this book deals with six major aspects of the short story, and of fiction in general: plot, character, point of view, tone, setting, and theme. Three short stories are used for illustration. One of them, James Thurber's "The Catbird Seat," is analyzed in some detail to give you a thorough understanding of how a story is put together. The other two, Frank O'Connor's "First Confession" and Shirley Jackson's "The Lottery," are discussed more briefly, but many questions are raised about them in connection with each of the major topics mentioned above.

First, read "The Catbird Seat."

The Catbird Seat

JAMES THURBER

Mr. Martin bought the pack of Camels on Monday night in the most 1. crowded cigar store on Broadway. It was theater time and seven or eight men were buying cigarettes. The clerk didn't even glance at Mr. Martin, who put the pack in his overcoat pocket and went out. If any of the staff at F & S had seen him buy the cigarettes, they would have been astonished, for it was generally known that Mr. Martin did not smoke, and never had. No one saw him.

It was just a week to the day since Mr. Martin had decided to rub out 2. Mrs. Ulgine Barrows. The term "rub out" pleased him because it suggested nothing more than the correction of an error—in this case an error of Mr. Fitweiler. Mr. Martin had spent each night of the past week working out his plan and examining it. As he walked home now he went over it again. For the hundredth time he resented the element of imprecision, the margin of guesswork that entered into the business. The project as he had worked it out was casual and bold, the risks were considerable. Something might go wrong anywhere along the line. And therein lay the cunning of his scheme. No one would ever see in it the cautious, painstaking hand of Erwin Martin, head of the filing department at F & S, of whom Mr. Fitweiler had once said, "Man is fallible but Martin isn't." No one would see his hand, that is, unless it were caught in the act.

Sitting in his apartment, drinking a glass of milk, Mr. Martin re- 3. viewed his case against Mrs. Ulgine Barrows, as he had every night for seven nights. He began at the beginning. Her quacking voice and braying laugh had first profaned the halls of F & S on March 7, 1941 (Mr. Martin had a head for dates). Old Roberts, the personnel chief, had introduced her as the newly appointed special adviser to the president of the firm, Mr. Fitweiler. The woman had appalled Mr. Martin instantly, but he hadn't shown it. He had given her his dry hand, a look of studious concentration, and a faint smile. "Well," she had said, looking at the papers on his desk, "are you lifting the oxcart out of the ditch?" As Mr. Martin recalled that moment, over his milk, he squirmed slightly. He must keep his mind on her crimes as a special adviser, not on her peccadillos as a personality. This he found difficult to do, in spite of entering an objection and sustaining it. The faults of the woman as a woman kept chattering on in his mind like an unruly witness. She had, for almost two years now, baited him. In the halls, in the elevator, even in his own office, into which she romped now and then like a circus horse, she was constantly shouting these silly questions at him. "Are you lifting the oxcart out of the ditch? Are you tearing up the pea patch? Are you hollering down the rain barrel? Are you scraping around the bottom of the pickle barrel? Are you sitting in the catbird seat?"

4.   It was Joey Hart, one of Mr. Martin's two assistants, who had explained what the gibberish meant. "She must be a Dodger fan," he had said. "Red Barber announces the Dodger games over the radio and he uses those expressions—picked 'em up down South." Joey had gone on to explain one or two. "Tearing up the pea patch" meant going on a rampage; "sitting in the catbird seat" meant sitting pretty, like a batter with three balls and no strikes on him. Mr. Martin dismissed all this with an effort. It had been annoying, it had driven him near to distraction, but he was too solid a man to be moved to murder by anything so childish. It was fortunate, he reflected as he passed on to the important charges against Mrs. Barrows, that he had stood up under it so well. He had maintained always an outward appearance of polite tolerance. "Why, I even believe you like the woman," Miss Paird, his other assistant, had once said to him. He had simply smiled.

5.   A gavel rapped in Mr. Martin's mind and the case proper was resumed. Mrs. Ulgine Barrows stood charged with willful, blatant, and persistent attempts to destroy the efficiency and system of F & S. It was competent, material, and relevant to review her advent and rise to power. Mr. Martin had got the story from Miss Paird, who seemed always able to find things out. According to her, Mrs. Barrows had met Mr. Fitweiler at a party, where she had rescued him from the embraces of a powerfully built drunken man who had mistaken the president of F & S for a famous retired Middle Western football coach. She had led him to a

sofa and somehow worked upon him a monstrous magic. The aging gentleman had jumped to the conclusion there and then that this was a woman of singular attainments, equipped to bring out the best in him and in the firm. A week later he had introduced her into F & S as his special adviser. On that day confusion got its foot in the door. After Miss Tyson, Mr. Brundage, and Mr. Bartlett had been fired and Mr. Munson had taken his hat and stalked out, mailing his resignation later, old Roberts had been emboldened to speak to Mr. Fitweiler. He mentioned that Mr. Munson's department had been "a little disrupted" and hadn't they perhaps better resume the old system there? Mr. Fitweiler had said certainly not. He had the greatest faith in Mrs. Barrows' ideas. "They require a little seasoning, a little seasoning, is all," he had added. Mr. Roberts had given it up. Mr. Martin reviewed in detail all the changes wrought by Mrs. Barrows. She had begun chipping at the cornices of the firm's edifice and now she was swinging at the foundation stones with a pickaxe.

Mr. Martin came now, in his summing up, to the afternoon of Monday, November 2, 1942—just one week ago. On that day, at 3 P.M., Mrs. Barrows had bounced into his office. "Boo!" she had yelled. "Are you scraping around the bottom of the pickle barrel?" Mr. Martin had looked at her from under his green eyeshade, saying nothing. She had begun to wander about the office, taking it in with her great, popping eyes. "Do you really need *all* these filing cabinets?" she had demanded suddenly. Mr. Martin's heart had jumped. "Each of these files," he had said, keeping his voice even, "plays an indispensable part in the system of F & S." She had brayed at him, "Well, don't tear up the pea patch!" and gone to the door. From there she had bawled, "But you sure have got a lot of fine scrap in here!" Mr. Martin could no longer doubt that the finger was on his beloved department. Her pickaxe was on the upswing, poised for the first blow. It had not come yet; he had received no blue memo from the enchanted Mr. Fitweiler bearing nonsensical instructions deriving from the obscene woman. But there was no doubt in Mr. Martin's mind that one would be forthcoming. He must act quickly. Already a precious week had gone by. Mr. Martin stood up in his living room, still holding his milk glass. "Gentlemen of the jury," he said to himself, "I demand the death penalty for this horrible person."

7.   The next day Mr. Martin followed his routine, as usual. He polished his glasses more often and once sharpened an already sharp pencil, but not even Miss Paird noticed. Only once did he catch sight of his victim; she swept past him in the hall with a patronizing "Hi!" At five-thirty he walked home, as usual, and had a glass of milk, as usual. He had never drunk anything stronger in his life—unless you could count ginger ale. The late Sam Schlosser, the S of F & S, had praised Mr. Martin at a staff meeting several years before for his temperate habits. "Our most efficient worker neither drinks nor smokes," he had said. "The results speak for themselves." Mr. Fitweiler had sat by, nodding approval.

8.   Mr. Martin was still thinking about that red-letter day as he walked over to the Schrafft's on Fifth Avenue near Forty-sixth Street. He got there, as he always did, at eight o'clock. He finished his dinner and the financial page of the *Sun* at a quarter to nine, as he always did. It was his custom after dinner to take a walk. This time he walked down Fifth Avenue at a casual pace. His gloved hands felt moist and warm, his forehead cold. He transferred the Camels from his overcoat to a jacket pocket. He wondered, as he did so, if they did not represent an unnecessary note of strain. Mrs. Barrows smoked only Luckies. It was his idea to puff a few puffs on a Camel (after the rubbing-out), stub it out in the ashtray holding her lipstick-stained Luckies, and thus drag a small red herring across the trail. Perhaps it was not a good idea. It would take time. He might even choke, too loudly.

9.   Mr. Martin had never seen the house on West Twelfth Street where Mrs. Barrows lived, but he had a clear enough picture of it. Fortunately, she had bragged to everybody about her ducky first-floor apartment in the perfectly darling three-story red-brick. There would be no doorman or other attendants; just the tenants of the second and third floors. As he walked along, Mr. Martin realized that he would get there before nine-thirty. He had considered walking north on Fifth Avenue from Schrafft's to a point from which it would take him until ten o'clock to reach the house. At that hour people were less likely to be coming in or going out. But the procedure would have made an awkward loop in the straight thread of his casualness, and he had abandoned it. It was impossible to figure when people would be entering or leaving the house, anyway. There was a great risk at any hour. If he ran into anybody, he would simply have to place the rubbing-out of Ulgine Barrows in the

inactive file forever. The same thing would hold true if there were someone in her apartment. In that case he would just say that he had been passing by, recognized her charming house, and thought to drop in.

It was eighteen minutes after nine when Mr. Martin turned into *10.* Twelfth Street. A man passed him, and a man and a woman, talking. There was no one within fifty paces when he came to the house, halfway down the block. He was up the steps and in the small vestibule in no time, pressing the bell under the card that said "Mrs. Ulgine Barrows." When the clicking in the lock started, he jumped forward against the door. He got inside fast, closing the door behind him. A bulb in a lantern hung from the hall ceiling on a chain seemed to give a monstrously bright light. There was nobody on the stair, which went up ahead of him along the left wall. A door opened down the hall in the wall on the right. He went toward it swiftly, on tiptoe.

"Well, for God's sake, look who's here!" bawled Mrs. Barrows, and *11.* her braying laugh rang out like the report of a shotgun. He pushed past her like a football tackle, bumping her. "Hey, quit shoving!" she said, closing the door behind them. They were in her living room, which seemed to Mr. Martin to be lighted by a hundred lamps. "What's after you?" she said. "You're as jumpy as a goat." He found he was unable to speak. His heart was wheezing in his throat. "I—yes," he finally brought out. She was jabbering and laughing as she started to help him off with his coat. "No, no," he said. "I'll put it here." He took it off and put it on a chair near the door. "Your hat and gloves, too," she said. "You're in a lady's house." He put his hat on top of the coat. Mrs. Barrows seemed larger than he had thought. He kept his gloves on. "I was passing by," he said. "I recognized—is there anyone here?" She laughed louder than ever. "No," she said, "we're all alone. You're as white as a sheet, you funny man. Whatever *has* come over you? I'll mix you a toddy." She started toward a door across the room. "Scotch-and-soda be all right? But say, you don't drink, do you?" She turned and gave him her amused look. Mr. Martin pulled himself together. "Scotch-and-soda will be all right," he heard himself say. He could hear her laughing in the kitchen.

Mr. Martin looked quickly around the living room for the weapon. *12.* He had counted on finding one there. There were andirons and a poker and something in a corner that looked like an Indian club. None of them would do. It couldn't be that way. He began to pace around. He came to a desk. On it lay a metal paper knife with an ornate handle. Would it be sharp enough? He reached for it and knocked over a small brass jar. Stamps spilled out of it and it fell to the floor with a clatter. "Hey," Mrs. Barrows yelled from the kitchen, "are you tearing up the pea patch?" Mr. Martin gave a strange laugh. Picking up the knife, he tried its point against his left wrist. It was blunt. It wouldn't do.

13.   When Mrs. Barrows reappeared, carrying two highballs, Mr. Martin, standing there with his gloves on, became acutely conscious of the fantasy he had wrought. Cigarettes in his pocket, a drink prepared for him—it was all too grossly improbable. It was more than that; it was impossible. Somewhere in the back of his mind a vague idea stirred, sprouted. "For heaven's sake, take off those gloves," said Mrs. Barrows. "I always wear them in the house," said Mr. Martin. The idea began to bloom, strange and wonderful. She put the glasses on a coffee table in front of a sofa and sat on the sofa. "Come over here, you odd little man," she said. Mr. Martin went over and sat beside her. It was difficult getting a cigarette out of the pack of Camels, but he managed it. She held a match for him, laughing. "Well," she said, handing him his drink, "this is perfectly marvelous. You with a drink and a cigarette."

14.   Mr. Martin puffed, not too awkwardly, and took a gulp of the highball. "I drink and smoke all the time," he said. He clinked his glass against hers. "Here's nuts to that old windbag, Fitweiler," he said, and gulped again. The stuff tasted awful, but he made no grimace. "Really, Mr. Martin," she said, her voice and posture changing, "you are insulting our employer." Mrs. Barrows was now all special adviser to the president. "I am preparing a bomb," said Mr. Martin, "which will blow the old goat higher than hell." He had only had a little of the drink, which was not strong. It couldn't be that. "Do you take dope or something?" Mrs. Barrows asked coldly. "Heroin," said Mr. Martin. "I'll be coked to the gills when I bump that old buzzard off." "Mr. Martin!" she shouted, getting to her feet. "That will be all of that. You must go at once." Mr. Martin took another swallow of his drink. He tapped his cigarette out in the ashtray and put the pack of Camels on the coffee table. Then he got up. She stood glaring at him. He walked over and put on his hat and coat. "Not a word about this," he said, and laid an

index finger against his lips. All Mrs. Barrows could bring out was "Really!" Mr. Martin put his hand on the doorknob. "I'm sitting in the catbird seat," he said. He stuck his tongue out at her and left. Nobody saw him go.

Mr. Martin got to his apartment, walking, well before eleven. No one 15. saw him go in. He had two glasses of milk after brushing his teeth, and he felt elated. It wasn't tipsiness, because he hadn't been tipsy. Anyway, the walk had worn off all effects of the whiskey. He got in bed and read a magazine for a while. He was asleep before midnight.

Mr. Martin got to the office at eight-thirty the next morning, as usual. 16. At a quarter to nine, Ulgine Barrows, who had never before arrived at work before ten, swept into his office. "I'm reporting to Mr. Fitweiler now!" she shouted. "If he turns you over to the police, it's no more than you deserve!" Mr. Martin gave her a look of shocked surprise. "I beg your pardon?" he said. Mrs. Barrows snorted and bounced out of the room, leaving Miss Paird and Joey staring after her. "What's the matter with that old devil now?" asked Miss Paird. "I have no idea," said Mr. Martin, resuming his work. The other two looked at him and then at each other. Miss Paird got up and went out. She walked slowly past the closed door of Mr. Fitweiler's office. Mrs. Barrows was yelling inside, but she was not braying. Miss Paird could not hear what the woman was saying. She went back to her desk.

Forty-five minutes later, Mrs. Barrows left the president's office and 17. went into her own, shutting the door. It wasn't until half an hour later that Mr. Fitweiler sent for Mr. Martin. The head of the filing department, neat, quiet, attentive, stood in front of the old man's desk. Mr. Fitweiler was pale and nervous. He took his glasses off and twiddled them. He made a small, bruffing sound in his throat. "Martin," he said, "you have been with us more than twenty years." "Twenty-two, sir," said Mr. Martin. "In that time," pursued the president, "your work and your —uh—manner have been exemplary." "I trust so, sir," said Mr. Martin. "I have understood, Martin," said Mr. Fitweiler, "that you have never taken a drink or smoked." "That is correct, sir," said Mr. Martin. "Ah, yes." Mr. Fitweiler polished his glasses. "You may describe what you did after leaving the office yesterday, Martin," he said. Mr. Martin allowed less than a second for his bewildered pause. "Certainly, sir," he said. "I walked home. Then I went to Schrafft's for dinner. Afterward I walked home again. I went to bed early, sir, and read a magazine for a while. I was asleep before eleven." "Ah, yes," said Mr. Fitweiler again. He was silent for a moment, searching for the proper words to say to the head of the filing department. "Mrs. Barrows," he said finally, "Mrs. Barrows has worked hard, Martin, very hard. It grieves me to report that she has suffered a severe breakdown. It has taken the form of a persecution complex accompanied by distressing hallucinations." "I am very sorry, sir," said Mr. Martin. "Mrs. Barrows is under the delusion," continued Mr. Fitweiler, "that you visited her last evening and behaved yourself in an—uh—unseemly manner." He raised his hand to silence Mr. Martin's little pained outcry. "It is the nature of these psychological diseases," Mr. Fitweiler said, "to fix upon the least likely and most innocent party as the—uh—source of persecution. These matters are not for the lay mind to grasp, Martin. I've just had my psychiatrist, Dr. Fitch, on the phone. He would not, of course, commit himself, but I suggested to Mrs. Barrows, when she had completed her—uh—story to me this morning, that she visit Dr. Fitch, for I suspected a condition at once. She flew, I regret to say, into a rage, and demanded—uh—requested that I call you on the carpet. You may not know, Martin, but Mrs. Barrows had planned a reorganization of your department—subject to my approval, of course, subject to my approval. This brought you, rather than anyone else, to her mind—but again that is a phenomenon for Dr. Fitch and not for us. So, Martin, I am afraid Mrs. Barrows' usefulness here is at an end." "I am dreadfully sorry, sir," said Mr. Martin.

18.   It was at this point that the door to the office blew open with the suddenness of a gas-main explosion and Mrs. Barrows catapulted through it. "Is the little rat denying it?" she screamed. "He can't get away with that!" Mr. Martin got up and moved discreetly to a point beside Mr. Fitweiler's chair. "You drank and smoked at my apartment," she bawled at Mr. Martin, "and you know it! You called Mr. Fitweiler an old wind-bag and said you were going to blow him up when you got coked to the gills on your heroin!" She stopped yelling to catch her breath and a new glint came into her popping eyes. "If you weren't such a drab, ordinary little man," she said, "I'd think you'd planned it all. Sticking your tongue out, saying you were sitting in the catbird seat, because you thought no

one would believe me when I told it! My God, it's really too perfect!" She brayed loudly and hysterically, and the fury was on her again. She glared at Mr. Fitweiler. "Can't you see how he has tricked us, you old fool? Can't you see his little game?" But Mr. Fitweiler had been surreptitiously pressing all the buttons under the top of his desk and employees of F & S began pouring into the room. "Stockton," said Mr. Fitweiler, "you and Fishbein will take Mrs. Barrows to her home. Mrs. Powell, you will go with them." Stockton, who had played a little football in high school, blocked Mrs. Barrows as she made for Mr. Martin. It took him and Fishbein together to force her out of the door into the hall, crowded with stenographers and office boys. She was still screaming imprecations at Mr. Martin, tangled and contradictory imprecations. The hubbub finally died out down the corridor.

"I regret that this has happened," said Mr. Fitweiler. "I shall ask *19.* you to dismiss it from your mind, Martin." "Yes, sir," said Mr. Martin, anticipating his chief's "That will be all" by moving to the door. "I will dismiss it." He went out and shut the door, and his step was light and quick in the hall. When he entered his department he had slowed down to his customary gait, and he walked quietly across the room to the W20 file, wearing a look of studious concentration.

Plot

I

The word *story* implies a series of tied-together events; and *plot* is the technical term that applies to these connected events in a story.   To build a plot the experienced writer carefully selects certain details and just as carefully rejects many more; he is interested not in compiling a precise record of a character's actions but in choosing only those details that have a direct bearing on the story.   In "The Catbird Seat," for instance, between the time Mr. Martin enters his office and the time Mr. Fitweiler summons him, many unimportant events might have occupied Mr. Martin— answering a phone, filing papers, addressing his assistants.   But Thurber wisely passes these over; he is interested only in Mrs. Barrows's eagerness to report Mr. Martin's behavior and in Mr. Martin's carefully prepared reaction.

Every detail selected must serve a specific purpose.   Had Thurber mentioned Mr. Martin's answering a phone, for instance, while awaiting Mr. Fitweiler's summons, that detail would have had to contribute somehow to the development of the plot or of Mr. Martin's character.   A famous Russian short-story writer, Anton Chekhov, made the point clear by saying that if a revolver is mentioned in the first paragraph of a story, it must be used sometime before the close.

But even a series of carefully chosen, related events does not necessarily constitute a plot. In paragraphs 16–19 of "The Catbird Seat," for instance, there is just such a carefully selected series. There is a richly drawn scene, the suggestion of a story, but no plot. A plot must deal with the straightening out of a question mark: some *conflict* must be dramatized that is in some way *resolved;* some *problem* must be set up that is in some way *solved,* at least for the moment. In "The Catbird Seat," the problem is that Mr. Martin must get rid of Mrs. Barrows before she gets rid of him. In the four paragraphs just cited we have the *resolution*—the account of his success. Read the paragraphs again with these comments in mind to see the difference between a well-organized *scene* as part of a story and a well-organized plot as the framework for a whole story.

II

Plot, then, refers to a series of interrelated events, during which some conflict or problem is resolved. Plot can be looked at for purposes of discussion as if isolated from the people concerned with those events and that conflict or problem. There are, of course, many ways in which an author can arrange the details he selects. Since events in the real world take place one after the other, the obvious way to tell a story is chronologically, in the manner of ". . , and then . . . and then . . . and then." Most simple tales are told this way, and there is no reason why a rather complex story cannot also be handled chronologically. Some very good stories in this book ("The Cask of Amontillado" and "Flight," for instance) are so handled. It would be foolish to say that Thurber would have had a less successful story had he followed a strictly chronological development; a skillful writer plays a skillful game no matter how he chooses to play it.

By avoiding a chronological treatment, however, Thurber plunges us into the heart of the story immediately. There is no point at which the focus is not directly on Mr. Martin. This concentration could not have been achieved had much time been spent establishing Mr. Martin's past and Mrs. Barrows's activities in a chronological ordering. Mr. Martin's behavior patterns, so necessary to the story, are revealed as he carries out his plan, rather than beforehand in scenes which would have no direct connection with events leading up to the "rubbing-out." As we shall see when we discuss *point of view*, there is almost no time when we are not viewing current actions as Mr. Martin is viewing them. Even though the story is not told by Mr. Martin directly, Thurber keeps him in the center of the stage virtually all the time.

Whatever background information Thurber might have given through a more chronological arrangement is made to come quite naturally out of the behavior we expect from a man like Mr. Martin faced with the problem he has. He has come to the point of decision. He knows that it is a question of his own survival and he has committed himself to "rubbing out" Mrs. Barrows, although he has not the foggiest notion of how to carry through his intentions once he is face to face with her. He has based his plan on the valid realization that no one could imagine him "rubbing out" anyone. He has spent a great many hours justifying to himself what he must do, and thus it is perfectly normal that he should review in his mind his justifications and his vague plan of action. Whatever we need to know about him, about F & S, and about Mrs. Barrows comes out effortlessly as the story moves along after the decision has been made.

III

Now notice specifically the details of the opening paragraph as illustrations of what it means to organize a story carefully. In a seemingly casual way, a great deal is revealed that a careless reader will miss. Mr. Martin does not buy *a* pack of *cigarettes*, he buys *"the* pack of *Camels."*

If *the* is used instead of *a* we are told that this pack has been planned for. It is not just any pack. Similarly, if Camels are mentioned in an opening sentence like this, more is meant than simply that Mr. Martin's brand happens to be Camel, though Thurber wisely leaves the reason unrevealed for the moment. The fact that Mr. Martin buys the Camels in "the most crowded cigar store on Broadway" makes us guess that he has picked a crowded store for a particular reason. The second and third sentences indicate that the guess is correct: he evidently does not want to be noticed buying the cigarettes. Sentence four tells us how unusual it is for Mr. Martin to buy cigarettes. His fellow employees would be "astonished," because they *knew* he "did not smoke, and never had"—and presumably never would. The last sentence in the paragraph increases the mystery by emphasizing Mr. Martin's strong desire not to be noticed.

Thurber uses his second paragraph to deepen the mystery and throw more light on Mr. Martin's character. Mrs. Barrows is introduced by name as the intended victim of a "rubbing-out," but no reason is yet given, and Mr. Martin hardly seems the kind of man who would do such a drastic thing. There must be great provocation. Mr. Fitweiler is mentioned, but so far only as someone who has made an error that needs correcting. Mr. Martin himself is further defined: his job is revealed, his efficiency and thoroughness are underscored, and the obsession with which he views his problem is drummed into the reader.

In paragraphs 3 through 6 the scene shifts to Mr. Martin's apartment. As is quite natural for a person of his temperament, Mr. Martin once again reviews his case against Ulgine Barrows. In the course of his presentation of the evidence, we get the necessary details about the brassy Mrs. Barrows and her reign at F & S. We see the inability of the faithful employees to counter her actions and of Mr. Fitweiler to see through them; we are introduced to the notion of "the catbird seat" (now occupied by Mrs. Barrows); and we get the complete picture of the hounded Mr. Martin, "drinking a glass of milk" and demanding the death penalty in the name of efficiency and system.

Several different approaches to revealing information are used in these paragraphs. Some of the details are of the present moment ("drinking a glass of milk," "A gavel rapped in Mr. Martin's mind"). Some are presented as *flashbacks* as Mr. Martin recalls his first meeting with Mrs. Barrows and subsequent dealings with that "horrible person." Some of the details are reported as hearsay from Miss Paird or old Roberts. Almost all are presented dramatically; that is, direct comments are given rather than simply recalled and listed, so that there is immediacy throughout the paragraphs even though Mr. Martin is reviewing the past in the quiet of his apartment.

From paragraph 7 to the end, the plot moves chronologically to the final dismissal of Mrs. Barrows and the enthronement of Mr. Martin in the catbird seat, with only an occasional reference to past time (as at the end of paragraph 7, for instance). In paragraph 7 we get reminders of Mr. Martin's fussiness and temperance, and a suggestion of his nervous anticipation. His recalling of Sam Schlosser's praise is carried over into paragraph 8, and we get the repeated phrase "as he always did" (echoed by "as usual" in other paragraphs) to keep uppermost in our minds the idea that Mr. Martin simply cannot do something that he has not been doing for years. Also in paragraph 8 the Camels, which have not been mentioned since the opening sentence, reappear in their proper place.

Paragraphs 9 and 10 get Mr. Martin to Mrs. Barrows's door. The emphasis is on whether or not he will be seen, and several phrases reassure us that all is well. The exact time of arrival on Twelfth Street is noted, and his fear of being found out is underscored by the fact that he "jumped forward against the door" when the lock clicked, and that the obviously dim bulb in the "lantern" hanging from the ceiling "seemed to give a monstrously bright light." Paragraph 10 closes with Mr. Martin going toward Mrs. Barrows's open door "swiftly, on tiptoe."

IV

The second major scene in the unfolding of the plot takes place in paragraphs 11 through 14, in Mrs. Barrows's apartment. We are aware that Mr. Martin has determined to "rub out" Mrs. Barrows, and we are vaguely aware that he is not the kind of man who can rub out anyone; but Thurber has kept us from bringing that awareness into focus by not letting Mr. Martin bring it into focus. Mr. Martin has no idea what he is going to do ("He had counted on finding [the weapon] there") or how he is going to do it.

Thurber's problem as author seems as impossible of solution as does Mr. Martin's. How does Thurber handle it? In paragraph 11 the starch goes out of Mr. Martin ("Mrs. Barrows seemed larger than he had thought"). Mrs. Barrows remarks on his appearance ("You're as white as a sheet") and offers to fix him a drink. Unaccountably—for him, for Mrs. Barrows, and for us—he accepts. While she is out of the room, he looks around for "the weapon." Every conceivable kind of weapon is available, but he rejects them all—naturally; he cannot possibly use *any* weapon. With this realization now clear to him, and with the probability of "the rubbing-out of Ulgine Barrows" being placed "in the inactive file forever," he sees her reenter with the drinks: "standing there with his gloves on" (murderers do not want to leave fingerprints), he "became acutely conscious of the fantasy he had wrought. Cigarettes in his pocket, a drink prepared for him—it was all too grossly improbable. It was more than that; it was impossible."

Mr. Martin's problem is solved, and so is Thurber's: no one will believe the situation possible. "Somewhere in the back of his mind a vague idea stirred, sprouted. . . . The idea began to bloom, strange and wonderful." We have been prepared for the idea by what Mr. Martin is and does, and we recognize it long before Mrs. Barrows blurts it out in paragraph 18: "If you weren't such a drab, ordinary little man, . . . I'd think you'd planned it all. . . . you thought no one would believe me when I told it! My God, it's really too perfect!" The words of paragraph 2—"And therein lay the cunning of his scheme"—are ironically appropriate because therein lies the cunning of Thurber's handling of his plot. Mr. Martin had vaguely planned to "rub out" Mrs. Barrows ("The project as he had worked it out was casual and bold, the risks were considerable"). Yet, in fact, he had worked out almost nothing. His only preparations were to maintain absolute secrecy and to count on his reputation for temperance and for being a "cautious, painstaking" person. In a manner which he could not have foreseen, his preparations and his reputation bring him success.

It is not until he realizes how thoroughly fantastic and impossible is his decision to murder Mrs. Barrows that he stumbles on the true solution to his problem; and that solution is ironically a product of his personality and his "planning," although totally different in kind from his vague, wishful daydreaming. What he has regretted in paragraph 2 about his plan now proves to be corrected: his plan now involves no "imprecision," no "guesswork," no "risks"; nothing can go wrong "anywhere along the line." Thurber has neatly worked out the solution, and Mr. Martin casually carries it through. Notice that in paragraph 14 the slang phrases become his and the straightforward comments are Mrs. Barrows's. He is definitely "sitting in the catbird seat," as he says when leaving her apartment.

Paragraphs 16–19 bring the final scene at F & S. We know that Mrs. Barrows will eagerly report Mr. Martin's behavior to Mr. Fitweiler, that he will not believe her, that Mrs. Barrows will "tear up the pea patch" in desperation, and that Mr. Martin will return to his beloved files satisfied and secure. The closing words are that "he walked quietly across the room to the W20 file, wearing a look of studious concentration." It is the same look of "studious concentration" he gave Mrs. Barrows (paragraph 3) when she was introduced to him as Mr. Fitweiler's special adviser twenty months before.

Exercises

1. What purpose is served by the following details?
   a. The repetition of "Mr. Martin," particularly in the first paragraph.

b. Mr. Martin's recollection of Miss Paird's remark: "Why, I even believe you like the woman." (Paragraph 4)

c. The fact that Mr. Munson has "taken his hat and stalked out, mailing his resignation later." (Paragraph 5)

d. The comment in paragraph 7 that "He had never drunk anything stronger in his life—unless you could count ginger ale."

e. The fact that Mrs. Barrows's apartment is located in a building where there will be "no doorman or other attendants." (Paragraph 9)

2. How is the action in the fourth and fifth sentences of paragraph 10 compressed to emphasize Mr. Martin's fearful haste? In other words, what do we know he actually must go through to get into Mrs. Barrows's apartment, and how does Thurber give the impression that it is all one simple, smooth, rapid movement?

Now read Frank O'Connor's "First Confession" and deal with the questions about plot that are raised at the end of the story.

First Confession[1]

FRANK O'CONNOR

It was a Saturday afternoon in early spring. A small boy whose face looked as though it had been but newly scrubbed was being led by the hand by his sister through a crowded street. The little boy showed a marked reluctance to proceed; he affected to be very interested in the shop-windows. Equally, his sister seemed to pay no attention to them. She tried to hurry him; he resisted. When she dragged him he began to bawl. The hatred with which she viewed him was almost diabolical, but when she spoke her words and tone were full of passionate sympathy.

"Ah, sha,[2] God help us!" she intoned into his ear in a whine of commiseration.

"Leave me go!" he said, digging his heels into the pavement. "I don't want to go. I want to go home."

"But, sure, you can't go home, Jackie. You'll have to go. The parish priest will be up to the house with a stick."

"I don't care. I won't go."

"Oh, Sacred Heart,[3] isn't it a terrible pity you weren't a good boy? Oh, Jackie, me heart bleeds for you! I don't know what they'll do to you at all, Jackie, me poor child. And all the trouble you caused your poor old nanny,[4] and the way you wouldn't eat in the same room with her, and the time you kicked her on the shins, and the time you went for me with the bread knife under the table. I don't know will he ever listen to you at all, Jackie. I think meself he might sind you to the bishop. Oh, Jackie, how will you think of all your sins?"

Half stupefied with terror, Jackie allowed himself to be led through the sunny streets to the very gates of the church. It was an old one with

---

[1] **confession:** the act of disclosing one's sins to a priest and asking forgiveness of God.

[2] **sha:** an expression of irritation, usually spelled *pshaw*.

[3] **Sacred Heart:** a mild oath (literally, "Heart of Jesus").

[4] **nanny:** grandmother.

two grim iron gates and a long, low, shapeless stone front. At the gates
he stuck, but it was already too late. She dragged him behind her across
the yard, and the commiserating whine with which she had tried to
madden him gave place to a yelp of triumph.

"Now you're caught! Now, you're caught. And I hope he'll give
you the pinitintial[5] psalms! That'll cure you, you suppurating little
caffler!"[6]

Jackie gave himself up for lost. Within the old church there was no
stained glass; it was cold and dark and desolate, and in the silence, the
trees in the yard knocked hollowly at the tall windows. He allowed
himself to be led through the vaulted silence, the intense and magical
silence which seemed to have frozen within the ancient walls, buttress-
ing them and shouldering the high wooden roof. In the street outside, yet seeming a million miles away, a ballad singer was drawling a
ballad.

Nora sat in front of him beside the confession box. There were a few
old women before her, and later a thin, sad-looking man with long hair
came and sat beside Jackie. In the intense silence of the church that
seemed to grow deeper from the plaintive moaning of the ballad singer,
he could hear the buzz-buzz-buzz of a woman's voice in the box, and
then the husky ba-ba-ba of the priest's. Lastly the soft thud of something
that signaled the end of the confession, and out came the woman, head
lowered, hands joined, looking neither to right nor left, and tiptoed up
to the altar to say her penance.

It seemed only a matter of seconds till Nora rose and with a whispered
injunction disappeared from his sight. He was all alone. Alone and
next to be heard and the fear of damnation in his soul. He looked at the
sad-faced man. He was gazing at the roof, his hands joined in prayer.
A woman in a red blouse and black shawl had taken her place below
him. She uncovered her head, fluffed her hair out roughly with her
hand, brushed it sharply back, then, bowing, caught it in a knot and
pinned it on her neck. Nora emerged. Jackie rose and looked at her
with a hatred which was inappropriate to the occasion and the place.

---

[5]**pinitintial:** penitential; the psalms are 6, 31, 37, 50, 101, 129, and 142 in
the Douay (Catholic) Bible. Nora hopes that the priest will make Jackie
repeat the psalms as penance.
[6]**caffler:** "brat."

Her hands were joined on her stomach, her eyes modestly lowered, and her face had an expression of the most rapt and tender recollection. With death in his heart he crept into the compartment she left open and drew the door shut behind him.

He was in pitch darkness. He could see no priest nor anything else. And anything he had heard of confession got all muddled up in his mind. He knelt to the right-hand wall and said: "Bless me, father, for I have sinned. This is my first confession." Nothing happened. He repeated it louder. Still it gave no answer. He turned to the opposite wall, genuflected first, then again went on his knees and repeated the charm. This time he was certain he would receive a reply, but none came. He repeated the process with the remaining wall without effect. He had the feeling of someone with an unfamiliar machine, of pressing buttons at random. And finally the thought struck him that God knew. God knew about the bad confession he intended to make and had made him deaf and blind so that he could neither hear nor see the priest.

Then as his eyes grew accustomed to the blackness, he perceived something he had not noticed previously: a sort of shelf at about the height of his head. The purpose of this eluded him for a moment. Then he understood. It was for kneeling on.

He had always prided himself upon his powers of climbing, but this took it out of him. There was no foothold. He slipped twice before he succeeded in getting his knee on it, and the strain of drawing the rest of his body up was almost more than he was capable of. However, he did at last get his two knees on it, there was just room for those, but his legs hung down uncomfortably and the edge of the shelf bruised his shins. He joined his hands and pressed the last remaining button. "Bless me, father, for I have sinned. This is my first confession."

At the same moment the slide was pushed back and a dim light streamed into the little box. There was an uncomfortable silence, and then an alarmed voice asked, "Who's there?" Jackie found it almost impossible to speak into the grille which was on a level with his knees, but he got a firm grip of the molding above it, bent his head down and sideways, and as though he were hanging by his feet like a monkey found himself looking almost upside down at the priest. But the priest was looking sideways at him, and Jackie, whose knees were being tortured by this new position, felt it was a queer way to hear confessions.

" 'Tis me, father," he piped, and then, running all his words together in excitement, he rattled off, "Bless me, father, for I have sinned. This is my first confession."

"What?" exclaimed a deep and angry voice, and the somber soutaned[7] figure stood bolt upright, disappearing almost entirely from Jackie's view. "What does this mean? What are you doing there? Who are you?"

And with the shock Jackie felt his hands lose their grip and his legs their balance. He discovered himself tumbling into space, and, falling, he knocked his head against the door, which shot open and permitted him to thump right into the center of the aisle. Straight on this came a small, dark-haired priest with a biretta[8] well forward on his head. At the same time Nora came skeltering madly down the church.

"Lord God!" she cried. "The sniveling little caffler! I knew he'd do it! I knew he'd disgrace me!"

Jackie received a clout over the ear which reminded him that for some strange reason he had not yet begun to cry and that people might possibly think he wasn't hurt at all. Nora slapped him again.

"What's this? What's this?" cried the priest. "Don't attempt to beat the child, you little vixen!"

"I can't do me pinance with him," cried Nora shrilly, cocking a shocked eye on the priest. "He have me driven mad. Stop your crying, you dirty scut! Stop it now or I'll make you cry at the other side of your ugly puss!"

"Run away out of this, you little jade!" growled the priest. He suddenly began to laugh, took out a pocket handkerchief, and wiped Jackie's nose. "You're not hurt, sure you're not. Show us the ould head. . . . Ah, 'tis nothing. 'Twill be better before you're twice married. . . . So you were coming to confession?"

"I was, father."

"A big fellow like you should have terrible sins. Is it your first?"

" 'Tis, father."

"Oh, my, worse and worse! Here, sit down there and wait till I get rid of these ould ones and we'll have a long chat. Never mind that sister of yours."

[7]**soutaned:** cassocked.
[8]**biretta:** a square cap worn by a Roman Catholic clergyman.

With a feeling of importance that glowed through his tears Jackie waited. Nora stuck out her tongue at him, but he didn't even bother to reply. A great feeling of relief was welling up in him. The sense of oppression that had been weighing him down for a week, the knowledge that he was about to make a bad confession, disappeared. Bad confession, indeed! He had made friends, made friends with the priest, and the priest expected, even demanded terrible sins. Oh, women! Women! It was all women and girls and their silly talk. They had no real knowledge of the world!

And when the time came for him to make his confession he did not beat about the bush. He may have clenched his hands and lowered his eyes, but wouldn't anyone?

"Father," he said huskily, "I made it up to kill me grandmother."

There was a moment's pause. Jackie did not dare to look up, but he could feel the priest's eyes on him. The priest's voice also seemed a trifle husky.

"Your grandmother?" he asked, but he didn't after all sound very angry.

"Yes, father."

"Does she live with you?"

"She do, father."

"And why did you want to kill her?"

"Oh, God, father, she's a horrible woman!"

"Is she now?"

"She is, father."

"What way is she horrible?"

Jackie paused to think. It was hard to explain.

"She takes snuff, father."

"Oh, my!"

"And she goes round in her bare feet, father."

"Tut-tut-tut!"

"She's a horrible woman, father," said Jackie with sudden earnestness. "She takes porter.[9] And she ates the potatoes off the table with her hands. And me mother do be out working most days, and since that one came 'tis she gives us our dinner and I can't ate the dinner." He found

---

[9] **porter:**   an inexpensive beverage, mildly alcoholic in content.

himself sniffling. "And she gives pinnies to Nora and she doesn't give no pinnies to me because she knows I can't stand her. And me father sides with her, father, and he bates[10] me, and me heart is broken and wan night in bed I made it up the way I'd kill her."

Jackie began to sob again, rubbing his nose with his sleeve, as he remembered his wrongs.

"And what way were you going to kill her?" asked the priest smoothly.

"With a hatchet, father."

"When she was in bed?"

"No, father."

"How, so?"

"When she ates the potatoes and drinks the porter she falls asleep, father."

"And you'd hit her then."

"Yes, father."

"Wouldn't a knife be better?"

" 'Twould, father, only I'd be afraid of the blood."

"Oh, of course, I never thought of the blood."

"I'd be afraid of that, father. I was near hitting Nora with the bread knife one time she came after me under the table, only I was afraid."

"You're a terrible child," said the priest with awe.

"I am, father," said Jackie noncommittally, sniffling back his tears.

"And what would you do with the body?"

"How, father?"

"Wouldn't someone see her and tell?"

"I was going to cut her up with a knife and take away the pieces and bury them. I could get an orange box for threepence and make a cart to take them away."

"My, my," said the priest. "You had it all well planned."

"Ah, I tried that," said Jackie with mounting confidence. "I borrowed a cart and practised it by meself one night after dark."

"And weren't you afraid?"

"Ah, no," said Jackie half-heartedly. "Only a bit."

"You have terrible courage," said the priest. "There's a lot of people

---

[10]**bates:** beats.

I want to get rid of, but I'm not like you. I'd never have the courage. And hanging is an awful death!"

"Is it?" asked Jackie, responding to the brightness of a new theme.

"Oh, an awful blooming death!"

"Did you ever see a fellow hanged?"

"Dozens of them, and they all died roaring."

"Jay!" said Jackie.

"They do be swinging out of them for hours and the poor fellows lepping[11] and roaring, like bells in a belfry, and then they put lime on them to burn them up. Of course, they pretend they're dead but sure, they don't be dead at all."

"Jay!" said Jackie again.

"So if I were you I'd take my time and think about it. In my opinion 'tisn't worth it, not even to get rid of a grandmother. I asked dozens of fellows like you that killed their grandmothers about it, and they all said, no, 'twasn't worth it. . . ."

Nora was waiting in the yard. The sunlight struck down on her across the high wall and its brightness made his eyes dazzle. "Well?" she asked. "What did he give you?"

"Three Hail Marys."[12]

"You mustn't have told him anything."

"I told him everything," said Jackie confidently.

"What did you tell him?"

"Things you don't know."

"Bah! He gave you three Hail Marys because you were a cry baby!"

Jackie didn't mind. He felt the world was very good. He began to whistle as well as the hindrance in his jaw permitted.

"What are you sucking?"

"Bull's eyes."[13]

"Was it he gave them to you?"

---

[11]**lepping:** leaping.
[12]**Hail Marys:** prayers; here, of penance.
[13]**Bull's eyes:** round, hard candies.

" 'Twas."

"Almighty God!" said Nora. "Some people have all the luck. I might as well be a sinner like you. There's no use in being good."

Exercises

1. We saw that "The Catbird Seat" was arranged in three major scenes: the first in Mr. Martin's apartment, the second in Mrs. Barrows's apartment, and the third at the office. Several minor scenes and connecting action fill out the story. Divide "First Confession" into major scenes, minor scenes, and necessary connecting action.
2. What is revealed about Jackie and his sister through the details of the opening paragraph?
3. What later details reveal the small boy's growing terror until the moment he enters the confessional? Consider the parts played by his sister and the other confessors, and the description of the church.
4. What specifically is the conflict in the story and how is it resolved? Why is it important to have the last scene with Nora and Jackie? What would be lost if O'Connor had ended the story with Jackie leaving the church in high spirits?
5. What details about Jackie's past are introduced and how are they brought in?
6. What purpose is served by the reference to the ballad singer, in the "street outside," who seemed to be "a million miles away"?
7. Comment on how the priest draws the details of Jackie's "good" confession out of him. What makes the details humorous?

Character

I

Stories happen to people. If there is ever a story concerned chiefly with a tree, or a stone, or an ape, the story will exist only because these things will be treated *as if* they were human rather than as what we know they are in nature.

We read fiction at least in part because we are interested in what happens to people. We do not ask that they necessarily be like ourselves, but we do ask that they be *believable,* and that they be *consistent.* We demand more reasonableness out of characters in fiction than we demand in real life, probably because we know that an author is in control of what his characters do and therefore can provide the kind of order and logic we would like to find in real life. In a sense, fiction *has* to be less strange than truth to be acceptable. We have to believe that characters *would* do what the writer has them do. As readers, we tend to reject the unlikely; the totally good hero pitted against the totally evil villain is not the stuff of serious fiction.

To be acceptable, a character also has to behave in a consistent manner. We will not accept in fiction a .400 yearly batting average from a .230 hitter or a miracle drug from the village pharmacist. Such behavior may be possible, but it is highly improbable. The probable impossible is a familiar feature of good fiction, but the possible improbable has no place in it.

Along with these general truths about characters in fiction, there are two other considerations that apply primarily to short stories. One is the obvious fact that the short-story writer can deal with only a few facets of a character's personality and only a few events of his life. We may feel that we know Mr. Martin pretty well when "The Catbird Seat" ends, and in one sense we do. But what does he look like? What are his politics? Who are his family and friends? Where did he come from? What made him the way he is? Mrs. Barrows is a noisy, self-possessed, insensitive woman; beyond that we know very little about her. We see only one or two sides of people we know are many-sided, as we all are.

Another truth about most short stories is that the focus is on one, central character. One of the first questions a reader should ask as he moves into a story is "Whose story is it?" In other words, whom is it principally about? The answer is usually obvious, but not always so. It is not impossible that there be more than one principal character, but it is unusual. The length of the short story does not often allow for the development of more than one primary focus. In "The Catbird Seat" two characters are revealed in some detail, but quite clearly the story is about Mr. Martin, and Mrs. Barrows serves only as the creator of Mr. Martin's problem. Mrs. Barrows remains almost completely static while he reacts against the threat she poses.

II

Keeping these general considerations in mind and using "The Catbird Seat" for illustration, let us look at the specific ways in which a writer can reveal character. (Questions on character in "First Confession" will come at the end of this section.) Each detail has to be looked at in relation to the total picture; taken alone a detail may not reveal accurately what the author means it to reveal. If a character jumps into the water with his watch on, the act may mean that he is absent-minded by nature, or it may mean that he has been momentarily distracted. Other details will support one interpretation or the other, or possibly a third. Thus, it is important that the reader hold off final judgment until he is sure what pattern is developing.

1. WHAT A CHARACTER DOES   Stories show characters in action. Therefore, the most obvious method for revealing character is through what a person does. For instance, Mr. Martin takes a drink of milk when he gets home from work and before going out to dinner. He is also shown drinking milk as he sits at home reviewing his case against Mrs. Barrows. When he returns from his successful evening at her apartment, he drinks *two* glasses of milk—in celebration. Now, all kinds of people drink milk; there should be nothing particularly revealing about it one way or another, taken as an isolated fact in the real world. But in the setting of this story, Mr. Martin's milk-drinking habits establish his temperance (fortified by the fact that he doesn't smoke) and also suggest that he is a timid, unaggressive little man—a Milquetoast. (As a matter of fact, it would be very difficult to show a man drinking milk in any story without raising the suggestion that he is timid and unaggressive even though in the real world a great many he-men drink milk.) Similar in nature to this detail is the fact that Mr. Martin eats dinner at Schrafft's, which in fiction is thought of as the timid man's restaurant.

Mr. Martin's timidity is further revealed by the very job he has: there is no risk, only peaceful obscurity, in being chief file clerk. More directly, his actions reveal his character in such incidents as his frightened behavior at Mrs. Barrows's apartment house: he jumps forward against the door when the lock clicks; he goes toward her opened apartment door "swiftly, on tiptoe"; he rushes past her "like a football tackle, bumping her." Another exposure of his timid nature comes in Mr. Fitweiler's office: when Mrs. Barrows screams, " 'Is the little rat denying it? . . . He can't get away with that!' " he gets up and moves "discreetly to a point beside Mr. Fitweiler's chair."

What do Mrs. Barrow's actions show? Her behavior is presented as Mr. Martin views it, and our judgment of her must take this fact into account. Still, we have to put faith in his observations. She never simply walks into a room, she romps, bounces, sweeps, or catapults. She does not just talk, she brays, bawls, or snorts. She is undoubtedly a noisy, blustering, overbearing shrew.

2. WHAT A CHARACTER SAYS   Another way of revealing what people are like is to show what they say. For instance, Mr. Martin's speech is definitely that of a precise and proper, even prissy, man—"Scotch-and-soda will be all right." "I beg your pardon?" "I trust so, sir." "That is correct, sir." "I will dismiss it." His pleasure over "rub out" (he associates it with erasure and correction, rather than killing; most of us would associate it only with the latter), his pained reaction to the Red Barber expressions, and his forced overuse of slang when he talks about Mr. Fitweiler in paragraph 14 all suggest that his normal behavior, like his verbal behavior, is extremely proper.

What Mrs. Barrows says and how she says it support Mr. Martin's projection of her as a rather hard-boiled, blustering woman. She delights in using the Red Barber expressions, perfectly fitting for descriptions of the Dodger games, but not natural or appropriate in the confines of a rather formal business office. Her voice evidently had the quality of a carnival barker's. Even her casual expressions have a hard-bitten ring about them—"Well, for God's sake, look who's here!" "Hey, quit shoving!"

3. WHAT A CHARACTER THINKS   A writer may also reveal the character of people by showing what they think. In "The Catbird Seat" we see only Mr. Martin this way, since the story is told almost completely through his consciousness. We learn about his passions for order, precision, caution, and self-control primarily through his own reflections on what is going on. He resents the fact that his plan has an "element of imprecision," a "margin of guesswork," but he knows that "therein" lies "the cunning of his scheme," because no one will ever see in it "the cautious, painstaking hand of Erwin Martin." The term "rub out" pleases him because it suggests "nothing more than the correction of an error. . . ." He feels that he is "too solid a man to be moved to murder by anything so childish" as Mrs. Barrows's

"gibberish," and he prides himself that he has "stood up under it so well" and "maintained always an outward appearance of polite tolerance." All of these judgments about Mr. Martin are made by Mr. Martin, and we take them at face value. We also take, with a smile, such self-observations as the one he makes when he mulls over the use of the Camels (paragraph 8): "He might even choke, too loudly." A very cautious man is Erwin Martin.

4. HOW OTHERS REACT TO A CHARACTER   Much can be shown about a character by the way others react to him, or by what they say about him. Direct comments provide the more obvious examples: Miss Paird refers to Mrs. Barrows as "that old devil," a characterization that supports Mr. Martin's opinion. Mr. Fitweiler has said, "Man is fallible but Martin isn't"; and Mr. Schlosser has said, "Our most efficient worker neither drinks nor smokes." Since Mr. Martin shows no signs of conceit or deceit as normal behavior, we can take these comments as correctly reported.

Refreshingly clear in this story are the reactions of one character to another. We see Mrs. Barrows almost completely through Mr. Martin's reactions to her, particularly in the language he uses to describe her behavior. The first detailed reference to her is "Her *quacking* voice and *braying* laugh had first *profaned* the halls of F & S. . . ." From then on she is referred to in similar terms: she "*appalled* [him] instantly"; he "*squirmed* slightly" at the thought of her "*silly* questions"; her activities at F & S are "*crimes*" and "*nonsensical* instructions deriving from the *obscene* woman." Words like *baited, brayed, bawled, jabbering,* and *snorted* are used to reveal his reaction to her behavior. In contrast, her reaction to him is mild until his unbelievable performance in her apartment. He amuses her the way a child would: she bounces into his office and says " 'Boo!' "; she calls him a "funny man" and an "odd little man"; she laughs at him.

5. HOW A CHARACTER REACTS TO HIS SURROUNDINGS   One of the commonest ways to reveal character is to show how a person reacts to his surroundings—to things and places. For instance, Mr. Martin's fear of discovery is shown by his thinking that "a bulb in a lantern hung from the hall ceiling on a chain" seems to give a "monstrously bright light." A fixture described in these terms gives off anything but a "monstrously bright light." In the same category is his feeling that Mrs. Barrows's living room seems to be "lighted by a hundred lamps."

6. DIRECT DESCRIPTION OR EXPLANATION   A final method of character revelation is through direct description or explanation by the author. It may seem odd to say that "direct description or explanation" is a separate way of portraying character, since an author is, after all, in complete con-

trol of everything that goes into his story. But as we shall soon see in detail, the way he chooses to reveal what he knows determines how "directly" he seems to be controlling his characters. We cannot illustrate this last method by reference to "The Catbird Seat," since the story is told through Mr. Martin's consciousness. The author speaks of Mr. Martin in the third person (he refers to him as "Mr. Martin" and "he"), but everything that is said only reveals what Mr. Martin sees, hears, or thinks. Thurber himself does not comment on people or events from the position of a detached observer.

In "First Confession" the same observation holds true. Most details are described as Jackie experiences them. In his terror, he *would* look upon the iron gates of the church as "grim." He *would* feel that the old church is "cold and dark and desolate." It is through his consciousness that the ballad singer, "seeming a million miles away," is drawling a ballad. Look carefully at the other descriptions in the first part of the story and notice how most are revealed as seen through the awareness of a very scared little boy.

In many good stories, however, the author does act as the detached observer and describes the looks and actions of his characters directly. We shall see this method illustrated in the third of our introductory stories, "The Lottery."

Exercises

1. How does O'Connor give insight into Jackie, Nora, and the priest through what they do? Consider, among other things, the following:
   a. The opening paragraphs centering around Nora's dragging Jackie to church.
   b. Jackie's behavior in the confessional.
   c. The priest's reaction when he pushes the slide back and when he leaves the confessional and finds Jackie sprawled on the floor, with his sister "skeltering" down the aisle bawling at him.
   d. Nora's behavior in church.
   e. The priest's parting gift.
2. a. How does Nora's choice of language reveal that she is certainly a "little vixen," as the priest calls her? Consider such comments as "me heart bleeds for you" as well as such outright vulgarities as "dirty scut."
   b. Jackie's age is revealed partly through his behavior on the way to church and in the confessional. How does what he says to Nora and to the priest further underscore the fact that he cannot be much more than seven or eight years old?

c. The priest's understanding of small boys is revealed primarily through his response to Jackie's "good" confession. Indicate how what he says shows that he knows how to handle small boys sympathetically.

3. As with "The Catbird Seat" we get into the mind of only one of the characters in "First Confession." Jackie does not tell his own story, but the story is told through his consciousness, although not in language that he would use. We learn most about him through his thoughts about his experience. For instance, when the church is described as "cold and dark and desolate," with an "intense and magical silence," that is the way he sees it. Thus, his terror is underscored by the way he thinks about the church.

For another example, he is the one who is aware that his look of hatred toward Nora is "inappropriate to the occasion and the place," even though it is her false piety that leads him to react the way he does.

Give five other examples in which Jackie's thoughts are revealed, and point out what these examples show about him. Use at least two examples from his troubles in the confessional.

4. a. What do the priest's immediate defense of Jackie and his harsh words to Nora show about Jackie and Nora? In other words, how does the priest's attitude help define their characters?

   b. How does Jackie's almost immediate recognition that the priest is a kindly man help define the priest's character?

5. Show how Jackie's reactions to the strangeness of the confessional give us some of the clearest clues about what kind of boy he is and how we are to take him. (Be sure you have a clear picture of what the inside of the confessional is like. How large is it? Where are the grille and the sliding door located? What are they for? What purpose does the shelf serve for adults? Exactly what does Jackie do?)

Point of View

I

Stories don't just happen; they are created. There are no stories in the everyday course of events; there are only the ingredients for stories—in the most dramatic of happenings or in the simplest of acts. A dozen people may watch a man standing on a fifth-floor ledge or a small child crying. There is no story involved in either case unless one of the dozen chooses to make one up—to surround the isolated event with a beginning and an end, thereby giving what we call a *meaning* to human action. In other words, there has to be a story-maker—a storyteller—if there is to be a story.

The story-maker (the writer, the author) is in complete control of all of the details of his story. He has control over who the characters are, what they do, and why they do it. He also has control over how the story is to be told, and who is going to tell it. He can adopt one of a number of *points of view*, each of which will give a quite different total story.

Broadly speaking, there are two major approaches the author can take: (1) he can present the story as if told by someone who is, himself, completely outside it, or (2) he can present the story as if told by one of its characters. Within these broad divisions there are several possibilities, all of them quite different in the kind of story they will produce. The chief ways of handling the first main approach are that the teller either (*a*) goes into the thoughts as well as the actions and speeches of the characters or (*b*) simply describes the characters' behavior while foregoing any personal interpretation or analysis of their thoughts. When the story is told by a character, the author usually either (*a*) assumes the role of the main character and tells the story in the first person ("I") or (*b*) acts as a minor character but still tells the story as a first-person observer. In any of the methods the teller's role is an *assumed* role.

Perhaps the idea of point of view will be clearer if we look specifically at "The Catbird Seat" as it stands to see what the point of view is. (Questions on "First Confession" will come at the end of this section.) Then we can show briefly what differences there would be if some of the other points of view had been used. Thurber has chosen to use a narrator who is not a character in the story. But he has severely limited the narrator's scope in a way that might not be obvious to a casual reader. This particular narrator operates through the mind of Mr. Martin almost completely. In a sense it is as if the story were being told by Mr. Martin directly. He is present when most of the events in the story take place; almost nothing is revealed by the narrator that Mr. Martin has not witnessed, has not thought, or has not been told.

Even more important than the fact that the narrator sticks to what Mr. Martin sees and hears is the fact that the story is told through his language and through the way he thinks. For one thing, the key words in reference to Mrs. Barrows's voice and behavior are words Mr. Martin would use, as we have already indicated. The exaggerated comparisons are his comparisons: "romped . . . like a circus horse"; "her braying laugh rang out like the report of a shotgun"; "the door to the office blew open with the suddenness of a gas-main explosion." The language is not the normal language of the formal, quiet, reserved Mr. Martin; rather it is the language of that kind of man driven "near to distraction" by a brassy, vulgar female. He would not use such language in talking to someone else, but he does *think* about her that way over his glass of milk.

The thought processes also are those of Mr. Martin and further reveal his personality. The most obvious example is his long review of "his case against Ulgine Barrows." He acts as prosecutor ("It was competent, material, and relevant to review her advent and rise to power"), defense attorney ("entering an objection"), judge ("and sustaining it"), and jury ("'Gentlemen of the jury,' he said to himself"). The extended metaphor shows him as he sees himself: a judicious, thorough, self-controlled man protecting order and stability from the onslaught of "the obscene woman."

Throughout the rest of the story, the reflections on his behavior and on the behavior of the other characters are the reflections Mr. Martin would make; the narrator stays in his mind. In paragraph 7, for instance, the second sentence reads: "He polished his glasses more often and once sharpened an already sharp pencil, *but not even Miss Paird noticed.*" It is Mr. Martin who is aware that Miss Paird seems "always able to find things out," and it reveals him as the cautious man he says he is to have him aware that Miss Paird has not noticed his nervousness. In paragraph 8 it is Mr. Martin who thinks that "He might even choke, too loudly," not a detached narrator laughing at the "odd little man." The humor of the whole story lies primarily in the fact that the narrator is not standing wholly apart from Mr. Martin commenting on his foolish behavior, laughing at him; rather, Thurber in his choice of point of view lets Mr. Martin reveal himself as a Milquetoast driven to desperate thoughts and potentially desperate action, all the while behaving outwardly as the timid little man he essentially is. Mr. Martin takes himself seriously—he is afraid he *will* "choke, too loudly"—and our amusement comes because we are aware of the discrepancy between what he feels he has to do and what he can by nature do.

II

The stress we have put on point of view is unduly heavy unless its importance can be proved. If, as we have said, a writer consciously chooses one point of view from a number of possible ones, there must be good reasons why one is more appropriate than another for any given story. We have seen how the combination of detachment-involvement that Thurber uses in "The Catbird Seat" enables him to make the treatment of Mr. Martin's predicament humorous rather than embarrassingly personal or coldly unsympathetic. Let us look now at what different impressions are given if parts of the story are told using other possible methods.

1. THE ALL-KNOWING OR OMNISCIENT POINT OF VIEW   In the case of the all-knowing point of view, the narrator sees all and knows all. Unlike the narrator in "The Catbird Seat" he is not limited to the consciousness of one character. He can refer whenever he chooses to any act of any character and to any thought of any character, and he can comment on actions and thoughts as he pleases. The following version of the first paragraphs illustrates this point of view:

Erwin Martin, head of the filing department at F & S, bought the pack of Camels on Monday night in the most crowded cigar store on Broadway. It was theater time and seven or eight men were buying cigarettes. The clerk didn't even glance at him, but wouldn't have given a second thought to such a nondescript little man anyway. Mr. Martin put the pack in his overcoat pocket and went out. If any of the staff at F & S had seen him buy the cigarettes, he thought, they would have been astonished, for it was generally known that he did not smoke, and never had. Joey Hart, his assistant, was sure that one drag on a cigarette would turn the poor guy green. Luckily for Mr. Martin and his plan, no one saw him.

A week before, he had decided to kill Mrs. Ulgine Barrows, who had been hired some twenty months previously as special adviser to Mr. Fitweiler, the president of F & S. How Mr. Fitweiler could ever have made such an error in judgment was beyond belief, as are many things in this world. She was brassy and self-satisfied, and was systematically destroying the efficiency and system of F & S. Poor Mr. Fitweiler didn't realize it, and Mrs. Barrows really didn't care. She had confided to a friend of hers on a weekend on Long Island that she would "put a little life into F & S or bury the stupid place."

Dozens of times Mr. Martin had gone over his plan to rub out Mrs. Barrows (as he liked to put it). He was hardly the kind of man who could rub out anything but a stray mark on a file card, but Mrs. Barrows's behavior had so upset the timid soul's cozy little world that he had to do something or go crazy. As he sat drinking his usual glass of milk after getting back from buying the pack of Camels, he thought through his plan again. The roar of the el trains outside his window didn't disturb his file clerk's concentration. There was no doubt that it was a risky business, but he felt sure that the very riskiness of it would keep suspicion from falling on him, since he had a twenty-two year reputation with F & S as being the kind of man who never made a mistake, never took a risk, and never did anything bad. When people have established certain reputations over a period of years—good or bad—the world at large finds it difficult to imagine them behaving otherwise. It's often a helpful position to be in. The only real danger, then, lay in the possibility that somebody might catch him in the act.

The point should be clear that in this method of storytelling the narrator moves freely in and out of the minds of all of the characters and freely adds his own specific observations on individuals or general comments on human nature. He brings in Joey Hart's thought, Mrs. Barrows's remark to a friend on Long Island, and Mr. Martin's musings over his plan. The narrator says, as an outside observer, that the clerk "wouldn't have given a second thought to such a nondescript little man" and that Mr. Martin "was hardly the kind of man who could rub out anything but a stray mark on a file card." Furthermore, the narrator as outside observer makes general comments on human nature: "as are many things in this world"; "When people have established certain reputations . . ."

There is nothing inherently good or bad about using the point of view of the all-knowing narrator or about using any other point of view. A skillful writer uses a particular method for a particular purpose and knows the advantages and disadvantages of each. However, a crude use of the all-knowing narrator, as here, points up some of the dangers of this method, which is usually the one used by unskilled writers who are not consciously aware of point of view at all. The danger is clutter: so much more is said than need be said that the really significant object or speech or event cannot be distinguished. Joey Hart's observation can serve no useful purpose, for instance, unless the relationship between him and Mr. Martin is to be an important one, which it is not. Then, too, Mrs. Barrows's feelings remain properly vague in the original: maybe F & S needs shaking up, but that possibility is irrelevant, and should be. The *story* of "The Catbird Seat," the basic problem, is wholly concerned with Mr. Martin's efforts at self-preservation. Mr. Martin thinks Mrs. Barrows is out to destroy him; we ought to reserve judgment on that point. The full weakness of the present omniscient version, however, is shown by the fact that it tells us specifically that Mrs. Barrows is only interested in putting "a little life" into F & S. If she says so, we cannot think otherwise, and therefore we will find no reason for her outburst against Mr. Martin when he goes into his act in her apartment. Why should she care how "a little life" gets put into F & S, so long as it does? One other point should be made about the revised version. The narrator's comment on reputations is wholly unnecessary. All of Mr. Martin's musings prior to the observation have been based on that truth. To have the obvious spelled out is insulting to the reader.

   2. DETACHED OBSERVER   A variant of the omniscient point of view allows the narrator to describe what the various characters look like and what they do and say as if he were a detached observer who knows no more about them than this. The reader is led to make judgments on what a character is thinking, but he is never *told* what anyone is thinking; he has to infer this from carefully observed behavior. If the detached method were used with "The Catbird Seat" there could obviously not be paragraphs like 2 and 3, for instance. The narrator would have to handle the "review" material in some such way as the following:

Erwin Martin had been a hard-working, loyal employee of F & S for over twenty years when Mr. Fitweiler, president of the firm, appointed Mrs. Ulgine Barrows his special adviser. Mr. Martin's painstaking attention to details, his inability to make a mistake in the exacting job of keeping the records at F & S, and his willingness to work late into the evenings if necessary had earned him his present position as head of the filing department. A quiet, mousy man whose nerves visibly jangled at the excessive noise if one of his assistants took more than a few turns to sharpen a pencil, Mr. Martin was nevertheless considered the ideal employee at F & S. He had never complained, at least not openly.
   Naturally, he had had no opinions about the hiring of Mrs. Barrows some twenty months ago. Old Roberts, the personnel chief, introduced her in Mr. Martin's office. He had risen when they entered, but remained behind his desk staring bug-eyed at the swing of her broad shoulders and the size of her toothy smile. She maneuvered around his desk and grabbed his small, dry hand in her tanned fist.
   "Well," she said, looking at the papers on his desk and jangling his nerves, "are you lifting the oxcart out of the ditch?"
   He smiled faintly and mumbled something that neither old Roberts nor Mrs. Barrows responded to. She was gone as rapidly as she had come, with old Roberts hurrying along behind her. Mr. Martin sat down and flexed his fingers.
   The months that followed . . .

   Here we notice that, as with paragraph 1 of the original, all the details are either descriptions of actual behavior ("He had risen when they entered, but remained behind the desk"; "grabbed his small, dry hand in her

tanned fist"; "Mr. Martin sat down and flexed his fingers") or else judgments on behavior that any outside observer would make ("hard-working,"
"loyal," "quiet," "bug-eyed," "smiled faintly," "mumbled"). If the narrator
sticks faithfully to the detached point of view, he must simply present
action as it can be observed or make judgments that will be generally
acceptable to other detached or neutral observers. If Thurber had used
this method in "The Catbird Seat," he could hardly have been so successful
in treating Mr. Martin in a humorously ironic way. As the story stands,
the humor lies in the contrast between Mr. Martin's thoughts and his
actions, both of which Thurber's method allows him to show.

III

Two other general points of view can be used by the fiction writer, and
both involve a narrator who is not outside the story but an actor in it.

3. FIRST PERSON NARRATOR: THE PRINCIPAL CHARACTER   The main character can tell his own story in the first person—as an "I." If we try this point
of view with the opening paragraphs of "The Catbird Seat," we get the
following as a possibility:

I bought the pack of Camels on Monday night in the most crowded cigar store
on Broadway. It was theater time and seven or eight men were buying cigarettes.
The clerk didn't even glance at me as I put the pack in my overcoat pocket
and went out. If any of the staff at F & S had seen me buy the cigarettes, they
would have been astonished, for it is generally known that I do not smoke, and
never have. No one saw me.

It was just a week to the day since I had decided to rub out Mrs. Ulgine
Barrows. The term "rub out" pleases me because it suggests nothing more than
the correction of an error—in this case an error of Mr. Fitweiler. I had spent
each night of the past week working out my plan and examining it. As I walked
home now I went over it again. For the hundredth time I resented the element
of imprecision, the margin of guesswork that entered into the business. The
project as I had worked it out was casual and bold, the risks were considerable.
Something might go wrong anywhere along the line. And therein lay the cunning of my scheme. No one would ever see in it the cautious, painstaking hand
of Erwin Martin, head of the filing department of F & S, of whom Mr. Fitweiler
had once said, "Man is fallible but Martin isn't." No one would see my hand,
that is, unless it were caught in the act.

Here we have done nothing but change the language from the third
person ("Mr. Martin," "he") to the first person ("I"). The effect is quite

revealing. If we use the phrasing of the original as if Mr. Martin were talking directly, we get the impression of a much more purposeful, scheming man than Mr. Martin is in the original. In other words, Thurber's Mr. Martin is not the kind of man who will talk so openly, so bluntly, even to himself; he likes the phrase "rub out," for instance, but he will not use it out loud or admit openly that he likes it. The impression given in the first-person point of view is that the speaker is telling his story directly to the reader; the assumption is that the reader is a listener. We are not saying that Thurber could not have chosen to have Mr. Martin tell his story directly; we are simply saying that had he done so, Mr. Martin would have appeared a quite different man: talkative, self-applauding, even boastful; much more calculating.

It is also difficult to treat a character like Mr. Martin with humor in the first person. He does not see himself humorously and does not see the situation that way. He cannot consciously reveal himself as timid and foolish. Telling his own story, he would be too baldly and embarrassingly revealed as a puffed-up Milquetoast; we might feel pity but not sympathy.

4. FIRST PERSON NARRATOR: A MINOR CHARACTER   Another first person technique is to let a minor character tell the story, say Miss Paird in "The Catbird Seat," or to have as narrator an unnamed observer who is assumed to be a direct witness of events, say a member of the F & S staff, but who does not have any active part in the story. The following suggests this latter point of view:

Mr. Martin returned to the file room and walked quietly across to the W20 file, wearing his usual look of studious concentration. If we hadn't witnessed most of the affair in Mr. Fitweiler's office after Mrs. Barrows started screaming, we might have thought he was simply returning with the latest reports on delinquent accounts: there were no signs of the ordeal he had gone through. We had hastened back to our desks after Mrs. Barrows was hustled downstairs screaming vulgar curses at Mr. Martin.

Ever since the day she had showed up as special adviser to Mr. Fitweiler some twenty months ago, Mr. Martin had been the one person on the staff who had shown her any real courtesy. We thought he even liked the woman. The rest of us completely despised her.

In this case, the narrator would observe directly the actions and comments of Mr. Martin, Mrs. Barrows, and Mr. Fitweiler, and would know how the staff felt about what went on in the office, but would not know what was going on in the minds of the principal characters and would not be aware of any of the events outside the office unless told about them by one of the principals or by someone who was a witness. This method is particularly effective if the author wants to keep direct insight into his chief character at a minimum so that he is revealed primarily as he affects others (perhaps a neighborhood or a whole community), whose direct reactions are presented. One of the dangers in this method is the possibility that the narrator's own personality may loom too large and take the focus off the chief character. The first person point of view, by its very nature, involves the reader quickly in the personality of the narrator if the personality is interesting in its own right and not merely neutral. Compare the following version with the previous one and notice the difference as suggested above:

I guess I know Erwin Martin as well as anyone at F & S knows him. Or anyone anywhere for that matter, since I'm sure the only close friend he ever had was his mother, and she left this world ten years ago at least. I never knew her, but from her picture on his desk and from the poems he's written about her (I don't usually like poems, but these I like because I know who wrote them and he let me see them and they make sense), I would say that she was the same kind of decent, quiet person that he is.

We get definite insight into the personality of Erwin Martin here, but we also get a strong picture of what kind of person the narrator is—too strong. This narrator would clash with Mr. Martin for the central position in the story unless the self-revelations were considerably toned down, and in that case this opening paragraph would be misleading.

Clearly the point of view from which a story is told—who tells the story and how—makes a great deal of difference to the writer and to the reader. For the writer it determines his selection of details and his choice of language. It sets up one kind of guideline to keep his story development believable and consistent. For the reader, recognition of what point of view the writer has adopted tells him how to interpret the language and how to assess behavior.

Exercises

1. We have already indicated that "First Confession" is told, as is "The Catbird Seat," through the consciousness of the chief character, although not in language he would use. What are the advantages for this story in using this point of view? For contrast, try writing the two paragraphs beginning "Jackie gave himself up for lost" first from the point of view of an all-knowing narrator,

and then from the first-person point of view, as if Jackie were telling his own story.

2. What do the following details reveal about Jackie's state of mind:
   a. "The hatred with which she viewed him was almost diabolical."
   b. ". . . she intoned into his ear in a whine of commiseration."
   c. ". . . a yelp of triumph."
   d. ". . . the trees in the yard knocked hollowly at the tall window."
   e. ". . . the buzz-buzz-buzz of a woman's voice . . . and then the husky ba-ba-ba of the priest's."
   f. "Nora stuck out her tongue at him, but he didn't even bother to reply."

The third of our introductory stories is Shirley Jackson's "The Lottery." Here the narrator seems to be completely detached from the characters in the story. The focus is on an event in a small American village observed directly, as if from a position above the crowd where all can be seen and heard. It may be helpful to think of the narrator as in some sense the combination director and cameraman in a locally produced one-scene movie. He manipulates and reveals all that goes on, focusing sometimes on one character and sometimes on the whole group.

At the end of the story there are questions on plot and character which will reinforce what has been said in the first two sections of the book. Then follow questions on point of view in connection with "The Lottery."

The Lottery
SHIRLEY JACKSON

The morning of June 27th was clear and sunny, with the fresh warmth of a full-summer day; the flowers were blossoming profusely and the grass was richly green. The people of the village began to gather in the square, between the post office and the bank, around ten o'clock; in some towns there were so many people that the lottery took two days and had to be started on June 26th, but in this village, where there were only about three hundred people, the whole lottery took less than two hours, so it could begin at ten o'clock in the morning and still be through in time to allow the villagers to get home for noon dinner.

The children assembled first, of course. School was recently over for the summer, and the feeling of liberty sat uneasily on most of them; they tended to gather together quietly for a while before they broke into boisterous play, and their talk was still of the classroom and the teacher, of books and reprimands. Bobby Martin had already stuffed his pockets full of stones, and the other boys soon followed his example, selecting the smoothest and roundest stones; Bobby and Harry Jones and Dickie Delacroix—the villagers pronounced this name "Dellacroy"—eventually made a great pile of stones in one corner of the square and guarded it against the raids of the other boys. The girls stood aside, talking among themselves, looking over their shoulders at the boys, and the very small children rolled in the dust or clung to the hands of their older brothers or sisters.

Soon the men began to gather, surveying their own children, speaking of planting and rain, tractors and taxes. They stood together, away from the pile of stones in the corner, and their jokes were quiet and they smiled rather than laughed. The women, wearing faded house dresses and sweaters, came shortly after their menfolk. They greeted one another and exchanged bits of gossip as they went to join their husbands. Soon the women, standing by their husbands, began to call to their

Reprinted from *The Lottery* by Shirley Jackson, by permission of Farrar, Straus & Giroux, Inc. Copyright 1948 by *The New Yorker* Magazine, 1949 by Shirley Jackson.

children, and the children came reluctantly, having to be called four or five times. Bobby Martin ducked under his mother's grasping hand and ran, laughing, back to the pile of stones. His father spoke up sharply, and Bobby came quickly and took his place between his father and his oldest brother.

The lottery was conducted—as were the square dances, the teen-age club, the Halloween program—by Mr. Summers, who had time and energy to devote to civic activities. He was a round-faced, jovial man and he ran the coal business, and people were sorry for him, because he had no children and his wife was a scold. When he arrived in the square, carrying the black wooden box, there was a murmur of conversation among the villagers, and he waved and called, "Little late today, folks." The postmaster, Mr. Graves, followed him, carrying a three-legged stool, and the stool was put in the center of the square and Mr. Summers set the black box down on it. The villagers kept their distance, leaving a space between themselves and the stool, and when Mr. Summers said, "Some of you fellows want to give me a hand?" there was a hesitation before two men, Mr. Martin and his oldest son, Baxter, came forward to hold the box steady on the stool while Mr. Summers stirred up the papers inside it.

The original paraphernalia for the lottery had been lost long ago, and the black box now resting on the stool had been put into use even before Old Man Warner, the oldest man in town, was born. Mr. Summers spoke frequently to the villagers about making a new box, but no one liked to upset even as much tradition as was represented by the black box. There was a story that the present box had been made with some pieces of the box that had preceded it, the one that had been constructed when the first people settled down to make a village here. Every year, after the lottery, Mr. Summers began talking again about a new box, but every year the subject was allowed to fade off without anything's being done. The black box grew shabbier each year; by now it was no longer completely black but splintered badly along one side to show the original wood color, and in some places faded or stained.

Mr. Martin and his oldest son, Baxter, held the black box securely on the stool until Mr. Summers had stirred the papers thoroughly with his hand. Because so much of the ritual had been forgotten or discarded,

Mr. Summers had been successful in having slips of paper substituted for the chips of wood that had been used for generations. Chips of wood, Mr. Summers had argued, had been all very well when the village was tiny, but now that the population was more than three hundred and likely to keep on growing, it was necessary to use something that would fit more easily into the black box. The night before the lottery, Mr. Summers and Mr. Graves made up the slips of paper and put them in the box, and it was then taken to the safe of Mr. Summers's coal company and locked up until Mr. Summers was ready to take it to the square next morning. The rest of the year, the box was put away, sometimes one place, sometimes another: it had spent one year in Mr. Graves's barn and another year underfoot in the post office, and sometimes it was set on a shelf in the Martin grocery and left there.

There was a great deal of fussing to be done before Mr. Summers declared the lottery open. There were the lists to make up—of heads of families, heads of households in each family, members of each household in each family. There was the proper swearing-in of Mr. Summers by the postmaster, as the official of the lottery;.at one time, some people remembered, there had been a recital of some sort, performed by the official of the lottery, a perfunctory, tuneless chant that had been rattled off duly each year; some people believed that the official of the lottery used to stand just so when he said or sang it, others believed that he was supposed to walk among the people, but years and years ago this part of the ritual had been allowed to lapse. There had been, also, a ritual salute, which the official of the lottery had had to use in addressing each person who came up to draw from the box, but this also changed with time, until now it was felt necessary only for the official to speak to each person approaching. Mr. Summers was very good at all this; in his clean white shirt and blue jeans, with one hand resting carelessly on the black box, he seemed very proper and important as he talked interminably to Mr. Graves and the Martins.

Just as Mr. Summers finally left off talking and turned to the assembled villagers, Mrs. Hutchinson came hurriedly along the path to the square, her sweater thrown over her shoulders, and slid into place in the back of the crowd. "Clean forgot what day it was," she said to Mrs. Delacroix, who stood next to her, and they both laughed softly.

"Thought my old man was out back stacking wood," Mrs. Hutchinson went on, "and then I looked out the window and the kids was gone, and then I remembered it was the twenty-seventh and came a-running." She dried her hands on her apron, and Mrs. Delacroix said, "You're in time though. They're still talking away up there."

Mrs. Hutchinson craned her neck to see through the crowd and found her husband and children standing near the front. She tapped Mrs. Delacroix on the arm as a farewell and began to make her way through the crowd, "Here comes your Missus, Hutchinson," and "Bill, she made it after all." Mrs. Hutchinson reached her husband, and Mr. Summers, who had been waiting, said cheerfully, "Thought we were going to have to get on without you, Tessie." Mrs. Hutchinson said, grinning, "Wouldn't have me leave m'dishes in the sink, now, would you, Joe?" and soft laughter ran through the crowd as the people stirred back into position after Mrs. Hutchinson's arrival.

"Well, now," Mr. Summers said soberly, "guess we better get started, get this over with, so's we can go back to work. Anybody ain't here?"

"Dunbar," several people said. "Dunbar, Dunbar."

Mr. Summers consulted his list. "Clyde Dunbar," he said. That's right. He's broke his leg, hasn't he. Who's drawing for him?"

"Me, I guess," a woman said, and Mr. Summers turned to look at her. "Wife draws for her husband," Mr. Summers said. 'Don't you have a grown boy to do it for you, Janey?" Although Mr. Summers and everyone else in the village knew the answer perfectly well, it was the business of the official of the lottery to ask such questions formally. Mr. Summers waited with an expression of polite interest while Mrs. Dunbar answered.

"Horace's not but sixteen yet," Mrs. Dunbar said regretfully. "Guess I gotta fill in for the old man this year."

"Right," Mr. Summers said. He made a note on the list he was holding. Then he asked, "Watson boy drawing this year?"

A tall boy in the crowd raised his hand. "Here," he said. "I'm drawing for m'mother and me." He blinked his eyes nervously and ducked his head as several voices in the crowd said things like "Good fellow, Jack," and "Glad to see your mother's got a man to do it."

"Well,'" Mr. Summers said, "guess that's everyone. Old Man Warner make it?"

"Here," a voice said, and Mr. Summers nodded.

mood atmosphere

A sudden hush fell on the crowd as Mr. Summers cleared his throat and looked at the list. "All ready?" he called. "Now, I'll read the names —heads of families first—and the men come up and take a paper out of the box. Keep the paper folded in your hand without looking at it until everyone has had a turn. Everything clear?"

The people had done it so many times that they only half listened to the directions; most of them were quiet, wetting their lips, not looking around. Then Mr. Summers raised one hand high and said, "Adams." A man disengaged himself from the crowd and came forward. "Hi, Steve," Mr. Summers said, and Mr. Adams said, "Hi, Joe." They grinned at one another humorlessly and nervously. Then Mr. Adams reached into the black box and took out a folded paper. He held it firmly by one corner as he turned and went hastily back to his place in the crowd, where he stood a little apart from his family, not looking down at his hand.

"Allen," Mr. Summers said. "Anderson.... Bentham."

"Seems like there's no time at all between lotteries any more," Mrs. Delacroix said to Mrs. Graves in the back row. "Seems like we got through with the last one only last week."

"Time sure goes fast," Mrs. Graves said.

"Clark.... Delacroix."

"There goes my old man," Mrs. Delacroix said. She held her breath while her husband went forward.

"Dunbar," Mr. Summers said, and Mrs. Dunbar went steadily to the box while one of the women said, "Go on, Janey," and another said, "There she goes."

"We're next," Mrs. Graves said. She watched while Mr. Graves came around from the side of the box, greeted Mr. Summers gravely, and selected a slip of paper from the box. By now, all through the crowd there were men holding the small folded papers in their large hands, turning them over and over nervously. Mrs. Dunbar and her two sons stood together, Mrs. Dunbar holding the slip of paper.

"Harburt.... Hutchinson."

"Get up there, Bill," Mrs. Hutchinson said, and the people near her laughed.

"Jones."

"They do say," Mr. Adams said to Old Man Warner, who stood next to him, "that over in the north village they're talking of giving up the lottery."

Old Man Warner snorted. "Pack of crazy fools," he said. "Listening to the young folks, nothing's good enough for *them*. Next thing you know, they'll be wanting to go back to living in caves, nobody work any more, live *that* way for a while. Used to be a saying about 'Lottery in June, corn be heavy soon.' First thing you know, we'd all be eating stewed chickweed and acorns. There's *always* been a lottery," he added petulantly. "Bad enough to see young Joe Summers up there joking with everybody."

"Some places have already quit lotteries," Mrs. Adams said.

"Nothing but trouble in *that*," Old Man Warner said stoutly. "Pack of young fools."

"Martin." And Bobby Martin watched his father go forward. "Over-dyke.... Percy."

"I wish they'd hurry," Mrs. Dunbar said to her older son. "I wish they'd hurry."

"They're almost through," her son said.

"You get ready to run tell Dad," Mrs. Dunbar said.

Mr. Summers called his own name and then stepped forward precisely and selected a slip from the box. Then he called, "Warner."

"Seventy-seventh year I been in the lottery," Old Man Warner said as he went through the crowd. "Seventy-seventh time."

"Watson." The tall boy came awkwardly through the crowd. Someone said, "Don't be nervous, Jack," and Mr. Summers said, "Take your time, son."

"Zanini."

After that, there was a long pause, a breathless pause, until Mr. Summers, holding his slip of paper in the air, said, "All right, fellows." For a minute, no one moved, and then all the slips of paper were opened. Suddenly, all the women began to speak at once, saying, "Who is it?" "Who's got it?" "Is it the Dunbars?" "Is it the Watsons?" Then the voices began to say, "It's Hutchinson. It's Bill." "Bill Hutchinson's got it."

"Go tell your father," Mrs. Dunbar said to her older son.

People began to look around to see the Hutchinsons. Bill Hutchinson was standing quiet, staring down at the paper in his hand. Suddenly, Tessie Hutchinson shouted to Mr. Summers, "You didn't give him time enough to take any paper he wanted. I saw you. It wasn't fair!"

"Be a good sport, Tessie," Mrs. Delacroix called, and Mrs. Graves said, "All of us took the same chance."

"Shut up, Tessie," Bill Hutchinson said.

"Well, everyone," Mr. Summers said, "that was done pretty fast, and now we've got to be hurrying a little more to get done in time." He consulted his next list. "Bill," he said, "you draw for the Hutchinson family. You got any other households in the Hutchinsons?"

"There's Don and Eva," Mrs. Hutchinson yelled. "Make *them* take their chance!"

"Daughters draw with their husbands' families, Tessie," Mr. Summers said gently. "You know that as well as anyone else."

"It wasn't *fair*," Tessie said.

"I guess not, Joe," Bill Hutchinson said regretfully. "My daughter draws with her husband's family, that's only fair. And I've got no other family except the kids."

"Then, as far as drawing for families is concerned, it's you," Mr. Summers said in explanation, "and as far as drawing for households is concerned, that's you, too. Right?"

"Right," Bill Hutchinson said.

"How many kids, Bill?" Mr. Summers asked formally.

"Three," Bill Hutchinson said. "There's Bill, Jr., and Nancy, and little Dave. And Tessie and me."

"All right, then," Mr. Summers said. "Harry, you got their tickets back?"

Mr. Graves nodded and held up the slips of paper. "Put them in the box, then," Mr. Summers directed. "Take Bill's and put it in."

"I think we ought to start over," Mrs. Hutchinson said, as quietly as she could. "I tell you it wasn't *fair*. You didn't give him time enough to choose. Everybody saw that."

Mr. Graves had selected the five slips and put them in the box, and he dropped all the papers but those onto the ground, where the breeze caught them and lifted them off.

"Listen, everybody," Mrs. Hutchinson was saying to the people around her.

"Ready, Bill?" Mr. Summers asked, and Bill Hutchinson, with one quick glance around at his wife and children, nodded.

"Remember," Mr. Summers said, "take the slips and keep them folded until each person has taken one. Harry, you help little Dave." Mr. Graves took the hand of the little boy, who came willingly with him up to the box. "Take a paper out of the box, Davy," Mr. Summers said. Davy put his hand into the box and laughed. "Take just *one* paper," Mr. Summers said. "Harry, you hold it for him." Mr. Graves took the child's hand and removed the folded paper from the tight fist and held it while little Dave stood next to him and looked up at him wonderingly.

"Nancy next," Mr. Summers said. Nancy was twelve, and her school friends breathed heavily as she went forward, switching her skirt, and took a slip daintily from the box. "Bill, Jr.," Mr. Summers said, and Billy, his face red and his feet overlarge, nearly knocked the box over as he got a paper out. "Tessie," Mr. Summers said. She hesitated for a minute, looking around defiantly, and then set her lips and went up to the box. She snatched a paper out and held it behind her.

"Bill," Mr. Summers said, and Bill Hutchinson reached into the box and felt around, bringing his hand out at last with the slip of paper in it.

The crowd was quiet. A girl whispered, "I hope it's not Nancy," and the sound of the whisper reached the edges of the crowd.

"It's not the way it used to be," Old Man Warner said clearly. "People ain't the way they used to be."

"All right," Mr. Summers said. "Open the papers. Harry, you open little Dave's."

Mr. Graves opened the slip of paper and there was a general sigh through the crowd as he held it up and everyone could see that it was blank. Nancy and Bill, Jr., opened theirs at the same time, and both beamed and laughed, turning around to the crowd and holding their slips of paper above their heads.

"Tessie," Mr. Summers said. There was a pause, and then Mr. Summers looked at Bill Hutchinson, and Bill unfolded his paper and showed it. It was blank.

"It's Tessie," Mr. Summers said, and his voice was hushed. "Show us her paper, Bill."

Bill Hutchinson went over to his wife and forced the slip of paper out of her hand. It had a black spot on it, the black spot Mr. Summers had made the night before with the heavy pencil in the coal-company office. Bill Hutchinson held it up, and there was a stir in the crowd.

"All right, folks," Mr. Summers said. "Let's finish quickly."

Although the villagers had forgotten the ritual and lost the original black box, they still remembered to use stones. The pile of stones the boys had made earlier was ready; there were stones on the ground with the blowing scraps of paper that had come out of the box. Mrs. Delacroix selected a stone so large she had to pick it up with both hands and turned to Mrs. Dunbar. "Come on," she said. "Hurry up."

Mrs. Dunbar had small stones in both hands, and she said, gasping for breath, "I can't run at all. You'll have to go ahead and I'll catch up with you."

The children had stones already, and someone gave little Davy Hutchinson a few pebbles.

Tessie Hutchinson was in the center of a cleared space by now, and she held her hands out desperately as the villagers moved in on her. "It isn't fair," she said. A stone hit her on the side of the head.

Old Man Warner was saying, "Come on, come on, everyone." Steve Adams was in the front of the crowd of villagers, with Mrs. Graves beside him.

"It isn't fair, it isn't right," Mrs. Hutchinson screamed, and then they were upon her.

Exercises

1. This story deals with horror in a very powerful way. The horror is built
    around the contrast between the simple plot outline and character portrayal
    and the terrible fact that at the end a woman is being stoned to death by her
    family, friends, and neighbors.
    a. State briefly what actually happens in the story. There is a conflict, but
        it is so casually presented on the surface that the word "conflict" hardly
        seems appropriate. What is the conflict? What specifically is being de-
        termined by the lottery? When in the story does the reader find out what
        is really going on? How has this outcome been specifically prepared for?
        In other words, what specific actions in the plot development point to this
        outcome even though the reader may have missed their significance the
        first time he read the story? Don't be satisfied with pointing out only the
        facts that Bobby Martin "stuffed his pockets full of stones" or that some
        boys "made a great pile of stones in one corner of the square."
    b. The plot is obviously completely unbelievable. What makes it seem as
        though it is real when the reader knows full well it cannot be?
2. There is little or no character differentiation in the story. Why is this so?
    What general statements can you make about the people in this small village,
    judging by the evidence in the story? What is their behavior like, apart from
    the stoning? More specifically, what kind of person is Mr. Summers? Old
    Man Warner? Mr. Hutchinson? Mrs. Hutchinson?
3. a. We said previously that the narrator seems to be completely detached
        from the story, as if he were simply recording an event as an uninvolved
        observer. What, specifically, is the nature of his noninvolvement?   He
        knows more than a stranger would know. For instance, he knows that
        Mr. Summers has "time and energy to devote to civic activities" and that
        people are "sorry for him." He also knows that there is "a great deal of
        fussing to be done" before Mr. Summers declares the lottery open. What
        else does he know that a completely detached observer would not know?
    b. Although the narrator has such personal information, he remains com-
        pletely neutral about what is going on. What is the advantage for this
        story in having such a point of view? What difference would there be if
        the narrator were not as familiar as he is with the people involved—perhaps
        a stranger who happens to stop in the town at the time the lottery is taking
        place and discovers to his horror what the whole thing is leading up to?

Tone

I

The common comment "It's not *what* he said that bothers me, it's *how* he said it" assumes that the "what" and the "how" are separate and distinct. There is obviously some validity in this assumption, since the same group of words can be uttered in quite different manners. The words "I love Hungarian goulash" can be spoken so that genuine delight in the dish or extreme distaste for it can be indicated. But since the "how" makes all the difference in meaning, it may be more valid to say that the "what" and the "how" are inseparable. In other words, any given comment can be looked at for purposes of analysis *as if* the *tone of voice*—the attitude of the speaker—were something apart from the group of words; but in any human situation, the meaning communicated depends on an inseparable combination of the way the words are put together and the way the speaker utters them.

Tone is a much more subtle thing than the "Hungarian goulash" example indicates. It involves not only tone of voice, but word choice and selection of detail. We all get quite accomplished at picking our words and phrases to give attitudes as well as information, and at recognizing when someone else is doing the same. Compare the statements or questions in each of the following groups:

How come you made that mistake?
What could possibly have made you do that?
Why is it you never do anything right?

Has there been a change in the rules?
Why doesn't someone let me in on it when the rules get changed?
I suppose that now anything goes!

I like the coat you're wearing, but I wonder if the tie goes with it.
I like the coat you're wearing, but the tie doesn't do much for it.
I like that coat, but oh brother! Where'd you get that tie?

Tone is largely a matter of language choice, but it can also depend on choice of detail. For instance, an observer's attitude toward an overdressed woman can be revealed as slightly amused or disgusted or shocked by the details he chooses to mention just as well as by the words he finds for describing those details. Similarly, a teacher's written comment on a student's paper can reveal his attitude toward that paper as much by the details he chooses to praise or censure as by the language he uses.

II

What has already been said in this introduction about language and selection of detail makes it quite clear that a writer of fiction cannot avoid a central concern with tone.

He *must* adopt an *attitude* toward his characters (and toward his readers). That attitude is usually spoken of in terms such as serious, playful, amused, sober, and the like. The reader must pay particular attention to tone in fiction, or he will seriously misunderstand what the writer is saying, just as in his everyday life he will misunderstand another person's intention if he takes a joking comment seriously, or vice versa.

Tone of voice in dialogue is only a small part of a writer's concern, and she is limited in how she can reveal it. She may use such phrases as "said Tom, curtly" or "snarled Mary," or she may write dialogue where the tone of voice is unmistakable from the context: " 'I've never been so humiliated in my life!' said Prudence." If the story is told in the first person, tone of voice in dialogue may be quite clear from the total impression given by the speaker.

It is the *overall* tone of a story, however, that is of greatest importance. This effect involves the total pattern of language usage and the total choice of details. What is the tone of "The Catbird Seat" and how is it developed? In other words, what is Thurber's attitude toward his characters and how does he expect the reader to react to them? In a first analysis, we might say that Thurber is on Mr. Martin's side and expects the reader to be, no matter how the reader might feel in general about mild-mannered, mousy little men. Mr. Martin is handled sympathetically. Despite his essential timidity, he is not going to stand aside and let his "beloved department" be destroyed; he will "rub out" the destroyer. We have to admire his spunk. His plan is psychologically sound: he knows himself and he knows how people will be blinded to the truth of his proposed act by his reputation. His justification for "rubbing out" Mrs. Barrows is thoroughly documented and thoroughly reasonable. His rapid revision of plan in her apartment is masterful, and he carries through the revision perfectly. We admire the neat simplicity of his clever plot and the self-control he shows as he sets the bait. At the end he accepts his victory with proper calm. We applaud his restraint.

The above analysis is valid, however, only if we ignore Thurber's treatment of the story, which is the same as ignoring the story. Mr. Martin wins, but he does not do it quite so handsomely as our first analysis would make it seem. And therein lies part of the humor. Mr. Martin intends to preserve his department, and Thurber shows him pondering his plan soberly and reviewing his case with the calm dignity of a courtroom participant. Most of the language and details reflect Mr. Martin's opinion of himself as a solid, judicious man. But at the same time other phrases and details remind us of the jarring presence of Mrs. Barrows ("quacking," "braying," "chattering") and of the timidity of Mr. Martin, so that our awareness of his vague determination to do something drastic about his dilemma is qualified by our realization that such a man cannot possibly do what he thinks he has to do. It is one thing to plan to "rub out" someone and another thing to commit murder. The term "rub out" is perfectly chosen. Used by a hoodlum it would suggest a callous indifference to killing. Used by Mr. Martin it suggests, in his own words, "nothing more than the correction of an error." The reality of murder is something he cannot possibly imagine even when he is supposedly planning one. This fact is underscored by his complete rejection of all the suitable weapons in Mrs. Barrows's apartment. He has "counted on finding one there," and she has a room full of the best, but he rapidly rejects them all for no good reason (a blunt knife is just as good a murder weapon as a sharp one).

His carrying through of his "plan" has the same amusing combination of serious, painstaking determination ("A gavel rapped in Mr. Martin's mind") and bumbling nervousness ("He rushed past her like a football tackle, bumping her"; he "knocked over a small brass jar"). This humorous clash between what is *intended* and what *happens* comes through most delightfully in the fact that even though his "plan" is really no plan at all (he cannot possibly harm Mrs. Barrows physically), still the preparations he makes for the "rubbing-out" pay off perfectly in a way he could not have foreseen. His psychology is right: no one will ever "see his hand"; the "small red herring" is right: the Camels prove very useful; and his precautions to remain unseen are right: Mrs. Barrows is the only witness, to her undoing. He stumbles into his perfect plot because he is what he is. We give him credit for the wit that he shows, while recognizing how lucky he is. The outcome is the result not only of his good sense but of his good fortune. His skill in playing his role at the end is the skill of a man who has been dealt a royal flush.

In short, Thurber asks us to take Mr. Martin the way he takes himself— seriously—but at the same time, through the tone created by the language, to recognize what a pathetic, helpless fellow he basically is. The combination brings laughter, but there is nothing harsh about the laughter. We do not despise Mr. Martin for being a Milquetoast: he does what he can do; he does not complain; he cleverly makes the most of his good luck;

he does not gloat. We do not feel revulsion at his frank admission that he is going to "rub out" Mrs. Barrows, because we are never allowed to think of the term any more seriously than Mr. Martin thinks of it. Most important, we do not laugh *at* him, although we smile along with Thurber at how serious Mr. Martin's predicament is to him and at how perfectly it turns out. He is a simple, sober, somewhat silly man, but no fool. He makes no pretense at being more than he is, and he has wit enough to get satisfaction out of "sitting in the catbird seat."

Tone is not always an easy matter to determine, and often such subtle distinctions are made by the writer that it is difficult for any but the most practiced readers to recreate the exact tone a writer wishes to convey. We are not concerned in this book with such subtleties, but we are concerned that those who use this book be aware of what to look for. Here is a seemingly uncomplicated paragraph from "The Catbird Seat" rewritten so as to show what differences a change in language and detail can make. Reread paragraph 8 in the original and then read the following version:

(1) Mr. Martin was still thinking about that red-letter day as he sauntered over to Schrafft's on Fifth Avenue near Forty-sixth Street. *(2)* He got there, as he always did, at eight o'clock, mumbled something indistinct to the girl who usually waited on him, and wiped the silver off carefully on the flap of the tablecloth. *(3)* He finished his dinner and the sports page of the *Sun* at a quarter to nine, as he always did, put a dime under his coffee cup, and left. *(4)* After eating, he normally went for a stroll. *(5)* This night he took off down Fifth Avenue at a deceptively unconcerned pace, whistling. *(6)* His gloved hands felt clammy and hot, his forehead cold. *(7)* He yanked the Camels out of his overcoat and stuffed them into his jacket pocket. *(8)* He wondered, as he did so, if he weren't overdoing the whole job. *(9)* Mrs. Barrows smoked only Luckies. *(10)* He had planned to take a few drags on a Camel (after the killing), stub it out in the ashtray holding her lipstick-stained Luckies, and thus drag a big red herring across the trail. *(11)* Maybe it wasn't such a hot idea. *(12)* It would take time. *(13)* He would decide what to do when he got there.

The revision clearly illustrates the importance of tone. "Sauntered" in sentence *(1)* is out of place; Mr. Martin would not "saunter" and certainly not at a time like this. The two details added at the end of sentence *(2)* show a boorish side to Mr. Martin and make him a less sympathetic character; if the "mumbling" is meant to show his involvement with his plan, then it is inconsistent with "sauntered" and with the fact that he has been trying hard not to draw attention to himself. The change from "financial" to "sports" page in sentence *(3)* is out of character, as is the mention of a "coffee cup." In sentence *(4)* the formal "It was his custom after dinner," which supports the picture of Mr. Martin as a quiet, mannerly man, is replaced by the folksy, "After eating, he normally went for a stroll." "Took off" in sentence (5) is an inappropriately jaunty expression and "deceptively unconcerned pace, whistling" is even more inappropriate. The "clammy" and "hot" of sentence (6) are vulgar in comparison with "moist" and "warm." Mr. Martin is not vulgar; Mrs. Barrows *is,* and that is partly what upsets him so much. "Yanked" and "stuffed" in sentence (7) are exaggerated for the simple act involved; he is not frantic at this moment, and it would be misleading to use such terms. "Represent an unnecessary note of strain" of the original sentence (8) is delightfully stilted, while "overdoing the whole job" is slangy by comparison. The same distinction can be made between "puff a few puffs" in sentence (10) and the revised "take a few drags." In the same sentence "rubbing-out" is replaced by "killing": the first is Mr. Martin's special term; the second suggests much more awareness of his supposed intentions that he really has. The use of "small" in front of "red herring" is consistent with what he considers the "cunning of his scheme"; "big" is too gross a word in this connection. In sentence (11) of the revision a "hot idea" is also out of keeping with Mr. Martin's language usage. Finally, in the revision it would not do at all to mention the choking. This is a charmingly subtle point, and nothing else about the revision has been even slightly subtle.

Good writers consider every sentence carefully for its contribution to the total effect of the story; good readers should be willing to consider every sentence with the same care. This does not mean lingering over every sentence; it simply means being aware that the language and the details have been chosen deliberately, with a particular overall effect in mind. The reader who reads simply to find out what happens and ignores how the story is put together will, in fact, miss most of the story.

Exercises

THE CATBIRD SEAT

What does the tone of the story tell us about how to take Mrs. Barrows? Mr. Fitweiler?

FIRST CONFESSION

1. What is the tone set for "First Confession" in the very first paragraph? Some strong language is used, but is the reader meant to feel any sense of fear or

even unpleasantness? Compare the tone of the paragraph as it appears with that of the following version:

> It was a dreary afternoon in late winter. A skinny little boy with a tear-stained face was being dragged by his sister through a crowded street. He tried to break free and scratched at her arm with his free hand. She repeatedly struck the back of his head glancing blows with the flat of her hand. When she yanked him half off his feet, he began to bawl. She viewed him with a cold and intense hatred.

2. What is the tone of Nora's words in the opening part of the story? What does "passionate sympathy" mean? How seriously is the reader meant to take the phrase? What does "intoned" mean and why is it appropriate here? What does "commiseration" mean? How does its meaning change when "whine of" is put in front of it? Show how Nora's words to Jackie are in keeping with the terms used to describe them.

3. If Jackie's fear is real to him, why is it that the reader can feel only sympathetic amusement with his predicament? In other words, how does the tone of the opening pages keep the reader from sharing the fear the small boy feels? It is not enough to say that there is no reason for a first confession to be a terrifying experience. It is perfectly possible to write a story that would make the reader share a sense of fear with a small boy over just such an experience.

4. The central scene in the story takes place in the confessional. Part of the humor in this scene grows out of Jackie's lack of familiarity with the confessional and his subsequent fumbled attempts to carry through with what he knows vaguely he should do. But a good deal of the humor comes from the way his reactions are described. What is humorous about the following reactions?
   a. "He had the feeling of someone with an unfamiliar machine, of pressing buttons at random."
   b. "He had always prided himself upon his powers of climbing, but this took it out of him."
   c. "He joined his hands and pressed the last remaining button."
   d. ". . . as though he were hanging by his feet like a monkey [he] found himself looking almost upside down at the priest."
   e. " 'Tis me, father,' he piped. . . ."

5. Look closely at the priest's answers to Jackie's "confession." Is the priest laughing at him? If not, how would you characterize the tone of the priest's answers?

6. How is the tone of the story further defined by words and phrases like "thump," "skeltering," "clout," "cocking a shocked eye," and "Oh, women! Women! It was all women and girls and their silly talk. They had no real knowledge of the world!"?

7. How does Jackie's "good confession" relate to the lighthearted tone O'Connor has developed? In what way does Nora think that Jackie is "bad"? In what way does Jackie think that he is? How does the contrast between the two help define the humorous tone of the story?

8. How would you answer an objection that the lightness of treatment of a serious subject is disrespectful toward a fundamental part of Catholic belief?

THE LOTTERY

1. What is the tone of "The Lottery"? Is it cheerful? Lighthearted? Business-like? Sober? Matter-of-fact? Homey? Flat? A combination of several of these? None of these? Explain. Consider, among other things, the following:
   a. The casual, almost irrelevant, observations ("the villagers pronounced this name 'Dellacroy,'" "She tapped Mrs. Delacroix on the arm as a farewell," "Mr. Summers waited with an expression of polite interest").
   b. The nature of the conversation.
   c. The word choice in general.
   d. The straightforwardness of the closing paragraphs.

2. What part does the tone play in creating the sense of horror that "The Lottery" conveys to the reader? Try rewriting sections of the story, using words and phrases that suggest tension and fear and conversations that are expressions of dislike and mistrust and even hatred. Comment on whether the change in tone affects the sense of terror that the original has.

Setting

Most stories are set in a particular place at a particular time. This localization is perfectly natural, since human actions do not occur in a vacuum. It is also wise, since we are more willing to believe in the "reality" of what we are witnessing if it does not have the fairy-tale flavor of "Once upon a time in a kingdom far away." There is more to the selection of setting, however, than simply the inevitable necessity of having events take place somewhere at some time. The setting is not merely a series of stage props in front of which the characters act out the story. It is as much a part of the story as are plot, character, point of view, and language.

"The Catbird Seat" offers a good example of the importance of setting, because at first glance it does not seem to be the kind of story that depends very much on where and when it takes place. Any large city in the United States would have served just as well as New York, and any time recent enough to include a business office like F & S and someone like Red Barber. The important consideration, however, is that the place and time are used specifically, not vaguely. For instance, Mr. Martin buys the Camels on Broadway near the theater district (the Times Square area), several long blocks from Fifth Avenue and Forty-sixth Street, where he "always" eats dinner. And he buys them at "theater time," exactly the time (most plays open at 8:40, and the crowds start to gather a little after 8:00) when he "always" eats dinner at Schrafft's (getting there "at eight o'clock" and leaving "at a quarter to nine"). The details tell us how thoroughly Mr. Martin has planned not to be seen buying cigarettes.

West Twelfth Street is also a good distance (down Fifth Avenue) from Forty-sixth Street. Thurber places Mrs. Barrows's apartment far enough away from Mr. Martin's neighborhood to let him feel reasonably sure that no one who knows him will see him. Her apartment is on the first floor of an apartment building small enough that there will not be a "doorman or other attendants."

Other details of the setting are essential to the story. The dates must be specific to show how precise a man Mr. Martin is ("Mr. Martin had a head for dates"). The times must be specific for the same reason ("It was eighteen minutes after nine when Mr. Martin turned into Twelfth Street"). The reference to Monday night in the first paragraph suggests that he had spent the week end bringing his courage to the point of action. Mrs. Barrows had "bounced" into his office at 3 P.M. of the Monday of the week before, and he then knew she was about to reorganize his department (Mr. Fitweiler later confirms this). He must act, but the fact that it takes him a whole week of reviewing his "case" to work up his courage shows what a mild little man he is.

Another aspect of the setting of "The Catbird Seat" is the nature of the office itself. A number of details tell us that F & S is a quiet, orderly, unhurried kind of firm. Mr. Fitweiler, "the aging gentleman," is an unaggressive man who is in complete control of the business but who does not have much idea of what is going on under Mrs. Barrows's special advice. Old Roberts, the personnel chief, is obviously a faithful employee but not a very forceful personality. Efficiency is more than a virtue at F & S; it is a way of life. Mrs. Barrows's bullish, boisterous behavior is horribly out of place in such a gentle, dignified firm. She does not simply upset a comfortable routine for a lot of people; she is a woman who begins, in Mr. Martin's phrasing, "chipping at the cornices of the firm's edifice" and who later starts "swinging at the foundation stones with a pickaxe." The setting thus created shows a mixture of quiet dignity and frenzy which is the perfect expression of Mr. Martin's frame of mind.

The humor of the story results from this mixture. The whole affair is incongruous: Mrs. Barrows's behavior is ridiculous in such a setting, and Mr. Martin's "plan" is ridiculous in the light of his previous behavior in that setting. The mixture in language creates and sustains the basic incongruity: wild words and outrageous comparisons are coupled with stilted and dignified phrasing.

In some stories, setting plays a more obvious role than it does in "The Catbird Seat." It would be stretching things to say that setting serves as more than a necessary environment in Thurber's story, important as that environment is. In other stories it might well dominate the action. If, for instance, a story were about a young man's growing sense of isolation from the small town in which he grew up, so strongly felt that everything about the town—its physical setting, its social codes, its people—seems to bear down upon him to stifle him, then the setting would be central to the story.

Exercises

1. "First Confession" takes place in Ireland, as is suggested by the speech patterns and the references to such things as the ballad singer in the streets. The place is not particularly important, but other details are. Point out what aspects of setting serve a definite and necessary purpose in the story.

2. a. Describe the setting of "The Lottery." What details suggest a small American village? What kind of day is it? When does the story take place? Is the time of year and the time of day important? Why? Why is the village setting itself important?

    b. As we have clearly suggested, the characters in "The Lottery" are hardly more than village types. In what way can they be considered part of the setting? How do they react toward each other? What details show their normal, friendly concern for each other, within families and between families? Why is it important that their normal relationships be emphasized?

    c. What part does the total setting of "The Lottery" play in defining the horror of the story?

Theme

No matter how simple a story may appear to be, we inevitably ask: What does it mean? Neither a series of exciting events which "get nowhere" nor an interesting character sketch is a story. Stories are written because writers have something to say about human experience, and they feel they can best say it by showing human beings living through a series of events that leave them different—perhaps wiser, perhaps not—from what they were before the events took place. The characters involved are treated as unique. If they were not so treated, few readers would show any interest in them at all. But they are at the same time representative. What happens to them and how they respond mirror general human behavior, providing a commentary on what it means to be a human being.

A commentary is not the same thing as a moral. A commentary is simply an observation, a recognition that there are general truths about human nature. Stories that are written entirely to teach a moral—a lesson—are more often than not flat and bloodless. The emphasis is on the lesson, and the characters are puppets who act out the lesson. The element of discovery is missing from preaching, which is what lesson-literature is.

The meaning of a story with this "element of discovery" is a comment on human values embodied *in* the story as an inseparable part of it, not something *apart* from it. The observation itself and the way in which it is made through the interrelationship of the various elements we have been discussing reveals what is called the *theme* of the story. The theme cannot be understood in isolation from the story which embodies it, but as with the other elements in a short story we have to talk about it *as if* it could be.

What is the theme of "The Catbird Seat"? One way of putting it might be that "there is a special providence that enables timid men to be masters of their fates despite themselves." There is some validity in putting it that way, because Mr. Martin does manage to save his job and his peace of mind by his own actions, however unplanned. But certainly such a sober statement has little connection with the spirit of "The Catbird Seat." Another statement of the theme might be that "brassy, insensitive people will sooner or later get what is coming to them, and rightly by the actions of those they have harmed the most." There is also some validity in this statement, but it, too, has hardly more than a minor connection with "The Catbird Seat." A third statement might be simply that "the worm will turn," which is closer in spirit to the story but still not very adequate. Still another way of putting it might focus on the implications of the title in this manner: "The most unlikely person may be found 'sitting in the catbird seat' simply because, being what he is, he is the person most unlikely to be found there." This last is a reasonable statement of the theme of Thurber's story for several reasons: first, it is a fair generalization about Mr. Martin's problem and the solution of it; second, it suggests, in the very way it is put, the reversal of the expected, which parallels the ironic way the story develops; and third, it has a playfully serious tone, which is the general tone of the story. Even this last statement of theme, however, does not wholly define the humorous yet sympathetic quality of "The Catbird Seat," which, in the final analysis, can be defined only in the repeated *experiencing* of the story through repeated readings.

What we have been saying about the theme of "The Catbird Seat" illustrates what attitude we should take toward any statement about the theme of a story. First, it *is* possible to make a generalization which can be called the "theme" of a story. Second, our judgment of the adequacy of this generalization will depend upon the degree to which it harmonizes with all the features of the story in which it is incorporated. Third, the full meaning of the theme—which is to say, the generalization modified and particularized in terms of human experience—can be realized only through the story itself as it stands.

Exercises

FIRST CONFESSION

What is the theme of "First Confession"? Notice that there are many of the same conditions here that are present in "The Catbird Seat." Both stories center around bullied victims of females. Both involve ill-formulated plans to "rub out" females. Both have central characters who are not clever but who prove to be delightfully resourceful. Both treat the hero's ordeal humorously. In what sense can it be said that the theme of "First Confession" is essentially the same as that of "The Catbird Seat"? In what sense is it different?

THE LOTTERY

What is the theme of "The Lottery"? Obviously, the story cannot be taken at face value. The specific event involved simply could not take place as described. How is the story to be taken, then? Consider the contrast between what these simple, straightforward, friendly villagers usually are, and what they do in the yearly lottery ceremony. Consider also: the contrast between what happens and the way it is described; the fact that this is the behavior of the whole village and that the lottery has been a "tradition" for as long as can be remembered; the behavior of those who do not draw the black dot, particularly the Hutchinson children and Mr. Hutchinson; the fact that no one except Tessie protests, and that her protest comes only after her family and then she herself have been singled out; the fact that Steve Adams shows doubt about the affair by commenting that "over in the north village they're talking of giving up the lottery," but that he is "in the front of the crowd of villagers" when the stoning starts. What is being suggested about the possibilities for good and evil that lie in every person?

PART TWO

Stories Gathered by Theme

Part One of this book focuses on the craft of the short story, the way a story is structured, shaped, created. However, as we have said, we see no value in analyzing form as an academic exercise for its own sake, and you will have noticed already that our discussions of the three stories in Part One have focused also on what they have to say about human behavior—about the mystery of what and who we are. Our conviction is that an awareness of form brings a deeper awareness of meaning—that the two are, essentially, one.

In Part Two, we focus more specifically on meaning, and the questions raised should help point up the relationship between form and meaning. The fifteen stories are quite different in point of view, subject matter, tone; but they have in common a thematic concern for our perverse ability to treat ourselves and others with calculated or uncalculated indifference, misunderstanding, disrespect, cruelty. The first set of five stories deals with individuals confronting themselves, and the world they have made for themselves, with a mixture of self-knowledge and self-delusion; the second set deals with a range of interpersonal encounters that explore the destructive effects of violence on the human spirit; the third set deals with individuals in conflict with the values and conventions of the society they live in.

Before each set of five stories we have included a few comments that should suggest a framework for discussing the stories in relation to each other or to those in the other sets. While there is no need to belabor thematic similarities, recognizing them can often throw new light on the stories concerned or reinforce impressions only vaguely sensed. There's nothing wrong, of course, with reading the whole lot as simply a collection of fifteen good short stories.

Detailed questions follow each story. Some of them get at matters of fact or reasonable deduction, matters which need to be gotten straight for intelligent interpretation to take place. Most of the questions, however, call for discussion and interpretation. There are no "right" answers as such, but rather the possibility for reasoned analysis and exchange of views. As with all art, successive experiences and sharing of insights lead to greater understanding. Occasional written responses to certain questions will allow students (and teachers) to sharpen perception through having to take a stand and explain it convincingly.

I The urge to know _oneself_ is ancient and honorable, and few themes have commanded as much literary attention. But writers have been concerned not so much with the necessity of knowing oneself as with the snares and delusions that line the way. Human beings have an infinite capacity for self-deception, for kidding themselves, for believing what is convenient and comfortable to believe, for making life bearable by pretending it is what it isn't.

Four of the five stories in this section show how complex is the problem of "being, or knowing oneself," what other legitimate claims conflict with that wish, what difficulties there are in seeing life whole. The fifth story deals with the most momentous matter human beings have to face—survival itself—and with the ultimate irony that it's possible to know too much and, therefore, too little.

PURPOSE OF THE COMPOSITION IS TO SHOW ALL OF THE STORY IN SECTION 1 HAVE THE IDEA OF KNOWING ONESELF

DISCUS THE PROTAGONIST THEME

IN EACH PARAGRAPH DISCUSS ONE STORY USE AT LEAST ONE QUOTATION FOR EACH STORY

I INTRO
II ENGAG P.
III 16
IV MITTY
V SENSE SHELTER
VI BABYLON
VII CONCLUSION
RESTATE PURPOSE
SUM UP

The Engagement Party

ROBERT BOLES

She was not a drinker, for she held her glass too carefully. My eyes fastened to a detail. Her fingernail polish. The red was put into check by its own too-even glaze, was held, suspended.

"Yes. Well, my husband's work is similar to yours," she continued.

"Is it really?" I asked, but not quite politely enough. Had it been the lines of her eyes which projected the effect of my lack of attention? Her makeup, though not overdone, was obvious. Immediately, a sense of having played this scene before.

I turned slightly away from her as a member of the combo walked by, and noticed Helen beckoning me.

"Excuse me, please," I said.

The woman smiled with closed jaws, shifted her weight and pivoted on a heel. Her last name was Nolan. I remembered that then. I had no intention of embarrassing her. One should be accustomed to that sort of thing at a party.

Smiling now, I worked my way towards Helen.

"By God! It's George! It's George himself!" The voice belonged to Helen's younger brother. I clapped him on the shoulder. "And you don't even have a drink!"

"I left it on the mantel."

"Have you had enough already?"

"I've hardly begun," I said.

Helen appeared. Her arms were in front of her as if she were holding an imaginary purse with both hands. "There's someone you have to meet. My father's partner."

"I'm starved," I said.

She took my hand and led me across the room and into another.

The people seemed plant-like, rooted in the carpet. Their motions seemed to have been caused by winds and crosswinds. Necks bent, backs; arms gestured in conversation. I had begun to perspire.

"I hope he doesn't get drunk," she confided without moving her lips or looking at me.

"Who?"

"My brother."

I bumped into the woman who wore the brocade dress, the one I had had the conversation with a moment before. Laughter and apologies, far in excess of what was called for. It was a brief bursting of her tension.

"Here he is," Helen announced.

"So, this is the young man who's going to carry you away." The man in his late forties or early fifties took my hand and shook it vigorously.

"Yes, sir," I said, assuming the bearing of a lower responding to an upper classman.

"It's about time I met you. Engineering, isn't it?"

"Yes, sir. Aeronautical."

"That's fine. You're a good-looking young man."

"Thank you, sir."

Helen moved away from me. I felt her absence as a hollow space beside me. Someone had asked her something and I had heard her say, "Certainly, Marie." That was all. I folded my arms, turned at the waist and followed her with my eyes. She escorted a woman to the foyer. The woman was a politician of some sort, I think. I believe I had seen her picture in the paper in regards to a "Culture March" on the Negro community.

"Wonderful girl, Helen."

"Yes, I agree," I said, and turned to face him again.

"Fine family."

"Yes, sir, I know," I said.

A group of men to my right were involved in a familiar and hearty political discussion. I tried to divide my attention.

"Your family's in . . . ?"

"California."

"Right. Ken told me. I had forgotten. Doctor, is he?"

"Not an M.D. He has a doctorate in education."

"I was in California for two years, you know."

"No, I didn't," I said. It was difficult for me to keep my eyes on him. His complexion was sallow, the color of coffee with heavy cream. I watched someone take a sip of a drink and felt thirsty again.

"I was in L.A.," he continued.

"We're from San Francisco."

"And what do you think of Boston?"

"It's fine. I like it," I said without much enthusiasm.

The music began. Bass throb, brushes on cymbals, then piano, vibes and saxophone in a long chorus. People separated. We stepped back. Some danced the High-Life, others the Bossa-Nova.

"I don't intend for us to stay here," I continued. "I've taken a job in Connecticut."

"I'm sure it's best. Best to get the bride away from her parents."

I nodded, then covered my mouth while belching.

I recognized the bellowing of Tommy's voice to my right. He was, perhaps, getting drunk. "Being colored doesn't have anything to do with color! It's a question of attitudes and history and all that crap!"

"It's a good life that's yours to lead," Helen's father's partner said. "When I was your age, I had to struggle. Not like you young people today."

"Yes," I said. "I realize how hard it must have been. I know how hard my father had to work."

The entire conversation was one often repeated. A needless formality. We were knowledgeably secure in the words we spoke. I felt a little disquiet.

"You youngsters have all of the opportunities, you know. And there are new ones opening every day. No worry about finding a job. If you're qualified, you'll get one."

Although it was not altogether true, I could do nothing but nod in solemn agreement and press my lips together in a gesture akin to a pout.

I thought I heard Helen call me, but I could not see her.

"What are your hobbies, son? I heard that you were a fine trackman in school."

"I swim, of course," I said, and struggled to say naturally, "and I'm a bit of a bug on sailing." It was the truth and it seemed to offend him. I had known that it would and that he would enjoy it.

A group of people parted in laughter. Helen entered between them. She came to my side. "Excuse me, Al. I'm going to take him away from you." Her voice sounded remarkably like her mother's.

"I understand." He extended his hand immediately and shook mine again quite vigorously.

Helen's hand was cool, as if it had been in cold water.

"You look fresh," I remarked.

"I just freshened up. I was wilting. It's so warm, and all of these people," she said. "Did you have a good conversation?"

"Yes. I suppose so. He's a very interesting man."

"What time is it?"

Instead of taking my hand away from her, I stood on my toes, stretched myself, and attempted to read the clock on the mantel in the other room. My drink had disappeared from in front of the mirror. "Quarter to eleven, I think."

There was a roar of laughter that was quickly muffled.

"Little brother is acting up again," she said.

"Leave Tommy alone," I said. "He's happy and well adjusted. Let him have some fun."

"You don't know what I go through with him!"

From across the room, a woman's voice calling Helen's name. The tone of it was comparable to the surface of a highly polished piece of wood. All of us, in a dense atmosphere of movements and poses, were beneath and supportive to it. "Helen!"

She looked.

Again, "Helen!"

I saw her at the other end of the room before Helen did. She sipped at a Manhattan and waved from her wrist as women, curiously, always wave.

Between smiles, I managed to repeat myself more forcefully than before. "I am starved, Helen. Famished!"

"You told me."

"I'm beginning to get a headache," I lied. "I didn't get a chance to eat this evening." But the evening was getting to me, the sensuous fugue, the cacophony of voices, the odors and light, the smoke. But something more than that. My disquietude.

"My poor dear," she mouthed, as she stroked my forehead with her fingertips. "I'm sure the caterer has some of those . . . things left. What were those things? Cabbage leaves stuffed with something and baked. Go into the kitchen."

"I think I will."

She had not really expected me to do so. "Dance with me first."

"No," I said. "You're cruel. I'm salivating and starved and you want me to burn more of my energy."

If she had pressed me, I would have danced. But she didn't.

"I'll see you in a few minutes."

We separated. She, it seemed, with misgivings. But I was relieved. I felt at once the dissolution of the effect of the hundred small embarrassments which had occurred between myself and others throughout the evening, the seconds of arbitrary inattentiveness which inflicted wounds, pinpricks, on each of us.

Perhaps I'm lying.

The kitchen door was on spring hinges. It closed itself after I had entered. I let my smile fall and imagined myself making an entrance onto a stage. I, as an actor with a small part in a play with Strindberg overtones.

I was at ease with the noise practically shut out. I hadn't noticed how sweaty I was. With a lot of room and air, it seemed to be present all at once. The white tiles of the floor and walls, glazed, flat and hard, made me doubly aware of my body and the bodies of the caterer and the girl. All of us were dark mobile beings set into this sterile chamber. The room was filled with the odors of smoke and powder and perfume in the other rooms.

"The groom-to-be is here!" the caterer said.

"You know it, dad," I said, slipping easily into the dialect to let him know that I was a member. "And I want me some f-o-o-d!"

"I hear you talkin', baby," the caterer said.

A metal chair painted white was against one of the walls. I sat in it and stretched out my legs. The caterer took a plate and began

SOUL TALK

filling it. His white uniform was badly fitted. It was large. His arms were lean. The girl stood beside him and waited to help. She was very dark. Her bones were large, her hair coarse and beautiful.

"Get some salad for the man, Celestine," he said to her.

The name was right for her. It suggested fragility. Her bearing in some remarkable way suggested the same thing. She went to the refrigerator. I pretended that I had had slightly too much to drink. Her uniform played on my mind. The name Celestine did also. Her uniform was white. Starched. The material at the seams was doubled. Something easily noticeable for it was whiter there. The cloth played on her hips.

She looked at me briefly. I returned her glance with a smile and wondered, while I was doing so, what she thought of me. My complexion is agreeable with a black or charcoal gray suit. I am brown in the way a Mexican is brown. I had my jacket open, my vest unbuttoned part of the way.

Celestine put some salad into a wooden bowl. I raised my hand in a political gesture when enough had been placed there. She added a spoonful more and offered the words, "For your health."

"This is my daughter Celestine," the caterer said proudly.

"She's a very attractive girl."

Celestine turned away from me in modesty. It suddenly seemed right to speak of her with her father in this manner, the masculine dominant, the female subservient. I was particularly aware of the roles we had assumed and had heightened.

I noticed that the caterer continued to put food on my plate. "Enough!" I said. "Man, when I want food for next year, I'll let you know."

He accepted my criticism with gentle laughter, but I was vaguely aware that I had overstepped myself.

"And what do you want to drink with that, sir?" he asked.

"Either Scotch or bourbon on the rocks," I said, with the full, coarse, American aplomb.

"I'll have to go to the bar to get some." He put the plate on the table near me. The top of the table was porcelain.

Celestine went to a drawer, pulled it open and began to remove a table mat.

"I don't need that," I said with an unintended sharpness. I smiled idiotically afterwards.

Her father left the kitchen.

I pulled my chair to the table and began to eat.

"Sit down," I said to her after a moment. "You make me nervous standing there."

She obeyed me. My voice still had a residue of sharpness. It was her father who had gotten beneath my skin. All of us had accepted Southern attitudes in a minute.

I wanted to speak to her as I ate, but nothing seemed worth saying. It was difficult to cut through the cloth of pretension we had woven together. I ate in silence and she watched me in silence.

My thoughts turned to Helen, but it was clearly an alternative—something to compensate for my failure to communicate normally with the breathing girl seated next to me.

I ate too quickly and when I was almost done her father returned with a double light Scotch. I thanked him with a full mouth, then finished eating, and drank half of the drink slowly, with my eyes on the walls and ceiling.

I smiled to myself. I almost laughed.

In another moment I was in one of the large rooms again.

"So you're the fiancé!" a woman said, pointing her finger at my chest.

"I am," I said, and smiled.

"Well, dance with me, darling!" All of her *a*'s were broad, and her voice rasped pleasantly.

"Only the High-Life," I said. "I don't want to put my drink down."

We walked into the other room and began the lilting African dance which had gained so much favor. She danced well, if a bit stiffly, but it became her.

"You know, I just learned this," she said. "I think it's marvelous! And you must tell me about Helen. You two go so well together."

The combo ended the song. We had hardly begun. I hoped that I could separate myself from her without appearing to be rude. I excused myself but she gave no indication of having noticed.

She continued as we walked to the side of the room, then she met someone I had met previously and introduced us. I slipped quietly away from her.

I wandered through groups of people as if I were looking for someone. I stopped briefly to chat with Helen's mother, and once again near a small group of men centered around a white civil rights worker who had just returned from the South. He emoted before his words as he told a story of an atrocity too vile to be printed in a newspaper.

It all seemed a circus I cared little about. Or a parade. I've never liked parades. I did something idiotic. I stamped my foot. When I did it, a little of the contents of my glass spilled out onto my thumb and fingers. There was no reason for it. Perhaps I wanted to hear the sound of my footsteps beneath the carpet. And I didn't know any longer if I loved Helen. I'd marry her in any case, but I wondered if love was possible. It had disappeared in a second. It was like walking out in the middle of one of those romantic screen comedies. Of course, tomorrow I would feel differently. In all likelihood this pattern would stay with me for the next forty or fifty years.

After finishing my drink, I went to the bar and asked for a Scotch-and-quinine. I was slapped on the back.

"By Jove, it's Georgie!" Helen's brother said.

"Hello, Tommy."

"Great party, is it not?"

"It is that," I said.

He posed unwittingly against the bar. There was a serenity in the moment or him. "Who am I going to play tennis with on Saturdays when you're hooked up to Helen and in Connecticut?"

"Where is she, by the way?" I asked.

"Upstairs. Mrs. Williams spilled a drink on her dress . . . well, I kind of knocked her arm a little. You know how those things happen."

"I'll bet Helen has it in for you."

"What the hell! She's getting married in a couple of months," he said, then added, "You lucky son of a . . . So, what's going to happen to tennis and me on Saturdays?"

"You'll find a better player." I feinted a left to his jaw, bent my knees and jabbed at his stomach with my right. He jackknifed a bit. Then I mussed up his hair. "Judging by your reflexes, you haven't had as much to drink as I thought."

The bartender placed my drink on the counter. I didn't really want it, but picked it up and returned to the area in which couples danced. I watched without seeing and heard without listening. My preoccupation was with nothing. Maybe only the restlessness which had no outlet.

"Nice combo," someone said.

I tried, but not very hard, to remember his name. "Yes, they're very good."

In another moment I rested my glass and danced again. I found that this woman whose hand I had taken when I had stepped onto the floor was a fervent dancer. After our first words, all conversation stopped.

I danced with her several times. I got warm. My legs perspired. I saw Helen once and waved at her. She smiled obligingly and waved back. Tommy also danced a lot. We stopped when our foreheads and shirts were wet.

"To hell with being sedate!" he said. "I know we're supposed to, but it is a party."

Both of us went to the bar again, ordered and waited. Helen shook a finger of warning at him. I walked to her and kissed her. She recoiled from lack of privacy and said, "Not now, darling. Not here in front of all of these people. Gracious!"

"Leave your brother alone," I said. "That's an order."

"Yes, dear."

I took my glass and began to mingle half-heartedly. The alcohol had worked its miniature wonder. I was dizzy. Still, I hadn't learned anything. I wanted to go swimming. That was all. The idea of it seized me at once. I could envision and feel it. I stood still in the center of the crowded room, closed my eyes and began a process of complete imagination. The voices, the laughter, the music intruded.

Upon opening my eyes, I walked without hesitation to the French doors that led to the patio and stepped out into the open.

The air was much colder than I had expected it to be, and it took me a few seconds to get used to it. I sat in a deck lounge and closed my eyes. Who would be the first to disturb me?, I wondered. Helen might come looking for me. Tommy might want to tell me the latest dirty joke.

I felt myself sinking into the pulsating deepness of intoxication that precedes sleep, but pulled myself up and out of it at the sound of footsteps. I did not look behind me. I took a swallow of my drink. I followed the motion of the person behind me with my hearing. After a moment I realized that whoever it was had no interest in me. I closed my eyes again.

The footsteps moved from here to there, stopped, moved from here to there again. There was the sound of one glass touching another. When the sound moved to the side of me and a little in front of me, I opened my eyes. It was the caterer's daughter. I couldn't remember her name right away. Celestine. I should have guessed that it might have been either she or her father. She was putting empty glasses left by guests onto a tray.

I watched her, unnoticed. There was a certain dignity in her manner I find difficult to explain. It was feminine without the feminine embellishments of gesture. It was not decadent. Her uniform, her darkness, and that she worked contributed to it. But there was much more. I was at ease. I decided to finish my drink so that she would have to take my glass.

She heard me move, turned and seemed surprised by my presence. I smiled at her. She returned the smile and continued. She picked up glasses in front and then to the right of me. When she had almost finished, I held up my glass and turned it upside down to demonstrate its emptiness. She came and took it from me.

"Sit down for a while," I said.

She looked to the patio doors before deciding to accept.

I swung my legs over and put them on the ground to make room for her.

"I meant what I said to your father," I told her. My words were sincere. "It's a bit cold out here, don't you think?"

She did not answer.

I said nothing for the next few seconds. I reached for her bare arm. The contact, through brief, was electric. She did not move and was facing away from me. I wanted very much to see her face. I put my hand to her chin and forced her to look at me. I could not read her expression. I let go of her and waited for her to get up. She sat completely still.

"This is where my engagement was announced," I said. "Everyone was assembled here and a toast was made."

The night spun softly. I was not even able to hear her breathe. She sat rigidly, with her eyes fastened to some immobile bit of shadow. My need for her then urged me. I would give her something afterwards. Money. Fifty dollars perhaps. I had that much in my wallet.

The moment seemed to lick us with a broad tongue. I felt strangely like someone from the Southern past of masters and servants. I did love her for the moment. To make love with her once would be all that I needed. I would never have to see her again.

I stood and took her arm. "Let's go into the garden," I whispered.

I pulled her gently. I beckoned. My whispering voice trembled.

She broke away from me. "No," she said firmly. Her head was lowered. Her chin touched the top of her dress, her uniform, and although I could not see her eyes I detected a look of betrayal on her face.

Had I read the moment so inaccurately? She picked up the tray of unclean glasses and walked with quick, sure steps back to the house.

I waited for a decent length of time before returning. I wanted to smoke a cigarette, but had no matches. My disquietude was inert. The guests would begin to leave in an hour or so. Then the evening could be forgotten.

Exercises

1. George tells his own story. What is his attitude toward the others at the party? In what terms does he describe them? *Are* they the way he describes them? Why or why not?

2. Define his attitude toward Helen. What is she like? Why does she fret about her brother? Why does that fact annoy George? How do you take his comment: "I didn't know any longer if I loved Helen. I'd marry her in any case, but I wondered if love was possible. . . . Of course, tomorrow I would feel differently. In all likelihood this pattern would stay with me for the next forty or fifty years." Are these the honest doubts and misgivings of any thoughtful man contemplating such a serious step as marriage? Or are they something else?

3. How does George see himself? How do you think he would describe himself if he were asked to? As he is the narrator, we would expect him to put himself in the best light—what specific evidence shows that he is trying to? What assumptions is he making about his audience? Does he expect our sympathy? Does he get yours? Why or why not?

4. Does he try to put Celestine and her father in a good light? Does he succeed? What does he feel toward them and toward his relationship to them? Characterize their behavior toward him (as seen through his eyes, remember).

5. George says of the kitchen encounter: "My voice still had a residue of sharpness. It was her father who had gotten beneath my skin. All of us had accepted Southern attitudes in a minute." Why does he say this? What does he mean by "Southern attitudes"? What "Southern attitudes" does he show here and later that he is not aware of? How are his "Northern attitudes" no different from what he likes to call "Southern attitudes"?

6. Will he tell Tommy about what happened on the patio? Why or why not?

7. When Celestine says "No" to him, he comments that "although I could not see her eyes I detected a look of betrayal on her face." Why does he use the word "betrayal"? Betrayal of whom or of what? Does the word mean anything to him? What is the deepest irony revealed in his behavior at the "engagement party"? Consider especially the paragraph near the end that begins: "The moment seemed to lick us with a broad tongue." Consider whether the final encounter is basically any different to him from the rest of the encounters he had as the evening progressed.

8. Boles unfolds the plot chronologically. What are the advantages of his doing so?

9. Does George think that he knows who he is? Does he know who he is? Explain.

Sixteen

JESSAMYN WEST

The steam from the kettle had condensed on the cold window and was running down the glass in tear-like trickles. Outside in the orchard the man from the smudge company was refilling the pots with oil. The greasy smell from last night's burning was still in the air. Mr. Delahanty gazed out at the bleak darkening orange grove; Mrs. Delahanty watched her husband eat, nibbling up to the edges of the toast, then stacking the crusts about his tea cup in a neat fence-like arrangement.

"We'll have to call Cress," Mr. Delahanty said, finally. "Your father's likely not to last out the night. She's his only grandchild. She ought to be here."

Mrs. Delahanty pressed her hands to the bones above her eyes. "Cress isn't going to like being called away from college," she said.

"We'll have to call her anyway. It's the only thing to do." Mr. Delahanty swirled the last of his tea around in his cup so as not to miss any sugar.

"Father's liable to lapse into unconsciousness any time," Mrs. Delahanty argued. "Cress'll hate coming and Father won't know whether she's here or not. Why not let her stay at Woolman?"

Neither wanted, in the midst of their sorrow for the good man whose life was ending, to enter into any discussion of Cress. What was the matter with Cress? What had happened to her since she went away to college? She, who had been open and loving? And who now lived inside a world so absolutely fitted to her own size and shape that she felt any intrusion, even that of the death of her own grandfather, to be an unmerited invasion of her privacy. Black magic could not have changed her more quickly and unpleasantly and nothing except magic, it seemed, would give them back their lost daughter.

Mr. Delahanty pushed back his cup and saucer. "Her place is here, Gertrude. I'm going to call her long distance now. She's a bright girl and it's not going to hurt her to miss a few days from classes. What's the dormitory number?"

"I know it as well as our number," Mrs. Delahanty said. "But at the minute it's gone. It's a sign of my reluctance, I suppose. Wait a minute and I'll look it up."

Mr. Delahanty squeezed out from behind the table. "Don't bother. I can get it."

Mrs. Delahanty watched her husband, his usually square shoulders sagging with weariness, wipe a clear place on the steamy windowpane with his napkin. Some of the green twilight appeared to seep into the warm dingy little kitchen. "I can't ever remember having to smudge before in February. I expect you're right," he added as he went toward the phone. "Cress isn't going to like it."

Cress didn't like it. It was February, the rains had been late and the world was burning with a green fire; a green smoke rolled down the hills and burst shoulder-high in the cover crops that filled the spaces between the trees in the orange orchards. There had been rain earlier in the day and drops still hung from the grass blades, sickle-shaped with their weight. Cress, walking across the campus with Edwin, squatted to look into one of these crystal globes.

"Green from the grass and red from the sun," she told him. "The whole world right there in one raindrop."

"As Blake observed earlier about a grain of sand," said Edwin.[1]

---

[1] The reference is to the opening lines of "Auguries of Innocence" by William Blake (1757–1827):

> To see a world in a grain of sand,
>   And a heaven in a wild flower;
> Hold infinity in the palm of your hand,
>   And eternity in an hour.

Later in the poem are the lines:

> We are led to believe a lie
> When we see *with* not *through* the eye,

"O.K., show off," Cress told him. "You know it—but I saw it." She took his hand and he pulled her up, swinging her in a semicircle in front of him. "Down there in the grass the world winked at me."

"Don't be precious, Cress," Edwin said.

"I will," Cress said, "just to tease you. I love to tease you, Edwin."

"Why?" Edwin asked.

"Because you love to have me," Cress said confidently, taking his hand. Being older suited Edwin. She remembered when she had liked him in spite of his looks; but now spindly had become spare, and the dark shadow of his beard—Edwin had to shave every day while other boys were still just fuzzy—lay under his pale skin; and the opinions, which had once been so embarrassingly unlike anyone else's, were now celebrated at Woolman as being "Edwinian." Yes, Edwin had changed since that day when she had knocked his tooth out trying to rescue him from the mush pot. And had she changed? Did she also look better to Edwin, almost slender now and the freckles not noticeable except at the height of summer? And with her new-found ability for light talk? They were passing beneath the eucalyptus trees and the silver drops, falling as the wind shook the leaves, stung her face, feeling at once both cool and burning. Meadow larks in the fields which edged the campus sang in the quiet way they have after the rain has stopped.

"Oh, Edwin," Cress said, "no one in the world loves the meadow lark's song the way I do!"

"It's not a competition," Edwin said, "you against the world in an 'I-love-meadow-larks' contest. Take it easy, kid. Love 'em as much as in you lieth, and let it go at that."

"No," she said. "I'm determined to overdo it. Listen," she exclaimed, as two birds sang together. "Not grieving, nor amorous, nor lost. Nothing to read into it. Simply music. Like Mozart. Complete. Finished. Oh, it is rain to listening ears." She glanced at Edwin to see how he took this rhetoric. He took it calmly. She let go his hand and capered amidst the fallen eucalyptus leaves.

"The gardener thinks you've got St. Vitus' dance," Edwin said.

Old Boat Swain, the college gardener whose name was really Swain, was leaning on his hoe, watching her hopping and strutting. She didn't give a hoot about him or what he thought.

"He's old," she told Edwin. "He doesn't exist." She felt less akin to him than to a bird or toad.

There were lights already burning in the dorm windows. Cress could see Ardis and Nina still at their tables, finishing their *Ovid* or looking up a final logarithm. But between five and six most of the girls stopped trying to remember which form of the sonnet Milton had used or when the Congress of Vienna had met, and dressed for dinner. They got out of their sweaters and jackets and into their soft bright dresses. She knew just what she was going to wear when she came downstairs at six to meet Edwin—green silk like the merman's wife. They were going to the Poinsettia for dinner, escaping salmon-wiggle night in the college dining room.

"At six," she told him, "I'll fly down the stairs to meet you like a green wave."

"See you in thirty minutes," Edwin said, leaving her at the dorm steps.

The minute she opened the door, she began to hear the dorm sounds and smell the dorm smells—the hiss and rush of the showers, the thud of the iron, a voice singing, "Dear old Woolman we love so well," the slap of bare feet down the hall, the telephone ringing.

And the smells! Elizabeth Arden and Cashmere Bouquet frothing in the showers; talcum powder falling like snow; *Intoxication* and *Love Me* and *Devon Violet*; rubber-soled sneakers, too, and gym T-shirts still wet with sweat after basketball practice, and the smell of the hot iron on damp wool.

But while she was still listening and smelling, Edith shouted from the top of the stairs. "Long distance for you, Cress. Make it snappy."

Cress took the stairs three at a time, picked up the dangling receiver, pressed it to her ear.

"Tenant calling Crescent Delahanty," the operator said. It was her father: "Grandfather is dying, Cress. Catch the 7:30 home. I'll meet you at the depot."

"What's the matter—Cressie?" Edith asked.

"I have to catch the 7:30 Pacific Electric. Grandfather's dying."

"Oh, poor Cress," Edith cried and pressed her arm about her.

Cress scarcely heard her. Why were they calling her home to watch Grandpa die, she thought, angrily and rebelliously. An old man, past eighty. He'd never been truly alive for her, never more than a rough, hot hand, a scraggly mustache that repelled her when he kissed her, an old fellow who gathered what he called "likely-looking" stones and kept them washed and polished, to turn over and admire. It was silly and unfair to make so much of his dying.

But before she could say a word, Edith was telling the girls. They were crowding about her. "Don't cry," they said. "We'll pack for you. Be brave, darling Cress. Remember your grandfather has had a long happy life. He wouldn't want you to cry."

"Brave Cress—brave Cress," they said. "Just frozen."

She wasn't frozen. She was determined. She was not going to go. It did not make sense. She went downstairs to meet Edwin as she had planned, in her green silk, ready for dinner at the Poinsettia. The girls had told him.

"Are you wearing that home?" he asked.

"I'm not going home," she said. "It's silly and useless. I can't help Grandfather. It's just a convention. What *good* can I do him, sitting there at home?"

"He might do you some good," Edwin said. "Had you thought about that?"

"Why, Edwin!" Cress said. "Why, Edwin!" She had the girls tamed, eating out of her hand, and here was Edwin who loved her—he said so, anyway—cold and disapproving. Looking at herself through Edwin's eyes, she hesitated.

"Go on," Edwin said. "Get what you need and I'll drive you to the station."

She packed her overnight bag and went with him; there didn't seem—once she'd had Edwin's view of herself—anything else to do.

But once on the train her resentment returned. The Pacific Electric was hot and smelled of metal and dusty plush. It clicked past a rickety Mexican settlement, through La Habra and Brea, where the pool hall signs swung in the night wind off the ocean. An old man in a spotted corduroy jacket, and his wife, with her hair straggling through the holes in her broken net, sat in front of her.

Neat, thought Cress, anyone can be neat, if he wants to.

Her father, bareheaded, but in his big sheepskin jacket, met her at the depot. It was after nine, cold and raw.

"This is a sorry time, Cress," he said. He put her suitcase in the back of the car and climbed into the driver's seat without opening the door for her.

Cress got in, wrapped her coat tightly about herself. The sky was clear, the wind had died down.

"I don't see any sense in my having to come home," she said at last. "What good can I do Grandpa? If he's dying, how can I help?"

"I was afraid that was the way you might feel about it. So was your mother."

"Oh, Mother," Cress burst out. "Recently she's always trying to put me . . ."

Her father cut her off. "That'll be about enough, Cress. Your place is at home and you're coming home and keeping your mouth shut, whatever you think. I don't know what's happened to you recently. If college does this to you, you'd better stay home permanently."

There was nothing more said until they turned up the palm-lined driveway that led to the house. "Here we are," Mr. Delahanty told her.

Mrs. Delahanty met them at the door, tired and haggard in her Indian design bathrobe.

"Cress," she said, "Grandfather's conscious now. I told him you were coming and he's anxious to see you. You'd better go in right away—this might be the last time he'd know you."

Cress was standing by the fireplace holding first one foot then the other toward the fire. "Oh, Mother, what am I to say?" she asked. "What can I say? Or does Grandfather just want to see me?"

Her father shook his head as if with pain. "Aren't you sorry your grandfather's dying, Cress? Haven't you any pity in your heart? Don't you understand what death means?"

"He's an old man," Cress said obstinately. "It's what we must expect when we grow old," though she, of course, would never grow old.

"Warm your hands, Cress," her mother said. "Grandfather's throat bothers him and it eases him to have it rubbed. I'll give you the ointment and you can rub it in. You won't need to say anything."

Cress slid out of her coat and went across the hall with her mother to visit her grandfather's room. His thin old body was hardly visible beneath the covers; his head, with its gray skin and sunken eyes, lay upon the pillow as if bodiless. The night light frosted his white hair but made black caverns of his closed eyes.

"Father," Mrs. Delahanty said. "Father." But the old man didn't move. There was nothing except the occasional hoarse rasp of an indrawn breath to show that he was alive.

Mrs. Delahanty pulled the cane-bottomed chair a little closer to the bed. "Sit here," she said to Cress, "and rub this into his throat and chest." She opened her father's nightshirt so that an inch or two of bony grizzled chest was bared. "He says that this rubbing relieves him, even if he's asleep or too tired to speak. Rub it in with a slow steady movement." She went out to the living room leaving the door a little ajar.

Cress sat down on the chair and put two squeamish fingers into the jar of gray ointment; but she could see far more sense to this than to any talking or being talked to. If they had brought her home from school because she was needed in helping to care for Grandpa, that she could understand—but not simply to be present at his death. What had death to do with her?

She leaned over him, rubbing, but with eyes shut, dipping her fingers often into the gray grease. The rhythm of the rubbing, the warmth and closeness of the room, after the cold drive, had almost put her to sleep when the old man startled her by lifting a shaking hand to the bunch of yellow violets Edith had pinned to the shoulder of her dress before she left Woolman. She opened her eyes suddenly at his touch, but the old man said nothing, only stroked the violets awkwardly with a trembling forefinger.

Cress unpinned the violets and put them in his hand. "There, Grandpa," she said, "there. They're for you."

The old man's voice was a harsh and faltering whisper and to hear what he said Cress had to lean very close.

"I used to—pick them—on Reservoir Hill. I was always sorry to—plow them up. Still—so sweet. Thanks," he said, "to bring them. To remember. You're like her. Your grandmother," he added after a pause. He closed his eyes, holding the bouquet against his face, letting the wilting blossoms spray across one cheek like a pulled-up sheet of flowering earth. He said one more word, not her name but her grandmother's.

The dikes about Cress's heart broke. "Oh, Grandpa, I love you," she said. He heard her. He knew what she said, his fingers returned the pressure of her hand. "You were always so good to me. You were young and you loved flowers." Then she said what was her great discovery. "And you still do. You still love yellow violets, Grandpa, just like me."

At the sound of her uncontrolled crying, Mr. and Mrs. Delahanty came to the door. "What's the matter, Cress?"

Cress turned, lifted a hand toward them. "Why didn't you tell me?" she demanded. And when they didn't answer, she said, "Edwin knew."

Then she dropped her head on to her grandfather's outstretched hand and said something, evidently to him, which neither her father nor her mother understood.

"It's just the same."

Exercises

1. The story is divided into four sections. What is the central concern of each one, how is it resolved, and how does it prepare for Cress's insight into herself and her world?

2. What is her relationship with her parents? How valid and how deep are her complaints about them and theirs about her?

3. Cress says to Edwin, "Green from the grass and red from the sun. . . . The whole world right there in one raindrop." And Edwin answers, "As Blake observed earlier about a grain of sand." How is his observation of a totally different dimension from hers and what does it suggest about her need for a deeper understanding of life than her delight in nature suggests? What other details in the second section reinforce this essential difference between them at this point? What is significant about the fact that she is so eager to impress him?

4. How is Edwin's response to the summons home different from that of the girls in the dormitory? Why is it ironic that the violets Edith pinned on Cress (why?) become the medium through which Cress comprehends her oneness with her grandfather?

5. What is the point of her observation about the old man and his wife on the train? With what other observations is it consistent? How does it square with her comment that "no one in the world loves the meadow lark's song the way I do"?

6. Explain the end of the story. What did Edwin know? Recall what he said to her when she said, "What *good* can I do him, sitting there at home?" She said to her parents, "Why didn't you tell me?" Had they told her? Did they *know,* as well as Edwin? What does she mean by her final words? And what does the comment that "neither her father nor her mother understood" have reference to? What has Cress learned? What has she still to learn?

A Sense of Shelter

JOHN UPDIKE

Snow fell against the high school all day, wet big-flaked snow that did not accumulate well. Sharpening two pencils, William looked down on a parking lot that was a blackboard in reverse, car tires had cut smooth arcs of black into the white, and wherever a school bus had backed around, it had left an autocratic signature of two V's. The snow, though at moments it whirled opaquely, could not quite bleach these scars away. The temperature must be exactly 32°. The window was open a crack, and a canted pane of glass lifted outdoor air into his face, coating the cedarwood scent of pencil shavings with the transparent odor of the wet window sill. With each revolution of the handle his knuckles came within a fraction of an inch of the tilted glass, and the faint chill this proximity breathed on them sharpened his already acute sense of shelter.

The sky behind the shreds of snow was stone-colored. The murk inside the high classroom gave the air a solidity that limited the overhead radiance to its own vessels; six globes of dull incandescence floated on the top of a thin sea. The feeling the gloom gave him was not gloomy but joyous: he felt they were all sealed in, safe; the colors of cloth were dyed deeper, the sound of whispers was made more distinct, the smells of tablet paper and wet shoes and varnish and face powder pierced him with a vivid sense of possession. These were his classmates sealed in, his, the stupid as well as the clever, the plain as well as the lovely, his enemies as well as his friends, his. He felt like a king and seemed to move to his seat between the bowed heads of subjects that loved him less than he loved them. His seat was sanctioned by tradition; for twelve years he had sat at the rear of classrooms, William Young, flanked by Marsha Wyckoff and Andy Zimmerman. Once there had been two Zimmermans, but one went to work in his father's greenhouse, and in some classes—Latin and Trig—there were none, and William sat at the edge of the class as if on the lip of a cliff, and Marsha Wyckoff became Marvin Wolf or Sandra Wade, but it was always the same desk, whose surface altered from hour to hour but from whose blue-stained ink-hole his mind could extract, like a chain of magicians' handkerchiefs, a continuity of years. As a senior he was a kind of king, and as a teacher's pet another kind, a puppet king, who gathered in appointive posts and even, when the moron vote split between two football heroes, some elective ones. He was not popular, he had never had a girl, his intense friends of childhood had drifted off into teams and gangs, and in large groups— when the whole school, for instance, went in the fall to the beautiful, dung-and-cotton-candy-smelling county fair—he was always an odd man, without a seat on the bus home. But exclusion is itself a form of inclusion. He even had a nickname: Mip, because he stuttered. Taunts no longer much frightened him; he had come late into his physical inheritance, but this summer it had arrived, and he at last stood equal with his enormous, boisterous parents, and had to unbutton his shirt cuffs to get his wrists through them, and discovered he could pick up a basketball with one hand. So, his long legs blocking two aisles, he felt regal even in size and, almost trembling with happiness under the high globes of light beyond whose lunar glow invisible snowflakes were drowning on the gravel roof of his castle, believed that the long delay of unpopularity had been merely a consolidation, that he was at last strong enough to make his move. Today he would tell Mary Landis he loved her.

He had loved her ever since, a fat-faced tomboy with freckles and green eyes, she deftly stole his rubber-lined schoolbag on the walk back from second grade along Jewett Street and outran him —simply had better legs. The superior speed a boy was supposed to have failed to come; his kidneys burned with panic. In front of the grocery store next to her home she stopped and turned. She was willing to have him catch up. This humiliation on top of the rest was too much to bear. Tears broke in his throat; he spun around and ran home and threw himself on the floor of the front parlor, where his grandfather, feet twiddling, perused the newspaper and soliloquized all morning. In time the letter slot rustled, and the doorbell rang, and Mary gave his mother the schoolbag and the two of them politely exchanged whispers. Their voices had been to him, lying there on the carpet with his head wrapped in his arms, indistinguishable. Mother had always liked Mary. From when she had been a tiny girl dancing along the hedge on the end of an older sister's arm, Mother had liked her. Out of all the children that flocked, similar as pigeons, through the neighborhood, Mother's heart had reached out with claws and fastened on Mary. He never took the schoolbag to school again, had refused to touch it. He supposed it was still in the attic, still faintly smelling of sweet pink rubber.

   Fixed high on the plaster like a wren clinging to a barn wall, the buzzer sounded the two-minute signal. In the middle of the classroom Mary Landis stood up, a Monitor badge pinned to her belly. He broad red belt was buckled with a brass bow and arrow. She wore a lavender sweater with the sleeves pushed up to expose her forearms, a delicately cheap effect. Wild stories were told about her; perhaps it was merely his knowledge of these that put the hardness in her face. Her eyes seemed braced for squinting and their green was frosted. Her freckles had faded. William thought she laughed less this year; now that she was in the Secretarial Course and he in the College Preparatory, he saw her in only one class a day, this one, English. She stood a second, eclipsed at the thighs by Jack Stephens' zebra-striped shoulders, and looked back at the class with a stiff worn glance, as if she had seen the same faces too many times before. Her habit of perfect posture emphasized the angularity she had grown into. There was a nervous edge, a boxiness in her bones, that must have been waiting all along under the childish fat. Her eye sockets were deeply indented and her chin had a prim square set that seemed in the murky air tremulous and defiant. Her skirt was cut square and straight. Below the waist she was lean; the legs that had outrun him were still athletic; she starred at hockey and cheerleading. Above, she was abundant: so stacked her spine curved backwards to keep her body balanced. She turned and in switching up the aisle encountered a boy's leg thrown into her path. She coolly looked down until it withdrew. She was used to such attentions. Her pronged chest poised, Mary proceeded out the door, and someone she saw in the hall made her smile, a wide smile full of warmth and short white teeth, and love scooped at William's heart. He would tell her.

In another minute, the second bell rasped. Shuffling through the perfumed crowds to his next class, he crooned to himself in the slow, over-enunciated manner of the Negro vocalist who had brought the song back this year:

> "Lah-vender blue, dilly dilly,
> Lavendih gree-heen;
> *Eef* I were king, dilly dilly,
> You would: be queen."

The song gave him an exultant sliding sensation that intertwined with the pleasures of his day. He knew all the answers, he had done all the work, the teachers called upon him only to rebuke the ignorance of the others. In Trig and Soc Sci both it was this way. In gym, the fourth hour of the morning, he, who was always picked near the last, startled his side by excelling at volleyball, leaping like a madman, shouting like a bully. The ball felt light as a feather against his big bones. His hair in wet quills from the shower, he walked in the icy air to Luke's Luncheonette, where he ate three hamburgers in a booth with three juniors. There was Barry Kruppman, a tall, thyroid-eyed boy who came on the school bus from the country town of Bowsville and who was an amateur hypnotist; he told the tale of a Portland, Oregon, businessman who under hypnosis had been taken back through sixteen reincarnations to the condition of an Egyptian concubine in the household of a high priest of Isis. There was his friend Lionel Griffin, a pudgy simp whose blond hair puffed out above his ears in two slick waxed wings. He was rumored to be a fairy, and in fact did seem most excited by the transvestite aspect of the soul's transmigration. And there was Lionel's girl Virginia, a drab little mystery who chain-smoked Herbert Tareytons and never said anything. She had sallow skin and smudged eyes and Lionel kept jabbing her and shrieking,

making William wince. He would rather have sat with members
of his own class, who filled the other booths, but he would have
had to force himself on them. These juniors admired him and
welcomed his company. He asked, "Wuh-well, was he ever a
c-c-c-cockroach, like Archy?"

Kruppman's face grew intense; his furry lids dropped down
over the bulge of his eyes, and when they drew back, his pupils
were as small and hard as BBs. "That's the really interesting thing.
There was this gap, see, between his being a knight under Charle-
magne and then a sailor on a ship putting out from Macedonia—
that's where Yugoslavia is now—in the time of Nero; there was
this gap, when the only thing the guy would do was walk around
the office snarling and growling, see, like this." Kruppman worked
his blotched ferret face up into a snarl and Griffin shrieked. "He
tried to bite one of the assistants and they think that for six hundred years"—the uncanny, unhealthy seriousness of his whisper
hushed Griffin momentarily—"for six hundred years he just was
a series of wolves. Probably in the German forests. You see, when
he was in Macedonia"—his whisper barely audible—"he murdered
a woman."

Griffin squealed in ecstasy and cried, "Oh, Kruppman! Kruppman, how you do go on!" and jabbed Virginia in the arm so hard
a Herbert Tareyton jumped from her hand and bobbled across
the Formica table. William gazed over their heads in pain.

The crowds at the soda counter had thinned so that when the
door to the outside opened he saw Mary come in and hesitate there
for a second where the smoke inside and the snow outside swirled
together. The mixture made a kind of—Kruppman's ridiculous
story had put the phrase in his head—wolf-weather, and she was
just a gray shadow caught in it alone. She bought a pack of cigarettes from Luke and went out again, a kerchief around her head,
the pneumatic thing above the door hissing behind her. For a long
time, always in fact, she had been at the center of whatever gang
was the one: in the second grade the one that walked home up
Jewett Street together, and in the sixth grade the one that went
bicycling as far away as the quarry and the Rentschler estate and
played touch football Saturday afternoons, and in the ninth grade

the one that went roller-skating at Candlebridge Park with the tenth-grade boys, and in the eleventh grade the one that held parties past midnight and that on Sundays drove in caravans as far as Philadelphia and back. And all the while there had been a succession of boy friends, first Jack Stephens and Fritz March in their class and then boys a grade ahead and then Barrel Lord, who was a senior when they were sophomores and whose name was in the newspapers all football season, and then this last summer someone out of the school altogether, a man she met while working as a waitress in the city of Alton. So this year her weekends were taken up, and the party gang carried on as if she had never existed, and nobody saw her much except in school and when she stopped by in Luke's to buy a pack of cigarettes. Her silhouette against the big window had looked wan, her head hooded, her face nibbled by light, her fingers fiddling on the veined counter with her coins. He yearned to reach out, to comfort her, but he was wedged deep in the shrill booths, between the jingling guts of the pinball machine and the hillbilly joy of the jukebox. The impulse left him with a disagreeable feeling. He had loved her too long to want to pity her; it endangered the investment of worship on which he had not yet realized any return.

The two hours of the school afternoon held Latin and a study hall. In study hall, while the five people at the table with him played tic-tac-toe and sucked cough drops and yawned, he did all his homework for the next day. He prepared thirty lines of Vergil, Aeneas in the Underworld. The study hall was a huge low room in the basement of the building; its coziness crept into Tartarus. On the other side of the fudge-colored wall the circular saw in the woodworking shop whined and gasped and then whined again; it bit off pieces of wood with a rising, somehow terrorized inflection—*bzzzzzup!* He solved ten problems in trigonometry. His mind cut neatly through their knots and separated them, neat stiff squares of answer, one by one from the long but finite plank of problems that connected Plane Geometry with Solid. Lastly, as the snow on a ragged slant drifted down into the cement pits outside the steel-mullioned windows, he read a short story by Edgar Allan Poe. He closed the book softly on the pleasing sonority of its final note of horror, gazed at the red, wet, menthol-scented inner membrane of Judy Whipple's yawn, rimmed with flaking pink lipstick, and yielded his conscience to the snug sense of his work done, of the snow falling, of the warm minutes that walked through their shelter so slowly./The perforated acoustic tiling above his head seemed the lining of a long tube that would go all the way: high school merging into college, college into graduate school, graduate school into teaching at a college—section man, assistant, associate, *full* professor, possessor of a dozen languages and a thousand books, a man brilliant in his forties, wise in his fifties, renowned in his sixties, revered in his seventies, and then retired, sitting in the study lined with acoustical books until the time came for the last transition from silence to silence, and he would die, like Tennyson, with a copy of *Cymbeline* beside him on the moon-drenched bed.

After school he had to go to Room 101 and cut a sports cartoon into a stencil for the school paper. He liked the building best when it was nearly empty, when the casual residents—the rural commuters, the do-nothings, the trash—had cleared out. Then the janitors went down the halls sowing seeds of red wax and making an immaculate harvest with broad brooms, gathering all the fluff and hairpins and wrappers and powder that the animals had dropped that day. The basketball team thumped in the hollow gymnasium; the cheerleaders rehearsed behind drawn curtains on the stage. In Room 101 two empty-headed typists with stripes bleached into their hair banged away between giggles and mistakes. At her desk Mrs. Gregory, the faculty sponsor, wearily passed her pencil through misspelled news copy on tablet paper. William took the shadow box from the top of the filing cabinet and the styluses and little square plastic shading screens from their drawer and the stencil from the closet where the typed stencils hung, like fragile scarves, on hooks. B-BALLERS BOW, 57-42, was the headline. He drew a tall b-baller bowing to a stumpy pagan idol, labelled "W" for victorious Weiserton High, and traced it in the soft blue wax with the fine loop stylus. His careful breath grazed his knuckles. His eyebrows frowned while his heart bobbed happily on the giddy prattle of the typists. The shadow box was simply a black frame holding a pane of glass and lifted at one end by two legs so the light bulb, fitted in a tin tray, could slide under; it was like a primitive lean-to sheltering a fire. As he worked, his eyes smarting, he mixed himself up with the light bulb, felt himself burning under a slanting roof upon which a huge hand scratched. The glass grew hot; the danger in the job was pulling the softened wax with your damp hand, distorting or tearing the typed letters. Sometimes the center of an *o* stuck to your skin like a bit of blue confetti. But he was expert and cautious. He returned the things to their places feeling airily tall, heightened by Mrs. Gregory's appreciation, which she expressed by keeping her back turned, in effect stating that other staff members were undependable but William did not need to be watched.

In the hall outside Room 101 only the shouts of a basketball scrimmage reverberated; the chant of the cheerleaders had been silenced. Though he had done everything, he felt reluctant to leave. Neither of his parents—both worked—would be home yet, and this building was as much his home. He knew all its nooks. On the second floor of the annex, beyond the art room, there was a strange, narrow boys' lavatory that no one ever seemed to use. It was here one time that Barry Kruppman tried to hypnotize him and cure his stuttering. Kruppman's voice purred and his irises turned tiny in the bulging whites and for a moment William felt himself lean backward involuntarily, but he was distracted by the bits of bloodshot pink in the corners of these portentous eyes; the folly of giving up his will to an intellectual inferior occurred to him; he refused to let go and go under, and perhaps therefore his stuttering had continued.

The frosted window at the end of the long room cast a watery light on the green floor and made the porcelain urinals shine like slices of moon. The semi-opacity of this window gave the room's air of secrecy great density. William washed his hands with exaggerated care, enjoying the lavish amount of powdered soap provided for him in this castle. He studied his face in the mirror, making infinitesimal adjustments to attain the absolutely most flattering angle, and then put his hands below his throat to get their strong, long-fingered beauty into the picture. As he walked toward the door he sang, closing his eyes and gasping as if he were a real Negro whose entire career depended upon this recording:

> "Who—told me so, dilly dilly,
> Who told me soho?
> *Aii* told myself, dilly dilly,
> I told: me so."

When he emerged into the hall it was not empty: one girl walked down its varnished perspective toward him, Mary Landis, a scarf on her head and books in her arms. Her locker was up here, on the second floor of the annex. His own was in the annex basement. A tickling sensation that existed neither in the medium of sound nor of light crowded against his throat. She flipped the scarf back from her hair and in a conversational voice that carried well down the clean planes of the hall said, "Hi, Billy." The name came from way back, when they were both children, and made him feel small but brave.

"Hi. How are you?"

"Fine." Her smile broadened out from the *F* of this word.

What was so funny? Was she really, as it seemed, pleased to see him? "Du-did you just get through cheer-cheer-cheerleading?"

"Yes. Thank God. *Oh* she's so awful. She makes us do the same stupid locomotives for every cheer; I told her, no wonder nobody cheers any more."

"This is M-M-Miss Potter?" He blushed, feeling that he made an ugly face in getting past the *M*. When he got caught in the middle of a sentence the constriction was somehow worse. He admired the way words poured up her throat, distinct and petulant.

"Yes, Potbottom Potter," she said, "she's just aching for a man and takes it out on us. I wish she would get one. Honestly, Billy, I have half a mind to quit. I'll be so glad when June comes, I'll never set foot in this idiotic building again."

Her lips, pale with the lipstick worn off, crinkled bitterly. Her face, foreshortened from the height of his eyes, looked cross as a cat's. It a little shocked him that poor Miss Potter and this kind, warm school stirred her to what he had to take as actual anger; this grittiness in her was the first abrasive texture he had struck today. Couldn't she see around teachers, into their fatigue, their poverty, their fear? It had been so long since he had spoken to her, he wasn't sure how coarse she had become. "Don't quit," he brought out of his mouth at last. "It'd be n-n-n-nuh—it'd be nothing without you."

He pushed open the door at the end of the hall for her and as she passed under his arm she looked up and said, "Why, aren't you sweet?"

The stairwell, all asphalt and iron, smelled of galoshes. It felt more secret than the hall, more specially theirs; there was something magical in its shifting multiplicity of planes as they descended that lifted the spell on his tongue, so that words came as quickly as his feet pattered on the steps.

"No I mean it," he said, "you're really a beautiful cheerleader. But then you're beautiful period."

"I've skinny legs."

"Who told you that?"

"Somebody."

"Well *he* wasn't very sweet."

"No."

"Why do you hate this poor old school?"

"Now Billy. You know you don't care about this junky place any more than I do."

"I love it. It breaks my heart to hear you say you want to get out, because then I'll never see you again."

"You don't care, do you?"

"Why sure I care; you *know*"—their feet stopped; they had reached bottom, the first-floor landing, two brass-barred doors and a grimy radiator—"I've always li-loved you."

"You don't mean that."

"I do too. It's ridiculous but there it is. I wanted to tell you today and now I have."

He expected her to laugh and go out the door, but instead she showed an unforeseeable willingness to discuss this awkward matter. He should have realized before this that women enjoy being talked to. "It's a very silly thing to say," she asserted tentatively.

"I don't see why," he said, fairly bold now that he couldn't seem more ridiculous, and yet picking his words with a certain strategic care. "It's not *that* silly to love somebody, I mean what the hell. Probably what's silly is not to do anything about it for umpteen years but then I never had an opportunity, I thought."

He set his books down on the radiator and she set hers down beside his. "What kind of opportunity were you waiting for?"

"Well, see, that's it; I didn't know." He wished, in a way, she would go out the door. But she had propped herself against the wall and plainly awaited more talking. "Yuh-you were such a queen and I was such a nothing and I just didn't really want to presume." It wasn't very interesting; it puzzled him that she seemed to be interested. Her face had grown quite stern, the mouth very small and thoughtful, and he made a gesture with his hands intended to release her from the bother of thinking about it; after all, it was just a disposition of his heart, nothing permanent or expensive; perhaps it was just his mother's idea anyway. Half in impatience to close the account, he asked, "Will you marry me?"

"You don't want to marry me," she said. "You're going to go on and be a great man."

He blushed in pleasure; is this how she saw him, is this how they all saw him; as worthless now, but in time a great man? Had his hopes always been on view? He dissembled, saying, "No I'm not. But anyway, you're great now. You're so pretty, Mary."

"Oh, Billy," she said, "if you were me for just one day you'd hate it."

She said this rather blankly, watching his eyes; he wished her voice had shown more misery. In his world of closed surfaces a panel, carelessly pushed, had opened, and he hung in this openness paralyzed, unable to think what to say. Nothing he could think of quite fit the abruptly immense context. The radiator cleared its throat; its heat made, in the intimate volume just this side of the doors on whose windows the snow beat limply, a provocative snugness; he supposed he should try, and stepped forward, his hands lifting toward her shoulders. Mary sidestepped between him and the radiator and put the scarf back on. She lifted the cloth like a broad plaid halo above her head and then wrapped it around her chin and knotted it so she looked, in her red galoshes and bulky coat, like a peasant woman in a movie of Europe. With her thick hair swathed, her face seemed pale and chunky, and when she recradled her books in her arms her back bent humbly under the point of her kerchief. "It's too hot in here," she said. "I've got to wait for somebody." The disconnectedness of the two statements seemed natural in the fragmented atmosphere his stops and starts had produced. She bucked the brass bar with her shoulder and the door slammed open; he followed her into the weather.

"For the person who thinks your legs are too skinny?"

"Uh-huh." As she looked up at him a snowflake caught on the lashes of one eye. She jerkily rubbed that cheek on the shoulder of her coat and stamped a foot, splashing slush. Cold water gathered on the back of his thin shirt. He put his hands in his pockets and pressed his arms against his sides to keep from shivering.

"Thuh-then you wo-won't marry me?" His wise instinct told him the only way back was by going forward, through absurdity.

"We don't know each other," she said.

"My God," he said. "Why not? I've known you since I was two."

"What do you know about me?"

This awful seriousness of hers; he must dissolve it. "That you're not a virgin." But instead of making her laugh this made her face go dead and turned it away. Like beginning to kiss her, it was a mistake; in part, he felt grateful for his mistakes. They were like loyal friends who are nevertheless embarrassing. "What do you know about *me*?" he asked, setting himself up for a finishing insult but dreading it. He hated the stiff feel of his smile between his cheeks; glimpsed, as if the snow were a mirror, how hateful he looked.

"That you're basically very nice."

Her returning good for evil blinded him to his physical discomfort, set him burning with regret. "Listen," he said, "I did love you. Let's at least get that straight."

"You never loved anybody," she said. "You don't know what it is."

"O.K." he said. "Pardon me."

"You're excused."

"You better wait in the school," he told her. "He's-eez-eez going to be a long time."

She didn't answer and walked a little distance, toeing out in the childish Dutch way common to the women in this county, along the slack cable that divided the parking lot from the softball field. One bicycle, rusted as if it had been there for years, leaned in the rack, its fenders supporting airy crescents of white.

The warmth inside the door felt heavy. William picked up his books and ran his pencil along the black ribs of the radiator before going down the stairs to his locker in the annex basement. The shadows were thick at the foot of the steps; suddenly it felt late, he must hurry and get home. He was seized by the irrational fear that they were going to lock him in. The cloistered odors of paper, sweat, and, from the woodshop at the far end of the basement hall, sawdust no longer flattered him. The tall green double lockers appeared to study him critically through the three air slits near their tops. When he opened his locker, and put his books on his shelf, below Marvin Wolf's and removed his coat from his hook, his self seemed to crawl into the long dark space thus made vacant, the humiliated, ugly, educable self. In answer to a flick of his great hand the steel door weightlessly floated shut and through the length of his body he felt so clean and free he smiled. Between now and the happy future predicted for him he had nothing, almost literally nothing, to do.

Exercises

1. William doesn't tell the story directly (in the "I" of his own voice), but it is told through his consciousness. Give the evidence for this statement.
2. What kind of person "sees" the scene in the first two paragraphs? What "sense of shelter" is communicated here? Who would find "shelter" in such an environment? Who wouldn't? The narrator says, "He felt like a king." How do the described surroundings make you feel? How do you react at the beginning toward someone who feels "like a king" in this environment? Are we meant to look down our noses at him? Why or why not?
3. What is meant by, "But exclusion is itself a form of inclusion"? How does

that statement underscore William's human relationships? How is it illustrated in the story?

4. What are Mary Landis' charms? We see her as William sees her. How accurate is the observation and description? Does she see herself the same way? How do you know? How does she see him? What is Mary Landis to him really? Consider the following: "He had loved her too long to want to pity her; it endangered the investment of worship on which he had not realized any return."

5. How is the school a symbol of what his life has been and will be? Consider the description of it already discussed. Consider also his behavior in class, in study hall, after school. Note also that "he liked the building best when it was nearly empty, when the casual residents—the rural commuters, the do-nothings, the trash—had cleared out." What is the difference between the language he uses about the building itself and about most of the people in it? Cite examples.

6. What does it tell us about Mary that she takes him seriously and listens to him through? How do we know that in many ways, perhaps in the most important ways, her education has been superior to his? One indication is that she wouldn't think so, and neither would he. Give others.

7. William refers to "this awful seriousness of hers" as he fumbles through his encounter with Mary. In what way is she serious that he is not? What does it mean to take someone seriously or to take life seriously? Who takes life seriously here? In this connection what is the difference between their two responses to the question: "What do you know about me?"

8. William says, "Listen. . . . I did love you. Let's at least get that straight." And Mary answers, "You never loved anybody. . . . You don't know what it is." Is that a cruel comment or not? How would you have her say it if you were recreating this encounter as a scene in a play (which some pairs in the class might try)?

9. What does his telling Mary "he loved her" do to him? Analyze the last paragraph carefully. He's come back into the "shelter" of the building, but it's no longer the "kind, warm" place it was until he removes his coat from his locker and "his self [seems] to crawl into the long dark space thus made vacant, the humiliated, ugly, educable self." Why those three words to define "self"? What is the difference between being "educable" and "educated"? Why does he then feel "so clean and free . . . through the length of his body"? What does it mean to say that William had nothing, almost literally nothing, to do between "now and the happy future predicted for him"? Has he changed at all at the end of the story? Would he still see life as "a long tube that would go all the way. . . until the time came for the last transition from silence to silence"? Discuss.

The Secret Life of Walter Mitty

JAMES THURBER

We're going through!" The Commander's voice was like thin ice breaking. He wore his full-dress uniform, with the heavily braided white cap pulled down rakishly over one cold gray eye. "We can't make it, sir. It's spoiling for a hurricane, if you ask me." "I'm not asking you, Lieutenant Berg," said the Commander. "Throw on the power lights! Rev her up to 8,500! We're going through!" The pounding of the cylinders increased; ta-pocketa-pocketa-pocketa-*pocketa-pocketa*. The Commander stared at the ice forming on the pilot window. He walked over and twisted a row of complicated dials. "Switch on No. 8 auxiliary!" he shouted. "Switch on No. 8 auxiliary!" repeated Lieutenant Berg. "Full strength in No. 3 turret!" shouted the Commander. "Full strength in No. 3 turret!" The crew, bending to their various tasks in the huge, hurtling eight-engined Navy hydroplane, looked at each other and grinned. "The Old Man'll get us through," they said to one another. "The Old Man ain't afraid of Hell!" . . .

"Not so fast! You're driving too fast!" said Mrs. Mitty. "What are you driving so fast for?"

"Hmm?" said Walter Mitty. He looked at his wife, in the seat beside him, with shocked astonishment. She seemed grossly unfamiliar, like a strange woman who had yelled at him in a crowd. "You were up to fifty-five," she said. "You know I don't like to go more than forty. You were up to fifty-five." Walter Mitty drove on toward Waterbury in silence, the roaring of the SN202 through the worst storm in twenty years of Navy flying fading in the remote, intimate airways of his mind. "You're tensed up again," said Mrs. Mitty. "It's one of your days. I wish you'd let Dr. Renshaw look you over."

Walter Mitty stopped the car in front of the building where his wife went to have her hair done. "Remember to get those overshoes while I'm having my hair done," she said. "I don't need overshoes," said Mitty.

She put her mirror back into her bag. "We've been all through that," she said, getting out of the car. "You're not a young man any longer." He raced the engine a little. "Why don't you wear your gloves? Have you lost your gloves?" Walter Mitty reached in a pocket and brought out the gloves. He put them on, but after she had turned and gone into the building and he had driven on to a red light, he took them off again. "Pick it up, brother!" snapped a cop as the light changed, and Mitty hastily pulled on his gloves and lurched ahead. He drove around the streets aimlessly for a time, and then he drove past the hospital on his way to the parking lot.

. . . "It's the millionaire banker, Wellington McMillan," said the pretty nurse. "Yes?" said Walter Mitty, removing his gloves slowly. "Who has the case?" "Dr. Renshaw and Dr. Benbow, but there are two specialists here, Dr. Remington from New York and Dr. Pritchard-Mitford from London. He flew over." A door opened down a long, cool corridor and Dr. Renshaw came out. He looked distraught and haggard. "Hello, Mitty," he said. "We're having the devil's own time with McMillan, the millionaire banker and close personal friend of Roosevelt. Obstreosis of the ductal tract. Tertiary. Wish you'd take a look at him." "Glad to," said Mitty.

In the operating room there were whispered introductions: "Dr. Remington, Dr. Mitty. Dr. Pritchard-Mitford, Dr. Mitty." "I've read your book on streptothricosis," said Pritchard-Mitford, shaking hands. "A brilliant performance, sir." "Thank you," said Walter Mitty. "Didn't know you were in the States, Mitty," grumbled Remington. "Coals to Newcastle, bringing Mitford and me up here for a tertiary." "You are very kind," said Mitty. A huge, complicated machine, connected to the operating table, with many tubes and wires, began at this moment to go pocketa-pocketa-pocketa. "The new anaesthetizer is giving away!" shouted an interne. "There is no one in the East who knows how to fix it!" "Quiet, man!" said Mitty, in a low, cool voice. He sprang to the machine, which was now going pocketa-pocketa-queep-pocketa-queep. He began fingering delicately a row of glistening dials. "Give me a fountain pen!" he snapped. Someone handed him a fountain pen. He pulled a faulty piston out of the machine and inserted the pen in its place. "That will hold for ten minutes," he said. "Get on with the operation." A nurse hurried over and whispered to Renshaw, and Mitty saw the man turn pale. "Coreopsis has set in," said Renshaw nervously. "If you would take over, Mitty?" Mitty looked at him and at the craven figure of Benbow, who drank, and at the grave, uncertain faces of the two great specialists. "If you wish," he said. They slipped a white gown on him; he adjusted a mask and drew on thin gloves; nurses handed him shining . . .

"Back it up, Mac! Look out for that Buick!" Walter Mitty jammed on the brakes. "Wrong lane, Mac," said the parking-lot attendant, looking at Mitty closely. "Gee. Yeh," muttered Mitty. He began cautiously to back out of the lane marked "Exit Only." "Leave her sit there," said the attendant. "I'll put her away." Mitty got out of the car. "Hey, better leave the key." "Oh," said Mitty, handing the man the ignition key. The attendant vaulted into the car, backed it up with insolent skill, and put it where it belonged.

They're so damn cocky, thought Walter Mitty, walking along Main Street; they think they know everything. Once he had tried to take his chains off, outside New Milford, and he got them wound around the axles. A man had had to come out in a wrecking car and unwind them, a young, grinning garage man. Since then Mrs. Mitty always made him drive to a garage to have the chains taken off. The next time, he thought, I'll wear my right arm in a sling; they won't grin at me then. I'll have my right arm in a sling and they'll see I couldn't possibly take the chains off myself. He kicked at the slush on the sidewalk. "Overshoes," he said to himself, and he began looking for a shoe store.

When he came out into the street again, with the overshoes in a box under his arm, Walter Mitty began to wonder what the other thing was his wife had told him to get. She had told him, twice before they set out from their house for Waterbury. In a way he hated these weekly trips to town—he was always getting something wrong. Kleenex, he thought, Squibb's, razor blades? No. Toothpaste, toothbrush, bicarbonate, carborundum, initiative and referendum? He gave it up. But she would remember it. "Where's the what's-its-name?" she would ask. "Don't tell me you forgot the what's-its-name." A newsboy went by shouting something about the Waterbury trial.

. . . "Perhaps this will refresh your memory." The District Attorney suddenly thrust a heavy automatic at the quiet figure on the witness stand. "Have you ever seen this before?" Walter Mitty took the gun and examined it expertly. "This is my Webley-Vickers 50.80," he said calmly. An excited buzz ran around the courtroom. The judge rapped for order. "You are a crack shot with any sort of firearms, I believe?" said the District Attorney, insinuatingly. "Objection!" shouted Mitty's attorney. "We have shown that the defendant could not have fired the shot. We have shown that he wore his right arm in a sling on the night of the fourteenth of July." Walter Mitty raised his hand briefly and the bickering attorneys were stilled. "With any known make of gun," he said evenly, "I could have killed Gregory Fitzhurst at three hundred feet *with my left hand.*" Pandemonium broke loose in the courtroom. A woman's scream rose above the bedlam and suddenly a lovely, dark-haired girl was in Walter Mitty's arms. The District Attorney struck at her savagely. Without rising from his chair, Mitty let the man have it on the point of the chin. "You miserable cur!" . . .

"Puppy biscuit," said Walter Mitty. He stopped walking and the buildings of Waterbury rose up out of the misty courtroom and surrounded him again. A woman who was passing laughed. "He said 'Puppy biscuit,'" she said to her companion. "That man said 'Puppy biscuit' to himself." Walter Mitty hurried on. He went into an A. & P., not the first one he came to but a smaller one farther up the street. "I want some biscuit for small, young dogs," he said to the clerk. "Any special brand, sir?" The greatest pistol shot in the world thought a moment. "It says 'Puppies Bark for It' on the box," said Walter Mitty.

His wife would be through at the hairdresser's in fifteen minutes, Mitty saw in looking at his watch, unless they had trouble drying it; sometimes they had trouble drying it. She didn't like to get to the hotel first; she would want him to be there waiting for her as usual. He found a big leather chair in the lobby, facing a window, and he put the overshoes and the puppy biscuit on the floor beside it. He picked up an old copy of *Liberty* and sank down into the chair. "Can Germany Conquer the World through the Air?" Walter Mitty looked at the pictures of bombing planes and of ruined streets.

. . . "The cannonading has got the wind up in young Raleigh, sir," said the sergeant. Captain Mitty looked up at him through tousled hair. "Get him to bed," he said wearily, "with the others. I'll fly alone." "But you can't, sir," said the sergeant anxiously. "It takes two men to handle that bomber and the Archies are pounding hell out of the air.

Von Richtman's circus is between here and Saulier." "Somebody's got to get that ammunition dump," said Mitty. "I'm going over. Spot of brandy?" He poured a drink for the sergeant and one for himself. War thundered and whined around the dugout and battered at the door. There was a rending of wood and splinters flew through the room. "A bit of a near thing," said Captain Mitty carelessly. "The box barrage is closing in," said the sergeant. "We only live once, sergeant," said Mitty, with his faint, fleeting smile. "Or do we?" He poured another brandy and tossed it off. "I never see a man could hold his brandy like you, sir," said the sergeant. "Begging your pardon, sir." Captain Mitty stood up and strapped on his huge Webley-Vickers automatic. "It's forty kilometers through hell, sir," said the sergeant. Mitty finished one last brandy. "After all," he said softly, "what isn't?" The pounding of the cannon increased; there was the rat-tat-tatting of machine guns, and from somewhere came the menacing pocketa-pocketa-pocketa of the new flame-throwers. Walter Mitty walked to the door of the dugout humming *"Après de Ma Blonde."* He turned and waved to the sergeant. "Cheerio!" he said. . . .

Something struck his shoulder. "I've been looking all over this hotel for you," said Mrs. Mitty. "Why do you have to hide in this old chair? How did you expect me to find you?" "Things close in," said Walter Mitty vaguely. "What?" Mrs. Mitty said. "Did you get the what's-its-name? The puppy biscuit? What's in that box?" "Overshoes," said Mitty. "Couldn't you have put them on in the store?" "I was thinking," said Walter Mitty. "Does it ever occur to you that I am sometimes thinking?" She looked at him. "I'm going to take your temperature when I get you home," she said.

They went out through the revolving doors that made a faintly derisive whistling sound when you pushed them. It was two blocks to the parking lot. At the drugstore on the corner she said, "Wait here for me. I forgot something. I won't be a minute." She was more than a minute. Walter Mitty lighted a cigarette. It began to rain, rain with sleet in it. He stood up against the wall of the drugstore, smoking. . . . He put his shoulders back and his heels together. "To hell with the handkerchief," said Walter Mitty scornfully. He took one last drag on his cigarette and snapped it away. Then, with that faint, fleeting smile playing about his lips, he faced the firing squad; erect and motionless, proud and disdainful, Walter Mitty the Undefeated, inscrutable to the last.

Exercises

1. What is the point of view? Show that the narrator handles the story very objectively despite the fact that he reveals Mitty's daydreams.
2. Point out how Mitty's daydreams have a direct relationship to what is happening to him in the real world. For instance, what is he actually doing while he dreams of himself as Commander Mitty piloting the "eight-engined Navy hydroplane"? Show how the other dream incidents are blended in with the realistic details of his trip to Waterbury.
3. The action is closely knit together in other ways. For instance, trace the references to his gloves or to having his right arm in a sling. What other repeated references do you find? How do they all combine to help underscore the dual world Mitty lives in?
4. Part of the humor of the story lies in the seemingly reasonable yet essentially ridiculous details of his daydreams. Notice the first one. What would a voice "like thin ice breaking" sound like? Why does the comparison *seem* to make sense? How is the Commander dressed? What kinds of things does he do and say? Why does it all seem to make sense? How much sense does it really make? Look at the other daydreams in the same light.
5. The story was written before the days of television (but not before radio soap operas and wild-eyed magazine adventure stories). To those familiar with most television drama the situations and language of Mitty's fantasies are not far different from what passes for reality on television. Name some instances you have recently seen where absurdity is presented as reality. What does Thurber gain by using such stock situations?
6. What kind of person is Walter Mitty? Why does he daydream? What kind of person is his wife? Why does she not daydream?
7. What is the tone of the story? How are we supposed to take Mitty? Obviously, he is a pathetic man in many ways, but is there any contempt expressed for him? How would you characterize the humor? Lighthearted? Cruel? Biting? Gentle? Sympathetic? Support your response to these questions by specific references to the language of the story.
8. What would you say the theme of the story is? In what sense is Walter Mitty "the Undefeated, inscrutable to the last"?
9. Discuss the following comment: "Doesn't Mitty win us to his side simply because we've all got more of Walter Mitty in us than we are willing or able to admit? To deny him honor is to deny ourselves."

By the Waters of Babylon

STEPHEN VINCENT BENÉT

The north and the west and the south are good hunting ground, but it is forbidden to go east. It is forbidden to go to any of the Dead Places except to search for metal and then he who touches the metal must be a priest or the son of a priest. Afterward, both the man and the metal must be purified. These are the rules and the laws; they are well made. It is forbidden to cross the great river and look upon the place that was the Place of the Gods—this is most strictly forbidden. We do not even say its name though we know its name. It is there that spirits live, and demons—it is there that there are the ashes of the Great Burning. These things are forbidden—they have been forbidden since the beginning of time.

My father is a priest; I am the son of a priest. I have been in the Dead Places near us, with my father—at first, I was afraid. When my father went into the house to search for the metal, I stood by the door and my heart felt small and weak. It was a dead man's house, a spirit house. It did not have the smell of man, though there were old bones in a corner. But it is not fitting that a priest's son should show fear. I looked at the bones in the shadow and kept my voice still.

Then my father came out with the metal—a good, strong piece. He looked at me with both eyes but I had not run away. He gave me the metal to hold—I took it and did not die. So he knew that I was truly his son and would be a priest in my time. That was when I was very young—nevertheless, my brothers would not have done it, though they are good hunters. After that, they gave me the good piece of meat and the warm corner by the fire. My father watched over me—he was glad that I should be a priest. But when I boasted or wept without a reason, he punished me more strictly than my brothers. That was right.

After a time, I myself was allowed to go into the dead houses and search for metal. So I learned the ways of those houses—and if I saw bones, I was no longer afraid. The bones are light and old—sometimes they will fall into dust if you touch them. But that is a great sin.

I was taught the chants and the spells—I was taught how to stop the running of blood from a wound and many secrets. A priest must know many secrets—that was what my father said. If the hunters think we do all things by chants and spells, they may believe so—it does not hurt them. I was taught how to read in the old books and how to make the old writings—that was hard and took a long time. My knowledge made me happy—it was like a fire in my heart. Most of all, I liked to hear of the Old Days and the stories of the gods. I asked myself many questions that I could not answer, but it was good to ask them. At night, I would lie awake and listen to the wind—it seemed to me that it was the voice of the gods as they flew through the air.

We are not ignorant like the Forest People—our women spin wool on the wheel, our priests wear a white robe. We do not eat grubs from the tree, we have not forgotten the old writings, although they are hard to understand. Nevertheless, my knowledge and my lack of knowledge burned in me—I wished to know more. When I was a man at last, I came to my father and said, "It is time for me to go on my journey. Give me your leave."

He looked at me for a long time, stroking his beard, then he said at last, "Yes. It is time." That night, in the house of the priesthood, I asked for and received purification. My body hurt but my spirit was a cool stone. It was my father himself who questioned me about my dreams.

He bade me look into the smoke of the fire and see—I saw and told what I saw. It was what I have always seen—a river, and, beyond it, a great Dead Place and in it the gods walking. I have always thought about that. His eyes were stern when I told him—he was no longer my father but a priest. He said, "This is a strong dream."

"It is mine," I said, while the smoke waved and my head felt light. They were singing the Star song in the outer chamber and it was like the buzzing of bees in my head.

He asked me how the gods were dressed and I told him how they were dressed. We know how they were dressed from the book, but I saw them as if they were before me. When I had finished, he threw the sticks three times and studied them as they fell.

"This is a very strong dream," he said. "It may eat you up."

"I am not afraid," I said and looked at him with both eyes. My voice sounded thin in my ears but that was because of the smoke.

He touched me on the breast and the forehead. He gave me the bow and the three arrows.

"Take them," he said. "It is forbidden to travel east. It is forbidden to cross the river. It is forbidden to go to the Place of the Gods. All these things are forbidden."

"All these things are forbidden," I said, but it was my voice that spoke and not my spirit. He looked at me again.

"My son," he said. "Once I had young dreams. If your dreams do not eat you up, you may be a great priest. If they eat you, you are still my son. Now go on your journey."

I went fasting, as is the law. My body hurt but not my heart. When the dawn came, I was out of sight of the village. I prayed and purified myself, waiting for a sign. The sign was an eagle. It flew east.

Sometimes signs are sent by bad spirits. I waited again on the flat rock, fasting, taking no food. I was very still—I could feel the sky above me and the earth beneath. I waited till the sun was beginning to sink. Then three deer passed in the valley going east—they did not mind me or see me. There was a white fawn with them—a very great sign.

I followed them, at a distance, waiting for what would happen. My heart was troubled about going east, yet I knew that I must go. My head hummed with my fasting—I did not even see the panther spring upon the white fawn. But, before I knew it, the bow was in my hand. I shouted and the panther lifted his head from the fawn. It is not easy to kill a panther with one arrow but the arrow went through his eye and into his brain. He died as he tried to spring—he rolled over, tearing at the ground. Then I knew I was meant to go east—I knew that was my journey. When the night came, I made my fire and roasted meat.

It is eight suns journey to the east and a man passes by many Dead Places. The Forest People are afraid of them but I am not. Once I made my fire on the edge of a Dead Place at night and, next morning, in the dead house, I found a good knife, little rusted. That was small to what came afterward but it made my heart feel big. Always when I looked for game, it was in front of my arrow, and twice I passed hunting parties of the Forest People without their knowing. So I knew my magic was strong and my journey clean, in spite of the law.

Toward the setting of the eighth sun, I came to the banks of the great river. It was half-a-day's journey after I had left the god-road— we do not use the god-roads now for they are falling apart into great blocks of stone, and the forest is safer going. A long way off, I had seen the water through trees but the trees were thick. At last, I came out upon an open place at the top of a cliff. There was the great river below, like a giant in the sun. It is very long, very wide. It could eat all the streams we know and still be thirsty. Its name is Ou-dis-sun, the Sacred, the Long. No man of my tribe had seen it, not even my father, the priest. It was magic and I prayed.

Then I raised my eyes and looked south. It was there, the Place of the Gods.

How can I tell what it was like—you do not know. It was there, in the red light, and they were too big to be houses. It was there with the red light upon it, mighty and ruined. I knew that in another moment the gods would see me. I covered my eyes with my hands and crept back into the forest.

Surely, that was enough to do, and live. Surely it was enough to spend the night upon the cliff. The Forest People themselves do not come near. Yet, all through the night, I knew that I should have to cross the river and walk in the places of the gods, although the gods ate me up. My magic did not help me at all and yet there was a fire in my bowels, a fire in my mind. When the sun rose, I thought, "My journey has been clean. Now I will go home from my journey." But, even as I thought so, I knew I could not. If I went to the Place of the Gods, I would surely die; if I did not go, I could never be at peace with my spirit again. It is better to lose one's life than one's spirit, if one is a priest and the son of a priest.

Nevertheless, as I made the raft, the tears ran out of my eyes. The Forest People could have killed me without fight, if they had come upon me then, but they did not come. When the raft was made, I said the sayings for the dead and painted myself for death. My heart was cold as a frog and my knees like water, but the burning in my mind would not let me have peace. As I pushed the raft from the shore, I began my death song—I had the right. It was a fine song.

"I am John, son of John," I sang. "My people are the Hill People.
   They are the men.
I go into the Dead Places but I am not slain.
I take the metal from the Dead Places but I am not blasted.
I travel upon the god-roads and am not afraid. E-yah! I have killed
   the panther, I have killed the fawn!
E-yah! I have come to the great river. No man has come there before.
It is forbidden to go east, but I have gone, forbidden to go on the great
   river, but I am there.
Open your hearts, you spirits, and hear my song.
Now I go to the place of the gods, I shall not return.
My body is painted for death and my limbs weak, but my heart is big
   as I go to the Place of the Gods!"

All the same, when I came to the Place of the Gods, I was afraid, afraid. The current of the great river is very strong—it gripped my raft with its hands. That was magic, for the river itself is wide and calm. I could feel evil spirits about me, in the bright morning; I could feel their breath on my neck as I was swept down the stream. Never have I been so much alone—I tried to think of my knowledge, but it was a squirrel's heap of winter nuts. There was no strength in my knowledge any more and I felt small and naked as a new-hatched bird—alone upon the great river, the servant of the gods.

Yet, after a while, my eyes were opened and I saw. I saw both banks of the river—I saw that once there had been god-roads across it, though now they were broken and fallen like broken vines. Very great they were, and wonderful and broken—broken in the time of the Great Burning when the fire fell out of the sky. And always the current took me nearer to the Place of the Gods, and the huge ruins rose before my eyes.

I do not know the customs of rivers—we are the People of the Hills. I tried to guide my raft with the pole but it spun around. I thought the river meant to take me past the Place of the Gods and out into the Bitter

Water of the legends. I grew angry then—my heart felt strong. I said aloud, "I am a priest and the son of a priest!" The gods heard me—they showed me how to paddle with the pole on one side of the raft. The current changed itself—I drew near to the Place of the Gods.

When I was very near, my raft struck and turned over. I can swim in our lakes—I swam to the shore. There was a great spike of rusted metal sticking out into the river—I hauled myself up upon it and sat there, panting. I had saved my bow and two arrows and the knife I found in the Dead Place but that was all. My raft went whirling downstream toward the Bitter Water. I looked after it, and thought if it had trod me under, at least I would be safely dead. Neverthless, when I had dried my bowstring and re-strung it, I walked forward to the Place of the Gods.

It felt like ground underfoot; it did not burn me. It is not true what some of the tales say, that the ground there burns forever, for I have been there. Here and there were the marks and stains of the Great Burning, on the ruins, that is true. But they were old marks and old stains. It is not true either, what some of our priests say, that it is an island covered with fogs and enchantments. It is not. It is a great Dead Place—greater than any Dead Place we know. Everywhere in it there are god-roads, though most are cracked and broken. Everywhere there are the ruins of the high towers of the gods.

How shall I tell what I saw? I went carefully, my strung bow in my hand, my skin ready for danger. There should have been the wailings of spirits and the shrieks of demons, but there were not. It was very silent and sunny where I had landed—the wind and the rain and the birds that drop seeds had done their work—the grass grew in the cracks of the broken stone. It is a fair island—no wonder the gods built there. If I had come there, a god, I also would have built.

How shall I tell what I saw? The towers are not all broken—here and there one still stands, like a great tree in a forest, and the birds nest high. But the towers themselves look blind, for the gods are gone. I saw a fish hawk, catching fish in the river. I saw a little dance of white butterflies over a great heap of broken stones and columns. I went there and looked about me—there was a carved stone with cut-letters, broken in half. I can read letters but I could not understand these. They said UBTREAS. There was also the shattered image of a man or a god. It had been made of white stone and he wore his hair tied like a woman's. His name was ASHING, as I read on the cracked half of a stone. I thought it wise to pray to ASHING, though I do not know that god.

How shall I tell what I saw? There was no smell of man left, on stone or metal. Nor were there many trees in that wilderness of stone. There are many pigeons, nesting and dropping in the towers—the gods must have loved them, or, perhaps, they used them for sacrifices. There are wild cats that roam the god-roads, green-eyed, unafraid of man. At night they wail like demons but they are not demons. The wild dogs are more dangerous, for they hunt in a pack, but them I did not meet until later. Everywhere there are the carved stones, carved with magical numbers or words.

I went North—I did not try to hide myself. When a god or a demon saw me, then I would die, but meanwhile I was no longer afraid. My hunger for knowledge burned in me—there was so much that I could not understand. After a while, I knew that my belly was hungry. I could have hunted for my meat, but I did not hunt. It is known that the gods did not hunt as we do—they got their food from enchanted boxes and jars. Sometimes these are still found in the Dead Places— once, when I was a child and foolish, I opened such a jar and tasted it and found the food sweet. But my father found out and punished me for it strictly, for, often, that food is death. Now, though, I had long gone past what was forbidden, and I entered the likeliest towers, look- ing for the food of the gods.

I found it at last in the ruins of a great temple in the mid-city. A mighty temple it must have been, for the roof was painted like the sky at night with its stars—that much I could see, though the colors were faint and dim. It went down into great caves and tunnels—perhaps they kept their slaves there. But when I started to climb down, I heard the squeaking of rats, so I did not go—rats are unclean, and there must have been many tribes of them, from the squeaking. But near there, I found food, in the heart of a ruin, behind a door that still opened. I ate only the fruits from the jars—they had a very sweet taste. There was drink, too, in bottles of glass—the drink of the gods was strong and made my head swim. After I had eaten and drunk, I slept on the top of a stone, my bow at my side.

When I woke, the sun was low. Looking down from where I lay, I saw a dog sitting on his haunches. His tongue was hanging out of his mouth; he looked as if he were laughing. He was a big dog, with a gray-brown coat, as big as a wolf. I sprang up and shouted at him but he did not move—he just sat there as if he were laughing. I did not like that. When I reached for a stone to throw, he moved swiftly out of the way of the stone. He was not afraid of me; he looked at me as if I were meat. No doubt I could have killed him with an arrow, but I did not know if there were others. Moreover, night was falling.

I looked about me—not far away there was a great, broken god-road, leading North. The towers were high enough, but not so high, and while many of the dead-houses were wrecked, there were some that stood. I went toward this god-road, keeping to the heights of the ruins, while the dog followed. When I had reached the god-road, I saw that there were others behind him. If I had slept later, they would have come upon me asleep and torn out my throat. As it was, they were sure enough of me; they did not hurry. When I went into the dead-house, they kept watch at the entrance—doubtless they thought they would have a fine hunt. But a dog cannot open a door and I knew, from the books, that the gods did not like to live on the ground but on high.

I had just found a door I could open when the dogs decided to rush. Ha! They were surprised when I shut the door in their faces—it was a good door, of strong metal. I could hear their foolish baying beyond it but I did not stop to answer them. I was in darkness—I found stairs and climbed. There were many stairs, turning around till my head was dizzy. At the top was another door—I found the knob and opened it. I was in a long small chamber—on one side of it was a bronze door that could not be opened, for it had no handle. Perhaps there was a magic word to open it but I did not have the word. I turned to the door in the opposite side of the wall. The lock of it was broken and I opened it and went in.

Within, there was a place of great riches. The god who lived there must have been a powerful god. The first room was a small anteroom— I waited there for some time, telling the spirits of the place that I came in peace and not as a robber. When it seemed to me that they had had time to hear me, I went on. Ah, what riches! Few, even, of the windows had been broken—it was all as it had been. The great windows that looked over the city had not been broken at all though they were dusty and streaked with many years. There were coverings on the floors, the colors not greatly faded, and the chairs were soft and deep. There were pictures upon the walls, very strange, very wonderful—I remember one of a bunch of flowers in a jar—if you came close to it, you could see nothing but bits of color, but if you stood away from it, the flowers might have been picked yesterday. It made my heart feel strange to look at this picture—and to look at the figure of a bird, in some hard clay, on a table and see it so like our birds. Everywhere there were books and writings, many in tongues that I could not read. The god who lived there must have been a wise god and full of knowledge. I felt I had right there, as I sought knowledge also.

Nevertheless, it was strange. There was a washing-place but no water —perhaps the gods washed in air. There was a cooking-place but no wood, and though there was a machine to cook food, there was no place to put fire in it. Nor were there candles or lamps—there were things that looked like lamps but they had neither oil nor wick. All these things were magic, but I touched them and lived—the magic had gone out of them. Let me tell one thing to show. In the washing-place, a thing said "Hot" but it was not hot to the touch—another thing said "Cold" but it was not cold. This must have been a strong magic but the magic was gone. I do not understand—they had ways—I wish that I knew.

It was close and dry and dusty in their house of the gods. I have said that the magic was gone but that is not true—it had gone from the magic things but it had not gone from the place. I felt the spirits about me, weighing upon me. Nor had I ever slept in a Dead Place before— and yet, tonight, I must sleep there. When I thought of it, my tongue felt dry in my throat, in spite of my wish for knowledge. Almost I would have gone down again and faced the dogs, but I did not.

I had not gone through all the rooms when the darkness fell. When it fell, I went back to the big room looking over the city and made fire. There was a place to make fire and a box with wood in it, though I do not think they cooked there. I wrapped myself in a floor-covering and slept in front of the fire—I was very tired.

Now I tell what is very strong magic. I woke in the midst of the night. When I woke, the fire had gone out and I was cold. It seemed to me that all around me there were whisperings and voices. I closed my eyes to shut them out. Some will say that I slept again, but I do not think that I slept. I could feel the spirits drawing my spirit out of my body as a fish is drawn on a line.

Why should I lie about it? I am a priest and the son of a priest. If there are spirits, as they say, in the small Dead Places near us, what spirits must there not be in that great Place of the Gods? And would not they wish to speak? After such long years? I know that I felt myself drawn as a fish is drawn on a line. I had stepped out of my body —I could see my body asleep in front of the cold fire, but it was not I. I was drawn to look out upon the city of the gods.

It should have been dark, for it was night, but it was not dark. Everywhere there were lights—lines of light—circles and blurs of light—ten thousand torches could not have been the same. The sky itself was alight—you could barely see the stars for the glow in the sky. I thought to myself "This is strong magic" and trembled. There was a roaring in my ears like the rushing of rivers. Then my eyes grew used to the light and my ears to the sound. I knew that I was seeing the city as it had been when the gods were alive.

That was a sight indeed—yes, that was a sight: I could not have seen it in the body—my body would have died. Everywhere went the gods, on foot and in chariots—there were gods beyond number and counting and their chariots blocked the streets. They had turned night to day for their pleasure—they did not sleep with the sun. The noise of their coming and going was the noise of many waters. It was magic what they could do—it was magic what they did.

I looked out of another window—the great vines of their bridges were mended and the god-roads went east and west. Restless, restless, were the gods and always in motion! They burrowed tunnels under rivers—they flew in the air. With unbelievable tools they did giant works—no part of the earth was safe from them, for, if they wished for a thing, they summoned it from the other side of the world. And always, as they labored and rested, as they feasted and made love, there was a drum in their ears—the pulse of the giant city, beating and beating like a man's heart.

Were they happy? What is happiness to the gods? They were great, they were mighty, they were wonderful and terrible. As I looked upon them and their magic, I felt like a child—but a little more, it seemed to me, and they would pull down the moon from the sky. I saw them with wisdom beyond wisdom and knowledge beyond knowledge. And yet not all they did was well done—even I could see that—and yet their wisdom could not but grow until all was peace.

Then I saw their fate come upon them and that was terrible past speech. It came upon them as they walked the streets of their city. I have been in the fights with the Forest People—I have seen men die. But this was not like that. When gods war with gods, they use weapons we do not know. It was fire falling out of the sky and a mist that poisoned. It was the time of the Great Burning and the Destruction. They ran about like ants in the streets of their city—poor gods, poor gods! Then the towers began to fall. A few escaped—yes, a few. The legends tell it. But, even after the city had become a Dead Place, for many years the poison was still in the ground. I saw it happen, I saw the last of them die. It was darkness over the broken city and I wept.

All this, I saw. I saw it as I have told it, though not in the body. When I woke in the morning, I was hungry, but I did not think first of my hunger for my heart was perplexed and confused. I knew the reason for the Dead Places but I did not see why it had happened. It seemed to me it should not have happened, with all the magic they had. I went through the house looking for an answer. There was so much in the house I could not understand—and yet I am a priest and the son of a priest. It was like being on one side of the great river, at night, with no light to show the way.

Then I saw the dead god. He was sitting in his chair, by the window, in a room I had not entered before and, for the first moment, I thought that he was alive. Then I saw the skin on the back of his hand—it was like dry leather. The room was shut, hot and dry—no doubt that had kept him as he was. At first I was afraid to approach him—then the fear left me. He was sitting looking out over the city—he was dressed in the clothes of the gods. His age was neither young nor old—I could not tell his age. But there was wisdom in his face and great sadness. You could see that he would have not run away. He had sat at his window, watching his city die—then he himself had died. But it is better to lose one's life than one's spirit—and you could see from the face that his spirit had not been lost. I knew that, if I touched him, he would fall into dust—and yet, there was something unconquered in the face.

That is all of my story, for then I knew he was a man—I knew then that they had been men, neither gods nor demons. It is a great knowledge, hard to tell and believe. They were men—they went a dark road, but they were men. I had no fear after that—I had no fear going home, though twice I fought off the dogs and once I was hunted for two days by the Forest People. When I saw my father again, I prayed and was purified. He touched my lips and my breast, he said, "You went away a boy. You come back a man and a priest." I said, "Father, they were men! I have been in the Place of the Gods and seen it! Now slay me, if it is the law—but still I know they were men."

He looked at me out of both eyes. He said, "The law is not always the same shape—you have done what you have done. I could not have done it in my time, but you come after me. Tell!"

I told and he listened. After that, I wished to tell all the people but he showed me otherwise. He said, "Truth is a hard deer to hunt. If you eat too much truth at once, you may die of the truth. It was not idly that our fathers forbade the Dead Places." He was right—it is better the truth should come little by little. I have learned that, being a priest. Perhaps, in the old days, they ate knowledge too fast.

Nevertheless, we make a beginning. It is not for the metal alone we go to the Dead Places now—there are the books and the writings. They are hard to learn. And the magic tools are broken—but we can look at them and wonder. At least, we make a beginning. And, when I am chief priest we shall go beyond the great river. We shall go to the Place of the Gods—the place newyork—not one man but a company. We shall look for the images of the gods and find the god ASHING and the others—the gods Lincoln and Biltmore and Moses. But they were men who built the city, not gods or demons. They were men. I remember the dead man's face. They were men who were here before us. We must build again.

HOTELS IN NEW YORK

Exercises

1. What purpose is served by the first paragraph? Why is the word *forbidden* used six times? What repetitions in phrasing are there? What kind of life is suggested? What would be lost if the story started with the second paragraph?

2. List at least ten words or phrases in the next five paragraphs that further define the kind of society the boy lives in.

3. How many sections would you divide the story into? Indicate the central idea of each section.

4. What virtues does the narrator have? Support your answer with references to what he does. Why is he able to become a priest? What does the word *priest* mean in this story? How do the narrator's people differ from the Forest People? At the end, in what sense is he a greater priest than his father? In what sense not?

5. In what ways is the narrator very much like the men of the vanished civilization? Refer to specific things he says and feels.

6. Why is it effective to have the boy tell his own story? Consider whether some other point of view might have been equally effective. Try writing the opening paragraphs of the story from another point of view.

7. Notice how carefully Benét has kept to the kind of language the boy would use. Point out other instances of the repetition of phrasing mentioned in question 1. What other words like *forbidden* and *spirits* echo the emphasis on primitive religious rites? How does the sentence structure and word choice underscore the boy's lack of what we would call formal learning? Notice that any comparison he uses is based on the simple experiences he has had: for example, "like the buzzing of bees in my head" and "my heart was cold as a frog." Find other comparisons which bear out this observation. On the basis of your answers to the above questions, would you say the tone of the story is childish, childlike, simple, fearful, majestic, religious? Several of these? None of these?

8. UBTREAS refers to the Subtreasury Building in downtown New York, in front of which is a statue of George Washington (ASHING). Lincoln and Biltmore refer to the Lincoln and Biltmore Hotels. Moses refers to Robert Moses, a well-known New York public official, Park Commissioner for many years and president of the 1964–65 New York World's Fair. What hints are there early in the story as to where the boy lives and what the Place of the Gods is? Identify all the specific references not already identified, such as "Ou-dis-sun," "god-roads," the "Bitter Water," and so on.

9. How does the boy know as much as he seems to know about the Place of the Gods? Upon what does he base his vision of the city as it used to be? The rest of the details in the story are realistic if the supposed destruction has

taken place. Is any advantage gained by including the vision that would be lost if it were not included? Discuss.

10. What convinced the boy that "they had been men, neither gods nor demons"?

11. The title is taken from Psalm 137. Read it, and then point out its relevance to the story.

12. What are "ignorance" and "wisdom" as used in this story? What details reveal the ignorance of the boy's people? The ignorance of the "gods"? What details reveal their wisdom?

13. What is the theme of the story? Why are the following statements inadequate as expressions of the theme: "The road to knowledge is also the road to destruction"; "When people deal with the forbidden, they will be punished"?

II *It takes only an evening in front of the TV set or a few minutes with the amusement section of a daily paper (or the funnies) to prove the public appetite for violence. We have always been fascinated by the human capacity for evil, given and received, even as we denounce its prevalence. Paradoxically, most violent crimes involve people who are well known to each other.*

Tales of individual violence dramatize in the simplest and most direct way that we hang eternally over the edge of the unknown, outside and inside us. They probe our deepest possibilities for self-destruction and other-destruction. Some are catalogues of terror, rivaling in explicitness the naked eye or the camera. Others explore, as no camera can, the workings of the twisted and tortured mind. Still others tell us that violence need not be explicit or physical or rise from the festering of a diseased mind to have its disastrous effect, an effect which is often the more horrible because it is slowly corrosive and hidden from view.

The five stories in this section involve intense personal relationships in which the human ties we like to call normal are shredded by other, abnormal, human needs or demands.

The Cask of Amontillado[1]

EDGAR ALLAN POE

The thousand injuries of Fortunato I had borne as I best could, but when he ventured upon insult, I vowed revenge. You, who so well know the nature of my soul, will not suppose, however, that I gave utterance to a threat. *At length* I would be avenged; this was a point definitely settled—but the very definitiveness with which it was resolved precluded the idea of risk. I must not only punish, but punish with impunity. A wrong is unredressed when retribution overtakes its redresser. It is equally unredressed when the avenger fails to make himself felt as such to him who has done the wrong.

It must be understood that neither by word nor deed had I given Fortunato cause to doubt my good will. I continued, as was my wont, to smile in his face, and he did not perceive that my smile *now* was at the thought of his immolation.

He had a weak point—this Fortunato—although in other regards he was a man to be respected and even feared. He prided himself on his connoisseurship in wine. Few Italians have the true virtuoso spirit. For the most part their enthusiasm is adopted to suit the time and opportunity to practice imposture upon the British and Austrian millionaires. In painting and gemmary Fortunato, like his countrymen, was a quack, but in the matter of old wines he was sincere. In this respect I did not differ from him materially;—I was skillful in the Italian vintages myself, and bought largely whenever I could.

It was about dusk, one evening during the supreme madness of the carnival season, that I encountered my friend. He accosted me with excessive warmth, for he had been drinking much. The man wore motley. He had on a tight-fitting parti-striped dress, and his head was surmounted by the conical cap and bells. I was so pleased to see him that I thought I should never have done wringing his hand.

[1]**Amontillado:** here, a rare wine; a type of sherry, but in this story it is distinguished from ordinary sherry.

I said to him—"My dear Fortunato, you are luckily met. How remarkably well you are looking today! But I have received a pipe of what passes for Amontillado, and I have my doubts."

"How?" said he, "Amontillado? A pipe? Impossible! And in the middle of the carnival?"

"I have my doubts," I replied; "and I was silly enough to pay the full Amontillado price without consulting you in the matter. You were not to be found, and I was fearful of losing a bargain."

"Amontillado!"

"I have my doubts."

"Amontillado!"

"And I must satisfy them."

"Amontillado!"

"As you are engaged, I am on my way to Luchesi. If anyone has a critical turn, it is he. He will tell me——"

"Luchesi cannot tell Amontillado from Sherry."

"And yet some fools will have it that his taste is a match for your own."

"Come, let us go."

"Whither?"

"To your vaults."

"My friend, no; I will not impose upon your good nature. I perceive you have an engagement. Luchesi——"

"I have no engagement; come."

"My friend, no. It is not the engagement, but the severe cold with which I perceive you are afflicted. The vaults are insufferably damp. They are encrusted with niter."

"Let us go, nevertheless. The cold is merely nothing. Amontillado! You have been imposed upon; and as for Luchesi, he cannot distinguish Sherry from Amontillado."

Thus speaking, Fortunato possessed himself of my arm. Putting on a mask of black silk, and drawing a *roquelaure*² closely about my person, I suffered him to hurry me to my palazzo.

There were no attendants at home; they had absconded to make merry in honor of the time. I had told them that I should not return

²*roquelaure:* a cloak which buttons down the front and reaches to the knees.

until the morning, and had given them explicit orders not to stir from the house. These orders were sufficient, I well knew, to insure their immediate disappearance, one and all, as soon as my back was turned.

I took from their sconces two flambeaux, and giving one to Fortunato, bowed him through several suites of rooms to the archway that led into the vaults. I passed down a long and winding staircase, requesting him to be cautious as he followed. We came at length to the foot of the descent, and stood together on the damp ground of the catacombs of the Montresors.

The gait of my friend was unsteady, and the bells upon his cap jingled as he strode.

"The pipe," said he.

"It is farther on," said I; "but observe the white web-work which gleams from these cavern walls."

He turned towards me, and looked into my eyes with two filmy orbs that distilled the rheum of intoxication.

"Niter?" he asked, at length.

"Niter," I replied. "How long have you had that cough?"

"Ugh! ugh! ugh!—ugh! ugh! ugh!—ugh! ugh! ugh!—ugh! ugh! ugh!—ugh! ugh! ugh!"

My poor friend found it impossible to reply for many minutes.

"It is nothing," he said, at last.

"Come," I said, with decision, "we will go back; your health is precious. You are rich, respected, admired, beloved; you are happy, as once I was. You are a man to be missed. For me it is no matter. We will go back; you will be ill, and I cannot be responsible. Besides, there is Luchesi——"

"Enough," he said; "the cough is a mere nothing: it will not kill me. I shall not die of a cough."

"True—true," I replied; "and, indeed, I had no intention of alarming you unnecessarily—but you should use all proper caution. A draught of this Médoc[3] will defend us from the damps."

Here I knocked off the neck of a bottle which I drew from a long row of its fellows that lay upon the mold.

"Drink," I said, presenting him the wine.

[3]**Médoc:**   red wine from Médoc, France, near Bordeaux.

He raised it to his lips with a leer. He paused and nodded to me familiarly, while his bells jingled.

"I drink," he said, "to the buried that repose around us."

"And I to your long life."

He again took my arm, and we proceeded.

"These vaults," he said, "are extensive."

"The Montresors," I replied, "were a great and numerous family."

"I forget your arms."

"A huge human foot d'or, in a field azure; the foot crushes a serpent rampant whose fangs are imbedded in the heel."

"And the motto?"

"Nemo me impune lacessit."[4]

"Good!" he said.

The wine sparkled in his eyes and the bells jingled. My own fancy grew warm with the Médoc. We had passed through walls of piled bones, with casks and puncheons[5] intermingling, into the inmost recesses of the catacombs. I paused again, and this time I made bold to seize Fortunato by an arm above the elbow.

"The niter!" I said; "see, it increases. It hangs like moss upon the vaults. We are below the river's bed. The drops of moisture trickle among the bones. Come, we will go back ere it is too late. Your cough——"

"It is nothing," he said; "let us go on. But first, another draught of the Médoc." I broke and reached him a flagon of De Grâve. He emptied it at a breath. His eyes flashed with a fierce light. He laughed and threw the bottle upwards with a gesticulation I did not understand.

I looked at him in surprise. He repeated the movement—a grotesque one. "You do not comprehend?" he said.

"Not I," I replied.

"Then you are not of the brotherhood."

"How?"

"You are not of the masons."[6]

---

[4]*Nemo me impune lacessit:* No one dare attack me with impunity.

[5]**puncheons:** large casks.

[6]**masons:** Freemasons, members of a secret all-male society which stresses brotherhood, faithfulness, and honor; Montresor is not a member, but is able to make a bitter joke out of the fact that he has a mason's (i.e., stoneworker's) trowel with him.

"Yes, yes," I said, "yes, yes."

"You? Impossible! A mason?"

"A mason," I replied.

"A sign," he said.

"It is this," I answered, producing a trowel from beneath the folds of my *roquelaure*.

"You jest," he explained, recoiling a few paces. "But let us proceed to the Amontillado."

"Be it so," I said, replacing the tool beneath the cloak, and again offering him my arm. He leaned upon it heavily. We continued our route in search of the Amontillado. We passed through a range of low arches, descended, passed on, and descending again, arrived at a deep crypt, in which the foulness of the air caused our flambeaux rather to glow than flame.

At the most remote end of the crypt there appeared another less spacious. Its walls had been lined with human remains piled to the vault overhead, in the fashion of the great catacombs of Paris. Three sides of this interior crypt were still ornamented in this manner. From the fourth the bones had been thrown down, and lay promiscuously upon the earth, forming at one point a mound of some size. Within the wall thus exposed by the displacing of the bones, we perceived a still interior recess, in depth about four feet, in width three, in height six or seven. It seemed to have been constructed for no especial use within itself, but formed merely the interval between two of the colossal supports of the roof of the catacombs, and was backed by one of their circumscribing walls of solid granite.

It was in vain that Fortunato, uplifting his dull torch, endeavored to pry into the depths of the recess. Its termination the feeble light did not enable us to see.

"Proceed," I said; "herein is the Amontillado. As for Luchesi——"

"He is an ignoramus," interrupted my friend, as he stepped unsteadily forward, while I followed immediately at his heels. In an instant he had reached the extremity of the niche, and finding his progress arrested by the rock, stood stupidly bewildered. A moment more and I had fettered him to the granite. In its surface were two iron staples, distant from each other about two feet, horizontally. From one of these depended a short chain, from the other a padlock. Throwing the links about his waist, it was but the work of a few seconds to secure it. He was too much astounded to resist. Withdrawing the key I stepped back from the recess.

"Pass your hand," I said, "over the wall; you cannot help feeling the niter. Indeed it is *very* damp. Once more let me *implore* you to return. No? Then I must positively leave you. But I must first render you all the little attentions in my power."

"The Amontillado!" ejaculated my friend, not yet recovered from his astonishment.

"True," I replied; "the Amontillado."

As I said these words I busied myself among the pile of bones of which I have before spoken. Throwing them aside, I soon uncovered a quantity of building-stone and mortar. With these materials and with the aid of my trowel, I began vigorously to wall up the entrance of the niche.

I had scarcely laid the first tier of the masonry when I discovered that the intoxication of Fortunato had in a great measure worn off. The earliest indication I had of this was a low moaning cry from the depth of the recess. It was *not* the cry of a drunken man. There was then a long and obstinate silence. I laid the second tier, and the third, and the fourth; and then I heard the furious vibrations of the chain. The noise lasted for several minutes, during which, that I might hearken to it with the more satisfaction, I ceased my labors and sat down upon the bones. When at last the clanking subsided, I resumed the trowel, and finished without interruption the fifth, the sixth, and the seventh tier. The wall was now nearly upon a level with my breast. I again paused, and holding the flambeaux over the masonwork, threw a few feeble rays upon the figure within.

A succession of loud and shrill screams, bursting suddenly from the throat of the chained form, seemed to thrust me violently back. For a brief moment I hesitated—I trembled. Unsheathing my rapier, I began to grope with it about the recess; but the thought of an instant reassured me. I placed my hand upon the solid fabric of the catacombs, and felt satisfied. I reapproached the wall. I replied to the yells of him who clamored. I re-echoed—I aided—I surpassed them in volume and in strength. I did this, and the clamorer grew still.

It was now midnight, and my task was drawing to a close. I had completed the eighth, the ninth, and the tenth tier. I had finished a portion of the last and the eleventh; there remained but a single stone to be fitted and plastered in. I struggled with its weight; I placed it partially in its destined position. But now there came from out the niche a low laugh that erected the hairs upon my head. It was succeeded by a sad voice, which I had difficulty in recognizing as that of the noble Fortunato. The voice said—

"Ha! ha! ha!—he! he! he!—a very good joke indeed—an excellent jest. We will have many a rich laugh about it at the palazzo—he! he! he! —over our wine—he! he! he!"

"The Amontillado!" I said.

"He! he! he!—he! he! he!—yes, the Amontillado. But is it not getting late? Will not they be awaiting us at the palazzo, the Lady Fortunato and the rest? Let us be gone."

"Yes," I said, "let us be gone."

"For the love of God, Montresor!"

"Yes," I said, "for the love of God!"

But to these words I hearkened in vain for a reply. I grew impatient. I called aloud; "Fortunato!"

No answer. I called again; "Fortunato!"

No answer still. I thrust a torch through the remaining aperture and let it fall within. There came forth in return only a jingling of the bells. My heart grew sick—on account of the dampness of the catacombs. I hastened to make an end of my labor. I forced the last stone into its position; I plastered it up. Against the new masonry I re-erected the old rampart of bones. For the half of a century no mortal has disturbed them. *In pace requiescat!*[7]

Exercises

1. How much is revealed about the first-person narrator in the very first paragraph? Why does he say, "You, who so well know the nature of my soul . . ."? To whom is he writing? Why is it significant that he is telling about something that happened a half-century earlier? What conditions must his

[7]*In pace requiescat:* May he rest in peace.

revenge meet to be considered successful by him? What does such an attitude reveal about him? Do you suppose that Fortunato had really "injured" or "insulted" him? Does it make any difference? Explain.

2. The language of the opening paragraph is very formal. What purpose is served by the use of such language? Consider the following revision, which is, by contrast, very informal. What is the difference in tone between the two? What differences in the character of the speaker are suggested by the difference in tone?

> I had put up with many injuries from Fortunato, but when he insulted me, I decided I would get my revenge. You know what I'm like, so you won't be surprised if I say that I had no intention of threatening him. When the right time came, I would get back at him; I was sure of that. But I wasn't going to take any risks. I had to get my revenge without getting caught at it. There's no satisfaction in getting even if one gets in trouble doing so. There's also no satisfaction if the victim isn't fully aware of who's getting even with whom.

3. Why has Montresor chosen a carnival night? Why is it appropriate that Fortunato is in a clown's outfit? Why is it significant that Fortunato is a "quack" in most things but a real expert about wines? How do we know that Montresor has carefully planned this particular evening?
4. What shows Fortunato's conceit?
5. What is meant by "Amontillado? A pipe? Impossible! And in the middle of the carnival?" and by the fact that Fortunato repeats "Amontillado!" three times?
6. What is the effect of the narrator's repeating at various times "my friend" and "my poor friend"? Of his repeated expressions of concern for Fortunato's health? Of the repeated references to the jingling of the bells upon Fortunato's cap (the final reference to Fortunato is "only a jingling of the bells")?
7. The narrator says in the opening paragraph that an avenger must "make himself felt as such to him who has done the wrong." This necessity is obviously fulfilled, but Montresor goes even further than this in reporting his enjoyment of his revenge. Many of the things he says have a double meaning in which he delights but which Fortunato does not understand. The repeated use of "my friend" and the expressed concern for Fortunato's health are two examples. Another is his report of Fortunato's comment: "The cough is a mere nothing: it will not kill me. I shall not die of a cough." Point out other examples of double meanings. What does Montresor's use of such double meanings tell about him as a person?
8. How does Montresor see himself? How is the reader's view of the man different from the one Montresor has of himself?
9. What is the significance of the Montresor coat of arms?
10. What part does the setting play in the story? Consider other settings in

which such a story of revenge might take place. What are the advantages of the setting Poe uses? Be specific. Do not be satisfied with the comment that there is something gloomy and ghoulish about the catacombs.

11. What do you think the theme is? Is the story more than a study in revenge and terror? Consider the fact that the story is told "half of a century" after it takes place. What has the deed done to Montresor? How does his way of telling the story tell us what the deed has done to him?

Footfalls

WILBUR DANIEL STEELE

This is not an easy story; not a road for tender or for casual feet. Better
the meadows. Let me warn you, it is as hard as that old man's soul
and as sunless as his eyes. It has its inception in catastrophe, and its end
in an act of almost incredible violence; between them it tells barely how
a man, being blind, can become also deaf and dumb.

He lived in one of those old Puritan sea towns where the strain has
come down austere and moribund, so that his act would not be quite
unbelievable. Except that the town is no longer Puritan and Yankee.
It has been betrayed; it has become an outpost of the Portuguese islands.

This man, this blind cobbler himself, was a Portuguese, from St.
Michael,[1] in the Western Islands, and his name was Boaz Negro.

He was happy. An unquenchable exuberance lived in him. When
he arose in the morning he made vast, as it were uncontrollable, gestures
with his stout arms. He came into his shop singing. His voice, strong
and deep at the chest from which it emanated, rolled out through the
doorway and along the street, and the fishermen, done with their morning work and lounging and smoking along the wharfs, said, "Boaz is to
work already." Then they came up to sit in the shop.

In that town a cobbler's shop is a club. One sees the interior always
dimly thronged. They sit on the benches watching the artisan at his
work for hours, and they talk about everything in the world. A cobbler
is known by the company he keeps.

Boaz Negro kept young company. He would have nothing to do
with the old. On his own head the gray hairs set thickly.

He had a grown son. But the benches in his shop were for the lusty
and valiant young, men who could spend the night drinking, and then
at three o'clock in the morning turn out in the rain and dark to pull
at the weirs, sing songs, buffet one another among the slippery fish in

[1]**St. Michael:**   largest of the Portuguese Azores (the Western Islands).

the boat's bottom, and make loud jokes about the fundamental things, love and birth and death. Harkening to their boasts and strong prophecies, his breast heaved and his heart beat faster. He was a large, full-blooded fellow, fashioned for exploits; the flame in his darkness burned higher even to hear of them.

It is scarcely conceivable how Boaz Negro could have come through this much of his life still possessed of that unquenchable and priceless exuberance; how he would sing in the dawn; how, simply listening to the recital of deeds in gale or brawl, he could easily forget himself a blind man, tied to a shop and a last; easily make of himself a lusty young fellow breasting the sunlit and adventurous tide of life.

He had had a wife, whom he had loved. Fate, which had scourged him with the initial scourge of blindness, had seen fit to take his Angelina away. He had had four sons. Three, one after another, had been removed, leaving only Manuel, the youngest. Recovering slowly, with infinite agony, from each of these recurrent blows, his unquenchable exuberance had lived. And there was another thing quite as extraordinary. He had never done anything but work, and that sort of thing may kill the flame where an abrupt catastrophe fails. Work in the dark. Work, work, work! And accompanied by privation; an almost miserly scale of personal economy. Yes, indeed, he had "skinned his fingers," especially in the earlier years. When it tells most.

How he had worked! Not alone in the daytime, but also, sometimes, when orders were heavy, far into the night. It was strange for one, passing along that deserted street at midnight, to hear issuing from the black shop of Boaz Negro the rhythmical tap-tap-tap of hammer on wooden peg.

Nor was that sound all: no man in town could get far past that shop in his nocturnal wandering unobserved. No more than a dozen footfalls, and from the darkness Boaz's voice rolled forth, fraternal, stentorian, "Good night, Antone!" "Good night to you, Caleb Snow!"

To Boaz Negro it was still broad day.

Now, because of this, he was what might be called a substantial man. He owned his place, his shop, opening on the sidewalk, and behind it the dwelling-house with trellised galleries upstairs and down.

And there was always something for his son, a "piece for the pocket," a dollar, five, even a ten-dollar bill if he had "got to have it." Manuel was "a good boy." Boaz not only said this; he felt that he was assured of it in his understanding, to the infinite peace of his heart.

It was curious that he should be ignorant only of the one nearest to him. Not because he was physically blind. Be certain he knew more of other men and of other men's sons than they or their neighbors did. More, that is to say, of their hearts, their understandings, their idiosyncrasies, and their ultimate weight in the balance-pan of eternity.

His simple explanation of Manuel was that Manuel "wasn't too stout." To others he said this, and to himself. Manuel was not indeed too robust. How should he be vigorous when he never did anything to make him so? He never worked. Why should he work, when existence was provided for, and when there was always that "piece for the pocket"? Even a ten-dollar bill on a Saturday night! No. Manuel "wasn't too stout."

In the shop they let it go at that. The missteps and frailties of everyone else in the world were canvassed there with the most shameless publicity. But Boaz Negro was a blind man, and in a sense their host. Those reckless, strong young fellows respected and loved him. It was allowed to stand at that. Manuel was "a good boy." Which did not prevent them, by the way, from joining later in the general condemnation of that father's laxity—"the ruination of the boy!"

"He should have put him to work, that's what."

"He should have said to Manuel, 'Look here, if you want a dollar, go earn it first.'"

As a matter of fact, only one man ever gave Boaz the advice direct. That was Campbell Wood. And Wood never sat in that shop.

In every small town there is one young man who is spoken of as "rising." As often as not he is not a native, but "from away."

In this town Campbell Wood was that man. He had come from another part of the State to take a place in the bank. He lived in the upper story of Boaz Negro's house, the ground floor now doing for Boaz and the meager remnant of his family. The old woman who came in to tidy up for the cobbler looked after Wood's rooms as well.

Dealing with Wood, one had first of all the sense of his incorruptibility. A little ruthless perhaps, as if one could imagine him, in defense of his integrity, cutting off his friend, cutting off his own hand, cutting off the very stream flowing out from the wellsprings of human kindness. An exaggeration, perhaps.

He was by long odds the most eligible young man in town, good-looking in a spare, ruddy, sandy-haired Scottish fashion, important, incorruptible, "rising." But he took good care of his heart. Precisely that; like a sharp-eyed duenna to his own heart. One felt that here was the man, if ever was the man, who held his destiny in his own hand. Failing, of course, some quite gratuitous and unforeseeable catastrophe.

Not that he was not human, or even incapable of laughter or passion. He was, in a way, immensely accessible. He never clapped one on the shoulder; on the other hand, he never failed to speak. Not even to Boaz.

Returning from the bank in the afternoon, he had always a word for the cobbler. Passing out again to supper at his boarding-place, he had another, about the weather, the prospects of rain. And if Boaz was at work in the dark when he returned from an evening at the Board of Trade, there was a "Good night, Mr. Negro!"

On Boaz's part, his attitude toward his lodger was curious and paradoxical. He did not pretend to anything less than reverence for the young man's position; precisely on account of that position he was conscious toward Wood of a vague distrust. This was because he was an uneducated fellow.

To the uneducated the idea of large finance is as uncomfortable as the idea of the law. It must be said for Boaz that, responsive to Wood's unfailing civility, he fought against the sensation of dim and somehow shameful distrust.

Nevertheless his whole parental soul was in arms that evening when, returning from the bank and finding the shop empty of loungers, Wood paused a moment to propose the bit of advice already referred to.

"Haven't you ever thought of having Manuel learn the trade?"

A suspicion, a kind of premonition, lighted the fires of defense.

"Shoemaking," said Boaz, "is good enough for a blind man."

"Oh, I don't know. At least it's better than doing nothing at all."

Boaz's hammer was still. He sat silent, monumental. Outwardly. For once his unfailing response had failed him, "Manuel ain't too stout, you know." Perhaps it had become suddenly inadequate.

He hated Wood; he despised Wood; more than ever before, a hundredfold more, quite abruptly, he distrusted Wood.

How could a man say such things as Wood had said? And where Manuel himself might hear!

Where Manuel *had* heard! Boaz's other emotions—hatred and contempt and distrust—were overshadowed. Sitting in darkness, no sound had come to his ears, no footfall, no infinitesimal creaking of a floorplank. Yet by some sixth uncanny sense of the blind he was aware that Manuel was standing in the dusk of the entry joining the shop to the house.

Boaz made a Herculean effort. The voice came out of his throat, harsh, bitter, and loud enough to have carried ten times the distance to his son's ears.

"Manuel is a good boy!"

"Yes—h'm—yes—I suppose so."

Wood shifted his weight. He seemed uncomfortable.

"Well, I'll be running along, I—ugh! Heavens!"

Something was happening. Boaz heard exclamations, breathings, the rustle of sleeve-cloth in large, frantic, and futile graspings—all without understanding. Immediately there was an impact on the floor, and with it the unmistakable clink of metal. Boaz even heard that the metal was minted, and that the coins were gold. He understood. A coin-sack, gripped not quite carefully enough for a moment under the other's overcoat, had shifted, slipped, escaped, and fallen.

And Manuel had heard!

It was a dreadful moment for Boaz, dreadful in its native sense, as full of dread. Why? It was a moment of horrid revelation, ruthless clarification. His son, his link with the departed Angelina, that "good boy"—Manuel, standing in the shadow of the entry, visible alone to the blind, had heard the clink of falling gold, and—*and Boaz wished that he had not!*

There, amazing, disconcerting, destroying, stood the sudden fact.

Sitting as impassive and monumental as ever, his strong, bleached hands at rest on his work, round drops of sweat came out on Boaz's forehead. He scarcely took the sense of what Wood was saying. Only fragments.

"Government money, understand—for the breakwater workings— huge—too many people know, here, everywhere—don't trust the safe— tin safe—'Noah's Ark'[2]—give you my word—Heavens, no!"

It boiled down to this—the money, more money than was good for that antiquated "Noah's Ark" at the bank—and whose contemplated sojourn there overnight was public to too many minds—in short, Wood was not only incorruptible, he was canny. To what one of those minds, now, would it occur that he should take away that money bodily, under casual cover of his coat, to his own lodgings behind the cobbler shop of Boaz Negro? For this one, this important, night!

He was sorry the coin-sack had slipped, because he did not like to have the responsibility of secret sharer cast upon anyone, even upon Boaz, even by accident. On the other hand, how tremendously fortunate that it had been Boaz and not another. So far as that went, Wood had no more anxiety now than before. One incorruptible knows another.

"I'd trust you, Mr. Negro" (that was one of the fragments which came and stuck in the cobbler's brain), "as far as I would myself. As long as it's only you. I'm just going up here and throw it under the bed. Oh, yes, certainly."

Boaz ate no supper. For the first time in his life food was dry in his gullet. Even under those other successive crushing blows of Fate the full and generous habit of his functionings had carried on unabated; he had always eaten what was set before him. Tonight, over his untouched plate, he watched Manuel with his sightless eyes, keeping track of his every mouthful, word, intonation, breath. What profit he expected to extract from this catlike surveillance it is impossible to say.

When they arose from the supper table Boaz made another Herculean effort. "Manuel, you're a good boy!"

The formula had a quality of appeal, of despair, and of command.

"Manuel, you should be short of money, maybe. Look, what's this? A tenner? Well, there's a piece for the pocket; go and enjoy yourself."

He would have been frightened had Manuel, upsetting tradition,

[2]**Noah's Ark:** term applied to any enclosure considered so old-fashioned as to be of little use; here it means that the bank's vaults could easily be broken into.

declined the offering. With the morbid contrariness of the human imagination, the boy's avid grasping gave him no comfort.

He went out into the shop, where it was already dark, drew to him his last, his tools, mallets, cutters, pegs, leather. And having prepared to work, he remained idle. He found himself listening.

It has been observed that the large phenomena of sunlight and darkness were nothing to Boaz Negro. A busy night was broad day. Yet there was a difference; he knew it with the blind man's eyes, the ears.

Day was a vast confusion, or rather a wide fabric, of sounds; great and little sounds all woven together, voices, footfalls, wheels, far-off whistles and foghorns, flies buzzing in the sun. Night was another thing. Still there were voices and footfalls, but rare, emerging from the large, pure body of silence as definite, surprising, and yet familiar entities.

Tonight there was an easterly wind, coming off the water and carrying the sound of waves. So far as other fugitive sounds were concerned it was the same as silence. The wind made little difference to the ears. It nullified, from one direction at least, the other two visual processes of the blind, the sense of touch and the sense of smell. It blew away from the shop, toward the living-house.

As has been said, Boaz found himself listening, scrutinizing with an extraordinary attention this immense background of sound. He heard footfalls. The story of that night was written, for him, in footfalls.

He heard them moving about the house, the lower floor, prowling here, there, halting for long spaces, advancing, retreating softly on the planks. About this aimless, interminable perambulation there was something to twist the nerves, something led and at the same time driven, like a succession of frail and indecisive charges.

Boaz lifted himself from his chair. All his impulse called him to make a stir, join battle, cast in the breach the reinforcement of his presence, authority, good will. He sank back again; his hands fell down. The curious impotence of the spectator held him.

He heard footfalls, too, on the upper floor, a little fainter, borne to the inner rather than the outer ear, along the solid causeway of partitions and floor, the legs of his chair, the bony framework of his body. Very faint indeed. Sinking back easily into the background of the wind.

They, too, came and went, this room, that, to the passage, the stair-head, and away. About them too there was the same quality of being led and at the same time of being driven.

Time went by. In his darkness it seemed to Boaz that hours must have passed. He heard voices. Together with the footfalls, that abrupt, brief, and (in view of Wood's position) astounding interchange of sentences made up his history of the night. Wood must have opened the door at the head of the stair; by the sound of his voice he would be standing there, peering below perhaps; perhaps listening.

"What's wrong down there?" he called. "Why don't you go to bed?"

After a moment, came Manuel's voice, "Ain't sleepy."

"Neither am I. Look here, do you like to play cards?"

"What kind? Euchre? I like euchre all right. Or pitch."

"Well, what would you say to coming up and having a game of pitch then, Manuel? If you can't sleep?"

"That'd be all right."

The lower footfalls ascended to join the footfalls on the upper floor. There was the sound of a door closing.

Boaz sat still. In the gloom he might have been taken for a piece of furniture, of machinery, an extraordinary lay-figure, perhaps, for the trying on of the boots he made. He seemed scarcely to breathe, only the sweat starting from his brow giving him an aspect of life.

He ought to have run, and leaped up that inner stair and pounded with his fists on that door. He seemed unable to move. At rare intervals feet passed on the sidewalk outside, just at his elbow, so to say, and yet somehow, tonight, immeasurably far away. Beyond the orbit of the moon. He heard Rugg, the policeman, noting the silence of the shop, muttering, "Boaz is to bed tonight," as he passed.

The wind increased. It poured against the shop with its deep, continuous sound of a river. Submerged in its body, Boaz caught the note of the town bell striking midnight.

Once more, after a long time, he heard footfalls. He heard them coming around the corner of the shop from the house, footfalls half swallowed by the wind, passing discreetly, without haste, retreating, merging step by step with the huge, incessant background of the wind.

Boaz's muscles tightened all over him. He had the impulse to start up, to fling open the door, shout into the night, "What are you doing? Stop there! Say! What are you doing and where are you going?"

And as before, the curious impotence of the spectator held him motionless. He had not stirred in his chair. And those footfalls, upon which hinged, as it were, that momentous decade of his life, were gone.

There was nothing to listen for now. Yet he continued to listen. Once or twice, half arousing himself, he drew toward him his unfinished work. And then relapsed into immobility.

As has been said, the wind, making little difference to the ears, made all the difference in the world with the sense of feeling and the sense of smell. From the one important direction of the house. That is how it could come about that Boaz Negro could sit, waiting and listening to nothing in the shop and remain ignorant of disaster until the alarm had gone away and come back again, pounding, shouting, clanging.

"Fire!" he heard them bawling in the street. *"Fire! Fire!"*

Only slowly did he understand that the fire was in his own house.

There is nothing stiller in the world than the skeleton of a house in the dawn after a fire. It is as if everything living, positive, violent, had been completely drained in the one flaming act of violence, leaving nothing but negation till the end of time. It is worse than a tomb. A monstrous stillness! Even the footfalls of the searchers cannot disturb it, for they are separate and superficial. In its presence they are almost frivolous.

Half an hour after dawn the searchers found the body, if what was left from that consuming ordeal might be called a body. The discovery came as a shock. It seemed incredible that the occupant of that house, no cripple or invalid, but an able man in the prime of youth, should not have awakened and made good his escape. It was the upper floor which had caught; the stairs had stood to the last. It was beyond calculation. Even if he had been asleep!

And he had not been asleep. This second and infinitely more appalling discovery began to be known. Slowly. By a hint, a breath of rumor here; there an allusion, half taken back. The man, whose incinerated body still lay curled in its bed of cinders, had been dressed at the moment of disaster; even to the watch, the cuff-buttons, the studs, the very scarf-pin. Fully clothed to the last detail, precisely as those who had dealings at the bank might have seen Campbell Wood any weekday morning for the past eight months. A man does not sleep with his clothes on. The skull of the man had been broken, as if with a blunt instrument of iron. On the charred lacework of the floor lay the leg of an old andiron with which Boaz Negro and his Angelina had set up housekeeping in that new house.

It needed only Mr. Asa Whitelaw, coming up the street from that gaping "Noah's Ark" at the bank, to round out the scandalous circle of circumstance.

"Where is Manuel?"

Boaz Negro still sat in his shop, impassive, monumental, his thick, hairy arms resting on the arms of his chair. The tools and materials of his work remained scattered about him, as his irresolute gathering of the night before had left them. Into his eyes no change could come. He had lost his house, the visible monument of all those years of "skinning his fingers." It would seem that he had lost his son. And he had lost something incalculably precious—that hitherto unquenchable exuberance of the man.

"Where is Manuel?"

When he spoke his voice was unaccented and stale, like the voice of a man already dead.

"Yes, where is Manuel?"

He had answered them with their own question.

"When did you last see him?"

Neither he nor they seemed to take note of that profound irony.

"At supper."

"Tell us, Boaz, you knew about this money?"

The cobbler nodded his head.

"And did Manuel?"

He might have taken sanctuary in a legal doubt. How did he know what Manuel knew? Precisely! As before, he nodded his head.

"After supper, Boaz, you were in the shop? But you heard something?"

"Yes."

He went on to tell them what he had heard, the footfalls, below and above, the extraordinary conversation which had broken for a moment the silence of the inner hall. The account was bare, the phrases monosyllabic. He reported only what had been registered on the sensitive tympanums of his ears, to the last whisper of footfalls stealing past the dark wall of the shop. Of all the formless tangle of thoughts, suspicions, interpretations, and the special and personal knowledge given to the blind which moved in his brain, he said nothing.

He shut his lips there. He felt himself on the defensive. Just as he distrusted the higher ramifications of finance (his house had gone down uninsured), so before the rites and processes of that inscrutable creature, the Law, he felt himself menaced by the invisible and the unknown, helpless, oppressed; in an abject sense, skeptical.

"Keep clear of the Law!" they had told him in his youth. The monster his imagination had summoned then still stood beside him in his age.

Having exhausted his monosyllabic and superficial evidence, they could move him no farther. He became deaf and dumb. He sat before them, an image cast in some immensely heavy stuff, inanimate. His lack of visible emotion impressed them. Remembering his exuberance, it was only the stranger to see him unmoving and unmoved. Only once did they catch sight of something beyond. As they were preparing to leave he opened his mouth. What he said was like a swan-song to the years of his exuberant happiness. Even now there was no color of expression in his words, which sounded mechanical.

"Now I have lost everything. My house. My last son. Even my honor. You would not think I would like to live. But I go to live. I go to work. That *cachorra*,[3] one day he shall come back again, in the dark night, to have to look. I shall go to show you all. That *cachorra!*"

(And from that time on, it was noted, he never referred to the fugitive by any other name than *cachorra,* which is a gender of dog. "That *cachorra!*" As if he had forfeited the relationship not only of the family, but of the very genus, the very race! "That *cachorra!*")

He pronounced this resolution without passion. When they assured him that the culprit would come back again indeed, much sooner than

[3] *cachorra:* as later indicated in the story, a Portuguese word for dog; in reference to a man it is a term of contempt: a vile person.

he expected, "with a rope around his neck," he shook his head slowly.

"No, you shall not catch that *cachorra* now. But one day——"

There was something about its very colorlessness which made it sound oracular. It was at least prophetic. They searched, laid their traps, proceeded with all their placards, descriptions, rewards, clues, trails. But on Manuel Negro they never laid their hands.

Months passed and became years. Boaz did not rebuild his house. He might have done so, out of his earnings, for upon himself he spent scarcely anything, reverting to his old habit of an almost miserly economy. Yet perhaps it would have been harder after all. For his earnings were less and less. In that town a cobbler who sits in an empty shop is apt to want for trade. Folk take their boots to mend where they take their bodies to rest and their minds to be edified.

No longer did the walls of Boaz's shop resound to the boastful recollections of young men. Boaz had changed. He had become not only different, but opposite. A metaphor will do best. The spirit of Boaz Negro had been a meadowed hillside giving upon the open sea, the sun, the warm, wild winds from beyond the blue horizon. And covered with flowers, always hungry and thirsty for the sun and the fabulous wind and bright showers of rain. It had become an entrenched camp, lying silent, sullen, verdureless, under a gray sky. He stood solitary against the world. His approaches were closed. He was blind, and he was also deaf and dumb.

Against that, what can young fellows do who wish for nothing but to rest themselves and talk about their friends and enemies? They had come and they had tried. They had raised their voices even higher than before. Their boasts had grown louder, more presumptuous, more preposterous, until, before the cold separation of that unmoving and as if contemptuous presence in the cobbler's chair, they burst of their own air, like toy balloons. And they went and left Boaz alone.

There was another thing which served, if not to keep them away, at least not to entice them back. That was the aspect of the place. It was not cheerful. It invited no one. In its way that fire-bitten ruin grew to be almost as great a scandal as the act itself had been. It was plainly an eyesore. A valuable property, on the town's main thoroughfare— and an eyesore! The neighboring owners protested.

Their protestations might as well have gone against a stone wall. That man was deaf and dumb. He had become, in a way, a kind of vegetable, for the quality of a vegetable is that, while it is endowed with life, it remains fixed in one spot. For years Boaz was scarcely seen to move foot out of that shop that was left him, a small, square, blistered promontory on the shores of ruin.

He must indeed have carried out some rudimentary sort of a domestic program under the debris at the rear (he certainly did not sleep or eat in the shop). One or two lower rooms were left fairly intact. The outward aspect of the place was formless; it grew to be no more than a mound in time; the charred timbers, one or two still standing, lean and naked against the sky, lost their blackness and faded to a silvery gray. It would have seemed strange, had they not grown accustomed to the thought, to imagine that blind man, like a mole, or some slow slug, turning himself mysteriously in the bowels of that gray mound—that time-silvered "eyesore."

When they saw him, however, he was in the shop. They opened the door to take in their work (when other cobblers turned them off), and they saw him seated in his chair in the half-darkness, his whole person, legs, torso, neck, head, as motionless as the vegetable of which we have spoken—only his hands and his bare arms endowed with visible life. The gloom had bleached the skin to the color of damp ivory, and against the background of his immobility they moved with a certain amazing monstrousness, interminably. No, they were never still. One wondered what they could be at. Surely he could not have had enough work now to keep those insatiable hands so monstrously in motion. Even far into the night. Tap-tap-tap! Blows continuous and powerful. On what! On nothing? On the bare iron last? And for what purpose? To what conceivable end?

Well, one could imagine those arms, growing paler, also growing thicker and more formidable with that unceasing labor; the muscles feeding themselves omnivorously on their own waste, the cords toughening, the bone-tissues revitalizing themselves without end. One could imagine the whole aspiration of that mute and motionless man pouring itself out into those pallid arms, and the arms taking it up with a kind of blind greed. Storing it up. Against a day!

"That *cachorra!* One day——"

What were the thoughts of the man? What moved within that motionless cranium covered with long hair? Who can say? Behind everything, of course, stood that bitterness against the world—the blind world—blinder than he would ever be. And against "that *cachorra.*" But this was no longer a thought; it was the man.

Just as all muscular aspiration flowed into his arms, so all the energies of his senses turned to his ears. The man had become, you might say, two arms and two ears. Can you imagine a man listening, intently, through the waking hours of nine years?

Listening to footfalls. Marking with a special emphasis of concentration the beginning, rise, full passage, falling away, and dying of all the footfalls. By day, by night, Winter and Summer and Winter again. Unraveling the skein of footfalls passing up and down the street!

For three years he wondered when they would come. For the next three years he wondered if they would ever come. It was during the last three that a doubt began to trouble him. It gnawed at his huge moral strength. Like a hidden seepage of water, it undermined (in anticipation) his terrible resolution. It was a sign perhaps of age, a slipping away of the reckless infallibility of youth.

Supposing, after all, that his ears should fail him. Supposing they were capable of being tricked, without his being able to know it. Supposing that that *cachorra* should come and go, and he, Boaz, living in some vast delusion, some unrealized distortion of memory, should let him pass unknown. Supposing precisely this thing had already happened!

Or the other way around. What if he should hear the footfalls coming, even into the very shop itself. What if he should be as sure of them as of his own soul? What, then, if he should strike? And what, then, if it were not that *cachorra* after all? How many tens and hundreds of millions of people were there in the world? Was it possible for them all to have footfalls distinct and different?

Then they would take him and hang him. And that *cachorra* might then come and go at his own will, undisturbed.

As he sat there sometimes the sweat rolled down his nose, cold as rain. Supposing!

146

Sometimes, quite suddenly, in broad day, in the booming silence of the night, he would start. Not outwardly. But beneath the pale integument of his skin all his muscles tightened and his nerves sang. His breathing stopped. It seemed almost as if his heart stopped.

Was that it? Were those the feet, there, emerging faintly from the distance? Yes, there was something about them. Yes! Memory was in travail. Yes, yes, yes! No! How could he be sure? Ice ran down into his empty eyes. The footfalls were already passing. They were gone, swallowed up already by time and space. Had that been the *cachorra?*

Nothing in his life had been so hard to meet as this insidious drain of distrust in his own powers; this sense of a traitor within the walls. His iron-gray hair had turned white. It was always this now, from the beginning of the day to the end of the night; how was he to know? How was he to be inevitably, unshakably sure? . . .

It was on an evening of the Winter holidays, the Portuguese festival of *Menin' Jesus*. Christ was born again in a hundred mangers on a hundred tiny altars; there was cake and wine; songs went shouting by to the accompaniment of mandolins and tramping feet. The wind blew cold under a clear sky. In all the houses there were lights; even in Boaz Negro's shop a lamp was lit just now, for a man had been in for a pair of boots which Boaz had patched. The man had gone out again. Boaz was thinking of blowing out the light. It meant nothing to him.

He leaned forward, judging the position of the lamp-chimney by the heat on his face, and puffed out his cheeks to blow. Then his cheeks collapsed suddenly, and he sat back again.

It was not odd that he had failed to hear the footfalls until they were actually within the door. A crowd of merrymakers was passing just then; their songs and tramping almost shook the shop.

Boaz sat back. Beneath his passive exterior his nerves thrummed; his muscles had grown as hard as wood. Yes! Yes! But no! He had heard nothing; no more than a single step, a single foot-pressure on the planks within the door. Dear God! He could not tell!

Going through the pain of an enormous effort, he opened his lips. "What can I do for you?"

"Well, I—I don't know. To tell the truth——"

The voice was unfamiliar, but it might be assumed. Boaz held himself. His face remained blank, interrogating, slightly helpless.

"I am a little deaf," he said. "Come nearer."

The footfalls came half-way across the intervening floor, and there appeared to hesitate. The voice, too, had a note of uncertainty.

"I was just looking around. I have a pair of—well, you mend shoes?"

Boaz nodded his head. It was not in response to the words, for they meant nothing. What he had heard were the footfalls on the floor.

Now he was sure. As has been said, for a moment at least after he had heard them he was unshakably sure. The congestion of his muscles had passed. He was at peace.

The voice became audible once more. Before the massive preoccupation of the blind man it became still less certain of itself.

"Well, I haven't got the shoes with me. I was—just looking around."

It was amazing to Boaz, this miraculous sensation of peace.

"Wait!" Then, bending his head as if listening to the Winter wind, "It's cold tonight. You've left the door open. But wait!" Leaning down, his hand fell on a rope's end hanging by the chair. The gesture was one continuous, undeviating movement of the hand. No hesitation. No groping. How many hundreds, how many thousands of times, had his hand schooled itself in that gesture!

A single strong pull. With a little *bang* the front door had swung to and latched itself. Not only the front door. The other door, leading to the rear, had closed too and latched itself with a little *bang*. And leaning forward from his chair, Boaz blew out the light.

There was not a sound in the shop. Outside, feet continued to go by, ringing on the frozen road; voices were lifted; the wind hustled about the corners of the wooden shell with a continuous, shrill note of whistling. All of this outside, as on another planet. Within the blackness of the shop the complete silence persisted.

Boaz listened. Sitting on the edge of his chair, half-crouching, his head, with its long, unkempt, white hair, bent slightly to one side, he concentrated upon this chambered silence the full powers of his senses. He hardly breathed. The other person in that room could not be breathing at all, it seemed.

No, there was not a breath, not the stirring of a sole on wood, not the infinitesimal rustle of any fabric. It was as if in this utter stoppage of sound, even the blood had ceased to flow in the veins and arteries of that man, who was like a rat caught in a trap.

It was appalling even to Boaz; even to the cat. Listening became more than a labor. He began to have to fight against a growing impulse to shout out loud, to leap, sprawl forward without aim in that unstirred darkness—do something. Sweat rolled down from behind his ears, into his shirt-collar. He gripped the chair-arms. To keep quiet he sank his teeth into his lower lip. He would not! He would not!

And of a sudden he heard before him, in the center of the room, an outburst of breath, an outrush from lungs in the extremity of pain, thick, laborious, fearful. A coughing up of dammed air.

Pushing himself from the arms of the chair, Boaz leaped.

His fingers, passing swiftly through the air, closed on something. It was a sheaf of hair, bristly and thick. It was a man's beard.

On the road outside, up and down the street for a hundred yards, merrymaking people turned to look at one another. With an abrupt cessation of laughter, of speech. Inquiringly. Even with an unconscious dilation of the pupils of their eyes.

"What was that?"

There had been a scream. There could be no doubt of that. A single, long-drawn note. Immensely high-pitched. Not as if it were human.

"God's sake! What was that? Where'd it come from?"

Those nearest said it came from the cobbler shop of Boaz Negro.

They went and tried the door. It was closed; even locked, as if for the night. There was no light behind the window-shade. But Boaz would not have a light. They beat on the door. No answer.

But from where, then, had that prolonged, as if animal, note come?

They ran about, penetrating into the side-lanes, interrogating, prying. Coming back at least, inevitably, to the neighborhood of Boaz Negro's shop.

The body lay on the floor at Boaz's feet, where it had tumbled down slowly after a moment from the spasmodic embrace of his arms; those ivory-colored arms which had beaten so long upon the bare iron surface of a last. Blows continuous and powerful! It seemed incredible. They were so weak now. They could not have lifted the hammer now.

But that beard! That bristly, thick, square beard of a stranger!

His hands remembered it. Standing with his shoulders fallen forward and his weak arms hanging down, Boaz began to shiver. The whole thing was incredible. What was on the floor there, upheld in the vast gulf of darkness, he could not see. Neither could he hear it; smell it. Nor (if he did not move his foot) could he feel it. What he did not hear, smell, or touch did not exist. It was not there. Incredible!

But that beard! All the accumulated doubtings of those years fell down upon him. After all, the thing he had been so fearful of in his weak imaginings had happened. He had killed a stranger. He, Boaz Negro, had murdered an innocent man!

And all on account of that beard. His deep panic made him light-headed. He began to confuse cause and effect. If it were not for that beard, it would have been that *cachorra*.

On this basis he began to reason with a crazy directness. And to act. He went and pried open the door into the entry. From a shelf he took down his razor. A big, heavy-heeled blade, made long ago for a beard which turned the jaw black again an hour after shaving. It would have to be cold water. But after all, he thought (light-headedly), at this time of night——

Outside, they were at the shop again. The crowd's habit is to forget a thing quickly, once it is out of sight and hearing. But there had been something about that solitary cry which continued to bother them, even in memory. Where had it been? Where had it come from? And those who had stood nearest the cobbler shop were heard again. They were certain now, dead certain. They could swear!

In the end they broke down the door.

If Boaz had heard them he gave no sign. An absorption as complete as it was monstrous wrapped him. Kneeling in the glare of the lantern they had brought, as impervious as his own shadow sprawling behind him, he continued to shave the dead man on the floor.

No one touched him. Their minds and imaginations were arrested by the gigantic proportions of the act. The unfathomable presumption of the act. As throwing murder in their faces to the tune of a jig in a barbershop. It is a fact that none of them so much as thought of touching him. No less than all of them, together with all other men, shorn of their imaginations—that is to say, the expressionless and imperturbable creature of the Law—would be sufficient to touch that ghastly man.

On the other hand, they could not leave him alone. They could not go away. They watched. They saw the damp, lather-soaked beard of that victimized stranger falling away, stroke by stroke of the flashing, heavy razor. The dead denuded by the blind!

It was seen that Boaz was about to speak. It was something important he was to utter; something, one would say, fatal. The words would not come all at once. They swelled his cheeks out. His razor was arrested. Lifting his face, he encircled the watchers with a gaze at once of imploration and of command. As if he could see them. As if he could read his answer in the expressions of their faces.

"Tell me one thing now. Is it that *cachorra?*"

For the first time those men in the room made sounds. They shuffled their feet. It was as if an uncontrollable impulse to ejaculation, laughter, derision, forbidden by the presence of death, had gone down into their boot soles.

"Manuel?" one of them said. "You mean *Manuel?*"

Boaz laid the razor down on the floor beside its work. He got up from his knees slowly, as if his joints hurt. He sat down in his chair, rested his hands on the arms, and once more encircled the company with his sightless gaze.

"Not Manuel. Manuel was a good boy. But tell me now, is it that *cachorra?*"

Here was something out of their calculations; something for them, mentally, to chew on. Mystification is a good thing sometimes. It gives the brain a fillip, stirs memory, puts the gears of imagination in mesh. One man, an old, tobacco-chewing fellow, began to stare harder at the face on the floor. Something moved in his intellect.

"No, but look here now, by God——"

He had even stopped chewing. But he was forestalled by another.

"Say now, if it don't look like that fellow Wood, himself. The bank fellow—that was burned—remember? Himself."

"That *cachorra* was not burned. Not that Wood. You damned fool!"

Boaz spoke from his chair. They hardly knew his voice, emerging from its long silence; it was so didactic and arid.

"That *cachorra* was not burned. It was my boy that was burned. It was that *cachorra* called my boy upstairs. That *cachorra* killed my boy. That *cachorra* put his clothes on my boy, and he set my house on fire. I knew that all the time. Because when I heard those feet come out of my house and go away, I knew they were the feet of that *cachorra* from the bank. I did not know where he was going to. Something said to me—you better ask him where he is going to. But then I said, you are foolish. He had the money from the bank. I did not know. And then my house was on fire. No, it was not my boy that went away; it was that *cachorra* all the time. You damned fools! Did you think I was waiting for my own boy?"

"Now I show you all," he said at the end. "And now I can get hanged."

No one ever touched Boaz Negro for that murder. For murder it was in the eye and letter of the Law. But the Law in a small town is sometimes a curious creature; it is sometimes blind only in one eye.

Their minds and imaginations in that town were arrested by the romantic proportions of the act. Simply, no one took it up. I believe the man, Wood, was understood to have died of heart failure.

When they asked Boaz why he had not told what he knew as to the identity of that fugitive in the night, he seemed to find it hard to say exactly. How could a man of no education define for them his own but half-defined misgivings about the Law, his sense of oppression, constraint and awe, of being on the defensive, even, in an abject way, his skepticism? About his wanting, come what might, to "keep clear of the Law"?

He did say this, "You would have laughed at me."

And this, "If I told folks it was Wood went away, then I say he would not dare come back again."

That was the last. Very shortly he began to refuse to talk about the thing at all. The act was completed. Like the creature of fable, it had consumed itself. Out of that old man's consciousness it had departed. Amazingly. Like a dream dreamed out.

Slowly at first, in a makeshift, piece-at-a-time, poor man's way, Boaz commenced to rebuild his house. That "eyesore" vanished.

And slowly at first, like the miracle of a green shoot pressing out from the dead earth, that priceless and unquenchable exuberance of the man was seen returning. Unquenchable, after all.

Exercises

1. The narrator says in the opening paragraph that after the first catastrophe Boaz became "deaf and dumb." What does he mean by the comment? In what sense is it true, and in what sense is it not true?
2. Characterize Boaz Negro. Why does he like to have young men around his shop? Why does he allow Manuel to be a loafer? Why did he work so hard before Manuel's killing? Why does he distrust "the Law"? What does his distrust of Campbell Wood reveal about him? Is there any self-pity in him over his blindness? Is the reader meant to sympathize with him, even when he commits murder? Discuss.
3. What details prove that Campbell Wood has carefully planned the robbery and the murder, that he truly is, as the narrator says, "the man, if ever was the man, who held his destiny in his own hand"? What is ironic about that statement? How well has Campbell Wood judged the townspeople? Why does he return to the cobbler's shop?
4. Why does Boaz conceal his own doubts about who the murderer is? Why does he leave the "fire-bitten ruin" as it is until after he gets his revenge on Wood? In what ways does he prepare himself for Wood's return?
5. a. From what point of view is the story told? Is the narrator one of the townspeople? Does he in any way identify himself with them? Explain. (Consider whether any of the townspeople are in any way personalized and if the narrator gives us any indications of what they are thinking.) Does the narrator get into Boaz's mind in any way? In other words, do we get indications of what Boaz is thinking at any time? Take a close look at the scene that deals with Manuel's murder and at the part of the plot that deals with Boaz's nine-year wait.
   b. In further consideration of point of view, discuss how Steele handles the difficult problem of suspense. He has to play up the town's perfectly normal reaction that Manuel could and would steal the money and kill Campbell Wood. Explain specifically how that interpretation is handled. Steele also has to suggest Boaz's interpretation without being too obvious about it. Discuss how Steele successfully manages to do so. With the

handling of this double problem in mind, discuss Steele's choice of narrator. If he had decided to make his narrator definitely one of the townspeople, what advantage would he have lost? If he had decided to have Boaz tell his own story, what would he have lost?

6. What is the tone of the story? The narrator says at the very beginning: "This is not an easy story. . . . it is as hard as that old man's soul and as sunless as his eyes." Is the telling of it "hard" and "sunless"? Consider the kind of vocabulary and the number of short, biting sentences. Consider especially the two central scenes, those in which the two killings are described, one indirectly as Boaz senses what is happening, and one directly as the "incredible violence" in the darkened shop is described.

7. What is the theme of the story? Consider the fact that Boaz has taken the law into his own hands, that he is an "outsider" in more than one way, that Campbell Wood is accepted and respected in ways Boaz can never be, and that in the eyes of the townspeople and the narrator justice has been served. Consider also the opening and closing paragraphs.

8. In both "The Cask of Amontillado" and "Footfalls" the element of suspense plays a key role in the story. In Poe's story there is no doubt about what will happen, since Montresor indicates from the very first paragraph what he intends to do, and it becomes obvious almost immediately that he has planned his evening well. In Steele's story the suspense is of a different kind, since it is not obvious that Boaz is waiting for Wood's return. The element of suspense, therefore, does not depend on keeping the reader in the dark. What does it depend on, and how have the two authors managed to maintain a high degree of suspense with different approaches?

The Man Child

JAMES BALDWIN

As the sun began preparing for her exit, and he sensed the waiting night, Eric, blond and eight years old and dirty and tired, started homeward across the fields. Eric lived with his father, who was a farmer and the son of a farmer, and his mother, who had been captured by his father on some far-off, unblessed, unbelievable night, who had never since burst her chains. She did not know that she was chained anymore than she knew that she lived in terror of the night. One child was in the churchyard, it would have been Eric's little sister and her name would have been Sophie: for a long time, then, his mother had been very sick and pale. It was said that she would never, really, be better, that she would never again be as she had been. Then, not long ago, there had begun to be a pounding in his mother's belly, Eric had sometimes been able to hear it when he lay against her breast. His father had been pleased. *I did that,* said his father, big, laughing, dreadful, and red, and Eric knew how it was done, he had seen the horses and the blind and dreadful bulls. But then, again, his mother had been sick, she had had to be sent away, and when she came back the pounding was not there anymore, nothing was there anymore. His father laughed less, something in his mother's face seemed to have gone to sleep forever.

Eric hurried, for the sun was almost gone and he was afraid the night would catch him in the fields. And his mother would be angry. She did not really like him to go wandering off by himself. She would have forbidden it completely and kept Eric under her eye all day but in this she was overruled: Eric's father liked to think of Eric as being curious about the world and as being daring enough to explore it, with his own eyes, by himself.

His father would not be at home. He would be gone with his friend, Jamie, who was also a farmer and the son of a farmer, down to the tavern. This tavern was called The Rafters. They went each night, as his father said, imitating an Englishman he had known during a war, *to destruct the Rafters, sir.* They had been destructing The Rafters long before Eric had kicked in his mother's belly, for Eric's father and Jamie had grown up together, gone to war together, and survived together—never, apparently, while life ran, were they to be divided. They worked in the fields all day together, the fields which belonged to Eric's father. Jamie had been forced to sell his farm and it was Eric's father who had bought it.

Jamie had a brown and yellow dog. This dog was almost always with him; whenever Eric thought of Jamie he thought also of the dog. They had always been there, they had always been together: in exactly the same way, for Eric, that his mother and father had always been together, in exactly the same way that the earth and the trees and the sky were together. Jamie and his dog walked the country roads together, Jamie walking slowly in the way of country people, seeming to see nothing, heads lightly bent, feet striking surely and heavily on the earth, never stumbling. He walked as though he were going to walk to the other end of the world and knew it was a long way but knew that he would be there by morning. Sometimes he talked to his dog, head bent a little more than usual and turned to one side, a slight smile playing about the edges of his granite lips; and the dog's head snapped up, perhaps he leapt upon his master, who cuffed him down lightly, with one hand. More often he was silent. His head was carried in a cloud of blue smoke from his pipe. Through this cloud, like a ship on a foggy day, loomed his dry and steady face. Set far back, at an unapproachable angle, were those eyes of his, smoky and thoughtful, eyes which seemed always to be considering the horizon. He had the kind of eyes which no one had ever looked into—except Eric, only once. Jamie had been walking these roads and across these fields, whistling for his dog in the evenings as he turned away from Eric's house, for years, in silence. He had been married once, but his wife had run away. Now he lived alone in a wooden house and Eric's mother kept his clothes clean and Jamie always ate at Eric's house.

Eric had looked into Jamie's eyes on Jamie's birthday. They had had a party for him. Eric's mother had baked a cake and filled the house with flowers. The doors and windows of the great kitchen all stood open on the yard and the kitchen table was placed outside. The ground was not muddy as it was in winter, but hard, dry, and light brown. The flowers his mother so loved and so labored for flamed in their narrow borders against the stone wall of the farmhouse; and green vines covered the grey stone wall at the far end of the yard. Beyond this wall were the fields and barns, and Eric could see, quite far away, the cows nearly motionless in the bright green pasture. It was a bright, hot, silent day, the sun did not seem to be moving at all.

This was before his mother had had to be sent away. Her belly had been beginning to grow big, she had been dressed in blue, and had seemed—that day, to Eric—younger than she was ever to seem again.

Though it was still early when they were called to table, Eric's father and Jamie were already tipsy and came across the fields, shoulders touching, laughing, and telling each other stories. To express disapproval and also, perhaps, because she had heard their stories before and was bored, Eric's mother was quite abrupt with them, barely saying, "Happy Birthday, Jamie" before she made them sit down. In the nearby village church bells rang as they began to eat.

It was perhaps because it was Jamie's birthday that Eric was held by something in Jamie's face. Jamie, of course, was very old. He was thirty-four today, even older than Eric's father, who was only thirty-two. Eric wondered how it felt to have so many years and was suddenly, secretly glad that he was only eight. For today, Jamie *looked* old. It was perhaps the one additional year which had done it, this day, before their very eyes—a metamorphosis which made Eric rather shrink at the prospect of becoming nine. The skin of Jamie's face, which had never before seemed so, seemed wet today, and that rocky mouth of his was loose; loose was the word for everything about him, the way his arms and shoulders hung, the way he sprawled at the table, rocking slightly back and forth. It was not that he was drunk. Eric had seen him much drunker. Drunk, he became rigid, as though he imagined himself in the army again. No. He was old. It had come upon him all at once, today, on his birthday. He sat there, his hair in his eyes, eating, drinking, laughing now and again, and in a very strange way, and teasing the dog at his feet so that it sleepily growled and snapped all through the birthday dinner.

"Stop that," said Eric's father.

"Stop what?" asked Jamie.

"Let that stinking useless dog alone. Let him be quiet."

"Leave the beast alone," said Eric's mother—very wearily, sounding as she often sounded when talking to Eric.

"Well, now," said Jamie, grinning, and looking first at Eric's father and then at Eric's mother, " it *is* my beast. And a man's got a right to do as he likes with whatever's his."

"That dog's got a right to bite you, too," said Eric's mother, shortly.

"This dog's not going to bite me," said Jamie, "he knows I'll shoot him if he does."

"That dog knows you're not going to shoot him," said Eric's father. "Then you *would* be all alone."

"All alone," said Jamie, and looked around the table. "All alone." He lowered his eyes to his plate. Eric's father watched him. He said, "It's pretty serious to be all alone at *your* age." He smiled. "If I was you, I'd start thinking about it."

"I'm thinking about it," said Jamie. He began to grow red.

"No, you're not," said Eric's father, "you're dreaming about it."

"Well, goddammit," said Jamie, even redder now, "it isn't as though I haven't tried!"

"Ah," said Eric's father, "that was a *real* dream, that was. I used to pick *that* up on the streets of town every Saturday night."

"Yes," said Jamie, "I bet you did."

"I didn't think she was as bad as all that," said Eric's mother, quietly. "*I* liked her. I was surprised when she ran away."

"Jamie didn't know how to keep her," said Eric's father. He looked at Eric and chanted: *"Jamie, Jamie, pumkin-eater, had a wife and couldn't keep her!"* At this, Jamie at last looked up, into the eyes of Eric's father. Eric laughed again, more shrilly, out of fear. Jamie said:

"Ah, yes, you can talk, you can."

"It's not my fault," said Eric's father, "if you're getting old— and haven't got anybody to bring you your slippers when night comes—and no pitter-patter of little feet."

"Oh, leave Jamie alone," said Eric's mother, "he's *not* old, leave him alone."

Jamie laughed a peculiar, high, clicking laugh which Eric had never heard before, which he did not like, which made him want to look away and, at the same time, want to stare. "Hell, no," said Jamie, "I'm not old. I can still do all the things we used to do." He put his elbows on the table, grinning. "I haven't ever told you, have I, about the things we used to do?"

"No, you haven't," said Eric's mother, "and I certainly don't want to hear about them now."

"He wouldnt tell you anyway," said Eric's father, "he knows what I'd do to him if he did."

"Oh, sure, sure," said Jamie, and laughed again. He picked up a bone from his plate. "Here," he said to Eric, "why don't you feed my poor mistreated dog?"

Eric took the bone and stood up, whistling for the dog, who moved away from his master and took the bone between his teeth. Jamie watched with a smile and opened the bottle of whiskey and poured himself a drink. Eric sat on the ground beside the dog, beginning to be sleepy in the bright, bright sun.

"Little Eric's getting big," he heard his father say.

"Yes," said Jamie, "they grow fast. It won't be long now."

"Won't be long *what*?" he heard his father ask.

"Why, before he starts skirt-chasing like his Daddy used to do," said Jamie. There was mild laughter at the table in which his mother did not join; he heard instead, or thought he heard, the familiar, slight, exasperated intake of her breath. No one seemed to care whether he came back to the table or not. He lay on his back, staring up at the sky, wondering—wondering what he would feel like when he was old—and fell asleep.

When he awoke his head was in his mother's lap, for she was sitting on the ground. Jamie and his father were still sitting at the table; he knew this from their voices, for he did not open his eyes. He did not want to move or speak. He wanted to remain where he was, protected by his mother, while the bright day rolled on. Then he wondered about the uncut birthday cake. But he was sure, from the sound of Jamie's voice, which was thicker now, that they had not cut it yet; or if they had, they had certainly saved a piece for him.

"—ate himself just as full as he could and then fell asleep in the sun like a little animal," Jamie was saying, and the two men laughed. His father—though he scarcely ever got as drunk as Jamie did, and had often carried Jamie home from The Rafters— was a little drunk, too.

Eric felt his mother's hand on his hair. By opening his eyes very slightly he would see, over the curve of his mother's thigh, as through a veil, a green slope far away and beyond it the everlasting, motionless sky.

"—she was a no-good *bitch*," said Jamie.

"She was beautiful," said his mother, just above him.

Again, they were talking about Jamie's wife.

"Beauty!" said Jamie, furious. "Beauty doesn't keep a house clean. Beauty doesn't keep a bed warm, neither."

Eric's father laughed. "You were so—poetical—in those days, Jamie," he said. "Nobody thought you cared much about things like that. I guess she thought you didn't care, neither."

"I cared," said Jamie, briefly.

"In fact," Eric's father continued, "I *know* she thought you didn't care."

"*How* do you know?" asked Jamie.

"She told me," Eric's father said.

"What do you mean," asked Jamie, "what do you mean, she told you?"

"I mean just that. She told me."

Jamie was silent.

"In those days," Eric's father continued after a moment, "all you did was walk around the woods by yourself in the daytime and sit around The Rafters in the evenings with me."

"You two were always together then," said Eric's mother.

"Well," said Jamie, harshly, "at least that hasn't changed."

"Now, you know," said Eric's father, gently, "it's not the same. Now I got a wife and kid—and another one coming—"

Eric's mother stroked his hair more gently, yet with something in her touch more urgent, too, and he knew that she was thinking of the child who lay in the churchyard, who would have been his sister.

"Yes," said Jamie, "you really got it all fixed up, you did. You got it all—the wife, the kid, the house, and all the land."

"I didn't steal your farm from you. It wasn't my fault you lost it. I gave you a better price for it than anybody else would have done."

"I'm not blaming you. I know all the things I have to thank you for."

There was a short pause, broken, hesitantly, by Eric's mother. "What I don't understand," she said, "is why, when you went away to the city, you didn't *stay* away. You didn't really have anything to keep you here."

There was the sound of a drink being poured. Then, "No. I didn't have nothing—*really*—to keep me here. Just all the things I ever knew—all the things—*all* the things—I ever cared about."

"A man's not supposed to sit around and mope," said Eric's father, wrathfully, "for things that are over and dead and finished, things that can't *ever* begin again, that can't ever be the same again. That's what I mean when I say you're a dreamer—and if you hadn't kept on dreaming so long, you might not be alone now."

"Ah, well," said Jamie, mildly, and with a curious rush of affection in his voice, "I know you're the giant-killer, the hunter, the lover—the real old Adam, that's you. I know you're going to cover the earth. I know the world depends on men like you."

"And you're damn right," said Eric's father, after an uneasy moment.

Around Eric's head there was a buzzing, a bee, perhaps, a blue-fly, or a wasp. He hoped that his mother would see it and brush it away, but she did not move her hand. And he looked out again, through the veil of his eyelashes, at the slope and the sky, and then saw that the sun had moved and that it would not be long now before she would be going.

"—just like you already," Jamie said.

"You think my little one's like me?" Eric knew that his father was smiling—he could almost feel his father's hands.

"Looks like you, walks like you, talks like you," said Jamie.

"*And* stubborn like you," said Eric's mother.

"Ah, yes," said Jamie, and sighed. "You married the stubbornest, most determined—most selfish—man I know."

"I didn't know you felt that way," said Eric's father. He was still smiling.

"I'd have warned you about him," Jamie added, laughing, "if there'd been time."

"Everyone who knows you feels that way," said Eric's mother, and Eric felt a sudden brief tightening of the muscle in her thigh.

"Oh, *you*," said Eric's father, "I know *you* feel that way, women like to feel that way, it makes them feel important. But," and he changed to the teasing tone he took so persistently with Jamie today, "I didn't know my fine friend, Jamie, here—"

It was odd how unwilling he was to open his eyes. Yet, he felt the sun on him and knew that he wanted to rise from where he was before the sun went down. He did not understand what they were talking about this afternoon, these grown-ups he had known all his life; by keeping his eyes closed he kept their conversation far from him. And his mother's hand lay on his head like a blessing, like protection. And the buzzing had ceased, the bee, the blue-fly, or the wasp seemed to have flown away.

"—if it's a boy this time," his father said, "we'll name it after you."

"That's touching," said Jamie, "but that really won't do me— or the kid—a hell of a lot of good."

"Jamie can get married and have kids of his own any time he decides to," said Eric's mother.

"No," said his father, after a long pause, "Jamie's thought about it too long."

And, suddenly, he laughed and Eric sat up as his father slapped Jamie on the knee. At the touch, Jamie leaped up, shouting, spilling his drink and overturning his chair, and the dog beside Eric awoke and began to bark. For a moment, before Eric's unbelieving eyes, there was nothing in the yard but noise and flame.

His father rose slowly and stared at Jamie. "What's the matter with you?"

"What's the matter with me!" mimicked Jamie, "what's the matter with me? what the hell do you care what's the matter with me! What the hell have you been riding me for all day like this? What do you want? what do you *want*?"

"I want you to learn to hold your liquor for one thing," said his father, coldly. The two men stared at each other. Jamie's face was red and ugly and tears stood in his eyes. The dog, at his legs, kept up a furious prancing and barking. Jamie bent down and, with one hand, with all his might, slapped his dog, which rolled over, howling, and ran away to hide itself under the shadows of the far grey wall.

Then Jamie stared again at Eric's father, trembling, and pushed his hair back from his eyes.

"You better pull yourself together," Eric's father said. And, to Eric's mother. "Get him some coffee. He'll be all right."

Jamie set his glass on the table and picked up the overturned chair. Eric's mother rose and went into the kitchen. Eric remained sitting on the ground, staring at the two men, his father and his father's best friend, who had become so unfamiliar. His father, with something in his face which Eric had never before seen there, a tenderness, a sorrow—or perhaps it was, after all, the look he sometimes wore when approaching a calf he was about to slaughter —looked down at Jamie where he sat, head bent, at the table. "You take things too hard," he said. "You always have. I was only teasing you for your own good."

Jamie did not answer. His father looked over to Eric, and smiled.

"Come on," he said. "You and me are going for a walk."

Eric, passing on the side of the table farthest from Jamie, went to his father and took his hand.

"Pull yourself together," his father said to Jamie. "We're going to cut your birthday cake as soon as me and the little one come back."

Eric and his father passed beyond the grey wall where the dog still whimpered, out into the fields. Eric's father was walking too fast and Eric stumbled on the uneven ground. When they had gone a little distance his father abruptly checked his pace and looked down at Eric, grinning.

"I'm sorry," he said. "I guess I said we were going for a walk, not running to put out a fire."

"What's the matter with Jamie?" Eric asked.

"Oh," said his father, looking westward where the sun was moving, pale orange now, making the sky ring with brass and copper and gold—which, like a magician, she was presenting only to demonstrate how variously they could be transformed—"Oh," he repeated, "there's nothing wrong with Jamie. He's been drinking a lot," and he grinned down at Eric, "and he's been sitting in the sun—you know, his hair's not as thick as yours," and he ruffled Eric's hair, "and I guess birthdays make him nervous. Hell," he said, "they make me nervous, too."

"Jamie's *very* old," said Eric, "isn't he?"

His father laughed. "Well, butch, he's not exactly ready to fall into the grave yet—he's going to be around awhile, is Jamie. Hey," he said, and looked down at Eric again, "you must think I'm an old man, too."

"Oh," said Eric, quickly, "I know you're not as old as Jamie."

His father laughed again. "Well, thank you, son. That shows real confidence. I'll try to live up to it."

They walked in silence for awhile and then his father said, not looking at Eric, speaking to himself, it seemed, or to the air: "No, Jamie's not so old. He's not as old as he should be."

"How old *should* he be?" asked Eric.

"Why," said his father, "he ought to be his age," and, looking down at Eric's face, he burst into laughter again.

"Ah," he said, finally, and put his hand on Eric's head again, very gently, very sadly, "don't you worry now about what you don't understand. The time is coming when you'll have to worry—but that time hasn't come yet."

Then they walked till they came to the steep slope which led to the railroad tracks, down, down, far below them, where a small train seemed to be passing forever through the countryside, smoke, like the very definition of idleness, blowing out of the chimney stack of the toy locomotive. Eric thought, resentfully, that he scarcely ever saw a train pass when he came here alone. Beyond the railroad tracks was the river where they sometimes went swimming in the summer. The river was hidden from them now by the high bank where there were houses and where tall trees grew.

"And this," said his father, "is where your land ends."

"What?" said Eric.

His father squatted on the ground and put one hand on Eric's shoulder. "You know all the way we walked, from the house?" Eric nodded. "Well," said his father, "that's your land."

Eric looked back at the long way they had come, feeling his father watching him.

His father, with a pressure on his shoulder made him turn; he pointed: "And over there. It belongs to you." He turned him again. "And that," he said, "that's yours, too."

Eric stared at his father. "Where does it end?" he asked.

His father rose. "I'll show you that another day," he said. "But it's further than you can walk."

They started walking slowly, in the direction of the sun.

"When did it get to be mine?" asked Eric.

"The day you were born," his father said, and looked down at him and smiled.

"My father," he said, after a moment, "had some of this land—and when he died, it was mine. He held on to it for me. And I did my best with the land I had, and I got some more. I'm holding on to it for you."

He looked down to see if Eric was listening. Eric was listening, staring at his father and looking around him at the great countryside.

"When I get to be a real old man," said his father, "even older than old Jamie there—you're going to have to take care of all this. When I die it's going to be yours." He paused and stopped; Eric looked up at him. "When you get to be a big man, like your Papa, you're going to get married and have children. And all this is going to be theirs."

"And when *they* get married?" Eric prompted.

"All this will belong to *their* children," his father said.

"Forever?" cried Eric.

"Forever," said his father.

They turned and started walking toward the house.

"Jamie," Eric asked at last, "how much land has *he* got?"

"Jamie doesn't have any land," his father said.

"Why not?" asked Eric.

"He didn't take care of it," his father said, "and he lost it."

"Jamie doesn't have a wife anymore, either, does he?" Eric asked.

"No," said his father. "He didn't take care of her, either."

"And he doesn't have any little boy," said Eric—very sadly.

"No," said his father. Then he grinned. "But *I* have."

"*Why* doesn't Jamie have a little boy?" asked Eric.

His father shrugged. "Some people do, Eric, some people don't."

"Will I?" asked Eric.

"Will you what?" asked his father.

"Will I get married and have a little boy?"

His father seemed for a moment both amused and checked. He looked down at Eric with a strange, slow smile. "Of course you will," he said at last. "Of course you will." And he held out his arms. "Come," he said, "climb up. I'll ride you on my shoulders home."

So Eric rode on his father's shoulders through the wide green fields which belonged to him, into the yard which held the house which would hear the first cries of his children. His mother and Jamie sat at the table talking quietly in the silver sun. Jamie had washed his face and combed his hair, he seemed calmer, he was smiling.

"Ah," cried Jamie, "the lord, the master of this house arrives! And bears on his shoulders the prince, the son, and heir!" He described a flourish, bowing low in the yard. "My lords! Behold your humble, most properly chastised servant, desirous of your—compassion, your love, and your forgiveness!"

"Frankly," said Eric's father, putting Eric on the ground, "I'm not sure that this is an improvement." He looked at Jamie and frowned and grinned. "Let's cut that cake."

Eric stood with his mother in the kitchen while she lit the candles—thirty-five, one, as they said, to grow on, though Jamie, surely, was far past the growing age—and followed her as she took the cake outside. Jamie took the great, gleaming knife and held it with a smile.

"Happy Birthday!" they cried—only Eric said nothing—and then Eric's mother said, "You have to blow out the candles, Jamie, before you cut the cake."

"It looks so pretty the way it is," Jamie said.

"Go ahead," said Eric's father, and clapped him on the back, "be a man."

Then the dog, once more beside his master, awoke, growling, and this made everybody laugh. Jamie laughed loudest. Then he blew out the candles, all of them at once, and Eric watched him as he cut the cake. Jamie raised his eyes and looked at Eric and it was at this moment, as the suddenly blood-red sun was striking the topmost tips of trees, that Eric had looked into Jamie's eyes. Jamie smiled that strange smile of an old man and Eric moved closer to his mother.

"The first piece for Eric," said Jamie, then, and extended it to him on the silver blade.

That had been near the end of summer, nearly two months ago. Very shortly after the birthday party, his mother had fallen ill and had had to be taken away. Then his father spent more time than ever at The Rafters; he and Jamie came home in the evenings, stumbling drunk. Sometimes, during the time that his mother was away, Jamie did not go home at all, but spent the night at the farm house; and once or twice Eric had awakened in the middle of the night, or near dawn, and heard Jamie's footsteps walking up and down, walking up and down, in the big room downstairs. It had been a strange and dreadful time, a time of waiting, stillness, and silence. His father rarely went into the fields, scarcely raised himself to give orders to his farm hands—it was unnatural, it was frightening, to find him around the house all day, and Jamie was there always, Jamie and his dog. Then one day Eric's father told him that his mother was coming home but that she would not be bringing him a baby brother or sister, not this time, nor in any time to come. He started to say something more, then looked at Jamie who was standing by, and walked out of the house. Jamie followed him slowly, his hands in his pockets and his head bent. From the time of the birthday party, as though he were repenting of that outburst, or as though it had frightened him, Jamie had become more silent than ever.

When his mother came back she seemed to have grown older— old; she seemed to have shrunk within herself, away from them all, even, in a kind of storm of love and helplessness, away from Eric; but, oddly, and most particularly, away from Jamie. It was in nothing she said, nothing she did—or perhaps it was in everything she said and did. She washed and cooked for Jamie as before, took him into account as much as before as a part of the family, made him take second helpings at the table, smiled good night to him as he left the house—it was only that something had gone out of her familiarity. She seemed to do all that she did out of memory and from a great distance. And if something had gone out of her ease, something had come into it, too, a curiously still attention, as though she had been startled by some new aspect of something she had always known. Once or twice at the supper table, Eric caught her regard bent on Jamie, who, obliviously, ate. He could not read her look, but it reminded him of that moment at the birthday party when he had looked into Jamie's eyes. She seemed to be looking at Jamie as though she were wondering why she had not looked at him before; or as though she were discovering, with some surprise, that she had never really liked him but also felt, in her weariness and weakness, that it did not really matter now.

Now, as he entered the yard, he saw her standing in the kitchen doorway, looking out, shielding her eyes against the brilliant setting sun.

"Eric!" she cried, wrathfully, as soon as she saw him. "I've been looking high and low for you for the last hour. You're getting old enough to have some sense of responsibility and I wish you wouldn't worry me so when you know I've not been well."

She made him feel guilty at the same time that he dimly and

resentfully felt that justice was not all on her side. She pulled him to her, turning his face up toward hers, roughly, with one hand.

"You're filthy," she said, then. "Go around to the pump and wash your face. And hurry, so I can give you your supper and put you to bed."

And she turned and went into the kitchen, closing the door lightly behind her. He walked around to the other side of the house, to the pump.

On a wooden box next to the pump was a piece of soap and a damp rag. Eric picked up the soap, not thinking of his mother, but thinking of the day gone by, already half asleep: and thought of where he would go tomorrow. He moved the pump handle up and down and the water rushed out and wet his socks and shoes—this would make his mother angry, but he was too tired to care. Nevertheless, automatically, he moved back a little. He held the soap between his hands, his hands beneath the water.

He had been many places, he had walked a long way and seen many things that day. He had gone down to the railroad tracks and walked beside the tracks for awhile, hoping that a train would pass. He kept telling himself that he would give the train one more last chance to pass; and when he had given a considerable number of last chances, he left the railroad bed and climbed a little and walked through the high, sweet meadows. He walked through a meadow where there were cows and they looked at him dully with their great dull eyes and moo'd among each other about him. A man from the far end of the field saw him and shouted, but Eric could not tell whether it was someone who worked for his father or not and so he turned and ran away, ducking through the wire fence. He passed an apple tree, with apples lying all over the ground—he wondered if the apples belonged to him, if he were still walking on his own land or had gone past it—but he ate an apple anyway and put some in his pockets, watching a lone brown horse in a meadow far below him nibbling at the grass and flicking his tail. Eric pretended that he was his father and was walking through the fields as he had seen his father walk, looking it all over calmly, pleased, knowing that everything he saw belonged to him. And he stopped and pee'd as he had seen his father do, standing wide-legged and heavy in the middle of the fields; he pretended at the same time to be smoking and talking, as he had seen his father do. Then, having watered the ground, he walked on, and all the earth, for that moment, in Eric's eyes, seemed to be celebrating Eric.

Tomorrow he would go away again, somewhere. For soon it would be winter, snow would cover the ground, he would not be able to wander off alone.

He held the soap between his hands, his hands beneath the water; then he heard a low whistle behind him and a rough hand on his head and the soap fell from his hands and slithered between his legs onto the ground.

He turned and faced Jamie, Jamie without his dog.

"Come on, little fellow," Jamie whispered. "We got something in the barn to show you."

"Oh, did the calf come yet?" asked Eric—and was too pleased to wonder why Jamie whispered.

"Your Papa's there," said Jamie. And then: "Yes. Yes, the calf is coming now."

And he took Eric's hand and they crossed the yard, past the closed kitchen door, past the stone wall and across the field, into the barn.

"But *this* isn't where the cows are!" Eric cried. He suddenly looked up at Jamie, who closed the barn door behind them and looked down at Eric with a smile.

"No," said Jamie, "that's right. No cows here." And he leaned against the door as though his strength had left him. Eric saw that his face was wet, he breathed as though he had been running.

"Let's go see the cows," Eric whispered. Then he wondered why he was whispering and was terribly afraid. He stared at Jamie, who stared at him.

"In a minute," Jamie said, and stood up. He had put his hands in his pockets and now he brought them out and Eric stared at his hands and began to move away. He asked, "Where's my Papa?"

"Why," said Jamie, "he's down at The Rafters, I guess. I have to meet him there soon."

"I have to go," said Eric. "I have to eat my supper." He tried to move to the door, but Jamie did not move. "I have to go," he repeated, and, as Jamie moved toward him the tight ball of terror in his bowels, in his throat, swelled and rose, exploded, he opened his mouth to scream but Jamie's fingers closed around his throat. He stared, stared into Jamie's eyes.

"That won't do you any good," said Jamie. And he smiled. Eric struggled for breath, struggled with pain and fright. Jamie relaxed his grip a little and moved one hand and stroked Eric's tangled hair. Slowly, wondrously, his face changed, tears came into his eyes and rolled down his face.

Eric groaned—perhaps because he saw Jamie's tears or because his throat was so swollen and burning, because he could not catch his breath, because he was so frightened—he began in sob in great, unchildish gasps. "Why do you hate my father?"

"I love your father," Jamie said. But he was not listening to Eric. He was far away—as though he were struggling, toiling inwardly up a tall, tall mountain. And Eric struggled blindly, with all the force of his desire to live, to reach him, to stop him before he reached the summit.

"Jamie," Eric whispered, "you can have the land. You can have all the land."

Jamie spoke, but not to Eric: "I don't want the land."

"I'll be your little boy," said Eric. "I'll be your little boy forever and forever and forever—and you can have the land and you can live forever! Jamie!"

Jamie had stopped weeping. He was watching Eric.

"We'll go for a walk tomorrow," Eric said, "and I'll show it to you, all of it—really and truly—if you kill my father I can be your little boy and we can have it all!"

"This land," said Jamie, "will belong to no one."

"Please!" cried Eric, "oh, please! Please!"

He heard his mother singing in the kitchen. Soon she would come out to look for him. The hands left him for a moment. Eric opened his mouth to scream, but the hands then closed around his throat.

Mama. Mama.

The singing was further and further away. The eyes looked

into his, there was a question in the eyes, the hands tightened. Then the mouth began to smile. He had never seen such a smile before. He kicked and kicked.

Mama. Mama. Mama. Mama. Mama.

Far away, he heard his mother call him.

Mama.

He saw nothing, he knew that he was in the barn, he heard a terrible breathing near him, he thought he heard the sniffling of beasts, he remembered the sun, the railroad tracks, the cows, the apples, and the ground. He thought of tomorrow—he wanted to go away again somewhere tomorrow. *I'll take you with me,* he wanted to say. He wanted to argue the question, the question he remembered in the eyes—wanted to say, *I'll tell my Papa you're hurting me.* Then terror and agony and darkness overtook him, and his breath went violently out of him. He dropped on his face in the straw in the barn, his yellow head useless on his broken neck.

Night covered the countryside and here and there, like emblems, the lights of houses glowed. A woman's voice called, "Eric! Eric!"

Jamie reached his wooden house and opened his door; whistled, and his dog came bounding out of darkness, leaping up on him; and he cuffed it down lightly, with one hand. Then he closed his door and started down the road, his dog beside him, his hands in his pockets. He stopped to light his pipe. He heard singing from The Rafters, then he saw the lights; soon, the lights and the sound of singing diminished behind him. When Jamie no longer heard the singing, he began to whistle the song that he had heard.

Exercises

1. Most of the "story" here is filtered through Eric's memory as he hurries "homeward across the fields." (Notice that he starts home in the first few lines and arrives there some 14 pages later.) What are the story's two main scenes? What plot details are important to remember in each one?
2. Repeated reference is made to the physical characteristics of the farm: buildings, fields, animals, sun, sky. Why? Characterize the descriptive

phrases used in reference to them. What role does the setting play in the story? Keep in mind that it is seen through Eric's eyes.

3. The title "The Man Child" can mean either the man who is a child or the child who is a man. To whom does the title refer in the story? Jamie? Eric? Eric's father? All three? Whose story is it? Discuss.

4. Do Eric's father and mother get any of the hints Eric gets about Jamie's dark side? Is Eric fearful only because any strident male behavior would be overwhelming to a child of eight even when in fun? Discuss.

5. Characterize the exchanges between Eric's father and Jamie. Are they needling? or kidding? Defend your position with specific examples. How genuine is their friendship? What is good about it? What is not good about it?

6. What is Eric's mother's role in the story? In the opening paragraph the narrator says that she "had been captured by his father on some far-off, unblessed, unbelievable night, [and] had never since burst her chains." What do you take that to mean? Can those be Eric's thoughts? If not, what are they doing here? Was Jamie's behavior toward his wife, who ran off, different from Eric's father's toward his wife?

7. What preparations are there for the final act of terror? Are Jamie's actions believable? What clues have there been that he could do such a thing? Why does he do it when he does? Why not before? Or perhaps never?

8. The story is told *through* Eric, although obviously not by him. The narrator sticks to Eric's experiences and understanding, though not his language, and gets inside him in a sense, most clearly so at the moment of strangulation. Discuss how the story's impact would be different if it were told either by or through any of the other characters. The discussion should suggest some of the ways in which Baldwin's choice of narrator intensifies the sense of terror that pervades the story even before the outcome is known.

9. Can you suggest reasons why the father and mother are nameless, why they are always referred to as "Eric's father" and "Eric's mother"?

10. How much of what is happening does Eric understand? Consider carefully what happens when Jamie takes him into the barn. Why does he sense so quickly what is going on? What kinds of bargains does he make for his life? How much of his father has he absorbed? (Jamie remarks several times how much Eric is like his father.) How did the day of the birthday party and his mother's miscarriage set inevitably in motion the final horror?

11. What details (in the light of the whole story) are particularly significant in the first four paragraphs (take them one by one). Consider language choice as well as story facts. What mood is set and how is it set?

12. Jamie says to Eric's father, "What the hell have you been riding me for all day like this? What do you want? What do you *want?*" What does he want and why does he want it? What connection is there between the father's wants and Jamie's terrible revenge?

The Rocking-Horse Winner

D. H. LAWRENCE

There was a woman who was beautiful, who started with all the advantages, yet she had no luck. She married for love, and the love turned to dust. She had bonny children, yet she felt they had been thrust upon her, and she could not love them. They looked at her coldly, as if they were finding fault with her. And hurriedly she felt she must cover up some fault in herself. Yet what it was that she must cover up she never knew. Nevertheless, when her children were present, she always felt the center of her heart go hard. This troubled her, and in her manner she was all the more gentle and anxious for her children, as if she loved them very much. Only she herself knew that at the center of her heart was a hard little place that could not feel love, no, not for anybody. Everybody else said of her: "She is such a good mother. She adores her children." Only she herself, and her children themselves, knew it was not so. They read it in each other's eyes.

There were a boy and two little girls. They lived in a pleasant house, with a garden, and they had discreet servants, and felt themselves superior to anyone in the neighborhood.

Although they lived in style, they felt always an anxiety in the house. There was never enough money. The mother had a small income, and the father had a small income, but not nearly enough for the social position which they had to keep up. The father went into town to some office. But though he had good prospects, these prospects never materialized. There was always the grinding sense of the shortage of money, though the style was always kept up.

At last the mother said: "I will see if *I* can't make something."

But she did not know where to begin. She racked her brains, and tried this thing and the other, but could not find anything successful. The failure made deep lines come into her face. Her children were growing up, they would have to go to school. There must be more money, there must be more money. The father, who was always very handsome and expensive in his tastes, seemed as if he never *would* be able to do anything worth doing. And the mother, who had a great belief in herself, did not succeed any better, and her tastes were just as expensive.

And so the house came to be haunted by the unspoken phrase: *There must be more money! There must be more money!* The children could hear it all the time, though nobody said it aloud. They heard it at Christmas, when the expensive and splendid toys filled the nursery. Behind the shining modern rocking-horse, behind the smart doll's house, a voice would start whispering: "There *must* be more money! There *must* be more money!" And the children would stop playing, to listen for a moment. They would look into each other's eyes, to see if they had all heard. And each one saw in the eyes of the other two that they too had heard. "There *must* be more money! There *must* be more money!"

It came whispering from the springs of the still-swaying rocking-horse, and even the horse, bending his wooden, champing head, heard it. The big doll, sitting so pink and smirking in her new pram, could hear it quite plainly, and seemed to be smirking all the more self-consciously because of it. The foolish puppy, too, that took the place of the teddy-bear, he was looking so extraordinarily foolish for no other reason but that he heard the secret whisper all over the house: "There *must* be more money!"

Yet nobody ever said it aloud. The whisper was everywhere, and therefore no one spoke it. Just as no one ever says: "We are breathing!" in spite of the fact that breath is coming and going all the time.

"Mother," said the boy Paul one day, "why don't we keep a car of our own? Why do we always use uncle's, or else a taxi?"

"Because we're the poor members of the family," said the mother.

"But why *are* we, mother?"

"Well—I suppose," she said slowly and bitterly, "It's because your father has no luck."

The boy was silent for some time.

"Is luck money, mother?" he asked, rather timidly.

"No, Paul. Not quite. It's what causes you to have money."

"Oh!" said Paul vaguely. "I thought when Uncle Oscar said *filthy lucker*, it meant money."

"*Filthy lucre* does mean money," said the mother. "But it's lucre, not luck.

"Oh!" said the boy. "Then what *is* luck, mother?

"It's what causes you to have money. If you're lucky you have money. That's why it's better to be born lucky than rich. If you're rich, you may lose your money. But if you're lucky, you will always get more money."

"Oh! Will you? And is father not lucky?"

"Very unlucky, I should say," she said bitterly.

The boy watched her with unsure eyes.

"Why?" he asked.

"I don't know. Nobody ever knows why one person is lucky and another unlucky."

"Don't they? Nobody at all? Does *nobody* know?

"Perhaps God. But He never tells."

"He ought to, then. And aren't you lucky either, mother?"

"I can't be, if I married an unlucky husband."

"But by yourself, aren't you?"

"I used to think I was, before I married. Now I think I am very unlucky indeed."

"Why?"

"Well—never mind! Perhaps I'm not really," she said.

The child looked at her to see if she meant it. But he saw, by the lines of her mouth, that she was only trying to hide something from him.

"Well, anyhow," he said stoutly, "I'm a lucky person."

"Why?" said his mother, with a sudden laugh.

He stared at her. He didn't even know why he had said it.

"God told me," he asserted, brazening it out.

"I hope He did, dear!" she said, again with a laugh, but rather bitter.

"He did, mother!"

"Excellent!" said the mother, using one of her husband's exclamations.

The boy saw she did not believe him; or rather, that she paid no attention to his assertion. This angered him somewhat, and made him want to compel her attention.

He went off by himself, vaguely, in a childish way, seeking for the clue to "luck." Absorbed, taking no heed of other people, he went about with a sort of stealth, seeking inwardly for luck. He wanted luck, he wanted it, he wanted it. When the two girls were playing dolls in the nursery, he would sit on his big rocking-horse, charging madly into space, with a frenzy that made the little girls peer at him uneasily. Wildly the horse careered, the waving dark hair of the boy tossed, his eyes had a strange glare in them. The little girls dared not speak to him.

When he had ridden to the end of his mad little journey, he climbed down and stood in front of his rocking-horse, staring fixedly into its lowered face. Its red mouth was slightly open, its big eye was wide and glassy-bright.

"Now!" he would silently command the snorting steed. "Now, take me to where there is luck! Now take me!"

And he would slash the horse on the neck with the little whip he had asked Uncle Oscar for. He *knew* the horse could take him to where there was luck, if only he forced it. So he would mount again and start on his furious ride, hoping at last to get there. He knew he could get there.

"You'll break your horse, Paul!" said the nurse.

"He's always riding like that! I wish he'd leave off!" said his elder sister[1] Joan.

But he only glared down on them in silence. Nurse gave him up. She could make nothing of him. Anyhow, he was growing beyond her.

One day his mother and his Uncle Oscar came in when he was on one of his furious rides. He did not speak to them.

"Hallo, you young jockey! Riding a winner?" said his uncle.

[1]**elder sister:** i.e., the older of his two sisters; both are younger than Paul.

"Aren't you growing too big for a rocking-horse? You're not a very little boy any longer, you know," said his mother.

But Paul only gave a blue glare from his big, rather close-set eyes. He would speak to nobody when he was in full tilt. His mother watched him with an anxious expression on her face.

At last he suddenly stopped forcing his horse into the mechanical gallop and slid down.

"Well, I got there!" he announced fiercely, his blue eyes still flaring and his sturdy long legs straddling apart.

"Where did you get to?" asked his mother.

"Where I wanted to go," he flared back at her.

"That's right, son!" said Uncle Oscar. "Don't you stop till you get there. What's the horse's name?"

"He doesn't have a name," said the boy.

"Gets on without all right?" asked the uncle.

"Well, he has different names. He was called Sansovino last week."

"Sansovino, eh? Won the Ascot.[2] How did you know his name?"

"He always talks about horse-races with Bassett," said Joan.

The uncle was delighted to find that his small nephew was posted with all the racing news. Bassett, the young gardener, who had been wounded in the left foot in the war and had got his present job through Oscar Cresswell, whose batman[3] he had been, was a perfect blade of the "turf."[4] He lived in the racing events, and the small boy lived with him.

Oscar Cresswell got it all from Bassett.

"Master Paul comes and asks me, so I can't do more than tell him, sir," said Bassett, his face terribly serious, as if he were speaking of religious matters.

"And does he ever put anything on a horse he fancies?"

"Well—I don't want to give him away—he's a young sport,[5] a

---

[2]**Ascot:**   a famous English horse race. The other races mentioned later on are also well-known yearly races.

[3]**batman:**   personal servant to an officer in the British army.

[4]**perfect . . . "turf":**   one thoroughly wrapped-up in horse-racing.

[5]**sport:**   a gambler.

fine sport, sir. Would you mind asking him yourself? He sort of takes a pleasure in it, and perhaps he'd feel I was giving him away, sir, if you don't mind."

Bassett was serious as a church.

The uncle went back to his nephew and took him off for a ride in the car.

"Say, Paul, old man, do you ever put anything on a horse?" the uncle asked.

The boy watched the handsome man closely.

"Why, do you think I oughtn't to?" he parried.

"Not a bit of it! I thought perhaps you might give me a tip for the Lincoln."

The car sped on into the country, going down to Uncle Oscar's place in Hampshire.

"Honor bright?" said the nephew.

"Honor bright, son!" said the uncle.

"Well, then, Daffodil."

"Daffodil! I doubt it, sonny. What about Mirza?"

"I only know the winner," said the boy. "That's Daffodil."

"Daffodil, eh?"

There was a pause. Daffodil was an obscure horse comparatively.

"Uncle!"

"Yes, son?"

"You won't let it go any further, will you? I promised Bassett."

"Bassett be damned, old man! What's he got to do with it?"

"We're partners. We've been partners from the first, uncle. He lent me my first five shillings, which I lost. I promised him, honor bright, it was only between me and him; only you gave me that ten-shilling note I started winning with, so I thought you were lucky. You won't let it go any further, will you?"

The boy gazed at his uncle from those big, hot, blue eyes, set rather close together. The uncle stirred and laughed uneasily.

"Right you are, son! I'll keep your tip private. Daffodil, eh? How much are you putting on him?"

"All except twenty pounds," said the boy. "I keep that in reserve."

The uncle thought it a good joke.

"You keep twenty pounds in reserve, do you, you young romancer? What are you betting, then?"

"I'm betting three hundred," said the boy gravely. "But it's between you and me, Uncle Oscar! Honor bright?"

The uncle burst into a roar of laughter.

"It's between you and me all right, you young Nat Gould,[6]" he said, laughing. "But where's your three hundred?"

"Bassett keeps it for me. We're partners."

"You are, are you! And what is Bassett putting on Daffodil?"

"He won't go quite as high as I do, I expect. Perhaps he'll go a hundred and fifty."

"What, pennies?" laughed the uncle.

"Pounds," said the child, with a surprised look at his uncle. "Bassett keeps a bigger reserve than I do."

Between wonder and amusement Uncle Oscar was silent. He pursued the matter no further, but he determined to take his nephew with him to the Lincoln races.

"Now, son," he said, "I'm putting twenty on Mirza, and I'll put five on for you on any horse you fancy. What's your pick?"

"Daffodil, uncle."

"No, not the fiver on Daffodil!"

"I should if it was my own fiver," said the child.

"Good! Good! Right you are! A fiver for me and a fiver for you on Daffodil."

The child had never been to a race-meeting before, and his eyes were blue fire. He pursed his mouth tight and watched. A Frenchman just in front had put his money on Lancelot. Wild with excitement, he flayed his arms up and down, yelling *"Lancelot! Lancelot!"* in his French accent.

Daffodil came in first, Lancelot second, Mirza third. The child, flushed and with eyes blazing, was curiously serene. His uncle brought him four five-pound notes, four to one.

"What am I to do with these?" he cried, waving them before the boy's eyes.

---

[6]**Nat Gould:**   British novelist (1857–1919); author of 130 novels, mostly on horse-racing.

"I suppose we'll talk to Bassett," said the boy. "I expect I have fifteen hundred now; and twenty in reserve; and this twenty."

His uncle studied him for some moments.

"Look here, son!" he said. "You're not serious about Bassett and that fifteen hundred, are you?"

"Yes, I am. But it's between you and me, uncle. Honor bright?"

"Honor bright all right, son! But I must talk to Bassett."

"If you'd like to be a partner, uncle, with Bassett and me, we could all be partners. Only, you'd have to promise, honor bright, uncle, not to let it go beyond us three. Bassett and I are lucky, and you must be lucky, because it was your ten shillings I started winning with...."

Uncle Oscar took both Bassett and Paul into Richmond Park for an afternoon, and there they talked.

"It's like this, you see, sir," Bassett said. "Master Paul would get me talking about racing events, spinning yarns, you know, sir. And he was always keen on knowing if I'd made or if I'd lost. It's about a year since, now, that I put five shillings on Blush of Dawn for him: and we lost. Then the luck turned, with that ten shillings he had from you: that we put on Singhalese. And since that time, it's been pretty steady, all things considering. What do you say, Master Paul?"

"We're all right when we're sure," said Paul. "It's when we're not quite sure that we go down.

"Oh, but we're careful then," said Bassett.

"But when are you *sure*?" smiled Uncle Oscar.

"It's Master Paul, sir," said Bassett in a secret, religious voice. "It's as if he had if from heaven. Like Daffodil, now, for the Lincoln. That was as sure as eggs."

"Did you put anything on Daffodil?" asked Oscar Cresswell.

"Yes, sir. I made my bit."

"And my nephew?"

Bassett was obstinately silent, looking at Paul.

"I made twelve hundred, didn't I, Bassett? I told uncle I was putting three hundred on Daffodil."

"That's right," said Bassett, nodding.

"But where's the money?" asked the uncle.

"I keep it safe locked up, sir. Master Paul he can have it any minute he likes to ask for it."

"What, fifteen hundred pounds?"

"And twenty! And *forty*, that is, with the twenty he made on the course."

"It's amazing!" said the uncle.

"If Master Paul offers you to be partners, sir, I would, if I were you: if you'll excuse me," said Bassett.

Oscar Cresswell thought about it.

"I'll see the money," he said.

They drove home again, and, sure enough, Bassett came round to the garden-house with fifteen hundred pounds in notes. The twenty pounds reserve was left with Joe Glee, in the Turf Commission deposit.

"You see, it's all right, uncle, when I'm *sure*! Then we go strong, for all we're worth. Don't we, Bassett?"

"We do that, Master Paul."

"And when are you sure?" said the uncle, laughing.

"Oh, well, sometimes I'm *absolutely* sure, like about Daffodil," said the boy; "and sometimes I have an idea; and sometimes I haven't even an idea, have I, Bassett? Then we're careful, because we mostly go down."

"You do, do you! And when you're sure, like about Daffodil, what makes you sure, sonny?"

"Oh, well, I don't know," said the boy uneasily. "I'm sure, you know, uncle; that's all."

"It's as if he had it from heaven, sir," Bassett reiterated.

"I should say so!" said the uncle.

But he became a partner. And when the Leger was coming on Paul was "sure" about Lively Spark, which was a quite inconsiderable horse. The boy insisted on putting a thousand on the horse, Bassett went for five hundred, and Oscar Cresswell two hundred. Lively Spark came in first, and the betting had been ten to one against him. Paul had made ten thousand.

"You see," he said, "I was absolutely sure of him."

Even Oscar Cresswell had cleared two thousand.

"Look here, son," he said, "this sort of thing makes me nervous."

"It needn't, uncle! Perhaps I shan't be sure again for a long time."

"But what are you going to do with your money?" asked the uncle.

"Of course," said the boy, "I started it for mother. She said she had no luck, because father is unlucky, so I thought if *I* was lucky, it might stop whispering."

"What might stop whispering?"

"Our house. I *hate* our house for whispering."

"What does it whisper?"

"Why—why"—the boy fidgeted—"why, I don't know. But it's always short of money, you know, uncle."

"I know it, son, I know it."

"You know people send mother writs, don't you, uncle?"

"I'm afraid I do," said the uncle.

"And then the house whispers, like people laughing at you behind your back. It's awful, that is! I thought if I was lucky—"

"You might stop it," added the uncle.

The boy watched him with big blue eyes, that had an uncanny cold fire in them, and he said never a word.

"Well, then!" said the uncle. "What are we doing?"

"I shouldn't like mother to know I was lucky," said the boy.

"Why not, son?"

"She'd stop me."

"I don't think she would."

"Oh!"—and the boy writhed in an odd way—"I *don't* want her to know, uncle."

"All right, son! We'll manage it without her knowing."

They managed it very easily. Paul, at the other's suggestion, handed over five thousand pounds to his uncle, who deposited it with the family lawyer, who was then to inform Paul's mother that a relative had put five thousand pounds into his hands, which sum was to be paid out a thousand pounds at a time, on the mother's birthday, for the next five years.

"So she'll have a birthday present of a thousand pounds for five successive years," said Uncle Oscar. "I hope it won't make it all the harder for her later."

Paul's mother had her birthday in November. The house had been "whispering" worse than ever lately, and, even in spite of his luck, Paul could not bear up against it. He was very anxious to see the effect of the birthday letter, telling his mother about the thousand pounds.

When there were no visitors, Paul now took his meals with his parents, as he was beyond the nursery control. His mother went into town nearly every day. She had discovered that she had an odd knack of sketching furs and dress materials, so she worked secretly in the studio of a friend who was the chief "artist" for the leading drapers. She drew the figures of ladies in furs and ladies in silk and sequins for the newspaper advertisements. This young woman artist earned several thousand pounds a year, but Paul's mother only made several hundreds, and she was again dissatisfied. She so wanted to be first in something, and she did not succeed, even in making sketches for drapery advertisements.

She was down to breakfast on the morning of her birthday. Paul watched her face as she read her letters. He knew the lawyer's letter. As his mother read it, her face hardened and became more expressionless. Then a cold, determined look came on her mouth. She hid the letter under the pile of others, and said not a word about it.

"Didn't you have anything nice in the post for your birthday, mother?" said Paul.

"Quite moderately nice," she said, her voice cold and absent.

She went away to town without saying more.

But in the afternoon Uncle Oscar appeared. He said Paul's mother had had a long interview with the lawyer, asking if the whole five thousand could not be advanced at once, as she was in debt.

"What do you think, uncle?" said the boy.

"I leave it to you, son."

"Oh, let her have it, then! We can get some more with the other," said the boy.

"A bird in the hand is worth two in the bush, laddie!" said Uncle Oscar.

"But I'm sure to *know* for the Grand National; or the Lincolnshire; or else the Derby.[7] I'm sure to know for *one* of them," said Paul.

So Uncle Oscar signed the agreement, and Paul's mother touched the whole five thousand. Then something very curious happened. The voices in the house suddenly went mad, like a chorus of frogs on a spring evening. There were certain new furnishings, and Paul had a tutor. He was *really* going to Eton, his father's school, in the following autumn. There were flowers in the winter, and a blossoming of the luxury Paul's mother had been used to. And yet the voices in the house, behind the sprays of mimosa and almond-blossom, and from under the piles of iridescent cushions, simply trilled and screamed in a sort of ecstacy: "There *must* be more money! Oh-h-h; there *must* be more money. Oh, now, now-w! Now-w-w—there *must* be more money!—more than ever! More than ever!"

It frightened Paul terribly. He studied away at his Latin and Greek with his tutor. But his intense hours were spent with Bassett. The Grand National had gone by: he had not "known," and had lost a hundred pounds. Summer was at hand. He was in agony for the Lincoln. But even for the Lincoln he didn't "know," and he lost fifty pounds. He became wild-eyed and strange, as if something were going to explode in him.

"Let it alone, son! Don't you bother about it!" urged Uncle Oscar. But it was as if the boy couldn't really hear what his uncle was saying.

"I've got to know for the Derby! I've got to know for the Derby!" the child reiterated, his big blue eyes blazing with a sort of madness.

His mother noticed how overwrought he was.

"You'd better go to the seaside. Wouldn't you like to go now to the seaside, instead of waiting? I think you'd better," she said, looking down at him anxiously, her heart curiously heavy because of him.

But the child lifted his uncanny blue eyes.

[7]**Derby:** the most famous horse race in England, at Epsom Downs. Comparable in importance in the United States is the Kentucky Derby, named after the English race.

"I couldn't possibly go before the Derby, mother!" he said. "I couldn't possibly!"

"Why not?" she said, her voice becoming heavy when she was opposed. "Why not? You can still go from the seaside to see the Derby with your Uncle Oscar, if that's what you wish. No need for you to wait here. Besides, I think you care too much about these races. It's a bad sign. My family has been a gambling family, and you won't know till you grow up how much damage it has done. But it has done damage. I shall have to send Bassett away, and ask Uncle Oscar not to talk racing to you, unless you promise to be reasonable about it: go away to the seaside and forget it. You're all nerves!"

"I'll do what you like, mother, so long as you don't send me away till after the Derby," the boy said.

"Send you away from where? Just from this house?"

"Yes," he said, gazing at her.

"Why, you curious child, what makes you care about this house so much, suddenly? I never knew you loved it."

He gazed at her without speaking. He had a secret within a secret, something he had not divulged, even to Bassett or to his Uncle Oscar.

But his mother, after standing undecided and a little bit sullen for some moments, said:

"Very well, then! Don't go to the seaside till after the Derby, if you don't wish it. But promise me you won't let your nerves go to pieces. Promise you won't think so much about horse-racing and *events*, as you call them!"

"Oh no," said the boy casually. "I won't think much about them, mother. You needn't worry. I wouldn't worry, mother, if I were you."

"If you were me and I were you," said his mother, "I wonder what we *should* do!"

"But you know you needn't worry, mother, don't you?" the boy repeated.

"I should be awfully glad to know it," she said wearily.

"Oh, well, you *can*, you know. I mean, you *ought* to know you needn't worry," he insisted.

"Ought I? Then I'll see about it," she said.

Paul's secret of secrets was his wooden horse, that which had no name. Since he was emancipated from a nurse and a nursery-governess, he had had his rocking-horse removed to his own bedroom at the top of the house.

"Surely you're too big for a rocking-horse!" his mother had remonstrated.

"Well, you see, mother, till I can have a *real* horse, I like to have *some* sort of animal about," had been his quaint answer.

"Do you feel he keeps you company?" she laughed.

"Oh yes! He's very good, he always keeps me company, when I'm there," said Paul.

So the horse, rather shabby, stood in an arrested prance in the boy's bedroom.

The Derby was drawing near, and the boy grew more and more tense. He hardly heard what was spoken to him, he was very frail, and his eyes were really uncanny. His mother had sudden strange seizures of uneasiness about him. Sometimes, for an hour, she would feel a sudden anxiety about him that was almost anguish. She wanted to rush to him at once, and know he was safe.

Two nights before the Derby, she was at a big party in town, when one of her rushes of anxiety about her boy, her first-born, gripped her heart till she could hardly speak. She fought with the feeling, might and main, for she believed in common sense. But it was too strong. She had to leave the dance and go downstairs to telephone to the country. The children's nursery-governess was terribly surprised and startled at being rung up in the night.

"Are the children all right, Miss Wilmot?"

"Oh yes, they are quite all right."

"Master Paul? Is he all right?"

"He went to bed as right as a trivet. Shall I run up and look at him?"

"No," said Paul's mother reluctantly. "No! Don't trouble. It's all right. Don't sit up. We shall be home fairly soon." She did not want her son's privacy intruded upon.

"Very good," said the governess.

It was about one o'clock when Paul's mother and father drove up to their house. All was still. Paul's mother went to her room and slipped off her white fur cloak. She had told her maid not to wait up for her. She heard her husband downstairs, mixing a whisky and soda.

And then, because of the strange anxiety at her heart, she stole upstairs to her son's room. Noiselessly, she went along the upper corridor. Was there a faint noise? What was it?

She stood, with arrested muscles, outside his door, listening. There was a strange, heavy, and yet not loud noise. Her heart stood still. It was a soundless noise, yet rushing and powerful. Something huge, in violent, hushed motion. What was it? What in God's name was it? She ought to know. She felt that she knew the noise. She knew what it was.

Yet she could not place it. She couldn't say what it was. And on and on it went, like a madness.

Softly, frozen with anxiety and fear, she turned the door-handle.

The room was dark. Yet in the space near the window, she heard and saw something plunging to and fro. She gazed in fear and amazement.

Then suddenly she switched on the light, and saw her son, in his green pajamas, madly surging on the rocking-horse. The blaze of light suddenly lit him up, as he urged the wooden horse, and lit her up, as she stood, blonde, in her dress of pale green and crystal, in the doorway.

"Paul!" she cried. "Whatever are you doing?"

"It's Malabar!" he screamed in a powerful, strange voice. "It's Malabar!"

His eyes blazed at her for one strange and senseless second, as he ceased urging his wooden horse. Then he fell with a crash to the ground, and she, all her tormented motherhood flooding upon her, rushed to gather him up.

But he was unconscious, and unconscious he remained, with some brain-fever. He talked and tossed, and his mother sat stonily by his side.

"Malabar! It's Malabar! Bassett, Bassett, I *know*! It's Malabar!"

So the child cried, trying to get up and urge the rocking-horse that gave him his inspiration.

"What does he mean by Malabar?" asked the heart-frozen mother.

"I don't know," said the father stonily.

"What does he mean by Malabar?" she asked her brother Oscar.

"It's one of the horses running for the Derby," was the answer.

And, in spite of himself, Oscar Cresswell spoke to Bassett, and himself put a thousand on Malabar: at fourteen to one.

The third day of the illness was critical: they were waiting for a change. The boy, with his rather long, curly hair, was tossing ceaselessly on the pillow. He neither slept nor regained consciousness, and his eyes were like blue stones. His mother sat, feeling her heart had gone, turned actually into a stone.

In the evening, Oscar Cresswell did not come, but Bassett sent a message, saying could he come up for one moment, just one moment? Paul's mother was very angry at the intrusion, but on second thought she agreed. The boy was the same. Perhaps Bassett might bring him to consciousness.

The gardener, a shortish fellow with a little brown moustache and sharp little brown eyes, tiptoed into the room, touched his imaginary cap to Paul's mother, and stole to the bedside, staring with glittering, smallish eyes at the tossing, dying child.

"Master Paul!" he whispered. "Master Paul! Malabar came in first all right, a clean win. I did as you told me. You've made over seventy thousand pounds, you have; you've got over eighty thousand. Malabar came in all right, Master Paul."

"Malabar! Malabar! Did I say Malabar, mother? Did I say Malabar? Do you think I'm lucky, mother? I knew Malabar, didn't I? Over eighty thousand pounds! I call that lucky, don't you, mother? Over eighty thousand pounds! I knew, didn't I know I knew? Malabar came in all right. If I ride my horse till I'm sure, then I tell you, Bassett, you can go as high as you like. Did you go for all you were worth, Bassett?"

"I went a thousand on it, Master Paul."

"I never told you, mother, that if I can ride my horse, and *get there*, then I'm absolutely sure—oh, absolutely! Mother, did I ever tell you? I *am* lucky!"

"No, you never did," said his mother.

But the boy died in the night.

And even as he lay dead, his mother heard her brother's voice saying to her: "My God, Hester, you're eighty-odd thousand to the good, and a poor devil of a son to the bad. But, poor devil, poor devil, he's best gone out of a life where he rides his rocking-horse to find a winner."

Exercises

1. The story is told in a kind of fairy-tale manner. Put the phrase "Once upon a time" in front of the first sentence and see if any change in tone is produced. What is the purpose of such a manner when used along with the characters' rather matter-of-fact, everyday language?

2. The story carries echoes of a well-known German legend about a doctor named Faust or Faustus, who pledges his soul to the devil in exchange for wealth and power. How is this story different? Why does Paul want what "luck" brings? Why is such a bargain more terrible under these circumstances?

3. What are the *whispers* in the house? Why do they grow louder when their demands seem to be satisfied?

4. What does Bassett's relationship to Paul represent in the working out of the implied bargain? Why does Lawrence use religious terms to describe the relationship?

5. What is Uncle Oscar's role? Why does he say what he does at the very end of the story? Are his remarks simply the insensitive reaction of a calloused man? If not, why not? Why does Lawrence end the story on that note?

6. What kind of person is Paul's mother? Point out details that give insight into her character. Why does she feel "the center of her heart go hard" when she is with her children? Why does she call home from the party to ask about Paul? In what sense is she "lucky" and yet blind to that fact?

7. If this is basically a kind of "morality tale," why does Lawrence go to such pains to give his characters clearly defined personalities?

8. As Paul puts it, he can "get there" on his rocking-horse. What is meant by the phrase? Is he doomed because he sought "luck" or because he used the power he found to satisfy greed? If the rocking-horse is the means of getting "there," what can it be said to symbolize?

9. Except for the descriptions of Paul on his rocking-horse and on his death bed, the story has a casual, childlike air to it, consistent with the kind of off-handedness we use when talking about someone's being "lucky." And yet the final impression is indeed terrible as we realize where Paul's "there" is. How do you account for the effect of terror in the story?

Winter Night

KAY BOYLE

There is a time of apprehension which begins with the beginning of darkness, and to which only the speech of love can lend security. It is there, in abeyance, at the end of every day, not urgent enough to be given the name of fear but rather of concern for how the hours are to be reprieved from fear, and those who have forgotten how it was when they were children can remember nothing of this. It may begin around five o'clock on a winter afternoon when the light outside is dying in the windows. At that hour the New York apartment in which Felicia lived was filled with shadows, and the little girl would wait alone in the living room, looking out at the winter-stripped trees that stood black in the park against the isolated ovals of unclean snow. Now it was January, and the day had been a cold one; the water of the artificial lake was frozen fast, but because of the cold and the coming darkness, the skaters had ceased to move across its surface. The street that lay between the park and the apartment house was wide, and the two-way streams of cars and busses, some with their head-lamps already shining, advanced and halted, halted and poured swiftly on to the tempo of the traffic signals' altering lights. The time of apprehension had set in, and Felicia, who was seven, stood at the window in the evening and waited before she asked the question. When the signals below would change from red to green again, or when the double-decker bus would turn the corner below, she would ask it. The words of it were already there, tentative in her mouth, when the answer came from the far end of the hall.

"Your mother," said the voice among the sound of kitchen things, "she telephoned up before you came in from nursery school.

She won't be back in time for supper. I was to tell you a sitter was coming in from the sitting parents' place."

Felicia turned back from the window into the obscurity of the living room, and she looked toward the open door, and into the hall beyond it where the light from the kitchen fell in a clear yellow angle across the wall and onto the strip of carpet. Her hands were cold, and she put them in her jacket pockets as she walked carefully across the living-room rug and stopped at the edge of light.

"Will she be home late?" she said.

For a moment there was the sound of water running in the kitchen, a long way away, and then the sound of the water ceased, and the high, Southern voice went on:

"She'll come home when she gets ready to come home. That's all I have to say. If she wants to spend two dollars and fifty cents and ten cents carfare on top of that three or four nights out of the week for a sitting parent to come in here and sit, it's her own business. It certainly ain't nothing to do with you or me. She makes her money, just like the rest of us does. She works all day down there in the office, or whatever it is, just like the rest of us works, and she's entitled to spend her money like she wants to spend it. There's no law in the world against buying your own freedom. Your mother and me, we're just buying our own freedom, that's all we're doing. And we're not doing nobody no harm."

"Do you know who she's having supper with?" said Felicia from the edge of the dark. There was one more step to take, and then she would be standing in the light that fell on the strip of carpet, but she did not take the step.

"Do I know who she's having supper with?" the voice cried out in what might have been derision, and there was the sound of dishes striking the metal ribs of the drainboard by the sink. "Maybe it's Mr. Van Johnson, or Mr. Frank Sinatra, or maybe it's just the Duke of Wincers for the evening. All I know is you're having soft-boiled egg and spinach and applesauce for supper, and you're going to have it quick now because the time is getting away."

The voice from the kitchen had no name. It was as variable as the faces and figures of the women who came and sat in the evenings. Month by month the voice in the kitchen altered to another voice, and the sitting parents were no more than lonely aunts of an evening or two who sometimes returned and sometimes did not to this apartment in which they had sat before. Nobody stayed anywhere very long any more, Felicia's mother told her. It was part of the time in which you lived, and part of the life of the city, but when the fathers came back, all this would be miraculously changed. Perhaps you would live in a house again, a small one, with fir trees on either side of the short brick walk, and Father would drive up every night from the station just after darkness set in. When Felicia thought of this, she stepped quickly into the clear angle of light, and she left the dark of the living room behind her and ran softly down the hall.

The drop-leaf table stood in the kitchen between the refrigerator and the sink, and Felicia sat down at the place that was set. The voice at the sink was speaking still, and while Felicia ate it did not cease to speak until the bell of the front door rang abruptly. The girl walked around the table and went down the hall, wiping her dark palms in her apron, and, from the drop-leaf table, Felicia watched her step from the angle of light into darkness and open the door.

"You put in an early appearance," the girl said, and the woman who had rung the bell came into the hall. The door closed behind her, and the girl showed her into the living room, and lit the lamp on the bookcase, and the shadows were suddenly bleached away. But when the girl turned, the woman turned from the living room too and followed her, humbly and in silence, to the threshold of the kitchen. "Sometimes they keep me standing around waiting after it's time for me to be getting on home, the sitting parents do," the girl said, and she picked up the last two dishes from the table and put them in the sink. The woman who stood in the doorway was a small woman, and when she undid the white silk scarf from around her head, Felicia saw that her hair was black. She wore it parted in the middle, and it had not been cut, but was drawn back loosely into a knot behind her head. She had very clean white gloves on, and her face was pale, and there was a look of sorrow in her soft black eyes. "Sometimes I have to stand out there in the hall with my hat and coat on, waiting for the sitting parents to turn up," the girl said, and, as she turned on the water in the sink, the contempt she had for them hung on the kitchen air. "But you're ahead of time," she said, and she held the dishes, first one and then the other, under the flow of steaming water.

The woman in the doorway wore a neat black coat, not a new-looking coat, and it had no fur on it, but had a smooth velvet collar and velvet lapels. She did not move, or smile, and she gave no sign that she had heard the girl speaking above the sound of water at the sink. She simply stood looking at Felicia, who sat at the table with the milk in her glass not finished yet.

"Are you the child?" she said at last, and her voice was low, and the pronunciation of the words a little strange.

"Yes, this here's Felicia," the girl said, and the dark hands dried the dishes and put them away. "You drink up your milk quick now, Felicia, so's I can rinse your glass."

"I will wash the glass," said the woman. "I would like to wash the glass for her," and Felicia sat looking across the table at the face in the doorway that was filled with such unspoken grief. "I will wash the glass for her and clean off the table," the woman was saying quietly. "When the child is finished, she will show me where her night things are."

"The others, they wouldn't do anything like that," the girl said, and she hung the dishcloth over the rack. "They wouldn't put their hand to housework, the sitting parents. That's where they got the name for them," she said.

Whenever the front door closed behind the girl in the evening, it would usually be that the sitting parent who was there would take up a book of fairy stories and read aloud for a while to Felicia; or else would settle herself in the big chair in the living room and begin to tell the words of a story in drowsiness to her, while Felicia took off her clothes in the bedroom, and folded them, and put her pajamas on, and brushed her teeth, and did her hair. But this time, that was not the way it happened. Instead, the woman sat down on the other chair at the kitchen table, and she began at once to speak, not of good fairies or bad, or of animals endowed with human speech, but to speak quietly, in spite of the eagerness behind her words, of a thing that seemed of singular importance to her.

"It is strange that I should have been sent here tonight," she said, her eyes moving slowly from feature to feature of Felicia's face, "for you look like a child that I knew once, and this is the anniversary of that child."

"Did she have hair like mine?" Felicia asked quickly, and she did not keep her eyes fixed on the unfinished glass of milk in shyness any more.

"Yes, she did. She had hair like yours," said the woman, and her glance paused for a moment on the locks which fell straight and thick on the shoulders of Felicia's dress. It may have been that she thought to stretch out her hand and touch the ends of Felicia's hair, for her fingers stirred as they lay clasped together on the table, and then they relapsed into passivity again. "But it is not the hair alone, it is the delicacy of your face, too, and your eyes the same, filled with the same spring lilac color," the woman said, pronouncing the words carefully. "She had little coats of golden fur on her arms and legs," she said, "and when we were closed up there, the lot of us in the cold, I used to make her laugh when I told her that the fur that was so pretty, like a little fawn's skin on her arms, would always help to keep her warm."

"And did it keep her warm?" asked Felicia, and she gave a little jerk of laughter as she looked down at her own legs hanging under the table, with the bare calves thin and covered with a down of hair.

"It did not keep her warm enough," the woman said, and now the mask of grief had come back upon her face. "So we used to take everything we could spare from ourselves, and we would sew them into cloaks and other kinds of garments for her and for the other children. . . ."

"Was it a school?" said Felicia when the woman's voice had ceased to speak.

"No," said the woman softly, "it was not a school, but still there were a lot of children there. It was a camp—that was the name the place had; it was a camp. It was a place where they put people until they could decide what was to be done with them." She sat with her hands clasped, silent a moment, looking at Felicia. "That little dress you have on," she said, not saying the words to anybody, scarcely saying them aloud. "Oh, she would have liked that little dress, the little buttons shaped like hearts, and the white collar—"

"I have four school dresses," Felicia said. "I'll show them to you. How many dresses did she have?"

"Well, there, you see, there in the camp," said the woman, "she did not have any dresses except the little skirt and the pullover. That was all she had. She had brought just a handkerchief of her belongings with her, like everybody else—just enough for three days away from home was what they told us, so she did not have enough to last the winter. But she had her ballet slippers," the woman said, and her clasped fingers did not move. "She had brought them because she thought during her three days away from home she would have the time to practice her ballet."

"I've been to the ballet," Felicia said suddenly, and she said it so eagerly that she stuttered a little as the words came out of her mouth. She slipped quickly down from the chair and went around the table to where the woman sat. Then she took one of the woman's hands away from the other that held it fast, and she pulled her toward the door. "Come into the living room and I'll do a pirouette for you," she said, and then she stopped speaking, her eyes halted on the woman's face. "Did she—did the little girl—could she do a pirouette very well?" she said.

"Yes, she could. At first she could," said the woman, and Felicia felt uneasy now at the sound of sorrow in her words. "But after that she was hungry. She was hungry all winter," she said in a low voice: "We were all hungry, but the children were the hungriest. Even now," she said, and her voice went suddenly savage, "when I see milk like that, clean, fresh milk standing in a glass, I want to cry out loud, I want to beat my hands on the table, because it did not have to be . . ." She had drawn her fingers abruptly away from Felicia now, and Felicia stood before her, cast off, forlorn, alone again in the time of apprehension. "That was three years ago," the woman was saying, and one hand was lifted, as in weariness, to shade her face. "It was somewhere else, it was in another country," she said, and behind her hand her eyes were turned upon the substance of a world in which Felicia had played no part.

"Did—did the little girl cry when she was hungry?" Felicia asked, and the woman shook her head.

"Sometimes she cried," she said, "but not very much. She was very quiet. One night when she heard the other children crying, she said to me, 'You know, they are not crying because they want something to eat. They are crying because their mothers have gone away.'"

"Did the mothers have to go out to supper?" Felicia asked, and she watched the woman's face for the answer.

"No," said the woman. She stood up from her chair, and now that she put her hand on the little girl's shoulder, Felicia was taken into the sphere of love and intimacy again. "Shall we go into the other room, and you will do your pirouette for me?" the woman said, and they went from the kitchen and down the strip of carpet on which the clear light fell. In the front room, they paused hand in hand in the glow of the shaded lamp, and the woman looked about her, at the books, the low tables with the magazines and ash trays on them, the vase of roses on the piano, looking with dark, scarcely seeing eyes at these things that had no reality at all. It was only when she saw the little white clock on the mantelpiece that she gave any sign, and then she said quickly: "What time does your mother put you to bed?"

Felicia waited a moment, and in the interval of waiting the woman lifted one hand and, as if in reverence, touched Felicia's hair.

"What time did the little girl you knew in the other place go to bed?" Felicia asked.

"Ah, God, I do not know, I do not remember," the woman said.

"Was she your little girl?" said Felicia softly, stubbornly.

"No," said the woman. "She was not mine. At least, at first she was not mine. She had a mother, a real mother, but the mother had to go away."

"Did she come back late?" asked Felicia.

"No, ah, no, she could not come back, she never came back,"

the woman said, and now she turned, her arm around Felicia's shoulders, and she sat down in the low soft chair. "Why am I saying all this to you, why am I doing it?" she cried out in grief, and she held Felicia close against her. "I had thought to speak of the anniversary to you, and that was all, and now I am saying these other things to you. Three years ago today, exactly, the little girl became my little girl because her mother went away. That is all there is to it. There is nothing more."

Felicia waited another moment, held close against the woman, and listening to the swift, strong heartbeats in the woman's breast.

"But the mother," she said then in the small, persistent voice, "did she take a taxi when she went?"

"This is the way it used to happen," said the woman, speaking in hopelessness and bitterness in the softly lighted room. "Every week they used to come into the place where we were and they would read a list of names out. Sometimes it would be the names of children they would read out, and then a little later they would have to go away. And sometimes it would be the grown people's names, the names of the mothers or big sisters, or other women's names. The men were not with us. The fathers were somewhere else, in another place."

"Yes," Felicia said. "I know."

"We had been there only a little while, maybe ten days or maybe not so long," the woman went on, holding Felicia against her still, "when they read the name of the little girl's mother out, and that afternoon they took her away."

"What did the little girl do?" Felicia said.

"She wanted to think up the best way of getting out so that she could go find her mother," said the woman, "but she could not think of anything good enough until the third or fourth day. And then she tied her ballet slippers up in the handkerchief again, and she went up to the guard standing at the door." The woman's voice was gentle, controlled now. "She asked the guard please to open the door so that she could go out. 'This is Thursday,' she said, 'and every Tuesday and Thursday I have my ballet lessons. If I miss a ballet lesson, they do not count the money off, so my mother would just be paying for nothing, and she cannot afford to pay for nothing. I missed my ballet lesson on Tuesday,' she said to the guard, 'and I must not miss it again today.' "

Felicia lifted her head from the woman's shoulder, and she shook her hair back and looked in question and wonder at the woman's face.

"And did the man let her go?" she said.

"No, he did not. He could not do that," said the woman. "He was a soldier and he had to do what he was told. So every evening after her mother went, I used to brush the little girl's hair for her," the woman went on saying. "And while I brushed it, I used to tell her the stories of the ballets. Sometimes I would begin with *Narcissus*," the woman said, and she parted Felicia's locks with her fingers, "so if you will go and get your brush now, I will tell it while I brush your hair."

"Oh, yes," said Felicia, and she made two whirls as she went quickly to the bedroom. On the way back, she stopped and held on to the piano with the fingers of one hand while she went up on her toes. "Did you see me? Did you see me standing on my toes?" she called to the woman, and the woman sat smiling in love and contentment at her.

"Yes, wonderful, really wonderful," she said. "I am sure I have never seen anyone do it so well." Felicia came spinning toward her, whirling in pirouette after pirouette, and she flung herself down in the chair close to her, with her thin bones pressed against the woman's soft, wide hip. The woman took the silver-backed, mono-grammed brush and the tortoise-shell comb in her hands, and now she began to brush Felicia's hair. "We did not have any soap at all and not very much water to wash in, so I never could fix her as nicely and prettily as I wanted to," she said, and the brush stroked regularly, carefully down, caressing the shape of Felicia's head.

"If there wasn't very much water, then how did she do her teeth?" Felicia said.

"She did not do her teeth," said the woman, and she drew the comb through Felicia's hair. "There were not any toothbrushes or tooth paste, or anything like that."

Felicia waited a moment, constructing the unfamiliar scene of it in silence, and then she asked the tentative question.

"Do I have to do my teeth tonight?" she said.

"No," said the woman, and she was thinking of something else, "you do not have to do your teeth."

"If I am your little girl tonight, can I pretend there isn't enough water to wash?" said Felicia.

"Yes," said the woman, "You can pretend that if you like. You do not have to wash," she said, and the comb passed lightly through Felicia's hair.

"Will you tell me the story of the ballet?" said Felicia, and the rhythm of the brushing was like the soft, slow rocking of sleep.

"Yes," said the woman. "In the first one, the place is a forest glade with little pale birches growing in it, and they have green veils over their faces and green veils drifting from their fingers, because it is the springtime. There is the music of a flute," said the woman's voice softly, softly, "and creatures of the wood dancing——"

"But the mother," Felicia said as suddenly as if she had been awaked from sleep. "What did the little girl's mother say when she didn't do her teeth and didn't wash at night?"

"The mother was not there, you remember," said the woman, and the brush moved steadily in her hand. "But she did send one little letter back. Sometimes the people who went away were able to do that. The mother wrote it in a train, standing up in a car that had no seats," she said, and she might have been telling the story of the ballet still, for her voice was gentle and the brush did not falter on Felicia's hair. "There were perhaps a great many other people standing up in the train with her, perhaps all trying to write their little letters on the bits of paper they had managed to hide on them, or that they had found in forgotten corners as they traveled. When they had written their letters, then they must try to slip them out through the boards of the car in which they journeyed, standing up," said the woman, "and these letters fell down on the tracks under the train, or they were blown into the fields or onto the country roads, and if it was a kind person who picked them up, he would seal them in envelopes and send them to where they were addressed to go. So a letter came back like this from the little girl's mother," the woman said, and the brush followed the comb, the comb the brush in steady pursuit through Felicia's hair. "It said good-by to the little girl, and it said please take care of her. It said: 'Whoever reads this letter in the camp, please take good care of my little girl for me, and please have her tonsils looked at by a doctor if this is possible to do.' "

"And then," said Felicia softly, persistently, "what happened to the little girl?"

"I do not know. I cannot say," the woman said. But now the brush and comb had ceased to move, and in the silence Felicia turned her thin, small body on the chair, and she and the woman suddenly put their arms around each other. "They must all be asleep now, all of them," the woman said, and in the silence that fell on them again, they held each other closer. "They must be quietly asleep somewhere, and not crying all night because they are hungry and because they are cold. For three years I have been saying, 'They must all be asleep, and the cold and the hunger and the seasons or night or day or nothing matters to them——' "

It was after midnight when Felicia's mother put her key in the lock of the front door, and pushed it open, and stepped into the hallway. She walked quickly to the living room, and just across the threshold she slipped the three blue foxskins from her shoulders and dropped them, with her little velvet bag, upon the chair. The room was quiet, so quiet that she could hear the sound of breathing in it, and no one spoke to her in greeting as she crossed toward the bedroom door. And then, as startling as a slap across her delicately tinted face, she saw the woman lying sleeping on the divan, and Felicia, in her school dress still, asleep within the woman's arms.

Exercises

1. How do the opening sentences set the tone of the whole story? Do you agree with the observations? For whom are the observations true? Is it only particularly sensitive or lonely children in isolated apartments who have this "concern for how the hours are to be reprieved from fear"? What is the narrator setting up here and what would be lost if the story started with paragraph two?

2. What kind of person is the "voice" from the kitchen? What do we learn through her about Felicia's mother besides factual information? In what ways especially does she contrast with the sitting parent?

3. Why is the "voice" from the kitchen nameless? Who else in the story is nameless? Why? In this connection, consider the parallel story the sitting parent tells.

4. The girl in the kitchen says: "There's no law in the world against buying your own freedom. Your mother and me, we're just buying our freedom, that's all we're doing. And we're not doing nobody no harm." What does "buying our own freedom" mean? What is "freedom" in this story? What is "doing . . . harm"? How much freedom has either the mother or the maid bought? At what expense?

5. How much of all that the sitter says does Felicia understand? How much could she understand if the sitter tried to explain further. In what sense is Felicia simply a substitute for the "anniversary" child, a springboard for memory? Does the sitter see her as more than that? Discuss.

6. Why does Felicia's innocence about what the sitter is relating make more terrible the enormity of that experience? How does the parallel story of the little girl in the camp help the reader comprehend Felicia's world? How does it comment on the world of Felicia's mother?

7. What is Felicia's mother's reaction when she returns home? What is the phrase, "as startling as a slap across her delicately tinted face," meant to convey? Why is she startled? Why *should* she be startled? Is she wrong for leaving Felicia with a sitter? Why or why not?

8. What does Felicia's name mean? Why is it appropriate to what Kay Boyle is saying and to how she says it (the carefully structured ironies of the situation)?

9. The apartment high above Central Park is perfectly safe for a little girl. What, then, causes her anxiety, her insecurity, her unwillingness to step beyond "the edge of light"? Compare her situation with that of the children in "The Man Child" and "The Rocking-Horse Winner."

III   *The popular metaphor for explaining our congenital failure to under-stand, appreciate, relate to, show compassion for—love—other human beings is some variety of "gap": "generation gap," "communication gap," "cultural gap," "spiritual gap." Most of us feel uncomfortable with the metaphor, at least as it applies to us individually, and maybe that's the greatest gap of all—the gap between what we like to think we are and what we really are. Whether or not the metaphor is a too mechanical and simplistic explanation, it illuminates an abiding truth about the human condition.*

The five stories that follow probe the alienation, the nonlove, created and sustained by the blindness and indifference of people to the ways and needs of other people. In some cases, the attitude is open and arrogant; in others, faceless and detached; in still others, simply ignorant and self-justifying. In all cases it is cruel, dehumanizing, unloving. The treatments vary from bitter to ironic to triumphantly humorous.

Flight

JOHN STEINBECK

About fifteen miles below Monterey, on the wild coast, the Torres family had their farm, a few sloping acres above a cliff that dropped to the brown reefs and to the hissing white waters of the ocean. Behind the farm the stone mountains stood up against the sky. The farm buildings huddled like little clinging aphids[1] on the mountain skirts, crouched low to the ground as though the wind might blow them into the sea. The little shack, the rattling, rotting barn were gray-bitten with sea salt, beaten by the damp wind until they had taken on the color of the granite hills. Two horses, a red cow and a red calf, half a dozen pigs and a flock of lean, multi-colored chickens stocked the place. A little corn was raised on the sterile slope, and it grew short and thick under the wind, and all the cobs formed on the landward sides of the stalks.

Mama Torres, a lean, dry woman with ancient eyes, had ruled the farm for ten years, ever since her husband tripped over a stone in the field one day and fell full length on a rattlesnake. When one is bitten on the chest there is not much that can be done.

Mama Torres had three children, two undersized black ones of twelve and fourteen, Emilio and Rosy, whom Mama kept fishing on the rocks below the farm when the sea was kind and when the truant officer was in some distant part of Monterey County. And there was Pepé, the tall smiling son of nineteen, a gentle, affectionate boy, but very lazy. Pepé had a tall head, pointed at the top, and from its peak, coarse black hair grew down like a thatch all around. Over his smiling little eyes Mama cut a straight bang so he could see. Pepé had sharp Indian cheekbones and an eagle nose, but his mouth was as sweet and shapely as a girl's mouth, and his chin was fragile and chiseled. He was loose and gangling, all legs and feet and wrists, and he was very lazy. Mama thought him

[1] **aphids:** insects that live on the juice of plants.

fine and brave, but she never told him so. She said, "Some lazy cow must have got into thy father's family, else how could I have a son like thee." And she said, "When I carried thee, a sneaking lazy coyote came out of the brush and looked at me one day. That must have made thee so."

Pepé smiled sheepishly and stabbed at the ground with his knife to keep the blade sharp and free from rust. It was his inheritance, that knife, his father's knife. The long heavy blade folded back into the black handle. There was a button on the handle. When Pepé pressed the button, the blade leaped out ready for use. The knife was with Pepé always, for it had been his father's knife.

One sunny morning when the sea below the cliff was glinting and blue and the white surf creamed on the reef, when even the stone mountains looked kindly, Mama Torres called out the door of the shack, "Pepé, I have a labor for thee."

There was no answer. Mama listened. From behind the barn she heard a burst of laughter. She lifted her full long skirt and walked in the direction of the noise.

Pepé was sitting on the ground with his back against a box. His white teeth glistened. On either side of him stood the two black ones, tense and expectant. Fifteen feet away a redwood post was set in the ground. Pepé's right hand lay limply in his lap, and in the palm the big black knife rested. The blade was closed back into the handle. Pepé looked smiling at the sky.

Suddenly Emilio cried, "Ya!"

Pepé's wrist flicked like the head of a snake. The blade seemed to fly open in mid-air, and with a thump the point dug into the redwood post, and the black handle quivered. The three burst into excited laughter. Rosy ran to the post and pulled out the knife and brought it back to Pepé. He closed the blade and settled the knife carefully in his listless palm again. He grinned self-consciously at the sky.

"Ya!"

The heavy knife lanced out and sunk into the post again. Mama moved forward like a ship and scattered the play.

"All day you do foolish things with the knife, like a toy-baby," she stormed. "Get up on thy huge feet that eat up shoes. Get up!" She

took him by one loose shoulder and hoisted at him. Pepé grinned sheepishly and came half-heartedly to his feet. "Look!" Mama cried. "Big
lazy, you must catch the horse and put on him thy father's saddle. You
must ride to Monterey. The medicine bottle is empty. There is no salt.
Go thou now, Peanut! Catch the horse."

A revolution took place in the relaxed figure of Pepé. "To Monterey,
me? Alone? *Sí,* Mama."

She scowled at him. "Do not think, big sheep, that you will buy
candy. No, I will give you only enough for the medicine and the salt."

Pepé smiled. "Mama, you will put the hatband on the hat?"

She relented then. "Yes, Pepé. You may wear the hatband."

His voice grew insinuating, "And the green handkerchief, Mama?"

"Yes, if you go quickly and return with no trouble, the silk green
handkerchief will go. If you make sure to take off the handkerchief
when you eat so no spot may fall on it. . . ."

"*Sí,* Mama. I will be careful. I am a man."

"Thou? A man? Thou art a peanut."

He went into the rickety barn and brought out a rope, and he walked
agilely enough up the hill to catch the horse.

When he was ready and mounted before the door, mounted on his
father's saddle that was so old that the oaken frame showed through
torn leather in many places, then Mama brought out the round black
hat with the tooled leather band, and she reached up and knotted the
green silk handkerchief about his neck. Pepé's blue denim coat was
much darker than his jeans, for it had been washed much less often.

Mama handed up the big medicine bottle and the silver coins. "That
for the medicine," she said, "and that for the salt. That for a candle to
burn for the papa. That for *dulces*[2] for the little ones. Our friend Mrs.
Rodriguez will give you dinner and maybe a bed for the night. When
you go to the church say only ten Paternosters[3] and only twenty-five
Ave Marias.[4] Oh! I know, big coyote. You would sit there flapping
your mouth over Aves all day while you looked at the candles and the
holy pictures. That is not good devotion to stare at the pretty things."

---

[2]*dulces:* candy.
[3]**Paternosters:** Our Fathers; i.e., Lord's Prayers.
[4]**Ave Marias:** Hail Marys.

The black hat, covering the high pointed head and black thatched hair of Pepé, gave him dignity and age. He sat the rangy horse well. Mama thought how handsome he was, dark and lean and tall. "I would not send thee now alone, thou little one, except for the medicine," she said softly. "It is not good to have no medicine, for who knows when the toothache will come, or the sadness of the stomach. These things are."

"Adios, Mama," Pepé cried. "I will come back soon. You may send me often alone. I am a man."

"Thou art a foolish chicken."

He straightened his shoulders, flipped the reins against the horse's shoulder and rode away. He turned once and saw that they still watched him, Emilio and Rosy and Mama. Pepé grinned with pride and gladness and lifted the tough buckskin horse to a trot.

When he had dropped out of sight over a little dip in the road, Mama turned to the black ones, but she spoke to herself. "He is nearly a man now," she said. "It will be a nice thing to have a man in the house again." Her eyes sharpened on the children. "Go to the rocks now. The tide is going out. There will be abalones to be found." She put the iron hooks into their hands and saw them down the steep trail to the reefs. She brought the smooth stone *metate*[5] to the doorway and sat grinding her corn to flour and looking occasionally at the road over which Pepé had gone. The noonday came and then the afternoon, when the little ones beat the abalones on a rock to make them tender and Mama patted the tortillas to make them thin. They ate their dinner as the red sun was plunging down toward the ocean. They sat on the doorsteps and watched the big white moon come over the mountain tops.

Mama said, "He is now at the house of our friend Mrs. Rodriguez. She will give him nice things to eat and maybe a present."

Emilio said, "Some day I too will ride to Monterey for medicine. Did Pepé come to be a man today?"

Mama said wisely, "A boy gets to be a man when a man is needed. Remember this thing. I have known boys forty years old because there was no need for a man."

Soon afterwards they retired, Mama in her big oak bed on one side

°*metate:* a stone used for grinding grain.

of the room, Emilio and Rosy in their boxes full of straw and sheepskins on the other side of the room.

The moon went over the sky and the surf roared on the rocks. The roosters crowed the first call. The surf subsided to a whispering surge against the reef. The moon dropped toward the sea. The roosters crowed again.

The moon was near down to the water when Pepé rode on a winded horse to his home flat. His dog bounced out and circled the horse yelping with pleasure. Pepé slid off the saddle to the ground. The weathered little shack was silver in the moonlight and the square shadow of it was black to the north and east. Against the east the piling mountains were misty with light; their tops melted into the sky.

Pepé walked wearily up the three steps and into the house. It was dark inside. There was a rustle in the corner.

Mama cried out from her bed. "Who comes? Pepé, is it thou?"

"*Sí*, Mama."

"Did you get the medicine?"

"*Sí*, Mama."

"Well, go to sleep, then. I thought you would be sleeping at the house of Mrs. Rodriguez." Pepé stood silently in the dark room. "Why do you stand there, Pepé? Did you drink wine?"

"*Sí*, Mama."

"Well, go to bed then and sleep out the wine."

His voice was tired and patient, but very firm. "Light the candle, Mama. I must go away into the mountains."

"What is this, Pepé? You are crazy." Mama struck a sulphur match and held the little blue burr until the flame spread up the stick. She set light to the candle on the floor beside her bed. "Now, Pepé, what is this you say?" She looked anxiously into his face.

He was changed. The fragile quality seemed to have gone from his chin. His mouth was less full than it had been, the lines of the lips were straighter, but in his eyes the greatest change had taken place. There was no laughter in them any more nor any bashfulness. They were sharp and bright and purposeful.

He told her in a tired monotone, told her everything just as it had happened. A few people came into the kitchen of Mrs. Rodriguez. There was wine to drink. Pepé drank wine. The little quarrel—the man started toward Pepé and then the knife—it went almost by itself. It flew, it darted before Pepé knew it. As he talked, Mama's face grew stern, and it seemed to grow more lean. Pepé finished. "I am a man now, Mama. The man said names to me I could not allow."

Mama nodded. "Yes, thou art a man, my poor little Pepé. Thou art a man. I have seen it coming on thee. I have watched you throwing the knife into the post, and I have been afraid." For a moment her face had softened, but now it grew stern again. "Come! We must get you ready. Go. Awaken Emilio and Rosy. Go quickly."

Pepé stepped over to the corner where his brother and sister slept among the sheepskins. He leaned down and shook them gently. "Come, Rosy! Come, Emilio! The mama says you must arise."

The little black ones sat up and rubbed their eyes in the candlelight. Mama was out of bed now, her long black skirt over her nightgown. "Emilio," she cried. "Go up and catch the other horse for Pepé. Quickly now! Quickly." Emilio put his legs in his overalls and stumbled sleepily out the door.

"You heard no one behind you on the road?" Mama demanded.

"No, Mama. I listened carefully. No one was on the road."

Mama darted like a bird about the room. From a nail on the wall she took a canvas water bag and threw it on the floor. She stripped a blanket from her bed and rolled it into a tight tube and tied the ends with string. From a box beside the stove she lifted a flour sack half full of black stringy jerky.[6] "Your father's black coat, Pepé. Here, put it on."

Pepé stood in the middle of the floor watching her activity. She reached behind the door and brought out the rifle, a long 38-56, worn shiny the whole length of the barrel. Pepé took it from her and held it in the crook of his elbow. Mama brought a little leather bag and counted the cartridges into his hand. "Only ten left," she warned. "You must not waste them."

Emilio put his head in the door. " *'Qui 'st 'l caballo,* Mama."

[6]**jerky:**   long slices of sun-dried meat.

"Put on the saddle from the other horse. Tie on the blanket. Here, tie the jerky to the saddle horn."

Still Pepé stood silently watching his mother's frantic activity. His chin looked hard, and his sweet mouth was drawn and thin. His little eyes followed Mama about the room almost suspiciously.

Rosy asked softly, "Where goes Pepé?"

Mama's eyes were fierce. "Pepé goes on a journey. Pepé is a man now. He has a man's thing to do."

Pepé straightened his shoulders. His mouth changed until he looked very much like Mama.

At last the preparation was finished. The loaded horse stood outside the door. The water bag dripped a line of moisture down the bay shoulder.

The moonlight was being thinned by the dawn and the big white moon was near down to the sea. The family stood by the shack. Mama confronted Pepé. "Look, my son! Do not stop until it is dark again. Do not sleep even though you are tired. Take care of the horse in order that he may not stop of weariness. Remember to be careful with the bullets— there are only ten. Do not fill thy stomach with jerky or it will make thee sick. Eat a little jerky and fill thy stomach with grass. When thou comest to the high mountains, if thou seest any of the dark watching men, go not near to them nor try to speak to them. And forget not thy prayers." She put her lean hands on Pepé's shoulders, stood on her toes and kissed him formally on both cheeks, and Pepé kissed her on both cheeks. Then he went to Emilio and Rosy and kissed both of their cheeks.

Pepé turned back to Mama. He seemed to look for a little softness, a little weakness in her. His eyes were searching, but Mama's face remained fierce. "Go now," she said. "Do not wait to be caught like a chicken."

Pepé pulled himself into the saddle. "I am a man," he said.

It was the first dawn when he rode up the hill toward the little canyon which let a trail into the mountains. Moonlight and daylight fought with each other, and the two warring qualities made it difficult to see. Before Pepé had gone a hundred yards, the outlines of his figure were misty; and long before he entered the canyon, he had become a gray, indefinite shadow.

Mama stood stiffly in front of her doorstep, and on either side of her stood Emilio and Rosy. They cast furtive glances at Mama now and then.

When the gray shape of Pepé melted into the hillside and disappeared, Mama relaxed. She began the high, whining keen[7] of the death wail. "Our beautiful—our brave," she cried. "Our protector, our son is gone." Emilio and Rosy moaned beside her. "Our beautiful—our brave, he is gone." It was the formal wail. It rose to a high piercing whine and subsided to a moan. Mama raised it three times and then she turned and went into the house and shut the door.

Emilio and Rosy stood wondering in the dawn. They heard Mama whimpering in the house. They went out to sit on the cliff above the ocean. They touched shoulders. "When did Pepé come to be a man?" Emilio asked.

"Last night," said Rosy. "Last night in Monterey." The ocean clouds turned red with the sun that was behind the mountains.

"We will have no breakfast," said Emilio. "Mama will not want to cook." Rosy did not answer him. "Where is Pepé gone?" he asked.

Rosy looked around at him. She drew her knowledge from the quiet air. "He has gone on a journey. He will never come back."

"Is he dead? Do you think he is dead?"

Rosy looked back at the ocean again. A little steamer, drawing a line of smoke, sat on the edge of the horizon. "He is not dead," Rosy explained. "Not yet."

FORESHADOWING

Pepé rested the big rifle across the saddle in front of him. He let the horse walk up the hill and he didn't look back. The stony slope took on a coat of short brush so that Pepé found the entrance to a trail and entered it.

When he came to the canyon opening, he swung once in his saddle and looked back, but the houses were swallowed in the misty light. Pepé jerked forward again. The high shoulder of the canyon closed in

---

[7]**keen:** a loud, wailing cry, mourning death.

on him. His horse stretched out its neck and sighed and settled to the trail.

It was a well-worn path, dark soft leaf-mold earth strewn with broken pieces of sandstone. The trail rounded the shoulder of the canyon and dropped steeply into the bed of the stream. In the shallows the water ran smoothly, glinting in the first morning sun. Small round stones on the bottom were as brown as rust with sun moss. In the sand along the edges of the stream the tall, rich wild mint grew, while in the water itself the cress, old and tough, had gone to heavy seed.

The path went into the stream and emerged on the other side. The horse sloshed into the water and stopped. Pepé dropped his bridle and let the beast drink of the running water.

Soon the canyon sides became steep and the first giant sentinel redwoods guarded the trail, great round red trunks bearing foliage as green and lacy as ferns. Once Pepé was among the trees, the sun was lost. A perfumed and purple light lay in the pale green of the underbrush. Gooseberry bushes and blackberries and tall ferns lined the stream, and overhead the branches of the redwoods met and cut off the sky.

Pepé drank from the water bag, and he reached into the flour sack and brought out a black string of jerky. His white teeth gnawed at the string until the tough meat parted. He chewed slowly and drank occasionally from the water bag. His little eyes were slumberous and tired, but the muscles of his face were hard set. The earth of the trail was black now. It gave up a hollow sound under the walking hoofbeats.

The stream fell more sharply. Little waterfalls splashed on the stones. Five-fingered ferns hung over the water and dripped spray from their fingertips. Pepé rode half over in his saddle, dangling one leg loosely. He picked a bay leaf from a tree beside the way and put it into his mouth for a moment to flavor the dry jerky. He held the gun loosely across the pommel.

Suddenly he squared in his saddle, swung the horse from the trail and kicked it hurriedly up behind a big redwood tree. He pulled up the reins tight against the bit to keep the horse from whinnying. His face was intent and his nostrils quivered a little.

A hollow pounding came down the trail, and a horseman rode by, a fat man with red cheeks and a white stubble beard. His horse put down its head and blubbered at the trail when it came to the place where Pepé had turned off. "Hold up!" said the man and he pulled up his horse's head.

When the last sound of the hoofs died away, Pepé came back into the trail again. He did not relax in the saddle any more. He lifted the big rifle and swung the lever to throw a shell into the chamber, and then he let down the hammer to half cock.

The trail grew very steep. Now the redwood trees were smaller and their tops were dead, bitten dead where the wind reached them. The horse plodded on; the sun went slowly overhead and started down toward the afternoon.

Where the stream came out of a side canyon, the trail left it. Pepé dismounted and watered his horse and filled up his water bag. As soon as the trail had parted from the stream, the trees were gone and only the thick brittle sage and manzanita and chaparral edged the trail. And the soft black earth was gone, too, leaving only the light tan broken rock for the trail bed. Lizards scampered away into the brush as the horse rattled over the little stones.

Pepé turned in his saddle and looked back. He was in the open now: he could be seen from a distance. As he ascended the trail the country grew more rough and terrible and dry. The way wound about the bases of great square rocks. Little gray rabbits skittered in the brush. A bird made a monotonous high creaking. Eastward the bare rock mountain-tops were pale and powder-dry under the dropping sun. The horse plodded up and up the trail toward a little V in the ridge which was the pass.

Pepé looked suspiciously back every minute or so, and his eyes sought the tops of the ridges ahead. Once, on a white barren spur, he saw a black figure for a moment, but he looked quickly away, for it was one of the dark watchers. No one knew who the watchers were, nor where they lived, but it was better to ignore them and never to show interest in them. They did not bother one who stayed on the trail and minded his own business.

The air was parched and full of light dust blown by the breeze from the eroding mountains. Pepé drank sparingly from his bag and corked it tightly and hung it on the horn again. The trail moved up the dry shale hillside, avoiding rocks, dropping under clefts, climbing in and out of old water scars. When he arrived at the little pass he stopped and looked back for a long time. No dark watchers were to be seen now. The trail behind was empty. Only the high tops of the redwoods indicated where the stream flowed.

Pepé rode on through the pass. His little eyes were nearly closed with weariness, but his face was stern, relentless and manly. The high mountain wind coasted sighing through the pass and whistled on the edges of the big blocks of broken granite. In the air, a red-tailed hawk sailed over close to the ridge and screamed angrily. Pepé went slowly through the broken jagged pass and looked down on the other side.

The trail dropped quickly, staggering among broken rock. At the bottom of the slope there was a dark crease, thick with brush, and on the other side of the crease a little flat, in which a grove of oak trees grew. A scar of green grass cut across the flat. And behind the flat another mountain rose, desolate with dead rocks and starving little black bushes. Pepé drank from the bag again for the air was so dry that it encrusted his nostrils and burned his lips. He put the horse down the trail. The hooves slipped and struggled on the steep way, starting little stones that rolled off into the brush. The sun was gone behind the westward mountain now, but still it glowed brilliantly on the oaks and on the grassy flat. The rocks and the hillsides still sent up waves of the heat they had gathered from the day's sun.

Pepé looked up to the top of the next dry withered ridge. He saw a dark form against the sky, a man's figure standing on top of a rock, and he glanced away quickly not to appear curious. When a moment later he looked up again, the figure was gone.

Downward the trail was quickly covered. Sometimes the horse floundered for footing, sometimes set his feet and slid a little way. They came at last to the bottom where the dark chaparral was higher than Pepé's head. He held up his rifle on one side and his arm on the other to shield his face from the sharp brittle fingers of the brush.

Up and out of the crease he rode, and up a little cliff. The grassy flat was before him, and the round comfortable oaks. For a moment he studied the trail down which he had come, but there was no movement and no sound from it. Finally he rode out over the flat, to the green streak, and at the upper end of the damp he found a little spring welling out of the earth and dropping into a dug basin before it seeped out over the flat.

Pepé filled his bag first, and then he let the thirsty horse drink out of the pool. He led the horse to the clump of oaks, and in the middle of the grove, fairly protected from sight on all sides, he took off the saddle and the bridle and laid them on the ground. The horse stretched his jaws sideways and yawned. Pepé knotted the lead rope about the horse's neck and tied him to a sapling among the oaks, where he could graze in a fairly large circle.

When the horse was gnawing hungrily at the dry grass, Pepé went to the saddle and took a black string of jerky from the sack and strolled to an oak tree on the edge of the grove, from under which he could watch the trail. He sat down in the crisp dry oak leaves and automatically felt for his big black knife to cut the jerky, but he had no knife. He leaned back on his elbow and gnawed at the tough strong meat. His face was blank, but it was a man's face.

The bright evening light washed the eastern ridge, but the valley was darkening. Doves flew down from the hills to the spring, and the quail came running out of the brush and joined them, calling clearly to one another.

Out of the corner of his eye Pepé saw a shadow grow out of the bushy crease. He turned his head slowly. A big spotted wildcat was creeping toward the spring, belly to the ground, moving like thought.

Pepé cocked his rifle and edged the muzzle slowly around. Then he looked apprehensively up the trail and dropped the hammer again. From the ground beside him he picked an oak twig and threw it toward the spring. The quail flew up with a roar and the doves whistled away. The big cat stood up: for a long moment he looked at Pepé with cold yellow eyes, and then fearlessly walked back into the gulch.

The dusk gathered quickly in the deep valley. Pepé muttered his prayers, put his head down on his arm and went instantly to sleep.

The moon came up and filled the valley with cold blue light, and the wind swept rustling down from the peaks. The owls worked up and down the slopes looking for rabbits. Down in the brush of the gulch a coyote gabbled. The oak trees whispered softly in the night breeze.

Pepé started up, listening. His horse had whinnied. The moon was just slipping behind the western ridge, leaving the valley in darkness behind it. Pepé sat tensely gripping his rifle. From far up the trail he heard an answering whinny and the crash of shod hooves on the broken rock. He jumped to his feet, ran to his horse and led it under the trees. He threw on the saddle and cinched it tight for the steep trail, caught the unwilling head and forced the bit into the mouth. He felt the saddle to make sure the water bag and the sack of jerky were there. Then he mounted and turned up the hill.

It was velvet dark. The horse found the entrance to the trail where it left the flat, and started up, stumbling and slipping on the rocks. Pepé's hand rose up to his head. His hat was gone. He had left it under the oak tree.

The horse had struggled far up the trail when the first change of dawn came into the air, a steel grayness as light mixed thoroughly with dark. Gradually the sharp snaggled edge of the ridge stood out above them, rotten granite tortured and eaten by the winds of time. Pepé had dropped his reins on the horn, leaving direction to the horse. The brush grabbed at his legs in the dark until one knee of his jeans was ripped.

Gradually the light flowed down over the ridge. The starved brush and rocks stood out in the half light, strange and lonely in high perspective. Then there came warmth into the light. Pepé drew up and looked back, but he could see nothing in the darker valley below. The sky turned blue over the coming sun. In the waste of the mountainside, the poor dry brush grew only three feet high. Here and there, big outcroppings of unrotted granite stood up like moldering houses. Pepé relaxed a little. He drank from his water bag and bit off a piece of jerky. A single eagle flew over, high in the light.

Without warning Pepé's horse screamed and fell on its side. He was almost down before the rifle crash echoed up from the valley. From a hole behind the struggling shoulder, a stream of bright crimson blood pumped and stopped and pumped and stopped. The hooves threshed on the ground. Pepé lay half stunned beside the horse. He looked slowly down the hill. A piece of sage clipped off beside his head and another crash echoed up from side to side of the canyon. Pepé flung himself frantically behind a bush.

He crawled up the hill on his knees and on one hand. His right hand held the rifle up off the ground and pushed it ahead of him. He moved with the instinctive care of an animal. Rapidly he wormed his way toward one of the big outcroppings of granite on the hill above him. Where the brush was high he doubled up and ran, but where the cover was slight he wriggled forward on his stomach, pushing the rifle ahead of him. In the last little distance there was no cover at all. Pepé poised and then he darted across the space and flashed around the corner of the rock.

He leaned panting against the stone. When his breath came easier he moved along behind the big rock until he came to a narrow slit that offered a thin section of vision down the hill. Pepé lay on his stomach and pushed the rifle barrel through the slit and waited.

The sun reddened the western ridges now. Already the buzzards were settling down toward the place where the horse lay. A small brown bird scratched in the dead sage leaves directly in front of the rifle muzzle. The coasting eagle flew back toward the rising sun.

Pepé saw a little movement in the brush far below. His grip tightened on the gun. A little brown doe stepped daintily out on the trail and crossed it and disappeared into the brush again. For a long time Pepé waited. Far below he could see the little flat and the oak trees and the slash of green. Suddenly his eyes flashed back at the trail again. A quarter of a mile down there had been a quick movement in the chaparral. The rifle swung over. The front sight nestled in the V of the rear sight. Pepé studied for a moment and then raised the rear sight a notch. The little movement in the brush came again. The sight settled on it. Pepé squeezed the trigger. The explosion crashed down the mountain and up the other side, and came rattling back. The whole side of the slope grew still. No more movement. And then a white streak cut into the granite of the slit and a bullet whined away and a crash sounded up from below. Pepé felt a sharp pain in his right hand. A sliver of granite was sticking out from between his first and second knuckles and the point protruded from his palm. Carefully he pulled out the sliver of stone. The wound bled evenly and gently. No vein nor artery was cut.

Pepé looked into a little dusty cave in the rock and gathered a handful of spider web, and he pressed the mass into the cut, plastering the soft web into the blood. The flow stopped almost at once.

The rifle was on the ground. Pepé picked it up, levered a new shell into the chamber. And then he slid into the brush on his stomach. Far to the right he crawled, and then up the hill, moving slowly and carefully, crawling to cover and resting and then crawling again.

In the mountains the sun is high in its arc before it penetrates the gorges. The hot face looked over the hill and brought instant heat with it. The white light beat on the rocks and reflected from them and rose up quivering from the earth again, and the rocks and bushes seemed to quiver behind the air.

Pepé crawled in the general direction of the ridge peak, zig-zagging for cover. The deep cut between his knuckles began to throb. He crawled close to a rattlesnake before he saw it, and when it raised its dry head and made a soft beginning whirr, he backed up and took another way. The quick gray lizards flashed in front of him, raising a tiny line of dust. He found another mass of spider web and pressed it against his throbbing hand.

Pepé was pushing the rifle with his left hand now. Little drops of sweat ran to the ends of his coarse black hair and rolled down his cheeks. His lips and tongue were growing thick and heavy. His lips writhed to draw saliva into his mouth. His little dark eyes were uneasy and suspicious. Once when a gray lizard paused in front of him on the parched ground and turned its head sideways he crushed it flat with a stone.

When the sun slid past noon he had not gone a mile. He crawled exhaustedly a last hundred yards to a patch of high sharp manzanita, crawled desperately, and when the patch was reached he wriggled in among the tough gnarly trunks and dropped his head on his left arm. There was little shade in the meager brush, but there was cover and safety. Pepé went to sleep as he lay and the sun beat on his back. A few little birds hopped close to him and peered and hopped away. Pepé squirmed in his sleep and he raised and dropped his wounded hand again and again.

The sun went down behind the peaks and the cool evening came, and then the dark. A coyote yelled from the hillside, Pepé started awake and looked about with misty eyes. His hand was swollen and heavy; a little thread of pain ran up the inside of his arm and settled in a pocket in his armpit. He peered about and then stood up, for the mountains were black and the moon had not yet risen. Pepé stood up in the dark. The coat of his father pressed on his arm. His tongue was swollen until it nearly filled his mouth. He wriggled out of the coat and dropped it in the brush, and then he struggled up the hill, falling over rocks and tearing his way through the brush. The rifle knocked against stones as he went. Little dry avalanches of gravel and shattered stone went whispering down the hill behind him.

After a while the old moon came up and showed the jagged ridge top ahead of him. By moonlight Pepé traveled more easily. He bent forward so that his throbbing arm hung away from his body. The journey uphill was made in dashes and rests, a frantic rush up a few yards and then a rest. The wind coasted down the slope rattling the dry stems of the bushes.

The moon was at meridian when Pepé came at last to the sharp backbone of the ridge top. On the last hundred yards of the rise no soil had clung under the wearing winds. The way was on solid rock. He clambered to the top and looked down on the other side. There was a draw like the last below him, misty with moonlight, brushed with dry struggling sage and chaparral. On the other side the hill rose up sharply and at the top the jagged rotten teeth of the mountain showed against the sky. At the bottom of the cut the brush was thick and dark.

Pepé stumbled down the hill. His throat was almost closed with thirst. At first he tried to run, but immediately he fell and rolled. After that he went more carefully. The moon was just disappearing behind the mountains when he came to the bottom. He crawled into the heavy brush feeling with his fingers for water. There was no water in the bed of the stream, only damp earth. Pepé laid his gun down and scooped up a handful of mud and put it in his mouth, and then he spluttered and scraped the earth from his tongue with his finger, for the mud drew at his mouth like a poultice. He dug a hole in the stream bed with his fingers, dug a little basin to catch water; but before it was very deep his head fell forward on the damp ground and he slept.

The dawn came and the heat of the day fell on the earth, and still Pepé slept. Late in the afternoon his head jerked up. He looked slowly around. His eyes were slits of wariness. Twenty feet away in the heavy brush a big tawny mountain lion stood looking at him. Its long thick tail waved gracefully, its ears erect with interest, not laid back dangerously. The lion squatted down on its stomach and watched him.

Pepé looked at the hole he had dug in the earth. A half inch of muddy water had collected in the bottom. He tore the sleeve from his hurt arm, with his teeth ripped out a little square, soaked it in the water and put it in his mouth. Over and over he filled the cloth and sucked it.

Still the lion sat and watched him. The evening came down but there was no movement on the hills. No birds visited the dry bottom of the cut. Pepé looked occasionally at the lion. The eyes of the yellow beast drooped as though he were about to sleep. He yawned and his long thin red tongue curled out. Suddenly his head jerked around and his nostrils quivered. His big tail lashed. He stood up and slunk like a tawny shadow into the thick brush.

A moment later Pepé heard the sound, the faint far crash of horses' hooves on gravel. And he heard something else, a high whining yelp of a dog.

Pepé took his rifle in his left hand and he glided into the brush almost as quietly as the lion had. In the darkening evening he crouched up the hill toward the next ridge. Only when the dark came did he stand up. His energy was short. Once it was dark he fell over the rocks and slipped to his knees on the steep slope, but he moved on and on up the hill, climbing and scrabbling over the broken hillside.

When he was far up toward the top, he lay down and slept for a little while. The withered moon, shining on his face, awakened him. He stood up and moved up the hill. Fifty yards away he stopped and turned back, for he had forgotten his rifle. He walked heavily down and poked about in the brush, but he could not find his gun. At last he lay down to rest. The pocket of pain in his armpit had grown more sharp. His arm seemed to swell out and fall with every heartbeat. There was no position lying down where the heavy arm did not press against his armpit.

With the effort of a hurt beast, Pepé got up and moved again toward the top of the ridge. He held his swollen arm away from his body with his left hand. Up the steep hill he dragged himself, a few steps and a rest, and a few more steps. At last he was nearing the top. The moon showed the uneven sharp back of it against the sky.

Pepé's brain spun in a big spiral up and away from him. He slumped to the ground and lay still. The rock ridge top was only a hundred feet above him.

The moon moved over the sky. Pepé half turned on his back. His tongue tried to make words, but only a thick hissing came from between his lips.

When the dawn came, Pepé pulled himself up. His eyes were sane again. He drew his great puffed arm in front of him and looked at the angry wound. The black line ran up from his wrist to his armpit. Automatically he reached in his pocket for the big black knife, but it was not there. His eyes searched the ground. He picked up a sharp blade of stone and scraped at the wound, sawed at the proud flesh[8] and then squeezed the green juice out in big drops. Instantly he threw back his head and whined like a dog. His whole right side shuddered at the pain, but the pain cleared his head.

In the gray light he struggled up the last slope to the ridge and crawled over and lay down behind a line of rocks. Below him lay a deep canyon exactly like the last, waterless and desolate. There was no flat, no oak trees, not even heavy brush in the bottom of it. And on the other side a sharp ridge stood up, thinly brushed with starving sage, littered with broken granite. Strewn over the hill there were giant outcroppings, and on the top the granite teeth stood out against the sky.

The new day was light now. The flame of sun came over the ridge and fell on Pepé where he lay on the ground. His coarse black hair was littered with twigs and bits of spider web. His eyes had retreated back into his head. Between his lips the tip of his black tongue showed.

He sat up and dragged his great arm into his lap and nursed it, rocking his body and moaning in his throat. He threw back his head and looked up into the pale sky. A big black bird circled nearly out of sight, and far to the left another was sailing near.

He lifted his head to listen, for a similar sound had come to him from the valley he had climbed out of; it was the crying yelp of hounds, excited and feverish, on a trail.

Pepé bowed his head quickly. He tried to speak rapid words but only a thick hiss came from his lips. He drew a shaky cross on his breast with his left hand. It was a long struggle to get to his feet. He crawled slowly and mechanically to the top of a big rock on the ridge peak.

IMAGE OF A SNAKE

[8] **proud flesh:** new tissue, very sensitive to the touch, that grows in open wounds.

CLIMAX

Once there, he arose slowly, swaying to his feet, and stood erect. Far below he could see the dark brush where he had slept. He braced his feet and stood there, black against the morning sky.

There came a ripping sound at his feet. A piece of stone flew up and a bullet droned off into the next gorge. The hollow crash echoed up from below. Pepé looked down for a moment and then pulled himself straight again.

His body jarred back. His left hand fluttered helplessly toward his breast. The second crash sounded from below. Pepé swung forward and toppled from the rock. His body struck and rolled over and over, starting a little avalanche. And when at last he stopped against a bush, the avalanche slid slowly down and covered up his head.

BURIAL

Exercises

1. Before looking closely at the way the plot is structured, it might be best to determine what the Torres family, especially Pepé, are like. How are they different from most Californians, even from their Mexican-American relatives living in Monterey? What kind of life do they lead? What values are most important to them? How do you know? In what ways is Mama Torres a strong character? What part in the story is played by the two younger children? In what sense are they children and at the same time very wise for their years? (Pay particular attention to the last words Rosy says.)

2. What is significant about the fact that Pepé is nineteen before his mother is willing to send him on a "man's" errand? In what sense is he both "a foolish chicken" and "nearly a man"? The narrator describes him as a "gentle, affectionate boy" and as "very lazy." How are both of these characterizations shown to be true? How is the reader prepared to expect him to react the way he does when he is insulted? Why does the whole family accept without question the fact that Pepé must try to escape into the mountains? That is, why is a return to Monterey unthinkable?

3. How does the description of the Torres farm play a key part in defining the character and situation of these people? Read the first paragraph carefully. How does it suggest that nature itself can be considered a character in the story? Notice, for instance, such words as *hissing, stood up, huddled, clinging,* and *gray-bitten.*

4. Outline carefully Pepé's flight. How many days are involved? What happens

each day? How does the terrain change as he goes further into the mountains? What significance does the change have? In what order and how does he lose the goods of civilization that he sets out with: horse, saddle, clothing, rifle, food? What is significant about the fact that he loses them? What part does his father's knife continue to play in the story? (Why doesn't he have it with him?)

5. As he moves into the mountains what increasing part does nature play in the story? Notice how often the terrain is described in human terms ("and on the other side a sharp ridge stood up, thinly brushed with starving sage, littered with broken granite. Strewn over the hill there were giant outcroppings, and on the top the granite teeth stood out against the sky.") How do the birds and animals respond to Pepé and his plight? What is significant about the fact that he crushes the lizard? In what sense, in the end, does he become like a wounded and hunted beast?

6. Why does he choose to die the way he does? When he left, his mother had said to him, "Do not wait to be caught like a chicken." How is the reader meant to take his final gesture? Is it the heroic defiance of a "man," standing erect against the sky to make a perfect target? Or is it the response of a cornered beast who dies uncringing and uncomplaining? Or is it something of both, or of neither? Discuss.

7. What is the effect of the final sentence in underscoring the role played by nature in the story?

8. The dark watchers are obviously people who live entirely apart from civilization in any form, untouched by it. What is the Torres family's relation to them and to the "civilized" world of Monterey? Why are the "dark watchers" in the story?

9. From what point of view is the story told? Do we ever get any inkling of what is going on in anyone's mind except when they speak? How detached is the narrator? Is it essential for this story that it be told as objectively as possible? Discuss.

10. Considering the kinds of questions raised previously, what is the theme of the story? It certainly is not that those who kill will be killed or that justice is relentless and unseen for those who transgress. Pepé reacts instinctively to the insults to his manhood and kills a man, but still our sympathies lie with him and his simple code of honor. There is a justice in what happens to him, but we feel that somehow it is the wrong kind of justice, and that people in his position can never get the right kind. In his simplicity he is as helpless in knowing how to handle the situation he faces as his father was when he fell on the rattlesnake. In framing an answer to the question of what the theme is, consider the kind of people involved, their relation to the larger world they live in, and the fact that the pursuer is faceless and nameless but certain to win.

Battle Royal

RALPH ELLISON

It goes a long way back, some twenty years. All my life I had been looking for something, and everywhere I turned someone tried to tell me what it was. I accepted their answers too, though they were often in contradiction and even self-contradictory. I was naïve. I was looking for myself and asking everyone except myself questions which I, and only I, could answer. It took me a long time and much painful boomeranging of my expectations to achieve a realization everyone else appears to have been born with: That I am nobody but myself. But first I had to discover that I am an invisible man!

And yet I am no freak of nature, nor of history. I was in the cards, other things having been equal (or unequal) eighty-five years ago. I am not ashamed of my grandparents for having been slaves. I am only ashamed of myself for having at one time been ashamed. About eighty-five years ago they were told that they were free, united with others of our country in everything pertaining to the common good, and, in everything social, separate like the fingers of the hand. And they believed it. They exulted in it. They stayed in their place, worked hard, and brought up my father to do the same. But my grandfather is the one. He was an odd old guy, my grandfather, and I am told I take after him. It was he who caused the trouble. On his deathbed he called my father to him and said, "Son, after I'm gone I want you to keep up the good fight. I never told you, but our life is a war and I have been a traitor all my born days, a spy in the enemy's country ever since I give up my gun back in the Reconstruction. Live with your head in the lion's mouth. I want you to overcome 'em with yeses, undermine 'em with grins, agree 'em to death and destruction, let 'em swoller you till they vomit or bust wide open." They thought the old man had gone out of his mind. He had been the meekest of men. The younger children were rushed from the room, the shades drawn and the flame of the lamp turned so low that it sputtered on the wick like the old man's breathing. "Learn it to the younguns," he whispered fiercely; then he died.

But my folks were more alarmed over his last words than over his dying. It was as though he had not died at all, his words caused so much anxiety. I was warned emphatically to forget what he had said and, indeed, this is the first time it has been mentioned outside the family circle. It had a tremendous effect upon me, however. I could never be sure of what he meant. Grandfather had been a quiet old man who never made any trouble, yet on his deathbed he had called himself a traitor and a spy, and he had spoken of his meekness as a dangerous activity. It became a constant puzzle which lay unanswered in the back of my mind. And whenever things went well for me I remembered my grandfather and felt guilty and uncomfortable. It was as though I was carrying out his advice in spite of myself. And to make it worse, everyone loved me for it. I was praised by the most lily-white men of the town. I was considered an example of desirable conduct—just as my grandfather had been. And what puzzled me was that the old man had defined it as *treachery*. When I was praised for my conduct I felt a guilt that in some way I was doing something that was really against the wishes of the white folks, that if they had understood they would have desired me to act just the opposite, that I should have been sulky and mean, and that that really would have been what they wanted, even though they were fooled and thought they wanted me to act as I did. It made me afraid that some day they would look upon me as a traitor and I would be lost. Still I was more afraid to act any other way because they didn't like that at all. The old man's words were like a curse. On my graduation day I delivered an oration in which I showed that humility was the secret, indeed, the very essence of progress. (Not that I believed this—how could I, remembering my grandfather? —I only believed that it worked.) It was a great success. Everyone praised me and I was invited to give the speech at a gathering of the town's leading white citizens. It was a triumph for our whole community.

It was in the main ballroom of the leading hotel. When I got there I discovered that it was on the occasion of a smoker, and I was told that since I was to be there anyway I might as well take part in the battle royal to be fought by some of my schoolmates as part of the entertainment. The battle royal came first.

All of the town's big shots were there in their tuxedoes, wolfing down the buffet foods, drinking beer and whiskey and smoking black cigars. It was a large room with a high ceiling. Chairs were arranged in neat rows around three sides of a portable boxing ring. The fourth side was clear, revealing a gleaming space of polished floor. I had some misgivings over the battle royal, by the way. Not from a distaste for fighting, but because I didn't care too much for the other fellows who were to take part. They were tough guys who seemed to have no grandfather's curse worrying their minds. No one could mistake their toughness. And besides, I suspected that fighting a battle royal might detract from the dignity of my speech. In those pre-invisible days I visualized myself as a potential Booker T. Washington.[1] But the other fellows didn't care too much for me either, and there were nine of them. I felt superior to them in my way, and I didn't like the manner in which we were all crowded together into the servants' elevator. Nor did they like my being there. In fact, as the warmly lighted floors flashed past the elevator we had words over the fact that I, by taking part in the fight, had knocked one of their friends out of a night's work.

We were led out of the elevator through a rococo hall into an anteroom and told to get into our fighting togs. Each of us was issued a pair of boxing gloves and ushered out into the big mirrored hall, which we entered looking cautiously about us and whispering, lest we might accidentally be heard above the noise of the room. It was foggy with cigar smoke. And already the whiskey was taking effect. I was shocked to see some of the most important men of the

---

[1]**Booker T. Washington (1856–1915):**   Black leader; founder of Tuskegee Institute (1881); leading advocate of the point of view expressed in the fifth sentence of the second paragraph of the story.

town quite tipsy. They were all there—bankers, lawyers, judges, doctors, fire chiefs, teachers, merchants. Even one of the more fashionable pastors. Something we could not see was going on up front. A clarinet was vibrating sensuously and the men were standing up and moving eagerly forward. We were a small tight group, clustered together, our bare upper bodies touching and shining with anticipatory sweat; while up front the big shots were becoming increasingly excited over something we still could not see. Suddenly I heard the school superintendent, who had told me to come, yell, "Bring up the shines, gentlemen! Bring up the little shines!"

We were rushed up to the front of the ballroom, where it smelled even more strongly of tobacco and whiskey. Then we were pushed into place. I almost wet my pants. A sea of faces, some hostile, some amused, ringed around us, and in the corner, facing us, stood a magnificent blonde—stark naked. There was dead silence. I felt a blast of cold air chill me. I tried to back away, but they were behind me and around me. Some of the boys stood with lowered heads, trembling. I felt a wave of irrational guilt and fear. My teeth chattered, my skin turned to goose flesh, my knees knocked. Yet I was strongly attracted and looked in spite of myself. Had the price of looking been blindness, I would have looked. The hair was yellow like that of a circus kewpie doll, the face heavily powdered and rouged, as though to form an abstract mask, the eyes hollow and smeared a cool blue, the color of a baboon's butt. I felt a desire to spit upon her as my eyes brushed slowly over her body. Her breasts were firm and round as the domes of East Indian temples, and I stood so close as to see the fine skin texture and beads of pearly perspiration glistening like dew around the pink and erected buds of her nipples. I wanted at one and the same time to run from the room, to sink through the floor, or go to her and cover her from my eyes and the eyes of the others with my body; to feel the soft thighs, to caress her and destroy her, to love her and murder her, to hide from her, and yet to stroke where below the small American flag tattooed upon her belly her thighs formed a capital V. I had a notion that of all in the room she saw only me with her impersonal eyes.

And then she began to dance, a slow sensuous movement; the smoke of a hundred cigars clinging to her like the thinnest of veils. She seemed like a fair bird-girl girdled in veils calling to me from the angry surface of some gray and threatening sea. I was transported. Then I became aware of the clarinet playing and the big shots yelling at us. Some threatened us if we looked and others if we did not. On my right I saw one boy faint. And now a man grabbed a silver pitcher from a table and stepped close as he dashed ice water upon him and stood him up and forced two of us to support him as his head hung and moans issued from his thick bluish lips. Another boy began to plead to go home. He was the largest of the group, wearing dark red fighting trunks much too small to conceal the erection which projected from him as though in answer to the insinuating low-registered moaning of the clarinet. He tried to hide himself with his boxing gloves.

And all the while the blonde continued dancing, smiling faintly at the big shots who watched her with fascination, and faintly smiling at our fear. I noticed a certain merchant who followed her hungrily, his lips loose and drooling. He was a large man who wore diamond studs in a shirtfront which swelled with the ample paunch underneath, and each time the blonde swayed her undulating hips he ran his hand through the thin hair of his bald head and, with his arms upheld, his posture clumsy like that of an intoxicated panda, wound his belly in a slow and obscene grind. This creature was completely hypnotized. The music had quickened. As the dancer flung herself about with a detached expression on her face, the men began reaching out to touch her. I could see their beefy fingers sink into the soft flesh. Some of the others tried to stop them and she began to move around the floor in graceful circles, as they gave chase, slipping and sliding over the polished floor. It was mad. Chairs went crashing, drinks were spilt, as they ran laughing and howling after her. They caught her just as she reached a door, raised her from the floor, and tossed her as college boys are tossed at a hazing, and above her red, fixed-smiling lips I saw the terror and disgust in her eyes, almost like my own terror and that which I saw in some of the other boys. As I watched, they tossed her twice and her soft breasts seemed to flatten against the air and her legs flung wildly as she spun. Some of the more sober ones helped her to escape. And I started off the floor, heading for the anteroom with the rest of the boys.

Some were still crying and in hysteria. But as we tried to leave we were stopped and ordered to get into the ring. There was nothing to do but what we were told. All ten of us climbed under the ropes and allowed ourselves to be blindfolded with broad bands of white cloth. One of the men seemed to feel a bit sympathetic and tried to cheer us up as we stood with our backs against the ropes. Some of us tried to grin. "See that boy over there?" one of the men said. "I want you to run across at the bell and give it to him right in the belly. If you don't get him, I'm going to get you. I don't like his looks." Each of us was told the same. The blindfolds were put on. Yet even then I had been going over my speech. In my mind each word was as bright as flame. I felt the cloth pressed into place, and frowned so that it would be loosened when I relaxed.

But now I felt a sudden fit of blind terror. I was unused to darkness. It was as though I had suddenly found myself in a dark room filled with poisonous cottonmouths. I could hear the bleary voices yelling insistently for the battle royal to begin.

"Get going in there!"

"Let me at that big nigger!"

I strained to pick up the school superintendent's voice, as though to squeeze some security out of that slightly more familiar sound.

"Let me at those black sonsabitches!" someone yelled.

"No, Jackson, no!" another voice yelled, "Here, somebody, help me hold Jack."

"I want to get at that ginger-colored nigger. Tear him limb from limb," the first voice yelled.

I stood against the ropes trembling. For in those days I was what they called ginger-colored, and he sounded as though he might crunch me between his teeth like a crisp ginger cookie.

Quite a struggle was going on. Chairs were being kicked about and I could hear voices grunting as with a terrific effort. I wanted to see, to see more desperately than ever before. But the blindfold was as tight as a thick skin-puckering scab and when I raised my gloved hands to push the layers of white aside a voice yelled, "Oh, no you don't, black bastard! Leave that alone!"

"Ring the bell before Jackson kills him a coon!" someone boomed in the sudden silence. And I heard the bell clang and the sound of the feet scuffling forward.

A glove smacked against my head. I pivoted, striking out stiffly as someone went past, and felt the jar ripple along the length of my arm to my shoulder. Then it seemed as though all nine of the boys had turned upon me at once. Blows pounded me from all sides while I struck out as best I could. So many blows landed upon me that I wondered if I were not the only blindfolded fighter in the ring, or if the man called Jackson hadn't succeeded in getting me after all.

Blindfolded, I could no longer control my motions. I had no dignity. I stumbled about like a baby or a drunken man. The smoke had become thicker and with each new blow it seemed to sear and further restrict my lungs. My saliva became like hot bitter glue. A glove connected with my head, filling my mouth with warm blood. It was everywhere. I could not tell if the moisture I felt upon my body was sweat or blood. A blow landed hard against the nape of my neck. I felt myself going over, my head hitting the floor. Streaks of blue light filled the black world behind the blindfold. I lay prone, pretending that I was knocked out, but felt myself seized by hands and yanked to my feet. "Get going, black boy! Mix it up!" My arms were like lead, my head smarting from blows. I managed to feel my way to the ropes and held on, trying to catch my breath. A glove landed in my mid-section and I went over again, feeling as though the smoke had become a knife jabbed into my guts. Pushed this way and that by the legs milling around me, I finally pulled erect and discovered that I could see the black sweat-washed forms weaving in the smoky-blue atmosphere like drunken dancers weaving to the rapid drum-like thuds of blows.

Everyone fought hysterically. It was complete anarchy. Everybody fought everybody else. No group fought together for long. Two, three, four, fought one, then turned to fight each other, were themselves attacked. Blows landed below the belt and in the

kidney, with the gloves open as well as closed, and with my eye
partly opened now there was not so much terror. I moved carefully, avoiding blows, although not too many to attract attention,
fighting from group to group. The boys groped about like blind,
cautious crabs crouching to protect their mid-sections, their heads
pulled in short against their shoulders, their arms stretched nervously before them, with their fists testing the smoke-filled air like
the knobbed feelers of hypersensitive snails. In one corner I
glimpsed a boy violently punching the air and heard him scream
in pain as he smashed his hand against a ring post. For a second I
saw him bent over holding his hand, then going down as a blow
caught his unprotected head. I played one group against the other,
slipping in and throwing a punch then stepping out of range while
pushing the others into the melee to take the blows blindly aimed
at me. The smoke was agonizing and there were no rounds, no bells
at three minute intervals to relieve our exhaustion. The room spun
round me, a swirl of lights, smoke, sweating bodies surrounded
by tense white faces. I bled from both nose and mouth, the blood
spattering upon my chest.

The men kept yelling, "Slug him, black boy! Knock his guts
out!"

"Uppercut him! Kill him! Kill that big boy!"

Taking a fake fall, I saw a boy going down heavily beside me
as though we were felled by a single blow, saw a sneaker-clad foot
shoot into his groin as the two who had knocked him down stumbled upon him. I rolled out of range, feeling a twinge of nausea.

The harder we fought the more threatening the men became.
And yet, I had begun to worry about my speech again. How would
it go? Would they recognize my ability? What would they give
me?

I was fighting automatically when suddenly I noticed that one
after another of the boys was leaving the ring. I was surprised,
filled with panic, as though I had been left alone with an unknown
danger. Then I understood. The boys had arranged it among
themselves. It was the custom for the two men left in the ring to
slug it out for the winner's prize. I discovered this too late. When
the bell sounded two men in tuxedoes leaped into the ring and
removed the blindfold. I found myself facing Tatlock, the biggest

of the gang. I felt sick at my stomach. Hardly had the bell stopped ringing in my ears than it clanged again and I saw him moving swiftly toward me. Thinking of nothing else to do I hit him smash on the nose. He kept coming, bringing the rank sharp violence of stale sweat. His face was a black blank of a face, only his eyes alive —with hate of me and aglow with a feverish terror from what had happened to us all. I became anxious. I wanted to deliver my speech and he came at me as though he meant to beat it out of me. I smashed him again and again, taking his blows as they came. Then on a sudden impulse I struck him lightly and as we clinched, I whispered, "Fake like I knocked you out, you can have the prize."

"I'll break your behind," he whispered hoarsely.

"For *them*?"

"For *me*, sonofabitch!"

They were yelling for us to break it up and Tatlock spun me half around with a blow, and as a joggled camera sweeps in a reeling scene, I saw the howling red faces crouching tense beneath the cloud of blue-gray smoke. For a moment the world wavered, unraveled, flowed, then my head cleared and Tatlock bounced before me. That fluttering shadow before my eyes was his jabbing left hand. Then falling forward, my head against his damp shoulder, I whispered,

"I'll make it five dollars more."

"Go to hell!"

But his muscles relaxed a trifle beneath my pressure and I breathed, "Seven?"

"Give it to your ma," he said, ripping me beneath the heart.

And while I still held him I butted him and moved away. I felt myself bombarded with punches. I fought back with hopeless desperation. I wanted to deliver my speech more than anything else in the world, because I felt that only these men could judge truly my ability, and now this stupid clown was ruining my chances. I began fighting carefully now, moving in to punch him and out again with my greater speed. A lucky blow to his chin and I had him going too—until I heard a loud voice yell, "I got my money on the big boy."

Hearing this, I almost dropped my guard. I was confused: Should I try to win against the voice out there? Would not this go against my speech, and was not this a moment for humility, for nonresistance? A blow to my head as I danced about sent my right eye popping like a jack-in-the-box and settled my dilemma. The room went red as I fell. It was a dream fall, my body languid and fastidious as to where to land, until the floor became impatient and smashed up to meet me. A moment later I came to. An hypnotic voice said FIVE emphatically. And I lay there, hazily watching a dark red spot of my own blood shaping itself into a butterfly, glistening and soaking into the soiled gray world of the canvas.

When the voice drawled TEN I was lifted up and dragged to a chair. I sat dazed. My eye pained and swelled with each throb of my pounding heart and I wondered if now I would be allowed to speak. I was wringing wet, my mouth still bleeding. We were grouped along the wall now. The other boys ignored me as they congratulated Tatlock and speculated as to how much they would be paid. One boy whimpered over his smashed hand. Looking up front, I saw attendants in white jackets rolling the portable ring away and placing a small square rug in the vacant space surrounded by chairs. Perhaps, I thought, I will stand on the rug to deliver my speech.

Then the M.C. called to us, "Come on up here boys and get your money."

We ran forward to where the men laughed and talked in their chairs, waiting. Everyone seemed friendly now.

"There it is on the rug," the man said. I saw the rug covered with coins of all dimensions and a few crumpled bills. But what excited me, scattered here and there, were the gold pieces.

"Boys, it's all yours," the man said. "You get all you grab."

"That's right, Sambo," a blond man said, winking at me confidentially.

I trembled with excitement, forgetting my pain. I would get the gold and the bills, I thought. I would use both hands. I would throw my body against the boys nearest me to block them from the gold.

"Get down around the rug now," the man commanded, "and don't anyone touch it until I give the signal."

"This ought to be good," I heard.

As told, we got around the square rug on our knees. Slowly the man raised his freckled hand as we followed it upward with our eyes.

I heard, "These niggers look like they're about to pray!"

Then, "Ready," the man said. "Go!"

I lunged for a yellow coin lying on the blue design of the carpet, touching it and sending a surprised shriek to join those rising around me. I tried frantically to remove my hand but could not let go. A hot, violent force tore through my body, shaking me like a wet rag. The rug was electrified. The hair bristled up on my head as I shook myself free. My muscles jumped, my nerves jangled, writhed. But I saw that this was not stopping the other boys. Laughing in fear and embarrassment, some were holding back and scooping up the coins knocked off by the painful contortions of the others. The men roared above us as we struggled.

"Pick it up, goddamnit, pick it up!" someone called like a bass-voiced parrot. "Go on, get it!"

I crawled rapidly around the floor, picking up the coins, trying to avoid the coppers and to get greenbacks and the gold. Ignoring the shock by laughing, as I brushed the coins off quickly, I discovered that I could contain the electricity—a contradiction, but it works. Then the men began to push us onto the rug. Laughing embarrassedly, we struggled out of their hands and kept after the coins. We were all wet and slippery and hard to hold. Suddenly I saw a boy lifted into the air, glistening with sweat like a circus seal, and dropped, his wet back landing flush upon the charged rug, heard him yell and saw him literally dance upon his back, his elbows beating a frenzied tattoo upon the floor, his muscles twitching like the flesh of a horse stung by many flies. When he finally rolled off, his face was gray and no one stopped him when he ran from the floor amid booming laughter.

"Get the money," the M.C. called. "That's good hard American cash!"

And we snatched and grabbed, snatched and grabbed. I was

careful not to come too close to the rug now, and when I felt the hot whiskey breath descend upon me like a cloud of foul air I reached out and grabbed the leg of a chair. It was occupied and I held on desperately.

"Leggo, nigger! Leggo!"

The huge face wavered down to mine as he tried to push me free. But my body was slippery and he was too drunk. It was Mr. Colcord, who owned a chain of movie houses and "entertainment palaces." Each time he grabbed me I slipped out of his hands. It became a real struggle. I feared the rug more than I did the drunk, so I held on, surprising myself for a moment by trying to topple *him* upon the rug. It was such an enormous idea that I found myself actually carrying it out. I tried not to be obvious, yet when I grabbed his leg, trying to tumble him out of the chair, he raised up roaring with laughter, and, looking at me with soberness dead in the eye, kicked me viciously in the chest. The chair leg flew out of my hand and I felt myself going and rolled. It was as though I had rolled through a bed of hot coals. It seemed a whole century would pass before I would roll free, a century in which I was seared through the deepest levels of my body to the fearful breath within me and the breath seared and heated to the point of explosion. It'll all be over in a flash, I thought as I rolled clear. It'll all be over in a flash.

But not yet, the men on the other side were waiting, red faces swollen as though from apoplexy as they bent forward in their chairs. Seeing their fingers coming toward me I rolled away as a fumbled football rolls off the receiver's fingertips, back into the coals. That time I luckily sent the rug sliding out of place and heard the coins ringing against the floor and the boys scuffling to pick them up and the M.C. calling, "All right, boys, that's all. Go get dressed and get your money."

I was limp as a dish rag. My back felt as though it had been beaten with wires.

When we had dressed the M.C. came in and gave us each five dollars, except Tatlock, who got ten for being last in the ring. Then he told us to leave. I was not to get a chance to deliver my speech, I thought. I was going out into the dim alley in despair when I was stopped and told to go back. I returned to the ballroom, where the men were pushing back their chairs and gathering in groups to talk.

The M.C. knocked on a table for quiet. "Gentlemen," he said, "we almost forgot an important part of the program. A most serious part, gentlemen. This boy was brought here to deliver a speech which he made at his graduation yesterday . . ."

"Bravo!"

"I'm told that he is the smartest boy we've got out there in Greenwood. I'm told that he knows more big words than a pocket-sized dictionary."

Much applause and laughter.

"So now, gentlemen, I want you to give him your attention."

There was still laughter as I faced them, my mouth dry, my eye throbbing. I began slowly, but evidently my throat was tense, because they began shouting, "Louder! Louder!"

"We of the younger generation extol the wisdom of the great leader and educator," I shouted, "who first spoke these flaming words of wisdom: 'A ship lost at sea for many days suddenly sighted a friendly vessel. From the mast of the unfortunate vessel was seen a signal: "Water, water; we die of thirst!" The answer from the friendly vessel came back: "Cast down your bucket where you are." The captain of the distressed vessel, at last heeding the injunction, cast down his bucket, and it came up full of fresh sparkling water from the mouth of the Amazon River.' And like him I say, and in his words, 'To those of my race who depend upon bettering their condition in a foreign land, or who underestimate the importance of cultivating friendly relations with the Southern white man, who is his next-door neighbor, I would say: "Cast down your bucket where you are"—cast it down in making friends in every manly way of the people of all races by whom we are surrounded . . .'"[2]

I spoke automatically and with such fervor that I did not realize that the men were still talking and laughing until my dry mouth, filling up with blood from the cut, almost strangled me. I coughed, wanting to stop and go to one of the tall brass, sand-

---

[2]The quotations are from Booker T. Washington's "Atlanta Exposition Address," often referred to as "The Atlanta Compromise."

filled spittoons to relieve myself, but a few of the men, especially the superintendent, were listening and I was afraid. So I gulped it down, blood, saliva and all, and continued. (What powers of endurance I had during those days! What enthusiasm! What a belief in the rightness of things!) I spoke even louder in spite of the pain. But still they talked and still they laughed, as though deaf with cotton in dirty ears. So I spoke with greater emotional emphasis. I closed my ears and swallowed blood until I was nauseated. The speech seemed a hundred times as long as before, but I could not leave out a single word. All had to be said, each memorized nuance considered, rendered. Nor was that all. Whenever I uttered a word of three or more syllables a group of voices would yell for me to repeat it. I used the phrase "social responsibility" and they yelled:

"What's that word you say, boy?"

"Social responsibility," I said.

"What?"

"Social . . ."

"Louder."

". . . responsibility."

"More!"

"Respon—"

"Repeat!"

"—sibility."

The room filled with the uproar of laughter until, no doubt, distracted by having to gulp down my blood, I made a mistake and yelled a phrase I had often seen denounced in newspaper editorials, heard debated in private.

"Social . . ."

"What?" they yelled.

". . . equality—"

The laughter hung smokelike in the sudden stillness. I opened my eyes, puzzled. Sounds of displeasure filled the room. The M.C. rushed forward. They shouted hostile phrases at me. But I did not understand.

A small dry mustached man in the front row blared out, "Say that slowly, son!"

"What sir?"

"What you just said!"

"Social responsibility, sir," I said.

"You weren't being smart, were you, boy?" he said, not un-kindly.

"No, sir!"

"You sure that about 'equality' was a mistake?"

"Oh, yes, sir," I said. "I was swallowing blood."

"Well, you had better speak more slowly so we can understand. We mean to do right by you, but you've got to know your place at all times. All right, now, go on with your speech."

I was afraid. I wanted to leave but I wanted also to speak and I was afraid they'd snatch me down.

"Thank you, sir," I said, beginning where I had left off, and having them ignore me as before.

Yet when I had finished there was a thunderous applause. I was surprised to see the superintendent come forth with a package wrapped in white tissue paper, and, gesturing for quiet, address the men.

"Gentlemen, you see that I did not overpraise this boy. He makes a good speech and some day he'll lead his people in the proper paths. And I don't have to tell you that that is important in these days and times. This is a good, smart boy, and so to encourage him in the right direction, in the name of the Board of Education I wish to present him a prize in the form of this . . ."

He paused, removing the tissue paper and revealing a gleaming calfskin brief case.

". . . in the form of this first-class article from Shad Whitmore's shop."

"Boy," he said, addressing me, "take this prize and keep it well. Consider it a badge of office. Prize it. Keep developing as you are and some day it will be filled with important papers that will help shape the destiny of your people."

I was so moved that I could hardly express my thanks. A rope of bloody saliva forming a shape like an undiscovered continent drooled upon the leather and I wiped it quickly away. I felt an importance that I had never dreamed.

"Open it and see what's inside," I was told.

My fingers a-tremble, I complied, smelling the fresh leather and finding an official-looking document inside. It was a scholarship to the state college for Negroes. My eyes filled with tears and I ran awkwardly off the floor.

I was overjoyed; I did not even mind when I discovered that the gold pieces I had scrambled for were brass pocket tokens advertising a certain make of automobile.

When I reached home everyone was excited. Next day the neighbors came to congratulate me. I even felt safe from grandfather, whose deathbed curse usually spoiled my triumphs. I stood beneath his photograph with my brief case in hand and smiled triumphantly into his stolid black peasant's face. It was a face that fascinated me. The eyes seemed to follow everywhere I went.

That night I dreamed I was at a circus with him and that he refused to laugh at the clowns no matter what they did. Then later he told me to open my brief case and read what was inside and I did, finding an official envelope stamped with the state seal; and inside the envelope I found another and another, endlessly, and I though I would fall of weariness. "Them's years," he said. "Now open that one." And I did and in it I found an engraved document containing a short message in letters of gold. "Read it," my grandfather said, "Out loud."

"To Whom It May Concern," I intoned. "Keep This Nigger-Boy Running."

I awoke with the old man's laughter ringing in my ears.

(It was a dream I was to remember and dream again for many years after. But at that time I had no insight into its meaning. First I had to attend college.)

Exercises

1. "Battle Royal" was originally published as a short story, but it is also the first chapter of Ellison's novel, *Invisible Man.* The narrator uses the phrase "invisible man" in the first paragraph. What do you think he means by it? Invisible to whom? For what? What connections are there with the usual connotations of "invisible man" in mystery stories? Has his grandfather been an "invisible man"? His father?

2. The narrator tells his own story some twenty years after it happened, and he tries to be as accurate as possible in sticking to the feelings he had as the incredible events took place. How successful is he? He says he was "naive." Show how this is borne out.

3. What is a "battle royal"? What meaning does the title have besides the obvious one?

4. What purpose is served by the framework of the "grandfather's curse" within which the story of the smoker takes place? Why does the narrator refer to his grandfather's dying words and their effect on him as a "curse"? Who in the story does not sense such a "curse" personally?

5. What kinds of "events" are listed for the smoker? List them in order, determining who is involved and how. If "obscene" can be defined as "abhorrent to morality and virtue, strongly repulsive to the sense of decency," comment on whether it is accurate to say that each succeeding event is more obscene than the one before it, culminating in the speech and the gift.

6. What is ironic about the narrator's elation over the scholarship? What is the meaning of his dream and of the message on the "engraved document": "To Whom It May Concern . . . Keep This Nigger-Boy Running"? He says that at that time he had no insight into its meaning. How does his response to the whole evening support that observation?

7. What is meant by the narrator's statement at the beginning of paragraph two: "And yet I am no freak of nature, nor of history. I was in the cards, other things having been equal (or unequal) eighty-five years ago." How is the time of that statement and of the rest of the first three paragraphs different from that of the rest of the story? Why is it?

8. The events of the smoker symbolize perfectly the human alienation that the story deals with (the alienation of black from white, but also of both from their humanity). Notice also how much of Ellison's imagery speaks directly to that dehumanization. Take a close look at the description of the naked blonde and the response to her. Note also such passages as the following, which describes the receipt of the gift: "A rope of bloody saliva forming a shape like an undiscovered continent drooled upon the leather and I wiped it quickly away. I felt an importance that I had never dreamed." Show that the image comments perfectly and, for the boy, unconsciously, on his naiveness and delusion.

9. This is a version of the great American success story. All it takes to succeed, the story goes, is ambition, drive, staying power, a "dream." How is it made clear that the hero of the story has all of these qualities? Does he still have them at the end? How is Booker T. Washington's "Atlanta Address" used as a comment on the dream and the reality? What is Ellison saying about the great American success story and its effect on blacks?

A Bottle of Milk for Mother
NELSON ALGREN

I feel I am of them—
I belong to those convicts and prostitutes myself,
And henceforth I will not deny them—
For how can I deny myself?

WHITMAN

Two months after the Polish Warriors S.A.C. had had their heads shaved, Bruno Lefty Bicek got into his final difficulty with the Racine Street police. The arresting officers and a reporter from the *Dziennik Chicagoski* were grouped about the captain's desk when the boy was urged forward into the room by Sergeant Adamovitch, with two fingers wrapped about the boy's broad belt: a full-bodied boy wearing a worn and sleeveless blue work shirt grown too tight across the shoulders; and the shoulders themselves with a loose swing to them. His skull and face were shining from a recent scrubbing, so that the little bridgeless nose glistened between the protective points of the cheekbones. Behind the desk sat Kozak, eleven years on the force and brother to an alderman.[1] The reporter stuck a cigarette behind one ear like a pencil.

"We spotted him followin' the drunk down Chicago—" Sergeant Comiskey began.

Captain Kozak interrupted. "Let the jackroller[2] tell us how he done it hisself."

"I ain't no jackroller."

"What you doin' here, then?"

Bicek folded his naked arms.

"Answer me. If you ain't here for jackrollin' it must be for strong-arm robb'ry—'r you one of them Chicago Av'noo moll-buzzers?"

---

[1]**alderman:** in Chicago, a member of the city legislature.
[2]**jackroller:** someone who robs a drunk or otherwise helpless person.

"I ain't that neither."

"C'mon, c'mon, I seen you in here before—what were you up to, followin' that poor old man?"

"I ain't been in here before."

Neither Sergeant Milano, Comiskey, nor old Adamovitch moved an inch; yet the boy felt the semicircle about him drawing closer. Out of the corner of his eye he watched the reporter undoing the top button of his mangy raccoon coat, as though the barren little query room were already growing too warm for him.

"What were you doin' on Chicago Av'noo in the first place when you live up around Division? Ain't your own ward big enough you have to come down here to get in trouble? What do you *think* you're here for?"

"Well, I was just walkin' down Chicago like I said, to get a bottle of milk for Mother, when the officers jumped me. I didn't see 'em drive up, they wouldn't let me say a word, I got no idea what I'm here for. I was just doin' a errand for Mother 'n——"

"All right, son, you want us to book you as a pickup 'n hold you overnight, is that it?"

"Yes sir."

"What about this, then?"

Kozak flipped a spring-blade knife with a five-inch blade onto the police blotter; the boy resisted an impulse to lean forward and take it. His own double-edged double-jointed spring-blade cuts-all genuine Filipino twisty-handled all-American gut-ripper.

"Is it yours or ain't it?"

"Never seen it before, Captain."

Kozak pulled a billy out of his belt, spread the blade across the bend of the blotter before him, and with one blow clubbed the blade off two inches from the handle. The boy winced as though he himself had received the blow. Kozak threw the broken blade into a basket and the knife into a drawer.

"Know why I did that, son?"

"Yes sir."

"Tell me."

" 'Cause it's three inches to the heart."

"No. 'Cause it's against the law to carry more than three inches of knife. C'mon, Lefty, tell us about it. 'N it better be good."

The boy began slowly, secretly gratified that Kozak appeared to know he was the Warriors' first-string left-hander: maybe he'd been out at that game against the Knothole Wonders the Sunday he'd finished his own game and then had relieved Dropkick Kodadek in the sixth in the second. Why hadn't anyone called him "Iron-Man Bicek" or "Fireball Bruno" for that one?

"Everythin' you say can be used against you," Kozak warned him earnestly. "Don't talk unless you want to." His lips formed each syllable precisely.

Then he added absently, as though talking to someone unseen, "We'll just hold you on an open charge[3] till you do."

And his lips hadn't moved at all.

The boy licked his own lips, feeling a dryness coming into his throat and a tightening in his stomach. "We seen this boobatch with his collar turned inside out cash'n his check by Konstanty Stachula's Tonsorial Palace of Art on Division. So I followed him a way, that was all. Just break'n the old monotony was all. Just a notion, you might say, that come over me. I'm just a neighborhood kid, Captain."

He stopped as though he had finished the story. Kozak glanced over the boy's shoulder at the arresting officers and Lefty began again hurriedly.

"Ever' once in a while he'd pull a little single-shot of Scotch out of his pocket, stop a second t' toss it down, 'n toss the bottle at the car tracks. I picked up a bottle that didn't bust but there wasn't a spider left in 'er, the boobatch'd drunk her dry. 'N do you know, he had his pockets *full* of them little bottles? 'Stead of buyin' hisself a fifth in the first place. Can't understand a man who'll buy liquor that way. Right before the corner of Walton 'n Noble he popped into a hallway. That was Chiney-Eye-the-Precinct-Captain's hallway, so I popped right in after him. Me 'n Chiney-Eye 'r just like that." The boy crossed two fingers of his left hand and asked innocently, "Has the alderman been in to straighten this out, Captain?"

"What time was all this, Lefty?"

"Well, some of the street lamps was lit awready 'n I didn't see nobody

<hr/>

[3] **open charge:**   a police measure by which persons are held in jail without being formally charged with a specific crime.

either way down Noble. It'd just started spitt'n a little snow 'n I couldn't see clear down Walton account of Wojciechowski's Tavern bein' in the way. He was a old guy, a dino you. He couldn't speak a word of English. But he started in cryin' about how every time he gets a little drunk the same old thing happens to him 'n he's gettin' fed up, he lost his last three checks in the very same hallway 'n it's gettin' so his family don't believe him no more . . ."

Lefty paused, realizing that his tongue was going faster than his brain. He unfolded his arms and shoved them down his pants pockets; the pants were turned up at the cuffs and the cuffs were frayed. He drew a colorless cap off his hip pocket and stood clutching it in his left hand.

"I didn't take him them other times, Captain," he anticipated Kozak.

"Who did?"

Silence.

"What's Benkowski doin' for a livin' these days, Lefty?"

"Just nutsin' around."

"What's Nowogrodski up to?"

"Goes wolfin' on roller skates by Riverview. The rink's open all year round."

"Does he have much luck?"

"Never turns up a hair. They go by too fast."

"What's that evil-eye up to?"

Silence.

"You know who I mean. Idzikowski."

"The Finger?"

"You know who I mean. Don't stall."

"He's hexin' fights,[4] I heard."

"Seen Kodadek lately?"

"I guess. A week 'r two 'r a month ago."

"What was *he* up to?"

"Sir?"

"What was Kodadek doin' the last time you seen him?"

"You mean Dropkick? He was nutsin' around."

"Does he nuts around drunks in hallways?"

---

⁴**hexin' fights:**   putting the evil sign (the hex) on the opponent.

Somewhere in the room a small clock or wrist watch began ticking distinctly.

"Nutsin' around ain't jackrollin'."

"You mean Dropkick ain't a jackroller but you are."

The boy's blond lashes shuttered his eyes.

"All right, get ahead with your lyin' a little faster."

Kozak's head came down almost neckless onto his shoulders, and his face was molded like a flatiron, the temples narrow and the jaws rounded. Between the jaws and the open collar, against the graying hair of the chest, hung a tiny crucifix, slender and golden, a shade lighter than his tunic's golden buttons.

"I told him I wasn't gonna take his check, I just needed a little change, I'd pay it back someday. But maybe he didn't understand. He kept hollerin' how he lost his last check, please to let him keep this one. 'Why you drink'n it all up, then,' I put it to him, 'if you're that anxious to hold onto it?' He gimme a foxy grin then 'n pulls out four of them little bottles from four different pockets, 'n each one was a different kind of liquor. I could have one, he tells me in Polish, which do I want, 'n I slapped all four out of his hands. All four. I don't like to see no full-grown man drinkin' that way. A Polak hillbilly he was, 'n certain'y no citizen.

"'Now let me have that change,' I asked him, 'n that wasn't so much t' ask. I don't go around just lookin' fer trouble, Captain. 'N my feet was slop-full of water 'n snow. I'm just a neighborhood fella. But he acted like I was gonna kill him 'r somethin'. I got one hand over his mouth 'n a half nelson behind him 'n talked polite-like in Polish in his ear, 'n he begun sweatin' 'n tryin' t' wrench away on me. 'Take it easy,' I asked him. 'Be reas'nable, we're both in this up to our necks now.' 'N he wasn't drunk no more then, 'n he was plenty t' hold onto. You wouldn't think a old boobatch like that'd have so much stren'th left in him, boozin' down Division night after night, year after year, like he didn't have no home to go to. He pulled my hand off his mouth 'n started hollerin', '*Mlody bandyta!*[5] *Mlody bandyta!*' 'n I could feel him slippin'. He was just too strong fer a kid like me to hold——"

---

[5] *Mlody bandyta:* young thief.

"Because you were reach'n for his wallet with the other hand?"

"Oh no. The reason I couldn't hold him was my right hand had the nelson 'n I'm not so strong there like in my left 'n even my left ain't what it was before I thrun it out pitchin' that double-header."

"So you kept the rod in your left hand?"

The boy hesitated. Then: "Yes sir." And felt a single drop of sweat slide down his side from under his armpit. Stop and slide again down to the belt.

"What did you get off him?"

"I tell you, I had my hands too full to get *anythin'*—that's just what I been tryin' to tell you. I didn't get so much as one of them little single-shots for all my trouble."

"How many slugs did you fire?"

"Just one, Captain. That was all there was in 'er. I didn't really fire, though. Just at his feet. T' scare him so's he wouldn't jump me. I fired in self-defense. I just wanted to get out of there." He glanced helplessly around at Comiskey and Adamovitch. "You do crazy things sometimes, fellas—well, that's all I was doin'."

The boy caught his tongue and stood mute. In the silence of the query room there was only the scraping of the reporter's pencil and the unseen wrist watch. "I'll ask Chiney-Eye if it's legal, a reporter takin' down a confession, that's my out," the boy thought desperately, and added aloud, before he could stop himself: " 'N beside I had to show him——"

"Show him what, son?"

Silence.

"Show him what, Left-hander?"

"That I wasn't just another greenhorn sprout like he thought."

"Did he say you were just a sprout?"

"No. But I c'd tell. Lot of people think I'm just a green kid. I show 'em. I guess I showed 'em now all right." He felt he should be apologizing for something and couldn't tell whether it was for strong-arming a man or for failing to strong-arm him.

"I'm just a neighborhood kid. I belonged to the Keep-Our-City-Clean Club at St. John Cant'us. I told him polite-like, like a Polish-American citizen, this was Chiney-Eye-a-Friend-of-Mine's hallway. 'No more after this one,' I told him. 'This is your last time gettin' rolled, old man. After this I'm pertectin' you, I'm seein' to it nobody touches you—but the people who live here don't like this sort of thing goin' on any more'n you 'r I do. There's gotta be a stop to it, old man—'n we all gotta live, don't we?' That's what I told him in Polish."

Kozak exchanged glances with the prim-faced reporter from the *Chicagoski,* who began cleaning his black tortoise-shell spectacles hurriedly yet delicately, with the fringed tip of his cravat. They depended from a black ribbon; he snapped them back onto his beak.

"You shot him in the groin, Lefty. He's dead."

The reporter leaned slightly forward, but perceived no special reaction and so relaxed. A pretty comfy old chair for a dirty old police station, he thought lifelessly. Kozak shaded his eyes with his gloved hand and looked down at his charge sheet. The night lamp on the desk was still lit, as though he had been working all night; as the morning grew lighter behind him lines came out below his eyes, black as though packed with soot, and a curious droop came to the St. Bernard mouth.

"You shot him through the groin—zip." Kozak's voice came, flat and unemphatic, reading from the charge sheet as though without understanding. "Five children. Stella, Mary, Grosha, Wanda, Vincent. Thirteen, ten, six, six, and one two months. Mother invalided since last birth, name of Rose. WPA[6] fifty-five dollars. You told the truth about *that,* at least."

Lefty's voice came in a shout: "You know *what?* That bullet must of bounced, that's what!"

"Who was along?"

"I was singlin'. Lone-wolf stuff." His voice possessed the first faint touch of fear.

"You said, 'We seen the man.' Was he a big man? How big a man was he?"

"I'd judge two hunerd twenty pounds," Comiskey offered, "at least. Fifty pounds heavier 'n this boy, just about. 'N half a head taller."

"Who's 'we,' Left-hander?"

[6] **WPA:** Work Projects Administration; public works program in the 1930s giving jobs to the unemployed.

"Captain, I said, 'We seen.' Lots of people, fellas, seen him is all I meant, cashin' his check by Stachula's when the place was crowded. Konstanty cashes checks if he knows you. Say, I even know the project that old man was on, far as that goes, because my old lady wanted we should give up the store so's I c'd get on it. But it was just me done it, Captain."

The raccoon coat readjusted his glasses. He would say something under a by-line like "This correspondent has never seen a colder gray than that in the eye of the wanton killer who arrogantly styles himself the *lone wolf of Potomac Street.*" He shifted uncomfortably, wanting to get farther from the wall radiator but disliking to rise and push the heavy chair.

"Where was that bald-headed pal of yours all this time?"

"Don't know the fella, Captain. Nobody got hair any more around the neighborhood, it seems. The whole damn Triangle went 'n got army haircuts by Stachula's."

"Just you 'n Benkowski, I mean. Don't be afraid, son—we're not tryin' to ring in anythin' you done afore this. Just this one you were out cowboyin' with Benkowski on; were you help'n him 'r was he help'n you? Did you 'r him have the rod?"

Lefty heard a Ford V-8 pull into the rear of the station, and a moment later the splash of the gas as the officers refueled. Behind him he could hear Milano's heavy breathing. He looked down at his shoes, carefully buttoned all the way up and tied with a double bowknot. He'd have to have new laces mighty soon or else start tying them with a single bow.

"That Benkowski's sort of a toothless monkey used to go on at the City Garden at around a hundred an' eighteen pounds, ain't he?"

"Don't know the fella well enough t' say."

"Just from seein' him fight once 'r twice is all. 'N he wore a mouth-piece, I couldn't tell about his teeth. Seems to me he came in about one thirty-three, if he's the same fella you're thinkin' of, Captain."

"I guess you fought at the City Garden once 'r twice yourself, ain't you?"

"Oh, once 'r twice."

"How'd you make out, Left'?"

"Won 'em both on K.O.s. Stopped both fights in the first. One was against that boogie from the Savoy. If he woulda got up I woulda killed him fer life. Fer Christ I would. I didn't know I could hit like I can."

"With Benkowski in your corner both times?"

"Oh no, sir."

"That's a bloodsuck'n lie. I seen him in your corner with my own eyes the time you won off Cooney from the C.Y.O. He's your manager, jackroller."

"I didn't say he wasn't."

"You said he wasn't secondin' you."

"He don't."

"Who does?"

"The Finger."

"You told me the Finger was your hex-man. Make up your mind."

"He does both, Captain. He handles the bucket 'n sponge 'n in between he fingers[7] the guy I'm fightin', 'n if it's close he fingers the ref 'n judges. Finger, he never losed a fight. He waited for the boogie outside the dressing room 'n pointed him clear to the ring. He win that one for me awright." The boy spun the frayed greenish cap in his hand in a concentric circle about his index finger, remembering a time when the cap was new and had earlaps. The bright checks were all faded now, to the color of worn pavement, and the earlaps were tatters.

"What possessed your mob to get their heads shaved, Lefty?"

"I strong-armed him myself, and I'm rugged as a bull." The boy began to swell his chest imperceptibly; when his lungs were quite full he shut his eyes, like swimming under water at the Oak Street beach, and let his breath out slowly, ounce by ounce.

"I didn't ask you that. I asked you what happened to your hair."

Lefty's capricious mind returned abruptly to the word "possessed" that Kozak had employed. That had a randy ring, sort of: "What possessed you boys?"

"I forgot what you just asked me."

"I asked you why you didn't realize it'd be easier for us to catch up with your mob when all of you had your heads shaved."

---

[7]**fingers:**   points at someone to put the evil sign (hex) on him.

"I guess we figured there'd be so many guys with heads shaved it'd be harder to catch a finger than if we all had hair. But that was some accident all the same. A fella was gonna lend Ma a barber chair 'n go fifty-fifty with her shavin' all the Polaks on P'tom'c Street right back of the store, for relief tickets. So she started on me, just to show the fellas, but the hair made her sicker 'n ever 'n back of the store's the only place she got to lie down 'n I hadda finish the job myself.

"The fellas begun giv'n me a Christ-awful razzin' then, ever' day. God oh God, wherever I went around the Triangle, all the neighborhood fellas 'n little niducks 'n old-time hoods by the Broken Knuckle, whenever they seen me they was pointin' 'n laughin' 'n sayin', 'Hi, Baldy Bicek!' So I went home 'n got the clippers 'n the first guy I seen was Bibleback Watrobinski, you wouldn't know him. I jumps him 'n pushes the clip right through the middle of his hair—he ain't had a haircut since the alderman got indicted you—'n then he took one look at what I done in the drugstore window 'n we both bust out laughin 'n laughin', 'n fin'lly Bible says I better finish what I started. So he set down on the curb 'n I finished him. When I got all I could off that way I took him back to the store 'n heated water 'n shaved him close 'n Ma couldn't see the point at all.

"Me 'n Bible prowled around a couple days 'n here come Catfoot Nowogrodski from Fry Street you, out of Stachula's with a spanty-new sideburner haircut 'n a green tie. I grabbed his arms 'n let Bible run it through the middle just like I done him. Then it was Catfoot's turn, 'n we caught Chester Chekhovaka fer *him,* 'n fer Chester we got Cowboy Okulanis from by the Nort'western Viaduct you, 'n fer him we got Mustang, 'n fer Mustang we got John from the Joint, 'n fer John we got Snake Baranowski, 'n we kep' right on goin' that way till we was doin' guys we never seen before even, Wallios 'n Greeks 'n a Flip from Clark Street he musta been, walkin' with a white girl we done it to. 'N fin'lly all the sprouts in the Triangle start comin' around with their heads shaved, they want to join up with the Baldheads A.C., they called it. They thought it was a club you.

"It got so a kid with his head shaved could beat up on a bigger kid because the big one'd be a-scared to fight back hard, he thought the Baldheads'd get him. So that's why we changed our name then, that's why we're not the Warriors any more, we're the Baldhead True American Social 'n Athletic Club.

"I played first for the Warriors when I wasn't on the mound," he added cautiously, " 'n I'm enterin' the Gold'n Gloves next year 'less I go to collitch instead. I went to St. John Cant'us all the way through. Eight' grade, that is. If I keep on gainin' weight I'll be a hunerd ninety-eight this time next year 'n be five-foot-ten—I'm a fair-size light-heavy right this minute. That's what in England they call a cruiser weight you."

He shuffled a step and made as though to unbutton his shirt to show his proportions. But Adamovitch put one hand on his shoulder and slapped the boy's hand down. He didn't like this kid. This was a low-class Polak. He himself was a high-class Polak because his name was Adamovitch and not Adamowski. This sort of kid kept spoiling things for the high-class Polaks by always showing off instead of just being good citizens like the Irish. That was why the Irish ran the City Hall and Police Department and the Board of Education and the Post Office while the Polaks stayed on relief and got drunk and never got anywhere and had everybody down on them. All they could do like the Irish, old Adamovitch reflected bitterly, was to fight under Irish names to get their ears knocked off at the City Garden.

"That's why I want to get out of this jam," this one was saying beside him. "So's it don't ruin my career in the rope arena. I'm goin' straight. This has sure been one good lesson fer me. Now I'll go to a big-ten collitch 'n make good you."

Now, if the college-coat asked him, "What big-ten college?" he'd answer something screwy like "The Boozological Stoodent-Collitch." That ought to set Kozak back awhile, they might even send him to a bug doc.[8] He'd have to be careful—not *too* screwy. Just screwy enough to get by without involving Benkowski.

He scuffed his shoes and there was no sound in the close little room save his uneasy scuffling; square-toed boy's shoes, laced with a button-hook. He wanted to look more closely at the reporter but every time

[8] **bug doc:** psychiatrist.

he caught the glint of the fellow's glasses he felt awed and would have to drop his eyes; he'd never seen glasses on a string like that before and would have given a great deal to wear them a moment. He took to looking steadily out of the barred window behind Kozak's head, where the January sun was glowing sullenly, like a flame held steadily in a fog. Heard an empty truck clattering east on Chicago, sounding like either a '38 Chevvie or a '37 Ford dragging its safety chain against the car tracks; closed his eyes and imagined sparks flashing from the tracks as the iron struck, bounced, and struck again. The bullet had bounced too. Wow.

"What do you think we ought to do with a man like you, Bicek?"

The boy heard the change from the familiar "Lefty" to "Bicek" with a pang; and the dryness began in his throat again.

"One to fourteen is all I can catch fer manslaughter." He appraised Kozak as coolly as he could.

"You like farm work the next fourteen years? Is that okay with you?"

"I said that's all I could get, at the most. This is a first offense 'n self-defense too. I'll plead the unwritten law."

"Who give you *that* idea?"

"Thought of it myself. Just now. You ain't got a chance to send me over the road 'n you know it."

"We can send you to St. Charles,[9] Bicek. 'N transfer you when you come of age. Unless we can make it first-degree murder."

The boy ignored the latter possibility.

"Why, a few years on a farm'd true me up fine. I planned t' cut out cigarettes 'n whisky anyhow before I turn pro—a farm'd be just the place to do that."

"By the time you're released you'll be thirty-two, Bicek—too late to turn pro then, ain't it?"

"I wouldn't wait that long. Hungry Piontek-from-by-the-Warehouse you, he lammed twice from that St. Charles farm. 'N Hungry don't have all his marbles even. He ain't even a citizen."

[9] **St. Charles:**   Illinois reformatory.

"Then let's talk about somethin' you couldn't lam out of so fast 'n easy. Like the chair. Did you know that Bogatski from Noble Street, Bicek? The boy that burned last summer, I mean."

A plain-clothes man stuck his head in the door and called confidently: "That's the man, Captain. That's the man."

Bicek forced himself to grin good-naturedly. He was getting pretty good, these last couple days, at grinning under pressure. When a fellow got sore he couldn't think straight, he reflected anxiously. And so he yawned in Kozak's face with deliberateness, stretching himself as effortlessly as a cat.

"Captain, I ain't been in serious trouble like this before . . ." he acknowledged, and paused dramatically. He'd let them have it straight from the shoulder now: "So I'm mighty glad to be so close to the alderman. Even if he is indicted."

There. Now they know. He'd told them.

"You talkin' about my brother, Bicek?"

The boy nodded solemnly. Now they knew who they had hold of at last.

The reporter took the cigarette off his ear and hung it on his lower lip. And Adamovitch guffawed.

The boy jerked toward the officer: Adamovitch was laughing openly at him. Then they were all laughing openly at him. He heard their derision, and a red rain danced one moment before his eyes; when the red rain was past, Kozak was sitting back easily, regarding him with the expression of a man who has just been swung at and missed and plans to use the provocation without undue haste. The captain didn't look like the sort who'd swing back wildly or hurriedly. He didn't look like the sort who missed. His complacency for a moment was as unbearable to the boy as Adamovitch's guffaw had been. He heard his tongue going, trying to regain his lost composure by provoking them all.

"Hey, Stingywhiskers!" He turned on the reporter. "Get your Eversharp goin' there, write down I plugged the old rumpot, write down Bicek carries a rod night 'n day 'n don't care where he points it. You, I go around slappin' the crap out of whoever I feel like——"

But they all remained mild, calm, and unmoved: for a moment he feared Adamovitch was going to pat him on the head and say something fatherly in Polish.

"Take it easy, lad," Adamovitch suggested. "You're in the query room. We're here to help you, boy. We want to see you through this thing so's you can get back to pugging. You just ain't letting us help you, son."

Kozak blew his nose as though that were an achievement in itself, and spoke with the false friendliness of the insurance man urging a fleeced customer toward the door.

"Want to tell us where you got that rod now, Lefty?"

"I don't want to tell you anything." His mind was setting hard now, against them all. Against them all in here and all like them outside. And the harder it set, the more things seemed to be all right with Kozak: he dropped his eyes to his charge sheet now and everything was all right with everybody. The reporter shoved his notebook into his pocket and buttoned the top button of his coat as though the questioning were over.

It was all too easy. They weren't going to ask him anything more, and he stood wanting them to. He stood wishing them to threaten, to shake their heads ominously, wheedle and cajole and promise him mercy if he'd just talk about the rod.

"I ain't mad, Captain. I don't blame you men either. It's your job, it's your bread 'n butter to talk tough to us neighborhood fellas— ever'body got to have a racket, 'n yours is talkin' tough." He directed this last at the captain, for Comiskey and Milano had left quietly. But Kozak was studying the charge sheet as though Bruno Lefty Bicek were no longer in the room. Nor anywhere at all.

"I'm still here," the boy said wryly, his lip twisting into a dry and bitter grin.

Kozak looked up, his big, wind-beaten, impassive face looking suddenly to the boy like an autographed pitcher's mitt he had once owned. His glance went past the boy and no light of recognition came into his eyes. Lefty Bicek felt a panic rising in him: a desperate fear that they weren't going to press him about the rod, about the old man, about his feelings. "Don't look at me like I ain't nowheres," he asked. And his voice was struck flat by fear.

Something else! The time he and Dropkick had broken into a slot machine! The time he and Casey had played the attention racket and made four dollars! Something! Anything else!

The reporter lit his cigarette.

"Your case is well disposed of," Kozak said, and his eyes dropped to the charge sheet forever.

"I'm born in this country. I'm educated here——"

But no one was listening to Bruno Lefty Bicek any more.

He watched the reporter leaving with regret—at least the guy could have offered him a drag—and stood waiting for someone to tell him to go somewhere now, shifting uneasily from one foot to the other. Then he started slowly, backward, toward the door: he'd make Kozak tell Adamovitch to grab him. Halfway to the door he turned his back on Kozak.

There was no voice behind him. Was this what "well disposed of" meant? He turned the knob and stepped confidently into the corridor; at the end of the corridor he saw the door that opened into the courtroom, and his heart began shaking his whole body with the impulse to make a run for it. He glanced back and Adamovitch was five yards behind, coming up catfooted like only an old man who has been a citizen-dress man can come up catfooted, just far enough behind and just casual enough to make it appear unimportant whether the boy made a run for it or not.

The Lone Wolf of Potomac Street waited miserably, in the long unlovely corridor, for the sergeant to thrust two fingers through the back of his belt. Didn't they realize that he might have Dropkick and Catfoot and Benkowski with a sub-machine gun in a streamlined cream-colored roadster right down front, that he'd zigzag through the courtroom onto the courtroom fire escape and—swish—down off the courtroom roof three stories with the chopper still under his arm and through the car's roof and into the driver's seat? Like that George Raft did that time he was innocent at the Chopin, and cops like Adamovitch had better start ducking when Lefty Bicek began making a run for it. He felt the fingers thrust overfamiliarly between his shirt and his belt.

A cold draft came down the corridor when the door at the far end opened; with the opening of the door came the smell of disinfectant from the basement cells. Outside, far overhead, the bells of St. John Cantius were beginning. The boy felt the winding steel of the staircase to the basement beneath his feet and heard the whining screech of a

Chicago Avenue streetcar as it paused on Ogden for the traffic lights and then screeched on again, as though a cat were caught beneath its back wheels. Would it be snowing out there still? he wondered, seeing the whitewashed basement walls.

"Feel all right, son?" Adamovitch asked in his most fatherly voice, closing the cell door while thinking to himself: "The kid don't *feel* guilty is the whole trouble. You got to make them *feel* guilty or they'll never go to church at all. A man who goes to church without feeling guilty for *something* is wasting his time, I say." Inside the cell he saw the boy pause and go down on his knees in the cell's gray light. The boy's head turned slowly toward him, a pious oval in the dimness. Old Adamovitch took off his hat.

"This place'll rot down 'n mold over before Lefty Bicek starts prayin', boobatch. Prays, squeals, 'r bawls. So run along 'n I'll see you in hell with yer back broke. I'm lookin' for my cap I dropped is all."

Adamovitch watched him crawling forward on all fours, groping for the pavement-colored cap; when he saw Bicek find it he put his own hat back on and left feeling vaguely dissatisfied.

He did not stay to see the boy, still on his knees, put his hands across his mouth, and stare at the shadowed wall.

Shadows were there within shadows.

"I knew I'd never get to be twenty-one anyhow," Lefty told himself softly at last.

Exercises

1. A few factual questions first. Where is Lefty being questioned? Why are they questioning him if they know already what they need to know? Did Lefty know when he was picked up that the bullet had killed the man? Had it "bounced" or not? Was he "singlin'" or not? How old is he?

2. Trace the changes in Lefty as the questioning proceeds. What attitude does he adopt at first? What does Kozak do and say that makes Lefty begin to talk? Through what steps does Kozak's questioning go? How much does he want to get Lefty to admit? What are the details that indicate that Lefty is losing his self-control?

3. What is Lefty like? There is no doubt that he "jackrolled" the old man and

that he is anything but an admirable citizen. But what other qualities does he have? What is important to him? What does he take pride in? Where does he get his values? He tells Adamovitch in the cell that "This place'll rot down 'n mold over before Lefty Bicek starts prayin', boobatch. Prays, squeals, 'r bawls." How do you know that this statement is probably true? What comes as the crowning blow to his ego in the query room? What do his interest in the reporter, his pride in his athletic achievement, and his fanciful thoughts of escape show about his values? How does his dress help define his character?

4. Characterize Kozak, Adamovitch, and the reporter. Cite specific examples of what they say or do or think that support your characterization. How is each one in his own way partly responsible for making Lefty what he is? What other elements in his society (including his victim) also have a hand in defining the world Lefty grew up in? In what ways?

5. The story could have been told differently. For instance, the jackrolling episode and Lefty's capture could have been dealt with dramatically. What different emphasis would there have been if Lefty had been shown in action? What is gained by having the whole action take place in the station house where Lefty is surrounded by five adults who have complete power over him? How does this restriction in the scope of the action direct the reader's sympathies toward Lefty?

6. The point of view is that of the all-knowing observer who occasionally enters into the thoughts of various characters, but who for the most part simply reports the proceedings in the query room. How is the point of view handled so that the reader's sympathies are directed toward the boy? What problems would there have been if Lefty had told his own story?

7. What is the tone of the story? Lefty's deed was certainly vicious, and the calloused indifference of the adult world is obvious, but the language seems rather casual and at times even humorous, certainly not in keeping with the brutality of the world it deals with. Given the seriousness of Lefty's situation and the author's obvious sympathy for him, how would you define the tone?

8. What has the opening quotation from Whitman got to do with the story? Would there be any difference in the reader's response if the quotation were omitted?

9. What is the significance of the title? Consider the fact that it echoes Lefty's first flippant response to Kozak's question about what Lefty was doing on Chicago Avenue. Consider also what the phrase means as a reference to a perfectly normal errand of a boy in some other environment and with some other kind of mother.

10. What is the theme of the story? Is Algren saying that boys like Lefty are really not bad but that some of them make foolish mistakes thinking they are

tougher than they are? Or that boys like Lefty are innocent victims of the corrupt adult world they live in? Or that young people will absorb the values of the society which surrounds them and that it is too bad when the values are not much good? If none of these exactly, then what?

Too Early Spring

STEPHEN VINCENT BENÉT

I'm writing this down because I don't ever want to forget the way
it was. It doesn't seem as if I could, now, but they all tell you things
change. And I guess they're right. Older people must have forgotten
or they couldn't be the way they are. And that goes for even the best
ones, like Dad and Mr. Grant. They try to understand but they don't
seem to know how. And the others make you feel dirty or else they
make you feel like a goof. Till, pretty soon, you begin to forget yourself—you begin to think, "Well, maybe they're right and it was that
way." And that's the end of everything. So I've got to write this down.
Because they smashed it forever—but it wasn't the way they said.

Mr. Grant always says in comp. class: "Begin at the beginning."
Only I don't know quite where the beginning was. We had a good
summer at Big Lake but it was just the same summer. I worked pretty
hard at the practice basket I rigged up in the barn, and I learned how
to do the back jackknife. I'll never dive like Kerry but you want to
be as all-around as you can. And when I took my measurements, at
the end of the summer, I was 5 ft. 9¾ and I'd gained 12 lbs. 6 oz.
That isn't bad for going on sixteen and the old chest expansion was
O.K. You don't want to get too heavy, because basketball's a fast game,
but the year before was the year when I got my height, and I was so
skinny, I got tired. But this year, Kerry helped me practice, a couple
of times, and he seemed to think I had a good chance for the team.
So I felt pretty set up—they'd never had a Sophomore on it before.
And Kerry's a natural athlete, so that means a lot from him. He's a
pretty good brother too. Most Juniors at State wouldn't bother with a
fellow in High.

It sounds as if I were trying to run away from what I have to write
down, but I'm not. I want to remember that summer, too, because it's

the last happy one I'll ever have. Oh, when I'm an old man—thirty or forty—things may be all right again. But that's a long time to wait and it won't be the same.

And yet, that summer was different, too, in a way. So it must have started then, though I didn't know it. I went around with the gang as usual and we had a good time. But, every now and then, it would strike me we were acting like awful kids. They thought I was getting the big head, but I wasn't. It just wasn't much fun—even going to the cave. It was like going on shooting marbles when you're in High.

I had sense enough not to try to tag after Kerry and his crowd. You can't do that. But when they all got out on the lake in canoes, warm evenings, and somebody brought a phonograph along, I used to go down to the Point, all by myself, and listen and listen. Maybe they'd be talking or maybe they'd be singing, but it all sounded mysterious across the water. I wasn't trying to hear what they said, you know. That's the kind of thing Tot Pickens does. I'd just listen, with my arms around my knees—and somehow it would hurt me to listen— and yet I'd rather do that than be with the gang.

I was sitting under the four pines, one night, right down by the edge of the water. There was a big moon and they were singing. It's funny how you can be unhappy and nobody know it but yourself.

I was thinking about Sheila Coe. She's Kerry's girl. They fight but they get along. She's awfully pretty and she can swim like a fool. Once Kerry sent me over with her tennis racket and we had quite a conversation. She was fine. And she didn't pull any of this big sister stuff, either, the way some girls will with a fellow's kid brother.

And when the canoe came along, by the edge of the lake, I thought for a moment it was her. I thought maybe she was looking for Kerry and maybe she'd stop and maybe she'd feel like talking to me again. I don't know why I thought that—I didn't have any reason. Then I saw it was just the Sharon kid, with a new kind of bob that made her look grown-up, and I felt sore. She didn't have any business out on the lake at her age. She was just a Sophomore in High, the same as me.

I chunked a stone in the water and it splashed right by the canoe, but she didn't squeal. She just said, "Fish," and chuckled. It struck me it was a kid's trick, trying to scare a kid.

"Hello, Helen," I said. "Where did you swipe the gunboat?"

"They don't know I've got it," she said. "Oh, hello, Chuck Peters. How's Big Lake?"

"All right," I said. "How was camp?"

"It was peachy," she said. "We had a peachy counselor, Miss Morgan. She was on the Wellesley field-hockey team."

"Well," I said, "we missed your society." Of course we hadn't, because they're across the lake and don't swim at our raft. But you ought to be polite.

"Thanks," she said. "Did you do the special reading for English? I thought it was dumb."

"It's always dumb," I said. "What canoe is that?"

"It's the old one," she said. "I'm not supposed to have it out at night. But you won't tell anybody, will you?"

"Be your age," I said. I felt generous. "I'll paddle a while, if you want," I said.

"All right," she said, so she brought it in and I got aboard. She went back in the bow and I took the paddle. I'm not strong on carting kids around, as a rule. But it was better than sitting there by myself.

"Where do you want to go?" I said.

"Oh, back towards the house," she said in a shy kind of voice. "I ought to, really. I just wanted to hear the singing."

"O.K.," I said. I didn't paddle fast, just let her slip. There was a lot of moon on the water. We kept around the edge so they wouldn't notice us. The singing sounded as if it came from a different country, a long way off.

She was a sensible kid, she didn't ask fool questions or giggle about nothing at all. Even when we went by Petters' Cove. That's where the lads from the bungalow colony go and it's pretty well populated on a warm night. You can hear them talking in low voices and then a laugh. Once Tot Pickens and a gang went over there with a flashlight, and a big Bohunk chased them for half a mile.

I felt funny, going by there with her. But I said, "Well, it's certainly Old Home Week"—in an offhand tone, because, after all, you've got to be sophisticated. And she said, "People are funny," in just the right sort of way. I took quite a shine to her after that and we talked.

The Sharons have only been in town three years and somehow I'd never really noticed her before. Mrs. Sharon's awfully good-looking but she and Mr. Sharon fight. That's hard on a kid. And she was a quiet kid. She had a small kind of face and her eyes were sort of like a kitten's. You could see she got a great kick out of pretending to be grown up—and yet it wasn't all pretending. A couple of times, I felt just as if I were talking to Sheila Coe. Only more comfortable, because, after all, we were the same age.

Do you know, after we put the canoe up, I walked all the way back home, around the lake? And most of the way, I ran. I felt swell too. I felt as if I could run forever and not stop. It was like finding something. I hadn't imagined anybody could ever feel the way I did about some things. And here was another person, even if it was a girl.

Kerry's door was open when I went by and he stuck his head out, and grinned.

"Well, kid," he said. "Stepping out?"

"Sure. With Greta Garbo," I said, and grinned back to show I didn't mean it. I felt sort of lightheaded, with the run and everything.

"Look here, kid—" he said, as if he was going to say something. Then he stopped. But there was a funny look on his face.

And yet I didn't see her again till we were both back in High. Mr. Sharon's uncle died, back East, and they closed the cottage suddenly. But all the rest of the time at Big Lake, I kept remembering that night and her little face. If I'd seen her in daylight, first, it might have been different. No, it wouldn't have been.

All the same, I wasn't even thinking of her when we bumped into each other, the first day of school. It was raining and she had on a green slicker and her hair was curly under her hat. We grinned and said hello and had to run. But something happened to us, I guess.

I'll say this now—it wasn't like Tot Pickens and Mabel Palmer. It wasn't like Junior David and Betty Page—though they've been going together ever since kindergarten. It wasn't like any of those things. We didn't get sticky and sloppy. It wasn't like going with a girl.

Gosh, there'd be days and days when we'd hardly see each other, except in class. I had basketball practice almost every afternoon and sometimes evenings and she was taking music lessons four times a week. But you don't have to be always twos-ing with a person, if you feel that way about them. You seem to know the way they're thinking and feeling, the way you know yourself.

Now let me describe her. She had that little face and the eyes like a kitten's. When it rained, her hair curled all over the back of her neck. Her hair was yellow. She wasn't a tall girl but she wasn't chunky —just light and well made and quick. She was awfully alive without being nervous—she never bit her fingernails or chewed the end of her pencil, but she'd answer quicker than anyone in the class. Nearly everybody liked her, but she wasn't best friends with any particular girl, the mushy way they get. The teachers all thought a lot of her, even Miss Eagles. Well, I had to spoil that.

If we'd been like Tot and Mabel, we could have had a lot more time together, I guess. But Helen isn't a liar and I'm not a snake. It wasn't easy, going over to her house, because Mr. and Mrs. Sharon would be polite to each other in front of you and yet there'd be something wrong. And she'd have to be fair to both of them and they were always pulling at her. But we'd look at each other across the table and then it would be all right.

I don't know when it was that we knew we'd get married to each other, some time. We just started talking about it, one day, as if we always had. We were sensible, we knew it couldn't happen right off. We thought maybe when we were eighteen. That was two years but we knew we had to be educated. You don't get as good a job, if you aren't. Or that's what people say.

We weren't mushy either, like some people. We got to kissing each other good-by, sometimes, because that's what you do when you're in love. It was cool, the way she kissed you, it was like leaves. But lots of the time we wouldn't even talk about getting married, we'd just play checkers or go over the old Latin, or once in a while go to the movies with the gang. It was really a wonderful winter. I played every game after the first one and she'd sit in the gallery and watch and I'd know she was there. You could see her little green hat or her yellow hair. Those are the class colors, green and gold.

And it's a queer thing, but everybody seemed to be pleased. That's what I can't get over. They liked to see us together. The grown people, I mean. Oh, of course, we got kidded too. And old Mrs. Withers would ask me about "my little sweetheart," in that awful damp voice of hers. But, mostly, they were all right. Even Mother was all right, though she didn't like Mrs. Sharon. I did hear her say to Father, once, "Really, George, how long is this going to last? Sometimes I feel as if I just couldn't stand it."

Then Father chuckled and said to her, "Now, Mary, last year you were worried about him because he didn't take any interest in girls at all."

"Well," she said, "he still doesn't. Oh, Helen's a nice child—no credit to Eva Sharon—and thank heaven she doesn't giggle. Well, Charles is mature for *his* age too. But he acts so solemn about her. It isn't natural."

"Oh, let Charlie alone," said Father. "The boy's all right. He's just got a one-track mind."

But it wasn't so nice for us after the spring came. In our part of the state, it comes pretty late, as a rule. But it was early this year. The little kids were out with scooters when usually they'd still be having snow-fights and, all of a sudden, the radiators in the classrooms smelt dry. You'd get used to that smell for months—and then, there was a day when you hated it again and everybody kept asking to open the windows. The monitors had a tough time, that first week—they always do when spring starts—but this year it was worse than ever because it came when you didn't expect it.

Usually, basketball's over by the time spring really breaks, but this year it hit us while we still had three games to play. And it certainly played hell with us as a team. After Bladesburg neary licked us, Mr. Grant called off all practice till the day before the St. Matthew's game. He knew we were stale—and they've been state champions two years. They'd have walked all over us, the way we were going.

The first thing I did was telephone Helen. Because that meant that there were six extra afternoons we could have, if she could get rid of her music lessons any way. Well, she said, wasn't it wonderful, her music teacher had a cold? And that seemed just like Fate.

Well, that was a great week and we were so happy. We went to the movies five times and once Mrs. Sharon let us take her little car. She knew I didn't have a driving license but of course I've driven ever since I was thirteen and she said it was all right. She was funny—sometimes she'd be awfully kind and friendly to you and sometimes she'd be like a piece of dry ice. She was that way with Mr. Sharon too. But it was a wonderful ride. We got stuff out of the kitchen—the cook's awfully sold on Helen—and drove way out in the country. And we found an old house, with the windows gone, on top of a hill, and parked the car and took the stuff up to the house and ate it there. There weren't any chairs or tables but we pretended there were.

We pretended it was our house, after we were married. I'll never forget that. She'd even brought paper napkins and paper plates and she set two places on the floor.

"Well, Charles," she said, sitting opposite me, with her feet tucked under, "I don't suppose you remember the days we were both in school."

"Sure," I said—she was always much quicker pretending things than I was—"I remember them all right. That was before Tot Pickens got to be President." And we both laughed.

"It seems very distant in the past to me—we've been married so long," she said, as if she really believed it. She looked at me.

"Would you mind turning off the radio, dear?" she said. "This modern music always gets on my nerves."

"Have we got a radio?" I said.

"Of course, Chuck."

"With television?"

"Of course, Chuck."

"Gee, I'm glad," I said. I went and turned it off.

"Of course, if you *want* to listen to the late market reports—" she said just like Mrs. Sharon.

"Nope," I said. "The market—uh—closed firm today. Up twenty-six points."

"That's quite a long way up, isn't it?"

"Well, the country's perfectly sound at heart, in spite of this damfool Congress," I said, like Father.

She lowered her eyes a minute, just like her mother, and pushed away her plate.

"I'm not very hungry tonight," she said. "You won't mind if I go upstairs?"

"Aw, don't be like that," I said. It was too much like her mother.

"I was just seeing if I could," she said. "But I never will, Chuck."

"I'll never tell you you're nervous, either," I said. "I—oh, gosh!"

She grinned and it was all right. "Mr. Ashland and I have never had a serious dispute in our wedded lives," she said—and everybody knows who runs *that* family. "We just talk things over calmly and reach a satisfactory conclusion, usually mine."

"Say, what kind of house have we got?"

"It's a lovely house," she said. "We've got radios in every room and lots of servants. We've got a regular movie projector and a library full of good classics and there's always something in the icebox. I've got a shoe closet."

"A what?"

"A shoe closet. All my shoes are on tipped shelves, like Mother's. And all my dresses are on those padded hangers. And I say to the maid, 'Elise, Madame will wear the new French model today.'"

"What are my clothes on?" I said. "Christmas trees?"

"Well," she said. "You've got lots of clothes and dogs. You smell of pipes and the open and something called Harrisburg tweed."

"I do not," I said. "I wish I had a dog. It's a long time since Jack."

"Oh, Chuck, I'm sorry," she said.

"Oh, that's all right," I said. "He was getting old and his ear was always bothering him. But he was a good pooch. Go ahead."

"Well," she said, "of course we give parties——"

"Cut the parties," I said.

"Chuck! They're grand ones!"

"I'm a homebody," I said. "Give me—er—my wife and my little family and—say, how many kids have we got, anyway?"

She counted on her fingers. "Seven."

"Good Lord," I said.

"Well, I always wanted seven. You can make it three, if you like."

"Oh, seven's all right, I suppose," I said. "But don't they get awfully in the way?"

"No," she said. "We have governesses and tutors and send them to boarding school."

"O.K.," I said. "But it's a strain on the old man's pocketbook, just the same."

"Chuck, will you ever talk like that? Chuck, this is when we're rich." Then suddenly, she looked sad. "Oh, Chuck, do you suppose we ever will?" she said.

"Why, sure," I said.

"I wouldn't mind if it was only a dump," she said. "I could cook for you. I keep asking Hilda how she makes things."

I felt awfully funny. I felt as if I were going to cry.

"We'll do it," I said. "Don't you worry."

"Oh, Chuck, you're a comfort," she said.

I held her for a while. It was like holding something awfully precious. It wasn't mushy or that way. I know what that's like too.

"It takes so long to get old," she said. "I wish I could grow up to-morrow. I wish we both could."

"Don't you worry," I said. "It's going to be all right."

We didn't say much, going back in the car, but we were happy enough. I thought we passed Miss Eagles at the turn. That worried me a little because of the driving license. But, after all, Mrs. Sharon had said we could take the car.

We wanted to go back again, after that, but it was too far to walk and that was the only time we had the car. Mrs. Sharon was awfully nice about it but she said, thinking it over, maybe we'd better wait till I got a license. Well, Father didn't want me to get one till I was seventeen but I thought he might come around. I didn't want to do anything that would get Helen in a jam with her family. That shows how careful I was of her. Or thought I was.

All the same, we decided we'd do something to celebrate if the team won the St. Matthew's game. We thought it would be fun if we could get a steak and cook supper out somewhere—something like that. Of course, we could have done it easily enough with a gang, but we didn't want a gang. We wanted to be alone together, the way we'd been at the house. That was all we wanted. I don't see what's wrong about that. We even took home the paper plates, so as not to litter things up.

Boy, that was a game! We beat them 36–34 and it took an extra period and I thought it would never end. That two-goal lead they had looked as big as the Rocky Mountains all the first half. And they gave me the full school cheer with nine Peters when we tied them up. You don't forget things like that.

Afterwards, Mr. Grant had a kind of spread for the team at his house and a lot of people came in. Kerry had driven down from State to see the game and that made me feel pretty swell. And what made me feel better yet was his taking me aside and saying, "Listen, kid, I don't want you to get the swelled head, but you did a good job. Well, just remember this. Don't let anybody kid you out of going to State. You'll like it up there." And Mr. Grant heard him and laughed and said, "Well, Peters, I'm not proselytizing. But your brother might think about some of the Eastern colleges." It was all like the kind of dream you have when you can do anything. It was wonderful.

Only Helen wasn't there because the only girls were older girls. I'd seen her for a minute, right after the game, and she was fine, but it was only a minute. I wanted to tell her about that big St. Matthew's forward and—oh, everything. Well, you like to talk things over with your girl.

Father and Mother were swell but they had to go on to some big shindy at the country club. And Kerry was going there with Sheila Coe. But Mr. Grant said he'd run me back to the house in his car and he did. He's a great guy. He made jokes about my being the infant phenomenon of basketball, and they were good jokes too. I didn't mind them. But, all the same, when I'd said good night to him and gone into the house, I felt sort of let down.

I knew I'd be tired the next day but I didn't feel sleepy yet. I was too excited. I wanted to talk to somebody. I wandered around downstairs and wondered if Ida was still up. Well, she wasn't, but she'd left half a chocolate cake, covered over, on the kitchen table, and a note on top of it, "Congratulations to Mister Charles Peters." Well, that was awfully nice of her and I ate some. Then I turned the radio on and got the time signal—eleven—and some snappy music. But still I didn't feel like hitting the hay.

So I thought I'd call up Helen and then I thought—probably she's asleep and Hilda or Mrs. Sharon will answer the phone and be sore. And then I thought—well, anyhow, I could go over and walk around the block and look at her house. I'd get some fresh air out of it, anyway, and it would be a little like seeing her.

So I did—and it was a swell night—cool and a lot of stars—and I felt like a king, walking over. All the lower part of the Sharon house was dark but a window upstairs was lit. I knew it was her window. I went around back of the driveway and whistled once—the whistle we made up. I never expected her to hear.

But she did, and there she was at the window, smiling. She made motions that she'd come down to the side door.

Honestly, it took my breath away when I saw her. She had on a kind of yellow thing over her night clothes and she looked so pretty. Her feet were so pretty in those slippers. You almost expected her to be carrying one of those animals kids like—she looked young enough. I know I oughtn't to have gone into the house. But we didn't think anything about it—we were just glad to see each other. We hadn't had any sort of chance to talk over the game.

We sat in front of the fire in the living room and she went out to the kitchen and got us cookies and milk. I wasn't really hungry, but it was like that time at the house, eating with her. Mr. and Mrs. Sharon were at the country club, too, so we weren't disturbing them or anything. We turned off the lights because there was plenty of light from the fire and Mr. Sharon's one of those people who can't stand having extra lights burning. Dad's that way about saving string.

It was quiet and lovely and the firelight made shadows on the ceiling. We talked a lot and then we just sat, each of us knowing the other was there. And the room got quieter and quieter and I'd told her about the game and I didn't feel excited or jumpy any more—just rested and happy. And then I knew by her breathing that she was asleep and I put my arm around her for just a minute. Because it was wonderful to hear that quiet breathing and know it was hers. I was going to wake her in a minute. I didn't realize how tired I was myself.

And then we were back in that house in the country and it was our home and we ought to have been happy. But something was wrong because there still wasn't any glass in the windows and a wind kept blowing through them and we tried to shut the doors but they wouldn't shut. It drove Helen distracted and we were both running through the house, trying to shut the doors, and we were cold and afraid. Then the sun rose outside the windows, burning and yellow and so big it covered the sky. And with the sun was a horrible, weeping voice. It was Mrs. Sharon's saying, "Oh, my God, oh, my God."

I didn't know what had happened, for a minute, when I woke. And then I did and it was awful. Mrs. Sharon was saying "Oh, Helen—I trusted you . . ." and looking as if she were going to faint. And Mr. Sharon looked at her for a minute and his face was horrible and he said, "Bred in the bone," and she looked as if he'd hit her. Then he said to Helen——

I don't want to think of what they said. I don't want to think of any of the things they said. Mr. Sharon is a bad man. And she is a bad woman, even if she is Helen's mother. All the same, I could stand the things he said better than hers.

I don't want to think of any of it. And it is all spoiled now. Everything is spoiled. Miss Eagles saw us going to that house in the country and she said horrible things. They made Helen sick and she hasn't been back at school. There isn't any way I can see her. And if I could, it would be spoiled. We'd be thinking about the things they said.

I don't know how many of the people know, at school. But Tot Pickens passed me a note. And, that afternoon, I caught him behind his house. I'd have broken his nose if they hadn't pulled me off. I meant to. Mother cried when she heard about it and Dad took me into his room and talked to me. He said you can't lick the whole town. But I will anybody like Tot Pickens. Dad and Mother have been all right. But they say things about Helen and that's almost worse. They're for me because I'm their son. But they don't understand.

I thought I could talk to Kerry but I can't. He was nice but he looked at me such a funny way. I don't know—sort of impressed. It wasn't the way I wanted him to look. But he's been decent. He comes down almost every weekend and we play catch in the yard.

You see, I just go to school and back now. They want me to go with the gang, the way I did, but I can't do that. Not after Tot. Of course my marks are a lot better because I've got more time to study now. But it's lucky I haven't got Miss Eagles though Dad made her apologize. I couldn't recite to her.

I think Mr. Grant knows because he asked me to his house once and we had a conversation. Not about that, though I was terribly afraid he would. He showed me a lot of his old college things and the gold football he wears on his watch chain. He's got a lot of interesting things.

Then we got talking, somehow, about history and things like that and how times had changed. Why, there were kings and queens who got married younger than Helen and me. Only now we lived longer and had a lot more to learn. So it couldn't happen now. "It's civilization," he said. "And all civilization's against nature. But I suppose we've got to have it. Only sometimes it isn't easy." Well somehow or other, that made me feel less lonely. Before that I'd been feeling that I was the only person on earth who'd ever felt that way.

I'm going to Colorado, this summer, to a ranch, and next year, I'll go East to school. Mr. Grant says he thinks I can make the basketball team, if I work hard enough, though it isn't as big a game in the East as it is with us. Well, I'd like to show them something. It would be some satisfaction. He says not to be too fresh at first, but I won't be that.

It's a boy's school and there aren't even women teachers. And, maybe, afterwards, I could be a professional basketball player or something, where you don't have to see women at all. Kerry says I'll get over that; but I won't. They all sound like Mrs. Sharon to me now, when they laugh.

They're going to send Helen to a convent—I found out that. Maybe they'll let me see her before she goes. But, if we do, it will be all wrong and in front of people and everybody pretending. I sort of wish they don't—though I want to, terribly. When her mother took her upstairs that night—she wasn't the same Helen. She looked at me as if she was afraid of me. And no matter what they do for us now, they can't fix that.

Man to society

1. What questions are raised in the reader's mind in the very first paragraph? What conflict, suggested in general terms, will be the subject of the story? How is the reader immediately involved in the conflict and subtly drawn to the narrator's side?

2. Before the first main scene in the story, the scene between Chuck and Helen,

what does the reader find out about Chuck? Is he conceited about his athletic ability? Does he have a "big head," as his friends think, because he is tiring of the gang's usual pleasures? Explain. What are his feelings about Kerry and his crowd, and what do those feelings show about him? How is he different from Tot Pickens? What part do his thoughts about Sheila Coe play in the plot development? What kind of person does he reveal himself to be?

3. What shows that there is a change in Helen similar to the one in Chuck? When does he begin to realize it? How do his feelings in general change (about Helen and about himself) after he paddles Helen across the lake?

4. Two brief comments in the first main scene foreshadow what is to come. One is about Helen's parents and one is about Kerry. What are they and why are they significant?

5. What does Chuck mean by the comment, "It wasn't like going with a girl"? What does the comment show about the two of them? What other details that he mentions show that their relationship is essentially strong and decent, that they are "in love" in the very best sense of the term?

6. In terms of the plot development after the first main scene, why is Miss Eagles mentioned? Why is reference made to the way the adult community reacts to Chuck and Helen? What is suggested further about the Sharons? What is the purpose of the brief comments by Chuck's mother and father?

7. What is the second main scene? What details reveal further the nature of their relationship? How would you characterize it in this scene? Since the story is told by Chuck, there is always the possibility that he may distort things. How is the reader convinced that he is not the kind of person who will distort things? Notice such a minor touch as Chuck's comment, "And they gave me the full school cheer with nine Peters after we [not *I*] tied them up."

8. How has Benét built his plot so that Chuck's walking over to Helen's house seems a perfectly natural thing to do? In other words, what else takes up his time after the game, and how is he gradually left alone still feeling elated over his victory? How is the scene in the living room also convincingly presented so that their falling asleep before the fire seems completely natural and innocent?

9. Show specifically how the reactions of the Sharons, the Peters, Miss Eagles, Kerry, and Tot Pickens have been completely prepared for.

10. What does Mr. Grant mean by "all civilization's against nature"? In what sense does his comment reveal that even he does not really understand? In what sense (not meant by him) does the comment state the theme of the story? What is it about the "civilization" represented by all the other characters in the story that is "against nature" as represented by Chuck and Helen?

11. What are the advantages of having Chuck tell his own story? What are the possible disadvantages? Consider, for one, the fact that the reader has to be convinced of Chuck's essential decency and that it is difficult to blow one's own horn convincingly.
12. The title refers partly to the fact that spring literally did come too early to the community. In what other sense did "spring" come too early to Chuck and Helen?
13. The event is written down by Chuck soon after it happens. Will writing it down prevent him from becoming one of the "older people . . . even the best ones" who "try to understand but . . . don't seem to know how"? Is the kind of lack of understanding which all of the "older people" have in varying degrees inevitable in "civilization"? Discuss.

Sun and Shadow

RAY BRADBURY

The camera clicked like an insect. It was blue and metallic, like a great fat beetle held in the man's precious and tenderly exploiting hands. It winked in the flashing sunlight.

"Hsst, Ricardo, come away!"

"You down there!" cried Ricardo out the window.

"Ricardo, stop!"

He turned to his wife. "Don't tell me to stop, tell them to stop. Go down and tell them, or are you afraid?"

"They aren't hurting anything," said his wife patiently.

He shook her off and leaned out the window and looked down into the alley. "You there!" he cried.

The man with the black camera in the alley glanced up, then went on focusing his machine at the lady in the salt-white beach pants, the white bra, and the green checkered scarf. She leaned against the cracked plaster of the building. Behind her a dark boy smiled, his hand to his mouth.

"Tomás!" yelled Ricardo. He turned to his wife. "Oh, Jesus the Blessed, Tomás is in the street, my own son laughing there." Ricardo started out the door.

"Don't do anything!" said his wife.

"I'll cut off their heads!" said Ricardo, and was gone.

In the street the lazy woman was lounging now against the peeling blue paint of a banister. Ricardo emerged in time to see her doing this. "That's my banister!" he said.

The cameraman hurried up. "No, no, we're taking pictures. Everything's all right. We'll be moving on."

"Everything's not all right," said Ricardo, his brown eyes flashing. He waved a wrinkled hand. "She's on my house."

"We're taking fashion pictures," smiled the photographer.

"*Now* what am I to do?" said Ricardo to the blue sky. "Go mad with this news? Dance around like an epileptic saint?"

"If it's money, well, here's a five-peso bill," smiled the photographer.

Ricardo pushed the hand away. "I *work* for my money. You don't understand. Please go."

The photographer was bewildered. "Wait ..."

"Tomás, get in the house!"

"But, Papa ... "

"Gahh!" bellowed Ricardo.

The boy vanished.

"This has *never* happened before," said the photographer.

"It is long past time! What are we? Cowards?" Ricardo asked the world.

A crowd was gathering. They murmured and smiled and nudged each other's elbows. The photographer with irritable good will snapped his camera shut, said over his shoulder to the model, "All right, we'll use that other street. I saw a nice cracked wall there and some nice deep shadows. If we hurry ..."

The girl, who had stood during this exchange nervously twisting her scarf, now seized her make-up kit and darted by Ricardo, but not before he touched at her arm. "Do not misunderstand," he said quickly. She stopped, blinked at him. He went on. "It is not you I am mad at. Or you." He addressed the photographer.

"Then why—" said the photographer.

Ricardo waved his hand. "You are employed; I am employed. We are all people employed. We must understand each other. But when you come to my house with your camera that looks like the complex eye of a black horsefly, then the understanding is over. I will not have my alley used because of its pretty shadows, or my sky used because of its sun, or my house used because there is an interesting crack in the wall, here. You *see!* Ah, how beautiful! Lean here! Stand there! Sit here! Crouch there! Hold it! Oh, I *heard* you. Do you think I am stupid? I have books up in my room. You see that window? Maria!"

His wife's head popped out. "Show them my books!" he cried.

She fussed and muttered, but a moment later she held out one, then two, then half a dozen books, eyes shut, head turned away, as if they were old fish.

"And two dozen more like them upstairs!" cried Ricardo. "You're not talking to some cow in the forest, you're talking to a man!"

"Look," said the photographer, packing his plates swiftly. "We're going. Thanks for nothing."

"Before you go, you must see what I am getting at," said Ricardo. "I am not a mean man. But I *can* be a very angry man. Do I look like a cardboard cutout?"

"Nobody said anybody looked like anything." The photographer hefted his case and started off.

"There is a photographer two blocks over," said Ricardo, pacing him. "They have cutouts. You stand in front of them. It says GRAND HOTEL. They take a picture of you and it looks like you are in the Grand Hotel. Do you see what I mean? My alley is my alley, my life is my life, my son is my son. My son is not cardboard! I saw you putting my son against the wall, so, and thus, in the background. What do you call it—for the correct air? To make the whole attractive, and the lovely lady in front of him?"

"It's getting late," said the photographer, sweating. The model trotted along on the other side of him.

"We are poor people," said Ricardo. "Our doors peel paint, our walls are chipped and cracked, our gutters fume in the street, the alleys are all cobbles. But it fills me with a terrible rage when I see you make over these things as if I had *planned* it this way, as if I had years ago induced the wall to crack. Did you think I knew you were coming and aged the paint? Or that I knew you were coming and put my boy in his dirtiest clothes? We are *not* a studio! We are people and must be given attention as people. Have I made it clear?" .

"With abundant detail," said the photographer, not looking at him, hurrying.

"Now that you know my wishes and my reasoning, you will do the friendly thing and go home?"

"You are a hilarious man," said the photographer. "Hey!" They had joined a group of five other models and a second photographer at the base of a vast stone stairway which in layers, like a bridal cake, led up to the white town square. "How are you doing, Joe?"

"We got some beautiful shots near the Church of the Virgin, some statuary without any noses, lovely stuff," said Joe. "What's the commotion?"

"Pancho here got in an uproar. Seems we leaned against his house and knocked it down."

"My name is Ricardo. My house is completely intact."

"We'll shoot it *here,* dear," said the first photographer. "Stand by the archway of that store. There's a nice antique wall going up there." He peered into the mysteries of his camera.

"So!" A dreadful quiet came upon Ricardo. He watched them prepare. When they were ready to take the picture he hurried forward, calling to a man in a doorway. "Jorge! What are you *doing?*"

"I'm standing here," said the man.

"Well," said Ricardo, "isn't that *your* archway? Are you going to let them *use* it?"

"I'm not bothered," said Jorge.

Ricardo shook his arm. "They're treating your property like a movie actor's place. Aren't you insulted?"

"I haven't thought about it." Jorge picked his nose.

"Jesus upon earth, man, *think!*"

"I can't see any harm," said Jorge.

"Am I the *only* one in the world with a tongue in my mouth?" said Ricardo to his empty hands. "And taste on my tongue? Is this a town of backdrops and picture sets? Won't *anyone* do something about this except me?"

The crowd had followed them down the street, gathering others to it as it came; now it was of a fair size and more were coming, drawn by Ricardo's bullish shouts. He stomped his feet. He made fists. He spat. The cameraman and the models watched him nervously. "Do you want a *quaint* man in the background?" he said wildly to the cameraman. "I'll pose back here. Do you want me near this wall, my hat *so,* my feet *so,* the light so and thus on my sandals which I made myself? Do you want me to rip this hole in my shirt a bit larger, eh, like *this? So!* Is my face smeared with enough perspiration? Is my hair long enough, kind sir?"

"Stand there if you want," said the photographer.

"I won't look in the camera," Ricardo assured him.

The photographer smiled and lifted his machine. "Over to your left one step, dear." The model moved. "Now turn your right leg. That's fine. Fine, fine. *Hold* it!"

The model froze, chin tilted up.

Ricardo dropped his pants.

"Oh, my God!" said the photographer.

Some of the models squealed. The crowd laughed and pummeled each other a bit. Ricardo quietly raised his pants and leaned against the wall.

"Was that quaint enough?" he said.

"Oh, my God!" muttered the photographer.

"Let's go down to the docks," said his assistant.

"I think *I'll* go there too," Ricardo smiled.

"Good God, what can we do with the idiot?" whispered the photographer.

"Buy him off!"

"I *tried* that!"

"You didn't go high enough."

"Listen, you run get a policeman. I'll put a stop to this."

The assistant ran. Everyone stood around smoking cigarettes nervously, eyeing Ricardo. A dog came by and briefly made water against the wall.

"Look at that!" cried Ricardo. "What art! What pattern! Quick, before the sun dries it!"

The cameraman turned his back and looked out to sea.

The assistant came rushing along the street. Behind him, a native policeman strolled quietly. The assistant had to stop and run back to urge the policeman to hurry. The policeman assured him with a gesture, at a distance, that the day was not yet over and in time they would arrive at the scene of whatever disaster lay ahead.

The policeman took up a position behind the two cameramen. "What seems to be the trouble?"

"That man up there. We want him removed."

"That man up there seems only to be leaning against a wall," said the officer.

"No, no, it's not the leaning, he—Oh hell," said the cameraman. "The only way to explain is to show you. Take your pose, dear."

The girl posed. Ricardo posed, smiling casually.

"Hold it!"

The girl froze.

Ricardo dropped his pants.

Click went the camera.

"Ah," said the policeman.

"Got the evidence right in this old camera if you need it!" said the cameraman.

"Ah," said the policeman, not moving, hand to chin. "So." He surveyed the scene like an amateur photographer himself. He saw the model with the flushed, nervous marble face, the cobbles, the wall, and Ricardo. Ricardo magnificently smoking a cigarette there in the noon sunlight under the blue sky, his pants where a man's pants rarely are.

"Well, officer?" said the cameraman, waiting.

"Just what," said the policeman, taking off his cap and wiping his dark brow, "do you want me to do?"

"Arrest that man! Indecent exposure!"

"Ah," said the policeman.

"Well?" said the cameraman.

The crowd murmured. All the nice lady models were looking out at the sea gulls and the ocean.

"That man up there against the wall," said the officer, "I know him. His name is Ricardo Reyes."

"Hello, Esteban!" called Ricardo.

The officer called back at him, "Hello, Ricardo."

They waved at each other.

"He's not doing anything *I* can see," said the officer.

"What do you mean?" asked the cameraman. "He's as naked as a rock. It's immoral!"

"That man is doing nothing immoral. He's just standing there," said the policeman. "Now if he were *doing* something with his hands or body, something terrible to view, I would act upon the instant. However, since he is simply leaning against the wall, not moving a single limb or muscle, there *is* nothing wrong."

"He's naked, *naked!*" screamed the cameraman.

"I don't understand." The officer blinked.

"You just don't go around naked, that's all!"

"There are naked people and naked people," said the officer. "Good and bad. Sober and with drink in them. I judge this one to be a man with no drink in him, a good man by reputation; naked, yes, but doing nothing with this nakedness in any way to offend the community."

"What *are* you, his *brother*? What are you, his confederate?" said the cameraman. It seemed that at any moment he might snap and bite and bark and woof and race around in circles under the blazing sun. "Where's the justice? What's going *on* here? Come on, girls, we'll go somewhere else!"

"France," said Ricardo.

"What!" The photographer whirled.

"I said France, or Spain," suggested Ricardo. "Or Sweden. I have seen some nice pictures of walls in Sweden. But not many cracks in them. Forgive my suggestion."

"We'll get pictures in spite of you!" The cameraman shook his camera, his fist.

"I will be there," said Ricardo. "Tomorrow, the next day, at the bullfights, at the market, anywhere, everywhere you go I go, quietly, with grace. With dignity, to perform my necessary task."

Looking at him, they knew it was true.

"Who are you—who in hell do you think you are?" cried the photographer.

"I have been waiting for you to ask me," said Ricardo. "Consider me. Go home and think of me. As long as there is one man like me in a town of ten thousand, the world will go on. Without me, all would be chaos."

"Good night, nurse," said the photographer, and the entire swarm of ladies, hatboxes, cameras, and make-up kits retreated down the street toward the docks. "Time out for lunch, dears. We'll figure something later!"

Ricardo watched them go, quietly. He had not moved from his position. The crowd still looked upon him and smiled.

Now, Ricardo thought, I will walk up the street to my house, which has paint peeling from the door where I have brushed it a thousand times in passing, and I shall walk over the stones I have worn down in forty-six years of walking, and I shall run my hand over the crack in the wall of my own house, which is the crack made by the earthquake in 1930. I remember well the night, us all in bed, Tomás as yet unborn, and Maria and I much in love, and thinking it was our love which moved the house, warm and great in the night; but it was the earth trembling, and in the morning, that crack in the wall. And I shall climb the steps to the lacework-grille balcony of my father's house, which grillwork he made with his own hands, and I shall eat the food my wife serves me on the balcony, with the books near at hand. And my son Tomás, whom I created out of whole cloth, yes, bed sheets, let us admit it, with my good wife. And we shall sit eating and talking, not photographs, not backdrops, not paintings, not stage furniture, any of us. But actors, all of us, very fine actors indeed.

As if to second this last thought, a sound startled his ear. He was in the midst of solemnly, with great dignity and grace, lifting his pants to belt them around his waist, when he heard this lovely sound. It was like the winging of soft doves in the air. It was applause.

The small crowd, looking up at him, enacting the final scene of the play before the intermission for lunch, saw with what beauty and gentlemanly decorum he was elevating his trousers. The applause broke like a brief wave upon the shore of the nearby sea.

Ricardo gestured and smiled to them all.

On his way home up the hill he shook hands with the dog that had watered the wall.

Exercises

1. What attitude toward the photographers is communicated in the very first paragraph by the way in which the camera is described?
2. The story is told in the third person. Is it told through the awareness of any particular character? Consider the description of the camera, and such phrases as "the lazy woman" (referring to a model), "Some of the models squealed," or (in reference to the photographer) "It seemed that at any moment he might snap and bite and bark and woof and race around in circles under the blazing sun."
3. What is being photographed? Why are they using this particular town? What does the town look like? Where is it?

4. What is Ricardo like? Why does he say, "Do you think I am stupid? I have books up in my room"? Why is he so anxious for the photographer and model to understand him? (He says to them: "It is not you I am mad at. Or you.") What proves that he well understands why the photographer chooses such backdrops for his pictures? How bright is he? What makes him likable? Point out examples of his ability to handle verbal barbs.

5. What is the photographer like? How do you know? Characterize his replies to Ricardo's attempts to explain his feelings. What is significant about the fact that he refers to Ricardo as "Pancho"?

6. How do the attitudes of Ricardo's wife, his son Tomás, Jorge, and Esteban help define Ricardo's attitude?

7. The fashion photographer has one concept of art and beauty. Ricardo has another. How do the two differ?

8. What is it that Ricardo objects to? It is more than invasion of privacy. Consider carefully what he says before and after the photographer (who remains nameless) says, "Who are you—who in hell do you think you are?" What is his "necessary task" without which "all would be chaos"?

9. The narrator says that Ricardo lifted his pants "with great dignity and grace" and that the applause of the crowd in response "was like the winging of soft doves in the air." How has the treatment of Ricardo's strange form of protest been consistent with the tone of these final comments? In other words, what keeps his action from seeming vulgar? Why is it that we can accept such comments as those quoted as being completely appropriate and can also appreciate fully the humor in the situation? Why is it that the last sentence is also perfectly in keeping with the spirit of the closing paragraphs and of the whole story? Consider what would be lost if the story closed with the sentence: "The crowd still looked upon him and smiled." (The action closes there insofar as Ricardo's triumph is concerned.)

10. Bradbury has made skillful use of the idea of "setting" in several senses. In the usual sense, how important is the physical setting of the story in a small Mexican town? In another sense, how has Bradbury built his story on the idea of *scenes*, making sharp distinctions between those which are frozen for the camera and those in which living people play a role?

11. What is the significance of the title? What has it got to do with the kind of photography involved? What has it got to do with the kind of people involved?

12. How would you define the theme in relation to what you have just said about the significance of the title?